JUST THEN FRED ... STABLE YARD, CA... COAT AND SILK H...

'Morning, Lord Fred.'

'You looking after me today, Tracie?'

'Yes, milord,' said Tracie demurely. Fred took in her pert face, her trim figure and tightly breeched bottom with appreciation. He knew from the village grapevine that she was nicknamed 'Pussy' – because she was so eminently strokable. He felt a brief twitch of lust beneath his breeches.

'Pull yourself together, lad,' he said to himself. 'We are going hunting.'

Willy Poole has had a varied life. Educated at Eton, he failed to become a Chartered Accountant. He has worked as a builder's labourer, a lorry driver and, for a brief, sickly period, as a deck hand. He spent twenty-five years as a full time Master of Foxhounds and part time shepherd. Foxhunting is the 'grand passion' of his life. In 1987 he started writing his column in the *Daily Telegraph* and since then he has written features, obituaries, op-eds, sports columns and food items for various magazines and newspapers. He says of himself: 'I used to be a farmer who wrote, now I am a writer who farms.'

The Hounds of Heaven is his seventh published book and his first novel. *A Backwoodsman's Year*, published in 1990, was followed by several collections of articles from the *Daily Telegraph* and *Shooting Times*; his last book was *The Fox's Prophecy*. His second novel is being hatched.

He is married and lives on his farm in 'deepest Northumberland', where he hunts, stalks, writes and smokes his pipe.

WILLY POOLE

The
HOUNDS
of HEAVEN

A SIGNET BOOK

SIGNET

Published by the Penguin Group
Penguin Books Ltd, 27 Wrights Lane, London W8 5TZ, England
Penguin Books USA Inc., 375 Hudson Street, New York, New York 10014, USA
Penguin Books Australia Ltd, Ringwood, Victoria, Australia
Penguin Books Canada Ltd, 10 Alcorn Avenue, Toronto, Ontario, Canada M4V 3B2
Penguin Books (NZ) Ltd, 182–190 Wairau Road, Auckland 10, New Zealand

Penguin Books Ltd, Registered Offices: Harmondsworth, Middlesex, England

First published by Nyali Press 1995
Published in Signet 1996
1 3 5 7 9 10 8 6 4 2

Copyright © R. W. F. Poole 1995

Set in 10/12pt Monotype Plantin Light
Typeset by RefineCatch Limited, Bungay, Suffolk
Printed in England by Clays Ltd, St Ives plc

A CIP catalogue record for this book is available from the British Library

ISBN 0451 18951 5

'The belief was widespread that on certain stormy nights the tumultuous gallop of the mysterious "savage hunt" could be heard in the sky.

'Wotan, in a flowing mantle and a wide-brimmed hat would range the sky in pursuit of fantastic game. From on high, he granted heroism and decided Man's fate.'

LAROUSSE
Encyclopaedia of Mythology

PART ONE

CHAPTER ONE

'A fire-bucket of whisky, Laslo, please, to save me from terminal boredom.'

'Very good, sir,' said the old Hungarian mess steward.

Major Lord Frederick FitzHugh dropped his forage cap and whip onto the table in the hall and sauntered towards the Six O'Clock News in the card room of the Officers' Mess at Hyde Park Barracks. The programme's signature tune was already playing, although it could hardly be heard above the noise of subalterns; there were only three of them, but where two or more are gathered there is always a noise.

John Humphreys was running through the headlines as Fred poured himself into a large armchair – a special report on the siege of Sarajevo was announced.

'Shut up, you reptiles! I want to listen to this!'

'Silence for the Squadron Leader!'

After a moment of muttering and a stifled laugh, relative calm descended on the room. Laslo appeared silently by Fred's side with a large and very strong whisky and water on a tray. Fred took a large swig and, watching the screen over the rim of his glass, saw Tatiana for the first time.

Fred lowered his glass and looked at the face on the television screen. He thought it was probably the most beautiful face that he had ever seen, even when streaked with filth and twisted with anger and grief as it was. The camera panned to two men in camouflaged combat kit who carried a large limp bundle wrapped in a blanket between them. The angle widened to include Kate Adie and a huddle of Croatian soldiers. Kate Adie approached the girl who was standing like a statue. The two men lowered their burden gently to the ground and stood silently, no expression on their blunt faces.

What happened next was carefully edited out of the transmission.

'BBC Television,' said Kate Adie, 'I wonder—' but she got no further.

'I know who you are,' snarled the girl in barely accented English. 'You fucking English, I hate the lot of you – you and your pathetic Carringtons and Hurds and Hoggs – pigs, more like. It is because of your stinking government that my husband is dead. It is because of your Old Etonian "gentlemen"' (she spat the word) 'that my husband and his comrades had to face the Chetnik tanks with a few old rifles. It is because of those feeble, limp old pricks whining about "fair treatment" that the Chetniks got their filthy hands on my husband. You want to see what they did to him? You want your nice, stupid people sitting in their comfortable home with beers and crisps to see?'

The woman motioned to the two soldiers who twitched the blanket away from the heap on the ground. The camera shied away.

'No, no! You won't show them, will you? So I will tell you and all those limp politicians what they did – they cut off his balls and cock and rammed them down his throat until he choked to death. I wish the same for all you bloody English lice!'

The viewers could plainly see the woman's grief-stricken rage, but all they could hear was Ms Adie's anodyne explanation that the woman's husband had been a Slovenian mercenary who had been captured by the Serbs and murdered in a particularly brutal way.

'I wonder what they did to him?' said Lieutenant Oakeford.

'They cut off his balls with a carving knife,' warbled Lieutenant Milton to the tune of 'Three Blind Mice', 'and his cock. Then they shoved the whole lot down his throat and choked him. They'd worked him over pretty badly first.'

'How the hell do you know that?' asked Lieutenant the Hon. Charles Luckington.

'Heard about from a chum in Bosnia who rang in this afternoon. He's out there with the Plods. He was there when they brought the body back. Pretty rum do, he said.'

The camera closed in on the woman's beautiful, distraught face.

'Jesus Christ!' said Fred, putting his glass down with a bang.

'What a woman!' said Lieutenant the Hon. Charles Luckington.

'I wouldn't mind getting my leg over that!' said Lieutenant Oakeford.

'Fwauugh! I bet she bangs like a stoat!' said Lieutenant Gracenote.

'Not with her husband no more, she won't – not with his kit in that state,' said the Honourable.

Fred had not been able to take his eyes off Tatiana's face. Now he felt the bile rise in his throat. Black humour is a military safety valve, but what he had seen triggered something deep inside him.

'Shut the fuck up, you little bastards,' he snarled. The subalterns stiffened. The Squadron Leader was notorious for seldom raising his voice, but when he did wise men took notice. Fred got to his feet and stamped for the door.

At the doorway, he paused. 'My compliments to the Riding Master and you are all on blanket ride in the morning!'

'Oh shit!' said the Honourable. 'Who rattled his cage?'

From the card room, Fred went to his room in the Mess to change his clothes.

'Kite!'

'Sah!' came a distant response, and Trooper Kite, Fred's long-standing Soldier Servant, appeared in the doorway.

'Where's Paddy?'

Trooper Kite looked at the empty dog basket in the room. 'The little sod was here, sir, fast asleep. I bet he's buggered off to the cook house again, sir.'

'Bloody hell, Kite, I told you to put a stop to that. He'll be like a bloody football. Go and grip the little bastard.'

'Sir!' said Trooper Kite to his officer – and to Trooper Dibben who, with spit, polish and duster, was hissing over the Colonel's boots, 'Who's been rattling his cage, then?'

'You never know with fuckin' officers,' said Trooper Dibben philosophically as he spat into a whirl of polish on the already mirror-like boots, 'or their bleedin' dogs.'

In the kitchens in the meantime: 'Now you 'orrible, idle little Paddy, you,' said Corporal of Horse Grummit, holding a piece of scrag-end in the air. 'This one for her Gracious Majesty. Die for the Queen, lad.'

The little brown terrier, who had been 'sitting to attention', promptly rolled over on his back, his already distended stomach and his 'wedding tackle' in the air, to an appreciative round of titters from the cooks. Kite appeared in the doorway.

'Excuse me, Corporal'orse, the Major wants 'is dog and he's in a fair taking.'

'My compliments to the Major,' said Grummit, managing to bend, in spite of his imposing belly, and handing a piece of meat to the now wriggling little dog, 'but the only way he's going to keep this chancy little character out of 'ere is by putting him under close arrest. In't that right, little Paddy?' With a huge fleshy hand he smoothed the terrier's rough coat.

'Right, fall out Trooper Paddy!'

Paddy wagged his disgracefully curly tail as he was tucked under Kite's arm.

'And tell the Major that dog's got an idle tail.' This was the Corporal of Horse's standard issue joke, and referred to the fact that Paddy had never had his tail docked.

'Your dog, sir!' said Kite moments later as Paddy wriggled from his arm, did a quick bounce on the bed and took a flying leap onto Fred's chest. Fred fielded him expertly and allowed his face to be licked.

'You are a nasty, evil, gungy little dog. Right, thank you, Kite. Good night.'

'Sir!'

A little later, Fred walked to his car parked outside the Mess, and opened the door for Paddy to jump in. As the BMW slid out through the gates, he automatically returned the salute of the MoD policeman and slid into a gap in the fast-moving traffic, causing a Fiesta to brake sharply, honk and mutter fiercely to itself about toffee-nosed bastards in flash cars. Fred was oblivious of this. He was driving and navigating on autopilot. His mind far away and in another place.

In fact, his melancholy lasted all the way to his mews house by Eaton Place. He could not get the scene in far-off Bosnia out of his mind and, at the centre of it, was always the girl with the golden hair and the flashing anger. 'Like a bloody wild cat,' he thought to himself.

As Fred parked his car in the mews, he saw the red Volkswagen outside his front door.

'Oh, shit!' he said to Paddy, who was standing up with his nose pressed against the windscreen. This may seem a little ungallant of him, since he knew well enough that the red car, with a green welly mascot on the bonnet, belonged to his fiancée Annabel Woodhouse. Fred was not in fiancée mood.

Fred was the younger son of the Marquis of Fowey, firmly family-seated at Bardwick Hall in the County of Gloucestershire. Fred's personal appearance has been variously described as 'pleasing' and 'dishy'. He was tall, lean, muscular and dark, with a fine narrow nose, amber eyes that changed to green in moments of tension and a mouth that certain women have described – with feeling – as 'sensual'. By nature he was quiet but with a dry, and sometimes acerbic, sense of humour. There was about him a sense of gentle melancholy and brooding. His father cordially disapproved of him at times: 'The young bugger reads too much, quotes poetry and stuff.' The Marquis himself had spent most of his life killing things – anything from foxes and pheasants, to foreigners – and felt that time not spent killing was time wasted. Other people said of Fred: 'Of course, what he needs is a good woman to bring him out of himself, to settle him down.' It was generally agreed that Annabel Woodhouse was just the ticket for the job.

The Woodhouses were neighbours of the Foweys. Fred and Annabel had grown up together, been in the same Pony Club, gone to their first hunt ball together. For some years it had been accepted by both families that they were a most suitable match, or as old Nanny Bardwick – a devoted Cartland reader – would say, 'made for

8

each other'. Their engagement had just 'growed', with a little skilful cultivation by Annabel and inertia on Fred's part.

Annabel was a forceful girl: she had been Head Girl and Captain of Lacrosse at St. Mary's, Ascot. She was used to taking charge of situations. She ran the Bardwick Hunt branch of the Pony Club with brisk, and sometimes ruthless, efficiency. She was bouncy and brunette, and tending to buxomness as she pushed twenty-seven. The Marquis described her as a 'damned good sort of brood bitch': this was high praise. Annabel was ready to brood, and determined to do it with Fred. As a preparation for this, she was prepared to submit to his carnal needs, but only within strictly defined limits.

'You want me to do what?' she had said to one of his more esoteric suggestions. 'What sort of a girl do you think I am?'

Fred had sighed inwardly, and silently accepted there was going to be nothing in his married life that any decent missionary would not have approved of. Annabel, for her part, secretly hoped that once she had popped out the 'four brats' she had set her mind on, all that sort of nonsense would quietly wither away anyway. Her mother had said: 'I know it's all rather disgusting, darling, but you will find that they lose interest after a few years, and then you can forget all about it.'

It may seem churlish for a chap not to welcome a surprise visit from his fiancée. Annabel was prone to make surprise visits; she felt they were good for discipline, and that they gave her a chance to make sure there were no unauthorized 'goings on' in Weeford Mews. 'Men are such ninnies,' her mother said.

'Hello, darling,' she said, throwing her arms round Fred's neck and giving him a large wet kiss. 'Surprise, surprise.'

'Oh shit,' thought Fred again. And in the same breath, 'Hello, Annabel,' and gently disengaged himself from her slightly clammy grip. 'How lovely to see you.'

He went into the drawing-room and poured himself a whisky, while Annabel prattled on about the vet's opinion of Pomeroy's tendon, about her experiences in the Harrods jungle and about the divine little French place that Daphne had told her about.

'Couldn't we go there tonight, darling, it's been an eternity since we had a lovely dins together? That's a very brown-looking whisky,' reprovingly, 'and your wretched little dog's been on the bed again – muddy paw marks. Darling, I really do think he will have to live outside when we are married.'

Paddy curled up into an even tighter ball in his basket.

Much later Fred lay on his back and looked at the ceiling dimly lit by the loom of a street lamp. Annabel snored happily beside him. She had had a lovely evening, although she wished that Fred would buck up and be more cheerful. 'You really should not let yourself get down in the dumps, you know.' She had let Fred do his thing, and had even had the sweetest little orgasm, before dropping straight into deep contented sleep.

And Fred? Was he contented as he watched the shadows? The far away image in his mind was definitely not brunette. 'That must be some girl to follow her husband like that. I wonder,' he mused, staring unseeingly at the ceiling, 'why he was there. They said he was from Slovenia.'

Many people had wondered why Francis had left his home and wife to fight a foreign war. The one person who had no doubts had been Francis himself, and perhaps the only person who understood was Tatiana.

For Francis, it had quite simply been a crusade, a 'call

of blood' from centuries of religious and family duty, that stretched far back into the mists of the Holy Roman Empire. It had always been the sacred duty of the Czernys to fight for what they believed in, and their ancestral lands at Lippitz. For these reasons his father, Gustav, had fought the Russians in the European War, and had gone on to fight against Stalin's rape of Czecho-slovakia. On both occasions he had been lucky to escape with his life, and to have been smuggled across the Dan-ube into Austria by a then young Tomislav, with nothing worse than a leg shattered by a Russian bullet and a head full of nuclear physics to bring with him.

The leg healed in time – although he always walked with a limp – and, his skills being much in demand in the post-war nuclear world, Francis's father prospered. Early on, he was sieved out of the displaced persons' camp by the Americans. He was transported to California but yearned endlessly for the schloss in the green hills above the village to which the blood of generations of Czernys tied him. He could never feel at home in the States. An offer from West Germany was received with enthusiasm. It brought him nearer home.

In Germany he became rich, having patented a design for encasing spent nuclear fuel rods in bronze. When quite middle-aged, he married a gentle and loving German woman whose family had come from Sudeten-land. Francis was born in 1960.

From an early age, the boy was steeped in the history and duties of his family. He was told of Vlad who had lost both legs in a battle against the Avares, and had fought to the death balanced on his stumps, held upright by his shield bearer. He learned of Mateus Twelve Heads, so called, not because he was cranially privileged, but because he rode home with twelve Turkish heads tied to his saddle. He heard of generation after generation of knights, crusaders and soldiers, of wars, invasions and pestilence, through all of which the Czernys did their duty to God and Emperor and held their lands, occasionally being flushed in and out by tides of invasion.

In time the Russian tide would also ebb, the old man said, and then it would be Francis's sacred duty to regain the family lands. The money rolling into the family coffers from a grateful nuclear industry must be used for this purpose.

So it came to be. Under Tito's regime the father of Francis was able to return to Slovenia, to be driven through a blank-faced and shuttered village of Lippitz in his Mercedes, and to limp once again through the courtyard of the castle. There was little to bring him joy. The land had gone to rack and ruin under the enlightened agricultural socialism, and the old castle had been a mess for officers of the Serbian garrison. It had not been well used, but there, standing in the yard, leaning on a stick, was a much older but unmistakable Tomislav; the two old men embraced. What they said to each other is not recorded, but Gustav's parting words were: 'My boy will come back here – look after him.'

So Francis was brought up to the belief that one day the Czernys would regain their ancestral lands, and he must be ready for that day. He read agriculture and estate management at university, and then went to work with a cousin who had a large estate high in the hills. He was supremely happy alone in the forests and mountains. An only child, he had turned solitude into pleasure, and seldom felt at ease in cities or crowds of people. He was a great bear of a man with immense physical strength and toughness. His rather clumsy appearance masked an ability to move with lightning speed when necessary. He was not handsome. His face looked as though it had been rough hewn from a block of granite. People tended to step aside when they saw Francis coming. You had to look at the soft brown eyes to see that this was a gentle giant. Sometimes the eyes twinkled with mischief; when he laughed the granite cracked into great fissures of mirth.

Women made Francis feel awkward. He always felt clumsy, as though his hands and feet were too big; this, coupled with a natural shyness, made him hold back. He did not realize the effect that his soft deep voice, quiet natural charm and gentle eyes had on women. He was always vaguely surprised when one finished up in his bed. The women were usually more than surprised.

'I thought I was going to split in two,' confided one lady to an intimate friend, 'and it went on and on. I came five times, and when he came – my God! – I thought I was going to dissolve.'

Tatiana Ludwigsdorf was the result of the passionate coupling between a count and a peasant girl with hair like ripening corn and flashing blue eyes. For a whole week, one fine autumn, the pair had fornicated with the intensity of animals. He had been bewitched by the girl's fire and passion. She had been aroused by the sophisticated refinements that he brought to their lovemaking. At the end of the week the girl was sore and aching from the intensity of their lust. She carried several weals from his whip on her bottom, and his baby inside her. The count's back was ripped to shreds and, for some time afterwards, he was forced to adopt the rolling gait of a sailor.

By the time that Tatiana came screaming and fighting into the world, discrete negotiations had taken place to ensure her the sort of education and financial security not usually accorded to a peasant child. Part of the deal was that there was to be no contact between the mother and the father.

Tatiana grew up wild amongst the mountains. She inherited fire and passion from both parents and was hard to handle; she also got a double portion of good looks. A series of smart schools shovelled her out of their doors with sincere prayers of thanks for delivery from such a scourge. However, the girl was clever and got to university where her behaviour left a swathe of destruction and mayhem behind her. The only man who could control her at all was her uncle, her mother's brother: a huge, unflappable man-mountain, who puffed his pipe, drank slivovitz like water, and who could calm his niece with the same feeling of security and gentleness that made a brood of baby chickens nestle down quietly when held in his huge hands. But even Uncle Sepp admitted, between puffs of his pipe, 'That girl is about as biddable as a lynx.'

Francis and Tatiana met by accident or, more correctly, in an accident. It was on the slopes at Kitzbühl where Tatiana rammed Francis extensively. She slid to a stop and, as he extracted himself from a snow drift, cursed him comprehensively as a clumsy, oafish, bear-like peasant. She then turned and disappeared down the mountain, and he promptly and devastatingly fell in love with her. He pursued her quietly, gently, relentlessly, in spite of the fact that she was entwined with a suave Arab oil princeling. Tatiana pretended not to notice him.

Francis was a skilled hunter. The old *Jäger* had taught him that a quarry is always curious about its pursuer. As long as the hunter keeps moving forward, the hunted animal will do the same thing instinctively. But if the hunter stops, and even retreats, inherent curiosity will force the animal to go back and see what has become of the pursuer. As often as the hunter repeats this patient process, the gap between the two will become progressively smaller, until the moment when the hunter – still and silent – brings his sights to bear on his quarry, squeezes the trigger and . . .

Our hunter was skilled in this process and reckoned that what worked for deer might well work for the human animal. Thus it was for a time; everywhere that Tatiana went, Francis was sure to follow. Tatiana would toss her golden head and pretend to ignore him completely. If she and a girl friend were drinking chocolate at her favourite café, Francis would be there reading a newspaper. If she went to a night club with her Prince, Francis would be there, sitting alone at a table. He never approached her, never spoke to her; he was just always there.

Then, one morning, he was not there at the café. That night he was not at Der Goldene Löwe. The next morning there was again no sign of him at the café. Not that Tatiana cared; after all, the man was nothing to her, just a nuisance, a big ugly peasant, a fly on the window of her patience that she would take great pleasure in swatting – if she could only get the chance. Yet, you cannot swipe a fly that is not there; this annoyed her.

She took to ski-ing every morning on the slope where she had first knocked the oaf into a drift. For the first two mornings he was not there. On the third morning she saw a familiar hulking figure in the queue for the ski-lift; so the miserable swine was back but, what was more, was having the impertinence to ignore her. That was intolerable. She would teach him another lesson in manners on the way down. She knew that he must be in front of her when she set off from the top of the run. She would cut him down and teach him manners – but he disappeared. All the way down she looked for the familiar figure. A great lump like that could not just vanish, but he had, bloody useless man.

Tatiana got a girl friend to make discreet enquiries. The girl friend discovered that the man was called

Francis Czerny and that he was at Kitzbühl with a small party of men from his university days.

'Ah ha!' said Tatiana, 'I bet they're queers.'

The girl friend said thoughtfully that recent experience, with certain members of the group, suggested this was not the case. She was also able to tell Tatiana that Francis was known amongst his friends as 'The Bear'; he was – according to legend – very big 'down there'. Mitzi Metzenegg, who knew about such things, had reported . . . and here she whispered some giggled details that made Tatiana choke in her chocolate. Her friend giggled some more . . .

'Mitzi said she nearly choked as well.'

In spite of herself, Tatiana felt an uninvited spreading warmth. This was nonsense and had to stop. She rose hastily from the table.

'The trouble with Mitzi and you is that you're sex-mad sluts,' said Tatiana disdainfully.

Matters came to a head one evening in Der Goldene Löwe to which Francis had followed Tatiana with the Arab and his sizable entourage. A discreet exchange of a bundle of schillings got him a single table. His arrival was not unnoticed, and earned him an icy glare from Tatiana and a heated conference amongst the Arabs. As a result, a very large minder, with a slight bulge under the left armpit, approached Francis and suggested he should escort him outside, and out of the *gnädiges Fräulein*'s life, for the sake of his health, which Allah preserve.

Francis agreed to accompany the Arab.

When Francis returned to his table, he was quite alone and apparently unruffled. He looked across at Tatiana and her escort, smiled, bowed slightly and resumed his meal.

Francis woke with the morning sun shining through his bedroom window. He had the farmer's and hunter's habit of early rising. Still naked, he opened the french

16

window to the balcony of his room, and felt the sun and the cold crisp air on his body. He felt a prickle of excitement.

The hunter settled himself behind the fallen tree trunk, his white coveralls blending in with the snow-covered ground. Below him in the forest was an area of clear fell, rough with scrub and herbage – an ideal place for deer to feed. The man savoured the sharp bite of the frosty air and the small warmth of the rising sun. Slipping open the bolt of the rifle, he slid a round into the breech and smoothly slid the bolt home behind it. Then the hunter very carefully and slowly raised his binoculars and began to scan the clearing. He felt a prickle of excitement.

Some instinct made Francis put on his dressing-gown and go out onto the balcony. In spite of the early hour there was a girl sitting alone on the terrace below, reading a newspaper and drinking a glass of tea through a straw. She was wearing huge reflective sunglasses, but the sun lit up her thick golden hair.

There was a flicker of movement in the birch scrub at the edge of the clearing, as it might be the flick of an ear. Infinitely slowly the hunter swung his glasses. The doe was feeding quietly, but always alert. Every now and then she would raise her head sharply, her nostrils licking the air for a taint of danger, her huge ears twitching for the slightest sound.

Tatiana lowered her newspaper slightly so that she could look over the top without appearing to. She could feel the bloody man watching her.

Always alert, the doe grazed her way slowly into the clearing. Very carefully the hunter eased up his rifle. A fallen tree gave a good firm rest for his left hand. He slipped the covers off the telescopic sights and nestled his beard-roughened cheek against the smooth wood of the stock.

Francis walked straight to the table.

'May I sit here, *gnädiges Fräulein*?'

The raised newspaper quivered slightly but was not lowered. 'The table does not belong to me, *mein Herr*.'

Francis sat. The newspaper was lowered, and he could see his image reflected in the huge glasses.

'You know that poor Yussuf cannot walk this morning?'

The doe had been behind the scrub, which prevented any chance of a safe shot, but there was a clear spot just in front of her and about 100 metres from the hunter. He brought the cross-hairs of the sight on to the open space and waited.

'I would be very surprised – and not a little unhappy – if he could,' said Francis. 'He was a clumsy oaf.'

'Like you! You are a clumsy oaf!'

The doe was moving.

'Ah! but I am a standing up, walking, clumsy oaf, *gnädiges Fräulein*.'

'You are a big, stupid bear.'

The doe moved into the clearing and stood side-on to the hunter. He brought the cross-hairs to bear just behind the shoulder of the doe. He eased off the safety catch.

'As you wish, *gnädiges Fräulein*.'

'So, what do you want from me, Bear?'

Deep breath, breath out slowly, steady the sight and squeeze the trigger.

'I want to make love to you, until *you* cannot walk, *gnädiges Fräulein*.'

'You think that you can do that, Bear?'

'Yes.'

The doe took one huge leap forward and crumpled; a heart shot and instantaneous death.

'You know,' said Tatiana, removing her sunglasses and teasing the end of the straw in her glass with the tip of her tongue, 'I have always had a soft spot for bears.'

Waidmannsheil!!!

'Why?' said Tatiana. '*Why* can't I come with you?'

Francis sighed with patient sadness and looked down at his wife's face. She was flushed with anger, her face streaked with tears and her mouth set in a stubborn line. The wings of corn-gold hair that framed her face were awry because of her habit of running her hands through her hair when she was angry or upset. She was a tall slim girl, but Francis towered above her with his powerful frame. It was easy to see why he had been nicknamed The Bear soon after his arrival at the village, soon after young Stanislaus had shot off his mouth to Francis in the inn. Francis had 'picked him up as though he were a bag of oats,' said old Tomislav, the *Jäger*, 'and hung him by his coat collar from a bacon hook in one of the beams'. The village had chortled at this; Stanislaus and his mouth were not popular. So Francis became The Bear behind his back, and Herr Graf – it was strange how old usages came back – to his face.

Francis sighed again and put his huge hands on his wife's shoulders to draw her to him, but she pulled back and spat at him like a cat, 'A wild cat,' he thought, 'who can tame a wild cat?' He reached down to stroke the thick gold hair. The angry hurt of her countenance softened and suddenly she was in his arms, her face buried against his shoulder and her tears hot through his shirt. God, how he loved her! The thought of leaving such beauty and love, and all they had both striven to achieve, for the mud, blood and nastiness of a foreign war, filled him with foreboding but he could not and must not admit to either.

'You know damn well why you can't come. It's because I want you safe, and I need to know that you're safe. And it's because I need to know that you are looking after the estate – all we've worked for. Do you want to sacrifice all of that?'

Her voice was muffled by his body: 'Sacrifice? And what the hell do you think you are going to be, eh? You want to fight? Well, we fought to get this land back, and now you go off like some over-grown boy scout for some stupid bloody idea.'

Francis smiled to himself. Tatiana's profanity when angry had come as a shock to him in the early days of their relationship. Very gently he bent and kissed her hair. She clutched him tighter and; as Francis held her, his eyes wandered through the window to the green wooded hills that he loved so much and had struggled so hard to regain. A deep sadness filled him, but even as it did he felt the warmth of her slim body, and felt himself hardening. His big hand found its way to her taut breast and found an answering hardness.

'Bed, darling, bed.'

Tatiana raised her tear-streaked face to him, her fury softening. She raised his hand to her mouth, and gently kissed each finger.

'You great, useless, stupid bear. Is that all you think about? Do you think that solves everything?'

'No, but it helps.'

A little later, old Tomislav paused in his hobble across the courtyard and listened to the ecstatic wail from the open window high above him. He crossed himself: 'God be thanked. The Bear is rutting well.'

CHAPTER TWO

'Farrier, Farrier, come on, lad. Baxter, Baxter, good old man, Baxter.' The eager hound came leaping over the gate, and Ted Ratchett opened it to let him through.

'Now then! Bike the rest of you, stand bike!'

The leaping hounds milled and bayed with excitement in the yard of the Bardwick Hunt kennels, as Ted consulted the little hand-written card in his hand.

'Seamstress! Seamstress! Come on, old gal!' He reached out with his stick and touched the grizzled head of the old heavy-dugged bitch who was standing, shivering with her head on one side, her eyes pleading. The old bitch bounded forward to the gate.

'Aye, we'll not leave you behind, old bitch,' said Ted affectionately.

Ted Ratchett, the long-time huntsman of the Bardwick, was 'drawing' his pack for the day's hunting. As each hound on the list had its name called, it came forward to be let through the gate to the next yard. As the hunting pack grew, so did its triumphal clamour. The chosen hounds were going hunting; they knew it and rejoiced accordingly.

'Cobweb! Crimson! Trumpeter!'

As the number of chosen grew, so did those hounds on the draw yard grow fewer and more crestfallen. One old doghound, with a deep hoarse voice, was especially pushy and vocal. Ted reached down and fondled the old dog's head.

'Poor old Tartar, lad! Not today my son. You're going to have a day off. You're starting to show your age, poor old lad.' The hound pleaded with his eyes to no avail.

Soon the only hounds left on the draw yard were the halt and lame, and those whose condition had attracted Ted's expert eye as needing a 'day back' – a foxhound may run up to one hundred miles in a hunting day. The 'rest hounds' would now be fed. Ted looked over the half-door to the feed room where Tony Flitch, the young whipper-in, was making a steaming pudding of oatmeal, vitamins and meat broth.

'That pudding ready yet, Tony? Come on, lad, come on, you're half a bloody sleep!'

'Yessir!' said Tony aloud, and, 'Miserable old git,' under his breath.

Ted Ratchett was notorious for being one of the 'old school' and desperately hard on his underlings. In spite of this, there was never a shortage of applicants for jobs at Bardwick. Ted was acknowledged as a brilliant professional huntsman, and the men who worked under him, and stuck to it, were usually able to get good jobs; to have whipped-in to Mr. Ratchett – 'evil old bastard' – carried a trade mark of smartness and excellence.

Everything to his grudging satisfaction, Ted rolled back along the gravel path to get his own breakfast. He was a wizened little man, who looked like a broken hawk. He limped from a damaged leg, and hunched from a smashed shoulder, whilst one eye was cloudy from being pierced by blackthorn when he had jumped through a seemingly impassable 'bullfinch'; but folk said that old Ratchett could see more from one eye than most buggers could with two – and an extra one stuck on their foreheads.

As Ted passed the stable yard, he met another wizened little man. Bert Spurrier, the stud groom, might have been a clone of Ted. He also hirpled from many broken bones, and he too was known as one of the 'old school'. Both men had worked for the Marquis of Fowey for many years – and woe betide the underling who forgot it – but they still spoke to each other as 'Mister', and were addressed as 'Sir' by lesser mortals. It was Bert who had made a famous remark when berated by Lord Fowey. The Marquis had returned from a heavy night in London – 'pricked out', as Bert succinctly remarked – and had not found his debility and crapulous state improved by having to ride two hard-fit and keen horses during a fast and demanding day's hunting.

'Spurrier!' he had bellowed, as he dropped stiffly off his second horse at the end of the day. 'You're giving these horses too much corn. They both pulled like buggery.'

''Scuse me, milord, 'scuse me, but if anyone round here's getting too many oats, it's not my bleedin' 'osses, milord.'

'Morning, Mr. Ratchett.'

'Morning, Mr. Spurrier.' The two men greeted each other briskly. 'Who have we got from the House today?'

'Well, His Lordship, of course, although how I'm supposed to keep him in 'osses with the weight he's carrying now, I don't know. I mean he must ride twenty stone now, and still tries to go like he did twenty years gone. I told him, I did, I said, "We'll need two new 'osses by the end of the season if it goes on like this, Milord." "Well find 'em, Spurrier, find 'em," says he. But where am I to find them sort of quality 'osses these days, Mr. Ratchett?'

Ted nodded sympathetically; the excesses of their employer were a hardy and happy topic of conversation for them both.

'Lord Tamar hunting?'

23

'Not bleeding likely. Two 'osses we keep up for him, and he ain't had a leg across them all season.'

'Nor anything else much, I shouldn't wonder.'

'I think you're right there, Mr. Ratchett. All he thinks about is them pink mice of his.'

Both men brooded for a moment, Earl Tamar, the eldest son and heir of the Marquis of Fowey, was a matter of some concern to an estate that was designed and maintained around hunting and shooting. The Earl did neither with enthusiasm. What verve there may have been in his flaccid frame seemed to be reserved for the exotic guinea pigs that he bred in the old orangery.

'But Lord Frederick's home. He's hunting.'

Both men brightened.

'Now there's a real hunting man, Mr. Spurrier. I've always said I'd die happy if I thought Lord Frederick was going to take the hounds on.'

'Ah well, we better get our breakfasts, I suppose.'

'Poor Lohengrin is not at all well again this morning,' said Lord Tamar, moodily pushing some museli around his plate.

'How nice, dear,' said Lady Fowey from behind her copy of *The Daily Telegraph*. This was her invariable answer to any comment made by her family at breakfast; partly because she was rather deaf, and partly because she had long since given up all hope of any of her family saying anything that might remotely be of interest to her.

Mavis Fowey had given up what was politely referred to as a 'promising career on the stage', to become the Marchioness of Fowey. The fact that it was a promise unlikely to have been honoured, was obscured by the mists of time and family disinterest. It was only her sister-in-law who, when the vodka was biting badly, was unkind enough to suggest that the 'career' had largely consisted of servicing the needs of any male actor whose tastes verged on the heterosexual. Mavis Fowey still trailed wispy clothes and an attraction to anything that might loosely be called the 'Arts'.

'Lohengrin? Who the hell's Lohengrin?' said the other *Daily Telegraph* at the end of the table.

There were always two *Daily Telegraphs* at breakfast in Bardwick Hall: one for the Marquis, and one for the family. Marcus Fowey's habit of shouting at bits of news that annoyed him, then tearing the offending page from the paper and scrumping it up into a ball, made it difficult to read a paper after him. On days when the Government had been more than usually tiresome, and had given in yet again to 'all those pinkos and poofters', the entire paper might well end up scattered about the room. Launder, the butler, kept a special waste-paper basket, complete with family coat of arms, for the daily paper.

'You know very well, Papa, that Lohengrin is the little Mauritian Brown with the colly-wobbles. I told you about him yesterday.'

'Oh, one of your damned rats. Oh damn that – d'yer see that, Mavis? They're going to use some of that lottery money to subsidize some damned lesbians.'

'Thespians, I think, darling.'

'Same thing, ain't it?'

And the page was ripped out, crumpled up, and went sailing across the breakfast room. Launder performed a nimble one-handed catch and dropped the offending ball in his basket.

'They're not damned rats, Papa, they're guinea pigs.'

Lord Tamar assumed the hurt air of the habitually misunderstood, and returned to his muesli-stirring.

'Good morning, all.' Enter Lord Frederick, already booted and breeched, and Paddy wagging his unfortunate tail.

25

'Morning, boy.'

'Good morning, darling.'

'Good morning, Fred.'

'Good morning, Lord Frederick.'

Fred kissed his mother on the top of her perfectly coifed head, and went to help himself from the chafing dishes on the side-board.

'That's it, my boy, always have a good breakfast before hunting. It might be your last.'

Lord Fowey burst into shuddering guffaws at his witticism, which had been produced on every hunting morning since time out of memory. He always found his own jokes immensely amusing. The family gave a gentle collective sigh, and the Marquis looked at his watch:

'You better be sharp about it, too. Mustn't be late for the meet. Are you coming with me?'

'No, thank you, Father. I'll go with Tracie in the Land Rover, then I can come home when I want to.'

'Time to go home is when hounds go home.'

The family gave another collective sigh.

'Come on, Moses!' said Tracie Eggar to the horse that was sidling away from the ramp of the two-horse trailer. 'Oh, come on you old bugger. You'd think you'd never been in one before. Old Sultan's up like a perfect gent.'

'Don't reckon there's been many perfect gents in your life, Trace,' said Mags, the second girl groom.

'That's all from you, Miss,' said Trace. 'I'm riding second horse for Lord Frederick today.'

'And we all know what that means, don't we?'

'Now then, girls! Ain't them 'osses loaded yet? Mags, get the yard broom.'

'Yes, Mr. Spurrier.'

Moses allowed himself one more bout of coyness about loading, rolled his eye at the sight of the yard broom, and, not wishing to have the bristle end applied to his rear, allowed himself to be led up the ramp without further demur.

Just then Fred appeared in the stable yard, carrying his red coat and silk hat. 'Morning all.'

'Morning, Lord Fred.'

'You looking after me today, Tracie?'

'Yes, milord,' said Tracie demurely. Fred took in her pert face, her trim figure and tightly breeched bottom with appreciation. He knew, from the village grapevine, that she was nicknamed 'Pussy' – because she was so eminently strokable. He felt a brief twitch of lust beneath his breeches.

'Pull yourself together, lad,' he said to himself. 'We are going hunting.'

Francis and Tatiana may have married with all due haste, but they certainly had very little leisure to repent, even supposing they had been so inclined – which they were not. Francis's father died not long after the young couple had married but, before he died, he completed negotiations with the Slovene Government for the transfer of Schloss Lippitz, with a substantial block of agriculturally viable land, back to the Czerny family. This only came after endless bureaucratic procrastination, a lot of slivovitz, much hard bargaining, and even more hard currency. There has to be a certain satisfaction in selling stolen property back to the people from whom it was stolen, and the Government was quite happy to pocket a good tranche of dollars in exchange for a crumbling estate. The officials were also pleased to waive responsibility for the local peasantry whom, as one put it, they had 'never managed to reconstruct totally into socialism', or, as another remarked more succinctly, were 'the bolshy lot of buggers up at Lippitz'.

This was true, and when Francis and Tatiana moved into the dilapidated castle, and set about picking up the pieces of the estate, they did not find it easy. It was not that the villagers and locals were overtly hostile, it was more that their faces and doors remained closed against the 'newcomers', as they perceived them. There was only a handful of old people who remembered the Czerny family, from their previous incumbency, and experience under a Communist government had taught them caution.

Only old Tomislav and his wife Katya showed friendly faces towards the young couple. Tomislav was installed as bailiff, adviser and general factotum; Katya became house-keeper at the castle.

Francis was disappointed by the silent reserve of the villagers.

'Give them time, Herr Graf,' said Tomislav. 'They have seen many changes and a lot of trouble since the time your family was forced out. In their experience change only means trouble. You must be patient.'

Tatiana was not patient. 'These people are like sheep,' she said. 'They cannot think for themselves. Surely they see that what we are doing is for their benefit as well as ours. We give them work and they are surly – they will not even look at me when I ride through the village.'

'We must give them time.'

'Huh,' said Tatiana.

The thaw came slowly. Old Manik's boy got into trouble with the police in the city. Francis went down and sorted it out, and the boy was released.

Those having problems with officialdom – and who does not? – gradually started bringing them to Francis and so he got a reputation for sorting things out. But still the villagers' faces stayed closed. He did not feel he was making as much headway as he would have liked, and this worried him.

'What do you expect from peasants?' said Tatiana, with a toss of her golden hair.

'Patience, Herr Graf,' advised Tomislav.

Then came the day when Francis's patience snapped. It had become his custom to call occasionally at the village inn. Whenever he entered and gave the traditional greeting of '*Grüss Gott*', he noticed that all conversation stopped at once, and eyes would drop. If he tried to talk to anyone, they would answer in monosyllables; the faces closed. He sighed and persevered.

Stanislaus was a known ne'er do well in the village who had left for the city but never managed to hold down a job. When things got too difficult for him, or he was short of money, he would return to the village and sponge off his widowed mother. Stanislaus was a small, ill-conditioned man, with a long tongue that was the cause of many of his troubles. He liked to boast of his important and successful life in the city, and how no one ever put one across on him – he always saw them off, oh yes.

Thus it was that Francis entered the inn one day, and noticed a strange face at the bar. It had become his custom to order a drink and just stand at the bar; he, too, could be stubborn and silent.

This day he was leaning on the bar, when he heard a voice at his elbow:

'So you're the new landlord, then.'

Francis turned to look. Stanislaus was standing beside him with a smirk on his face. He noted the purple-veined temples, the drink-stained breath, and the leery eye; he suspected trouble. Having got some money from his mother, Stanislaus was at that stage of drunkenness when he had became tiresome.

'So you're the new high and mighty landlord, then? You think you can just waltz in here and lord it over us.'

He turned to the audience to show what a fine fellow he was.

The villagers kept their eyes fixed on the floor and waited.

'Well,' Stanislaus continued, 'we threw your lot out once before and we can do it again,' he took another swig from his glass, 'and don't think you bloody parasites can come creeping back here to suck our blood.'

It was this that made Francis's patience finally snap. With one huge hand, he reached out and grabbed the front of Stanislaus's coat.

Stanislaus panicked.

He was a runt of a man and he had roused a giant.

Then he made a mistake.

He was a knife man; his dexterity with the blade had often got him in and out of trouble before. The flick-knife came out of his pocket with an evil crack.

Francis's reaction was a blur of speed. With a massive forearm, he blocked Stanislaus's knife hand and forced his arm up behind his back. Francis then pivoted slightly, forcing his biceps under Stanislaus's armpit and, locking the hand with the knife up behind his shoulder, bent the man forward. With the other hand he forced the little finger of the knife hand to breaking point.

Stanislaus screamed with pain, dropping the flick-knife which clattered to the stone floor. Still without saying a word, Francis kicked away the knife and, seizing him by the hair, marched him to the centre of the room.

Across the roof of the bar were huge ancient beams, with big iron hooks from which hams were hung. Francis stopped below one of these and, without apparent effort, lifted the smaller man up by his shoulders and hung him up by the collar of his coat. Then, without a backward glance, he returned to his drink at the bar.

'Help! comrades, help!' cried the wriggling little man.

No one moved. Then there was a titter, a snigger, and finally a great roar of laughter. The whole bar rocked as the peasants shook and slapped each other's back with mirth, pointing at the wriggling and revolving Stanislaus.

Francis drained his glass and pushed some money across the bar. The landlord pushed the money back and, without a word, refilled Francis's glass.

'This one is on the house, Herr Graf,' he said, and broke into peals of laughter.

As the relationship between the Czernys and the village improved, the relationship between Francis and Tatiana became more difficult. There was no doubt of the very real physical passion and gentle affection that existed between them, but temperamentally they were exact opposites. Francis liked to do everything after calm deliberation, and at a steady pace. Tatiana was by nature impulsive and mercurial; if she set her mind on something, she wanted it here and now and done yesterday. She would get furious at what she considered Francis's rather plodding approach.

These clashes became more frequent as the reclaiming of Lippitz, and all the work that attended upon repairs to the castle and getting the estate back in working order, progressed.

Tatiana's incandescent rages seemed to make very little impression against Francis's monumental calm. He always managed to dodge the crockery that sometimes went whizzing past his ear.

'The Gräfin is very hard on the glass and china,' said Katya to Tomislav, as she returned to the kitchen with yet another pan full of shards.

'It keeps The Bear on his toes,' said Tomislav. 'He ought to take a stick to her. That's what I would have done to you, old woman.'

Katya cackled with laughter. 'You? You old fool! I would have bent it round your scrawny neck, and if I had thrown something at you, I would not have missed.'

Tatiana's rages went as quickly as they came, then Francis would wrap her in his arms, and hold her as her fury died in her and she was content to bury her head on his shoulder.

'Oh Bear,' she would say, 'I do love you.'

In spite of this love, their relationship became more and more stormy. Old Uncle Sepp came to visit them, and watched what was going on through his usual cloud of pipe smoke.

After one of Tatiana's flare-ups, when she had stormed out of the room, Francis sat down at the table where the old man was puffing away, seemingly as imperturbable as ever. Francis put his head in his hands, and his huge body seemed to sag with tiredness and sadness.

'Uncle, what am I doing wrong?'

The old man got up and went to the sideboard where a bottle of slivovitz always stood. He poured two glasses and put one in front of Francis.

'*Prosit*,' he said. 'That girl is a wild cat,' he continued, 'always has been. I knew her from a kid and I was probably the only one who had any control over her. Now, I know that you love her, and that she loves you, but if you don't gaffer her, boy, she is going to trample all over you. It's her nature. If you don't keep her at your feet, she will always be at your throat. Think about it for both your sakes. Well, I must be going. But mind on what I have told you.'

'And do you have any practical suggestion as to how I set about this taming?'

Uncle Sepp stood silent for a moment, and then walked to a side-table in the hall where there was a jumble of dog leads and whips. From the pile he selected

32

a cutting-whip and, without another word, placed it on the table in front of Francis.

The storm broke the next day. It began as a little squall over a minor domestic matter, which progressed with lightning speed to one of Tatiana's more spectacular electrical storms. Francis, in his usual way, let the storm break over him and said nothing. He was sitting in his usual place at the table in the great hall, with estate papers spread in front of him. Tatiana had just returned from her morning ride and, as the storm raged and her eyes flashed, she came and stood over him. Francis sat silent, his eyes on the table.

'You are a dumb ox,' Tatiana screamed, 'can't you answer? You just sit there. You see, you have no answer!'

Francis sighed and looked up. Dear God, but she was lovely with her tossing hair and flashing eyes, but, but . . .

'Enough,' he said.

'Enough! Oh, you've had enough have you, you great bullock? Well let me tell you –'

'Stop it!'

'I'll stop when I bloody well want to –' She stopped.

Francis had risen to his feet. His face was stony. 'I said, enough.'

Tatiana looked at the face. She looked at the eyes which had developed a strange greeny light. She felt a tremor.

Without another word, Francis walked across to the side-table and picked up the cutting-whip that Uncle Sepp had put in front of him. He turned again to Tatiana.

Tatiana looked. She saw the whip. She saw Francis's face. In spite of herself, she backed away, back against the table. 'You wouldn't dare!'

Francis said nothing. He walked towards her.

'No!'

She swung a hand at his face.

He grabbed her by the wrist.

'No!'

Still that fearful silence. Francis loosed her wrist and seized a handful of her golden hair.

'No! Don't!'

He unbuckled the belt of her buckskin breeches, and then forced her face-down across the table.

'No! You bastard, I'll kill you!'

She felt her breeches being pulled down roughly around her knees – then her pants. His hand was gripping her hair, hurting her.

She began to scream.

The first blow seared her buttocks.

Her screams were clearly heard in the kitchen.

'Dear God,' said Tomislav, who was enjoying a cup of coffee. 'There's murder on!'

Katya seized the big cleaver from beside the stove, and they rushed to the door of the hall and opened it just as the second blow fell.

Tatiana screamed again.

'Holy Mother of God!' said Katya, pushing forward.

Tomislav caught her arm, pulled her firmly back and shut the door.

'My coffee's getting cold,' he said.

Francis released his hold on Tatiana's hair, and she collapsed sobbing to the stone flags of the floor. She looked up through her tears. Silent and motionless, Francis towered above her, the whip still in his hand. Still sobbing, she reached up and clasped his knees.

'Please!' she said.

Francis neither spoke nor moved. She raised her tear-wet eyes to his face. It was expressionless, but she could not miss the bulge in his trousers.

Still watching his face, she raised herself and brought

34

her lips to the bulge. Her hair was roughly seized and her head forced back.

'Beg!' said Francis.

Tatiana gave a little sob. 'Please.'

'Please what?'

'Please, Master.'

'That's better,' and he let go of her hair.

'Morning, George.'

'Morning, Fred.'

'Morning, sir.'

'Thanks, Stan, one of those whiskies looks good. Need a bit of spirit for the Vale.'

The meet at the Knackerman's Arms was a favourite fixture of the Bardwick Hunt. The pub stood amongst a scattering of houses on a little knoll that overlooked the Evenrush Vale, – a wide expanse of grass fields with stout thorn hedges. It was dotted with little coverts that had been planted long ago as a haven for wildlife in general, and foxes in particular. For those who came hunting to gallop and jump fences, the Vale was a mouth-watering prospect. For those who came to watch hounds hunt a fox, the wide open vistas, and the multiplicity of quarry, offered a chance for Ted Ratchett and his famous hounds to deploy their best skills.

The Vale was on the Bardwick estate, where vulpicide ranked as a capital offence. Thus there was a large gathering of well-mounted 'thrusters', and an even larger gathering of dedicated car followers. All of which added to the already strung-out nerves of 'Cardiac' Ponsonby, the Field Master. It was his unfortunate duty to act as buffer between the hard-riding field and the human grenade that the Marquis became out hunting. Cardiac was pouring large brown libations into his nervous system in the bar.

On the other side of the mêlée: 'Morning, Ratchett.'

'Morning, Lord Frederick. Very good to see you.'

'Good to be out. How many?'

'Twenty-two and a half. Might be some scent.'

'Hope so! Tamar's Whins first?'

'That's what your father said, sir.'

Tamar's Whins was a gorse covert on the bank below the pub. It had been planted on the occasion of Lord Tamar's birth, when his father had hoped that his heir's addiction to fur and feather would match his own. Tamar's penchant for small furry things in cages was not quite what his father had had in mind. However, Tamar's Whins had developed a formidable reputation as a source from which good hunts flowed.

'Hounds, gentlemen, please,'

Now there was a flurry of draining glasses, heaving into saddles, tightening girths. Horses sweated and became restive in the air of excitement and anticipation. Nerves twanged like bowstrings as they clattered and jostled down the narrow lane from the pub, and debouched onto a wide grassy field that ran along the top of the whins. Below them the Vale stretched away, the thorn and timber fences standing out black and sharp in the clear winter light.

'Fences look black.'

'Aye, I bet the buggers'll run today.'

'You never know with scent.'

'Nothing as queer as scent, 'cept a woman.'

'Oh, hold up, you bloody horse.'

'Darling! My curb chain's too loose, I'm sure. Jump off and check it for me.'

'Oh, shit, Myrtle! You always do this!'

'Well really, darling, I do think . . .'

Fred slipped away from the chattering throng to go on point.

'You'll take your usual spot, sir?' Ratchett had muttered to him at the meet. 'That big old dog fox is still lying in the whins! Get us on him if you can. He always goes right into the Vale.'

The 'usual spot' was at a bottom corner of the covert, where a wicket and a bridge crossed a broad and weed-strewn rhyne. This was a favourite spot for foxes to exit into the Vale. Fred crossed the bridge and settled himself. From there he could watch two sides of the square-shaped covert and, on a hill above him, a black-coated farmer, on a sharp cob, was settled at the top corner. At the other corner, Fred could see the red coat of Tony.

Old Moses had been quite skittish, and had even essayed a rather feeble buck coming down the hill. Now he stood like a rock, his ears pricked, his eye bright – Old Moses loved hunting. Fred cocked his leg forward and checked his girth straps for the tenth time; he could feel the tight knot of nerves in his stomach.

Above him he could see the tiny scarlet figure of Ratchett as he slowly moved along the ride in the covert. His voice came floating down the hill as he encouraged his hounds to enter the depths of the gorse: 'Leu in – leu in – try,' a huntsman's cry since the time it was Norman-French *loupe*. 'Wouldn't mind seeing a wolf go away,' thought Fred, 'bet it'd give a cracking hunt.'

The Hunter looked at the tracks in the snow with interest and surprise. With his stick he very carefully circled the outline of a pad print and then, kneeling down, he delicately touched the impression with his finger. So the wolves were back. The time of the wolf was returning, and this was a big one from the size of its prints – as big as he had ever seen. The Hunter slowly rubbed his beard, feeling a tingle of excitement. There were interesting times ahead. There would be blood on the snow before long.

'Yeu find him, my lovers – yohoote try!'

The whins were shaking as the eager hounds forced their way underneath them, their delicate noses whiffing for a taint of fox. There were stale lines everywhere. Then Cobweb felt a rank blast of scent in her nose – a fresh waft of fox scent. 'Fox! Fox!' she shouted.

Far below, Fred heard the old bitch's opening whimper and stiffened. Moses heard it too and stamped a foot. Fred smoothed the horse's neck.

Trumpeter had flown to Cobweb's squeak and his bass bellow endorsed her find. The gorse swayed and crackled as the other hounds scrambled to join in. The cry grew and swelled as the whole pack settled on the line and rejoiced in the scent they had been bred to triumph in – *Fox*.

It was quickly obvious that there was a scent – scent, that strange effervescent thing that foxes hunt by, and are hunted by. The hound voices became a mighty chorus, the urgent 'doubling' of Ratchett's horn, and his high-pitched 'On—on—on—on' driving them.

Fred concentrated on his corner. He glimpsed the farmer above him raise his cap and point it back into the whins; the fox had showed at that corner.

Back and forth the cry surged in the covert.

'If he don't go soon,' said Fred to Moses, 'they'll slot him in the whins.'

The lithe red shape slipped quietly out of the bottom of the whins, and leaped the rhyne effortlessly. For a moment he paused, with one paw raised, as he listened to the racket in the covert behind him. Fred and Moses stood like a rock. The fox cocked an eye at them, then set off across the field at a steady lope. 'One—two—three,' Fred chanted to himself. He was a big fox, a huge dog fox – almost as big as a wolf.

The Hunter smiled to himself.

'Twenty-eight, twenty-nine, thirty.' The fox slipped through the fence at the end of the field. Fred rose in his stirrups and holloaed. A good 'view holloa' cannot be reduced to print; it is a spine-tingling, nerve-jangling screech – a long descanting scream, as old as hunting itself, that tells everybody that the quarry has 'gone away'.

Even as Fred holloaed, the first hounds came bursting over the covert fence in a wave of white, black, lemon and brown. They were feasting on the scent of the fox and declaring their ecstasy to all the world. As they did so, Ratchett came rocketing over the hunt jump at the bottom of the ride.

'Forrard away—forrard away—forrard awaaay,' Fred chanted, and Ratchett's horn chorused that most thrilling of all calls, the 'gone away'.

'Twenty-two and a half, all on,' shouted Fred as he galloped beside Ratchett, 'and he's a corker.'

The little man gave Fred a twisted grin as he thrust the hunting horn back into the case on the pommel of his saddle, and the first big black fence loomed up before them.

Fred took one glance behind him. The field was galloping down the hill and filing over the bridge. He could imagine the nervous shouting, impatience and jostling, then he dismissed the thought.

Moses cocked his ears as the fence loomed up – a thick well-trimmed thorn fence with a ditch on the take-off side. Fred dropped his hands. Moses sized up the obstacle and, standing well back, launched himself, the momentum of the gallop and the great power of his quarters taking horse and rider soaring out over ditch and fence.

High up on the ancient earthworks of Woodman's Hill, the Hunter could see the whole Vale spread below him. Leaning on his stick, he was able to see the panorama of the hunt take shape.

He could see the fox, still going easily but with a sense of urgency.

He could see the hounds, flying like a flock of vari-coloured birds across the green fields, their wild cry floating up to him on the breeze. He could see two red-coated figures taking fence after fence, with deceptive ease, on the flank of the flying pack.

He could see the thrusters in the first flight of the field, riding with desperate valour to try and catch up with those elusively flitting scarlet figures before them. He could see the grief and pain behind them, as the pace and the big fences took their toll on the old and not so bold.

He could see the little knot of figures, and the cloud of steam and blasphemy, which indicated that the Marquis and his horse were down in a ditch.

He could see Doctor Matcham, and his horse Teddy, who between them demolished every fence that they came across and, as a consequence, always attracted a deferential follow-ing of the timorous.

He could see the column of motorized followers snaking its way along the road that skirted the Vale.

He could see the green lane where Tracie and the other second horsemen were proceeding at a decorous pace to keep in touch. His eye paused for a moment on the distant trim form of Tracie.

The Hunter lifted his binoculars and focused on Fred as he sailed over yet another fence. 'A true hunter,' thought the Hunter.

There is a moment in every great hunt when those who take part in it know that it has ceased to be a hunt, and has become a HUNT.

The pace had slowed a bit, but hounds were still hunt-ing steadily and inexorably, their fierce music floating back to Fred and Ratchett, who were taking fence for fence as they came. Behind them, the mounted field was spread and tailed off. Hounds were heading down into the Marsh.

The Vale lies between the hills and the big river. The part that lies beside the river is known as the 'Marsh', and here the ground is wetter and floods at times. The fields are divided by rhynes – wide water-filled dikes, green with weed and bottomless with primeval ooze; get a horse into one of those and you need a tractor, time and strong men to pull it out. One needs a bold horse and a stout heart to ride that country.

Fred thought of nothing except the hounds in front of him, the wind in his face, and the powerful feeling of his horse galloping beneath him. At each rhyne, he would drop his hands, and Moses would cock his ears and sail out across the scum-filled water with a crack of his nostrils; then on, on across the wet fields, with hooves sending up mud and spray.

At the bottom of the Marsh, alongside the river, were the Low Woods – a rough expanse of boggy woodland and withy beds which was a haven for all wildlife, especially foxes. That was where the fox was obviously heading. There he would find plenty of fresh brethren to divert the hounds.

The pace and deep going were beginning to tell on Moses. A glance to the side showed Fred that Ratchett's horse was obviously in trouble, and they were heading for the 'Black Rhyne'. This was a particularly wide rhyne, with a straggling thorn hedge on both sides. Not many attempted to jump it. Fred knew that the nearest gate and bridge were half a mile to the right; to divert might mean losing hounds. He looked at Ratchett. The little man gave a wry smile and then a jerk of his head.

'We've got to have it, sir,' he shouted.

Both men collected their horses and settled down to

ride at the Black Rhyne; only speed, boldness and impulsion would get them over.

Fred felt Moses gather himself; then came a great soaring leap, a crash through the straggling thorns, a glimpse of black, weedy water far below, and the exhilaration of landing safely. Then there was a mighty crash on Fred's left. Ratchett's horse had not made it. Its hindquarters had dropped into the water, and Ratchett himself had been pitched forward onto the bank.

Fred reined in. Ratchett's horse scrambled gamely, then slid back into the ooze so that it sat in the water like a begging dog. The small crumpled figure in the bog-stained coat lay still for a minute. 'Christ!' thought Fred. 'He's knacked,' but the little man stirred and rose groggily to his feet.

'Here,' Fred said, kicking his feet from the stirrup irons, 'take Moses.'

'No, milord, I'm done. My bloody shoulder's gone. Here.'

He held out his battered hunting horn to Fred. Fred naturally hesitated. 'Take it, man, take it, for fuck's sake, and don't come back without that bloody brush.'

The two men grinned at each other, then Fred took the horn. As he galloped away, a glance over his shoulder showed the little man standing forlornly beside his horse's head.

Moses was failing, game though he was. Fred knew that the horse would go on till he dropped, but he would not allow that. Oh, for his second horse! But Tracie must be miles away.

He galloped over a farm bridge and onto a green drove road. Hounds were splashing through a rhyne two fields in front of him. He could keep in touch with them on the lane for a bit, anyway until the next bend . . . round the bend came Tracie, trotting demurely along on Sultan. Oh, Fabolous Day!

'How the bloody hell did you find us?'

The Hunter smiled.

Tracie wasted no time with words, and she had never been able to spell 'intuition' anyway. She brought Sultan up on Moses's off-side and slipped out of the saddle. Like a flash she was round and holding both horses by their heads. Fred put his hands on the pommel of Sultan's saddle and vaulted across onto his back.

'Good luck, Lord Fred!'

'You're a fucking marvel, Tracie!'

'That's all you know about, milord,' said Tracie to herself as Sultan plunged eagerly forwards.

The Hunter had been watching the action. He saw Fred change horses and nodded approval. Then he stuck two fingers in his mouth and whistled as a shepherd whistles to his collie.

Fred could never understand why the fox had suddenly turned away from the almost certain sanctuary of the Low Woods, but there was no doubt about it; hounds were running away from the Marsh, and now heading back towards the steep-sided cone of Woodman's Hill that stuck out into the Vale like a promontory. 'My God, what a hunt,' he thought, and still the cry urged him on.

The short winter's day was starting to close.

The pace of the pack was beginning to falter, and a big flock of ewes, in a field below Woodman's Hill, brought them to a check. It was dimpsey now.

'I better try and pick them up,' Fred said to himself, looking at the hounds doggedly picking out the line through the sheep foil, 'but surely that fox can't be far in front of them now?' He pulled out the horn from the front of his coat.

43

From the lane at the bottom of the hill came a spine-tingling view holloa; someone had seen the fox.

Fred did not hesitate. He galloped up to the pack. 'Yere! Yere! Yere!' with a short staccato note on the horn. Hounds flew to the note, and they galloped to the lane.

Fred had never seen the big bearded man before, but he was pointing with his long stick.

'He's crossed the lane just by the holly bush. He's only just before you, and he's done for.'

'Thank you so much.' Fred turned Sultan's head and, as he did so, little Gossamer squeaked at the gap in the hedge. The pack flew to her.

Fred popped the post-and-rails off the lane, and onto the sweeping slope of Woodman's Hill. He saw the fox toiling up the hillside a hundred yards above him. Hounds saw him at the same time and surged forwards. Fred sat quietly. A snap and a snarl, and it was all over; a swirl of hounds came tumbling down the steep slope worrying at the carcass.

'Who whoop! worry! worry! worry!' Fried cried, leaping off the back of the heaving Sultan, and rattling his horn over the tugging, growling pack. The brush! he must have the brush for Ted Ratchett! He felt for his pocket knife and cursed. It was not there: 'never go hunting without a knife, a shilling and a piece of string.'

'Use mine,' said the bearded man, handing him a well-worn horn-handled clasp knife.

'Thanks,' said Fred, thinking who the hell is he? 'Stand bike, hounds.'

Ringed by the baying pack, he began peeling off the brush of the gallant fox.

'Waidmannsheil!'

Fred had hunted in Germany. *'Waidmannsdank,'* he said automatically, 'Who –'

There was no one there.

44

But Fred stood looking at the bone-handled knife in his hand.

Fred was drunk when Tracie found him. After she had watched him gallop off, she studied the direction that hounds had taken, and then set off back to the meet to get the Land Rover and trailer.

As she hacked along on a loose rein with a very tired Moses, she met scattered refugees from the hunt, and frustrated car-followers who had been completely thrown out by the strange turn that hounds had made 'down the Marsh'.

'Heading for Woodman's Hill?' they said. 'They never are! My Gor! That would be some bliddy hunt! Come Denis, boy! Git on down this bliddy road! Ta-ra Trace.'

'What! what!' cried old Colonel Huffley, leading a lame horse, with his top hat looking more like a concertina. 'Woodman's Hill, you say? But hounds never run that way from the Marsh, what? By Jove, what an absolute corker!'

Tracie got back to the box, and had Moses rugged-up and pulling at his haynet. The horse was tired, but he was such a tough old bugger she did not reckon he would come to much harm. Now it was just a case of finding her wandering Lord. She had a fair idea where he might be.

Old Harold Truscott farmed Woodman's Hill and the surrounding land. He had hunted all his life, but now what he referred to as 'age, vice and unsoundness' kept him grounded. He had been to the meet. His son Gilbert, and his grandson, Young Harold, were both amongst the mounted field. Harold had seen hounds find, and had watched, with a pang of nostalgia, as the hunt streamed away across the Vale.

'Oh God, what wouldn't I give to get on a horse again,'

he said to his old crony and sparring partner, Jimmy Robins.

'You'd only fall straight off the other side,' said that unfeeling man. 'Why, I minds the time after the Hunt Ball, when it took two of us to get 'ee on the horse, and one t'other side to stop 'ee falling off again.'

'Well, what about that time you was so drunk that you went head-first in the rhyne over to Gidley? If Frank and I hadn't pulled 'ee out, you'd still be there blowing bubbles.'

Quarrelling happily the two men hobbled back to the pub.

'They'm heading for Low Woods, certain sure – they'll be there for the day, I reckon.'

Thus it was a very surprised Harold Truscott who, hobbling about the yard back at Lower Wodton, heard the distant music of hounds.

'Lordy-pips, it never be hounds? Not right back yere!' Then he heard the holloa and the horn. 'Damn, but they've killed him, I reckon, and right back yere. Well, I be damned! Get the kettle on, Mother, and get the whisky out – hounds'll be yere d'rectly, I reckon.'

And so it came to pass. Fred collected the hounds and, knowing they were miles from the meet and transport, set out to find a place where there might be shelter and, perhaps, a little something else for man and beast.

At Lower Wodton he found it all: a well-strawed loose box for hounds, another for Sultan, along with a rug and a bran mash, and for himself a seat by the roaring fire and whisky, tea, cake and more whisky, as he re-lived 'The Great Tamar's Whin Day' for the benefit of the family Truscott.

'Now then, my dear, bless my soul, look. His Lordship's glass is empty. Fetch another bottle out the cupboard. Now, sir, you had the Black Rhyne? Why, I remember when Jimmy Robins and me . . .' and another wave of whisky and reminiscence flooded over the company.

By the time Tracie discovered that her hunch was correct, and had pulled up in the Lower Wodton yard, Fred was flying on a high-octane mixture of adrenaline and alcohol.

Various telephone calls had also brought Tony Flitch and the hound lorry to the farm. Poor Ted Ratchett, with his shoulder strapped and a powerful sedative administered, was spending the night in hospital 'for observation' but, judging from some of his observations to the nursing staff, they would not be keeping him in for any longer than was strictly necessary.

After hounds and Sultan had been loaded in their respective boxes, it became a question of loading Fred and this was proving slightly more problematical. He was definitely 'walking wounded', and determined to sing 'John Peel'. However, between the Truscotts and Tony, with Tracie directing manoeuvres, and with a lot of 'Now, sir, watch your head' and 'left hand down a bit', with, 'Now he ish gone! gone far, far away and we'll ne'er hear his horn in the moooorning – ishn't that a grand shong, Mish Truscott?', Fred was eventually installed in the passenger seat of the Land Rover and firmly strapped in.

'Do you think you'll be all right, Trace?' asked Tony.

'Don't you worry. I can handle him.'

'Thank you, thank you all you lovely Trushcotts.'

'Good bye, milord.'

In the Land Rover, the conversation continued: 'That wash a smashing hunt, Tracie, a smashing hunt, do you know that, do you?'

'Yes, Lord Frederick.'

'And you're a smashing girl, Tracie, an absolute corker, d'yer know that, do you?'

'Very kind, I'm sure.'

'I would like to be very kind to you, Tracie.'

Fred felt a whisky-induced rekindling of the flash of lust which he had felt that morning. He put out a hand, and gently stroked Tracie's slim thigh.

'Lord Frederick,' reprimanded Tracie, 'what *are* you doing?'

'Shtroking your thigh, Old Thing.'

'And what would Miss Annabel say, if she knew?'

'Well, I'm not going to tell her, Tracie. Gosh you're pretty, Tracie.'

With a determined expression on her face, Tracie pulled the Land Rover and trailer into a gateway, and turned to face her troublesome passenger. 'Look, I'm not having this all the way home – we'll finish up in the ditch – so I'm going to put a stop to it now. Now, you just sit back in your seat, like a good Lord Frederick, behave yourself and let me get on with it. You're in no fit state for anything. Aren't you ashamed?'

'Yes,' said Fred.

'Well, you just sit back and be quiet.'

Then, a few moments later, Fred said, 'What are you doing, Tracie?'

Tracie, who had been bought up never to talk with her mouth full, vouchsafed no coherent reply.

'Miss Annabel wouldn't like this, Tracie. But oh! That is lovely!'

Tracie raised her head for a moment. 'I'm not going to tell her, Lord Frederick.'

'For the purposes of this exercise, Tracie, you may call me "Frederick" – Yes! Yes! Yes! Go on! Go on!'

And she did.

CHAPTER THREE

'Wolves,' said Francis, 'are you sure?' Tomislav shrugged: 'The Hunter says so. He has seen the signs. He knows.'

'Ah, the Hunter,' said Francis.

He knew of the Hunter. Everybody knew of the Hunter; he was a local legend, but few people had ever met him. He was supposed to live in a remote house high in the forested foothills, but if you asked anyone where the house was exactly, they would shrug their shoulders and say: 'Up there somewhere,' pointing to the high peaks of the mountains, streaked with snow even in high summer. It seemed that no one had actually been to the Hunter's house, they just knew it was 'up there'.

'You know the Hunter, then?' said Francis with interest.

'No one *knows* him Herr Graf, but I have met him now and again over the years. But now that I am old and lame, I cannot get out into the hills like I used to. The Hunter, however, never seems to change.'

'You've seen him recently, though?'

'Yes, Herr Graf. Yesterday he brought a deer for the schloss with his compliments. That is a great honour, Herr Graf. He used to bring a deer for your grandfather and your father occasionally. He used to get on well with your father. They talked a lot. It was the Hunter who warned us when the Russians were coming, so that your father could get away over the Border. He guided us, too. He knows all the secret ways over the hills.'

'But surely this cannot be the same man? This must be a son or something?'

Tomislav shrugged again and said nothing, his face closed like a door. Francis knew that expression, and knew that it was a waste of time asking any more questions.

'I would like to meet this man.'

Tomislav's face remained closed, but he said, 'He sent you a message. He said he wanted to meet the son of the father, and to take you hunting. He will meet you and the Frau Gräfin at the Wolf's Slack at dawn any morning you like. He said to tell you that he knows of a good buck for you to take. I am to let him know.'

'How will you let him know?'

Tomislav remained silent and impassive.

'Very well,' said Francis, 'tell him Wednesday morning.'

'Wednesday would be a good choice, Herr Graf.'

'But who is this man, darling?' asked Tatiana a little while later.

'No one really knows. He's a bit of a mystery man – lives all alone up in the hills. If it's the same man that Father knew, he must be as old as those same hills by now. I think that this must be a son.'

'Do you really think there are wolves?'

'There's always been the odd few up in the mountains, but they never bothered us down here. I suppose it could be that the fighting has disturbed them and driven them over their side of the Border. Anyway, let's go and meet this mystery man and hear what he has to say.'

'What is this Wolf's Slack?'

'It's a steep rocky gully with a river running through it, right up in the foothills of the mountains. It's so deep and steep that the sun hardly ever gets in there. I've only been there once myself, it's a creepy place. The story is that there was once a Devil Wolf that lived there and caused a lot of damage, until it was killed.'

'How do you kill a Devil Wolf?'

'With difficulty, according to the legend. The locals tried all ways, without success, and then a mysterious stranger came with some hounds, and there was a great hunt at the end of which the Devil Wolf was killed. I can't remember all the details. I haven't heard the story since I was a child. So, shall you come on Wednesday?'

'Of course. I want to meet this mysterious man.'

'There is a wood-cutters' track that will take us nearly to the bottom of the slack. We can get up in 4-wheel-drive.'

The Hunter sat on the big rock at the bottom of the Wolf's Slack. His rifle and deer sack lay on the ground beside him. He had wrapped his loden cape around him against the chill of the pre-dawn. His nose twitched as he sifted through the scents of the summer early morning; the smells of pine, bracken and wet woodland were pleasing to him, and then the rank dog-like smell hit his palate all the harder – there was no doubt about the smell – wolf! The Hunter felt the old tingle of excitement – the Wolf Days were coming back, and with them the days of the Wild Hunt. The game was afoot.

His keen hearing caught the far-off sound of an engine grinding up-hill in low gear. The hunters were coming.

His nose smelled blood.

As Francis and Tatiana got out of the jeep, the man rose from the rock where he had been sitting.

'*Waidmannsheil!*'

'*Waidmannsdank!*' said Francis.

They shook hands and Francis took a good look at the Hunter. He was a huge man with a bushy beard. He looked upright and fit. Francis would have put him in his forties, but with that beard it was hard to tell. This *must* be the son of the Hunter whom his father had known.

'I knew your father well,' said the Hunter.

'But . . .' began Francis.

The man smiled, crinkling up the corners of his eyes, his white teeth gleaming through his beard. 'You think that I don't look old enough?'

'Well . . .' said Francis.

'Looks can be very deceptive. I may be older than you think.' The man gave a bark of laughter. 'I must might be much older. And now, greetings Gräfin.'

The Hunter took Tatiana's small white hand in his huge weather-beaten paw and bowed over it formally.

'The Gräfin is very beautiful, Graf. I hope that you make the most of each other while you can.'

His eyes twinkled.

Francis was bemused by all this; the man spoke and behaved like a gentleman, yet his clothes seemed to be more patch than cloth; then again, the rifle lying on the ground looked like a custom-made job.

'I had it made for me,' said the Hunter, apparently reading Francis's thoughts. 'It is one of the perks of my position.'

'And what position?' Francis longed to ask, but there was something about the man that prevented questions, a sense that he would only tell you what he thought you needed to know. Francis kept his silence.

There might have been many questions that both Francis and Tatiana could have put to the Hunter, but he gave them neither chance nor encouragement. The greetings over, he shrugged himself into the shoulder-straps of his deer sack, slung his rifle over his right shoulder, picked his stick up in his left hand and waited silently whilst Francis hurriedly got his own rifle out of the jeep and loaded it. Then, without another word, the Hunter turned away and set off up the steep, broken hillside to the left of the Wolf's Slack.

The Hunter climbed with the slow, steady stride of an experienced hill man – a deceptively slow gait, that the unaccustomed find impossible to match.

'My God,' said Francis to himself, 'I don't know how old this chap is, but he is certainly fit.' He paused to offer Tatiana a hand over a tumble of boulders strewn down the hillside. 'I wish the bugger would stop for a minute.' As though he had heard, the Hunter stopped and turned round, leaning on his stick as his two followers panted up the steep slope to where he was waiting.

'He's not even breathing hard enough to blow out a candle,' thought Francis.

'Rest a moment,' said the man as they came up to him, 'it's a steep slope.'

'Now,' he said, when Francis and Tatiana had got their breath back, 'there is something I want to show you.'

He led them along the hillside, ducking and weaving through a scrub of stunted birch trees to a little clearing, a dip in the gradient through which ran a small stream. Half in and half out of the stream lay a deer, or rather the remains of a deer; its throat had been torn out, its entrails and most of its hind quarters had been eaten, and bits of hide and bone lay scattered across the blood-stained grass, trampled and flattened where the death struggle had taken place. The wet soil by the edge of the stream, where the carcass lay, had been well trampled. The Hunter knelt down and beckoned to Francis. In the confusion of trampled mud there were some distinct prints; they might have been the pad marks of a dog, a very large dog. The Hunter carefully traced the outline of one of the marks with his finger.

'Wolf,' he said, 'and a very big one.'

'Perhaps it's another Devil Wolf,' said Tatiana with a rather nervous laugh.

'If it is,' said the Hunter, 'you won't find much to laugh about.'

'Are there many?' asked Francis.

'There will be more. The fighting is driving them over the Border. It is the time of the wolf. Right, we must get on.'

At the top of the steep slope they came to a flower-scattered stretch of meadow land. The early sun was already warm upon their backs, and the breeze blew fresh and cool in their faces, carrying with it the scent of field and woods.

The Hunter skirted the edge of the meadow, keeping to the tree line. After about a mile, a small valley began to open up in front of them, into which the meadow dipped and was divided by a rushing, boulder-strewn hill stream. Beyond the stream, the meadow rose again through a scattering of scrubby birch and willow that merged into a straggling wood of beech and pine on the far slope.

The Hunter paused and turned to his followers. 'Now we must go very quietly, and no more talking.'

In single file, they crept down the side of the wood to where the trees came to a point. Here there was a tumble of boulders. The Hunter held up his hand and motioned for Francis and Tatiana to stay where they were whilst he crept forward to the rocks. Crouching behind one of the bigger boulders, he raised his field glasses and looked at the valley below him. Then he waved the waiting couple to come quietly. Bent double, they crept forward to the cover of the rocks.

'We wait,' whispered the Hunter.

Very carefully he slipped off the deer sack and, putting it to the ground, motioned Tatiana to sit on it.

They waited in silence, well-screened by the rocks

from the valley below. The sky was blue with scattered clouds. There was an increasing warmth from the sun. Finches twittering in the pines behind them, and almost every tree top seemed to have a thrush singing its heart out. A hare came lolloping through the lush grass below them. Tatiana put her hand on Francis's arm, and he put his big hand over hers: a moment of contentment in this peaceful place.

The Hunter kept scanning the valley with his binoculars. He stiffened and concentrated on a spot. Patting Francis on the knee, he pointed. Very slowly, so as to make no sudden movement. Francis raised his binoculars in the direction the Hunter was pointing. There was a scattered stand of young silver birch down by the stream, about two hundred yards to the left of the rocks where they were sitting. At first Francis saw nothing. Then a glimpse of movement caught his eye, an ear flicked against an early morning fly. A buck was browsing in the birch. He was a fine mature beast, with a very good six-pointed head of antlers, which could now be seen as he stretched up to reach some especially juicy leaf from high in the scrub. Most of his body was screened by the bushes. The Hunter held out his hand as a signal to wait. The buck was feeding quietly, moving slowly through the birch, stopping and then moving on. The Hunter pointed to a gap in the scrub towards which the buck was moving.

A rock in front of Francis provided a perfect rest for his left hand. He worked the rifle into position very carefully and, nestling his cheek against the stock, lined up the cross-hairs of the telescopic sight on the opening. The buck was suddenly alert, his head raised, his nose feeling the wind; some sound, some scent had disturbed him. He moved forward and paused again, still testing the wind.

'Now, Graf!' whispered the Hunter.

The cross-hairs steadied on the point just below the shoulder. Francis squeezed the trigger.

'A good shot Graf,' said the Hunter as Francis unloaded his rifle. 'I have paced it at a hundred and fifty metres. You were right to take him then, something had disturbed him.

The buck lay in the lush grass, his brown eyes already glazed in death.

'It does always seem so sad,' said Tatiana, 'life snuffed out like that.'

The Hunter had snapped open the worn-bladed knife with the horn-scaled hilt; he turned back to look at Tatiana. 'He had a good life and quick death. There's many a human that would like to be able to claim the same.'

He bent to the gralloch.

'Look, look!' said Tatiana suddenly. Both men were bent over the buck; they jerked up and followed the line of her pointing finger.

The wolf was standing in the fringe of the wood on the far side of the valley. He was watching them, and he looked huge.

'Shoot, man! Shoot!'

Francis grabbed his rifle from the ground, took quick aim and squeezed the trigger. Click! Damn! Damn! Damn! Of course he had unloaded the rifle when they arrived at the buck. He worked the bolt and pushed a round into the chamber, but as he fired the wolf frisked his tail and disappeared into the wood.

The Hunter turned back to the buck. 'In the time of the wolf, Graf, you cannot afford to miss. Remember that.'

They left the Hunter by the boulder where they had met him. After they had loaded the carcass into the back of the jeep, the huge man shook hands with both of them.

Francis started to thank him.

'No thanks are necessary. It has been a good morning – a happy morning, and one I hope you will both remember.'

'Do you think the wolves will be a problem?'

'Wolves are always a problem. I think there will be difficult times ahead.'

'When shall we meet you again?'

The Hunter did not answer at once, and frowned as though trying to listen to some far off sound. Then he said, 'Oh, I shall be about. I'm always about. I will let Tomislav know about the wolves.'

'Will you be able to shoot some?'

The Hunter paused again, and again seemed to listen. 'There may have to be a different answer. Now I must go. God go with you both!'

And he turned and walked to the edge of the trees, where the thicket seemed to swallow him up.

'What a strange man,' said Francis.

'Yes, but I liked him.'

'You just like big men!'

'Yes, Bear, and when we get home I will show you just how much.'

'You randy minx! Is that all you think about?'

'I can't think what you mean,' said Tatiana demurely.

'Humbug!' said Francis, slamming the driver's door and starting the engine. He put the jeep into gear and moved forward, then suddenly stopped and, without a word, leaped out, walked back to the boulder, and stood looking at the boggy ground, his brow furrowed. He came slowly back to the vehicle, and sat for a moment, staring forward with his knuckles white on the steering wheel.

'What is it, darling?'

Francis shook his head, then said slowly, 'You know where the Hunter walked off? The wet ground?'

'Yes, so what?'

'There were no footprints.'

Tatiana put down her coffee cup and giggled. Francis put some cheese on his slice of rye bread and looked up. 'What's the slut been up to now?'

'You're not to call Mitzi a slut. She's a friend of mine!'

'Exactly.'

'You are saying that I am a slut?'

Francis grinned at his wife across the table. 'Let us say you have interesting habits that you would hardly have picked up in your smart finishing school.'

'Name one!'

Francis did.

Tatiana pouted. 'What do you think finishing schools are for? That's exactly where you learn that sort of thing.'

'I thought they were meant to teach you to curtsy.'

'Well, I can curtsy as well.'

'Well, you can damn well curtsy to me the next time you do that particular piece of sluttishness!'

Tatiana threw a piece of bread at her husband. 'You're a boorish bear.'

'Slut!'

'Impotent worm!'

'Enough! enough!' said Francis laughing. 'Just calm down and tell me what that slut Mitzi's been up to now.'

As he listened to the on-going saga of Mitzi's extremely lurid love life, he took a letter from the pile of post in front of him: postmark Bosnia.

Aunt Helga was not really Francis's aunt. She was his father's first cousin, but Francis always called her 'Aunt'. As a child he had spent a lot of time with Aunt Helga.

Her husband had disappeared in one of Tito's purges, and Helga had escaped to settle in Austria with her daughter, Maria, who was the same age as Francis. They had played together as children. Then, as Maria grew from a solemn little dark-haired child into a voluptuous and extremely desirable teenager, she and Francis had experimented with the wonders of their developing bodies in a mutually pleasurable and light-hearted way. Maria's confessions caused a great deal of sighing from her worthy parish priest.

Aunt Helga had always yearned for Bosnia, the home of her ancestors, and when the political situation allowed it, she and Maria returned to take up their lives. Maria had married, and now had a solemn little dark-haired child of her own. Through all the years the cousins had remained close and, whilst they saw each other less often, regular letters were exchanged between Bosnia and Lippitz.

Francis recognized his aunt's strong handwriting. He buttered another slice of toast, took a sip of coffee and opened the letter.

A moment later, there was a crash as the coffee cup Francis had been holding to his lips fell to the table, smashed and sent the coffee flooding across the breakfast things.

Tatiana looked up in shock. What she saw shocked her even further. Her husband's ruddy and cheerful face had suddenly become ashen and drawn as he read the letter.

'Darling! What is it?'

Francis did not reply. He sat fixed, staring at the page.

Tatiana slipped from her chair, went round the table and, kneeling beside her husband's chair, put a hand on his arm. 'Darling, tell me!'

Without a word, Francis handed her the letter.

'Ethnic Cleansing' is a useful euphemism. It is a

convenient coverall for a great horror, and great horrors are usually built of myriad smaller horrors. Aunt Helga's was only a little horror, just a small statistic on a great print-out of terror.

Aunt Helga's small farm was in a mixed area. For some 300 years Bosnian Croats, Muslims and Serbs had mixed more or less amicably. They went to school together, played together, drank in the cafés together. Sometimes they even intermarried. This made the horror even worse. The Serbs who came to 'cleanse' Aunt Helga's farm were neighbours.

It was the village postman who had smashed her in the face with a rifle butt.

The men who had shot Maria's husband had played with him in the same football team.

They showed the same sense of team spirit when they successively raped Maria. It was the goal keeper who had cut her throat.

Maria's child had screamed hysterically at what was happening to her mother. The same shop keeper who had given her sweets in the past had quietened her now by staving her skull in with a blow from a heavy rake.

Aunt Helga had been left for dead, as the laughing, cheering mob had celebrated their victory in slivovitz.

Aunt Helga was not dead, but the next few days had been lost in a mist of pain and grief, until she had stumbled upon a Bosnian Army patrol who had got her to the overcrowded hospital. From there she had been able to write to Francis, using the one good eye that remained to her.

Francis had struggled through a slough of bureaucracy to get the old lady out of a refugee camp and installed at Schloss Lippitz. Her appearance had shocked them both profoundly. Her sightless eye and battered twisted face had been bad enough, but the psychological damage was worse. At times Helga was quite lucid, and her accounts of the horrors of Bosnia were shocking in the extreme. At other times the black cloud of her experiences would overwhelm her, and she would descend into a nightmare pit – a pit full of blood and terror. Sometimes her screams would echo round the castle, at other times she would crouch sobbing in a corner, endlessly moaning the names of her family.

Francis wondered whether she should be in hospital, but Tatiana furiously opposed this. The hospital had repaired such of the physical damage as it could; it was now a matter of the mind. She summoned a friend from her student days in Vienna, a man now regarded as one of the leading psychiatric lights. He shook his head; Aunt Helga was permanently scarred. The only thing was to let her work out her trauma through time, allowing the emotional scar tissue to form. In the meantime, it was a question of rest, kindness and patience. There were some drugs which could ease the suffering, but Tatiana protested about using drugs.

Dr Kunz shrugged. 'Look,' he said, 'when that woman goes down towards Hell, at least the drugs will help her into Purgatory. You are a good Catholic. You should understand that.'

'You always were a bastard to argue with.'

'That is because where you apply faith, I apply logic.'

'I prefer faith.'

'I think you're going to need it.'

'You know that I have to go,' said Francis one morning, some weeks after Aunt Helga had come to live with them at the castle.

Tatiana did not reply but concentrated on licking his armpit. Her hand began to fondle his testicles.

'Dammit, woman, will you listen for a moment!'

'I am listening,' came a muffled voice.

The questing fingers reached up.

'Well then, you know that I have to go.'

The hand was now working the sensitive area towards the end of his penis, which was excreting a little. With her forefinger and thumb, Tatiana expertly massaged the moistness into the glans.

Francis moaned.

Tatiana straddled him and bent her lips to his.

'I know,' she said.

And, as she felt him slide into her hot, yielding body, she began to cry.

The day before Francis left for Bosnia, he walked alone up through the hanging beech woods on the steep banks of the River Lipp. A path wound up through the woods and out onto a hilltop meadow. At one end of this was a rocky outcrop from which the fertile valley with strips of fields, multi-hued from different crops, and with the river winding between them, could be seen. In the foreground below him, above the river, was the square of the castle built round its central courtyard, with its first and second floor galleries running round the courtyard on three sides. He saw the distant figure of Tomislav hobbling across the courtyard. He looked down on this, and on the steep pitched, red tiled roof of the circular tower with the spiral staircase of worn stones, which had been built by his ancestors so that a right-handed swordsman had the advantage when defending the stair.

Behind the hilltop meadow, forested hills climbed higher still, fold after fold, until they merged into the rocky slopes of the mountains.

This had always been a favourite spot for Francis. Here he could watch the butterflies in summer, see the eagles soaring over the distant crags, hear the birdsong of the woods. In the valley, toy-like tractors crawled about the fields, while a horse-drawn cart rumbled along a distant road.

Here Francis came, on his last morning at home, for a moment of solitary reflection, sitting on the rocks in the sun: so much to think about.

He was annoyed to see a figure already sitting on the rocks, with his back to him, as he approached. A curl of pipe smoke rose from the figure which was huddled in a cape in spite of the rising warmth of the sun.

As Francis approached, the figure turned; it was the Hunter.

The large man rose and doffed his battered green hat.

'Good morning, Graf, I apologize for intruding on your place of solitude.'

'Good morning ... Look, I don't even know your name.'

'Names are not important – just call me Hunter – it serves, although some people call me the Wanderer.'

'Did you want to see me, er, Hunter?'

'Just for a moment, and then I will leave you to your thoughts. You have a lot to think about.'

'Yes.'

'First I wanted to wish you good luck, and if I thought I could persuade you not to go, I would try, but I know that that would be a waste of time, eh?'

'Yes, but why would you want to?'

'Because this is a bad war, Graf. War is not a crime, but this is a war of criminals. You are going in search of honour in a place where it cannot be found.'

'I have to go.'

'You're worried about many things.'

'Yes.'

'There is one thing you must not worry about. The

63

Gräfin is surrounded by my protection and everybody knows that. I cannot do the same for you, but remember that, whatever happens, your wife will come to no harm.'

Francis stared at the man in his patched old clothing. Why did he not ask the Hunter how he knew all these things? Why did he not ask him what he meant by his 'protection'? Why didn't he ask him . . . ? He did not know why, but he didn't. All he said was: 'Thank you.'

The Hunter rose to his feet and held out a huge hand. 'Now I shall leave you in peace. God go with you, Graf Francis.'

'I'm not sure that I believe in God.'

'Gods have their uses,' said the Hunter.

CHAPTER FOUR

Major Smith-Watson was bemused. 'Good heavens, Jimbo! D'you really think that this is a good idea?'

Lieutenant-Colonel Paxton, Commanding Officer of The Household Cavalry Mounted Regiment, was leaning back in his office chair trying to do a trick with two pencils that he had learned from a 'Woodentop' – Officer of the Coldstream Guards – at a Quarter Masters' dinner.

'Damn,' he said, as the pencils spun across the room. Then: 'Jones!'

'The door opened and the Clerk entered. 'Yessir!'

The Colonel pointed silently at the far-flung pencils, and Jones, sighing inwardly, replaced them on the desk for the fifth time that morning.

'Thank you, Jones.'

'Very good, sir,' said the retreating Jones.

Once through the door he shook his head. He wished officers would not try to learn tricks from Foot Guards officers; that simply was not seemly. It was well-known that tricks in the Cavalry were for non-commissioned ranks only.

'Yes,' said the Colonel, 'I consider it a damn good idea. Think of all that lovely free Champagne. Do you a power of good, Benjy, you really should let down your hair occasionally.'

'But what about London District? What will they

think?' worried the Major, twisting his small moustache: a sure sign of inner turmoil.

'No problem. I cleared it with the Silver Stick and he's all for it. You know what Tom's like – he loves a party.'

'Yes, but I foresee all sorts of problems. I mean all those media persons and reptiles from the gossip columns, and God knows what other riffraff in the Mess. Think of the security – they might even pinch things.'

Colonel Paxton sighed to himself. His Second-in-Command was something of a worrier, and something of an anxiety himself. One of the Major's problems was that he was 'not quite out of the hanky drawer,' as one of his fellow officers had once rather delicately put it. The Commanding Officer of the day had been rather more blunt when Smith-Watson first joined the Regiment. He had said, 'I've got several officers with common names, but now I've got one with *two* common names.' Not that this worried Jimbo Paxton; it was just that Smith-Watson was such a wet blanket. Mind, when he considered that perfectly frightful wife of his, he could see the poor bugger had a lot to worry about.

The plan to hold a publisher's party in the Officers' Mess at Hyde Park Barracks occasioned Major Smith-Watson's particular worry at the present time. This party was to be a celebration of Jilly Cooper's new blockbuster, *Striders* – a stirring tale of love, laughter, tears and passion in the Ramblers Association – 'Hairy legs that go all the way'. Champagne was literally going to haemorrhage from the publisher's entertainment account.

'Calm down, Benjy. It will be all right. Just think how your wife will enjoy it.'

'Yes, well I suppose so.'

Pencils clattered across the floor once again.

'Jones!'

★

The pile of letters was pushed into a fan as Fred opened the door of his London house. He bent down and picked up the pile, giving Paddy a double glazing circular to savage. Up in the drawing room, he dumped the pile on his desk and went to pour himself a glass of whisky. He then lit a cigarette and sat down to sort through the pile.

All circulars went straight into the basket. There were several stiff-carded invitations – 'Lady Counteswear At Home for Sarah . . .' etc – which Fred skimmed through. Boring, boring, fancy dress: ugh! He put them in a separate pile for future consideration and sorting into 'must', 'maybe' and 'they would have to carry me there in a coffin'.

The next letter in the pile commanded immediate attention. The envelope had 'ABLE & ROBB' printed on it. Able and Robb were Fred's Members' Agents at Lloyds, and they wrote thus:

My Lord
Underwriting results as at 31st December.
Please find enclosed your Underwriting Statement which sets out your underwriting results as at 31st December. Managing Agents have requested that losses be settled by the end of July . . .

Fred turned to the statement pinned to the back of the letter.

'Holy shit!' he uttered.

Mr Octavius Rankin, senior partner in Hoggsmith & Shower, sighed deeply, removed a large silk handkerchief from his sleeve and vigorously began to polish his half-moon spectacles: a sure sign of worry. Mr Rankin had, in fact, no need of spectacles, but he found them useful as an aid to gravitas, and for peering at clients over the top of; he felt this made them believe they were getting their money's worth. In view of the scale of Hoggsmith &

Shower's charges, he deemed that the clients were entitled to a little butter on their bun.

H. & S. had looked after the affairs of the various Marquises of Fowey and their families since Queen Victoria's accession to the throne. The firm had a good reputation as shrewd handlers of funds for those whose worldly wealth far exceeded their financial acumen. Mr Rankin was renowned, not just as a 'man of business', who provided a convenient excuse for many backwoodsmen to visit the flesh pots of the metropolis, but also for having a 'way with him' when it came to dealing with some of the more encrusted members of the landed classes: 'the feller's a sort of Gent,' they felt.

Mr Rankin kept his ear finely tuned to the jungle drums which pass really important intelligence in the City of London. When Lord Frederick FitzHugh required a meeting with him, he had a pretty shrewd idea of what was in store. He turned to the file on his desk, flicked through the pages, then sighed again. Being a kindly man, he regarded his clients, on the whole, as children wandering about in the bomb site of the 'civilisation' that makes up the modern world. He did his best to ensure they did not fall down and graze their knees but, judging from Lord Frederick's file, the lad was going to finish up a casualty with his leg in plaster.

The intercom on his desk flashed. 'Yes?'

'Lord Frederick FitzHugh is here, Mr Rankin.'

'Please ask him in.' Another sigh.

Mr Rankin had always liked Fred, whom he had known since boyhood: such a pleasant and easy-going young man, and if only all his clients were such.

'Good morning, Lord Frederick.'

'Good morning, Mr Rankin. I trust that you are well, and Mrs Rankin?'

'In robust health, when I last saw her. She plays a lot of

golf, you know. Not a pastime that enthuses me, but we must always be grateful for anything that keeps our women folk fulfilled and content. Not a problem for you yet, eh?'

Fred thought of Annabel and agreed it was not yet a problem for him; however he did have other problems.

Mr Rankin looked down at the letter from Able & Robb which Fred handed him, and sighed once more. He leaned back in his chair, steepled his fingers, and looked at Fred over the top of his spectacles as a prelude to his 'this is going to hurt you more than it hurts me' routine. He looked sadly at the young man opposite him – silk tie, very well-cut dark suit, highly-polished and unmistakably Lobb shoes – and inwardly feared that there were going to be some changes.

'Frederick, there is no way I can soften the blow. These underwriting losses are terrible. You will bear in mind that I did advise your family against having any truck with Lloyds. I gave it as my firm opinion that the only competent underwriters are the crooked ones, and I regret to say this seems to have been borne our recently. Many of our noble and landed families are facing various degrees of distress at the present time.'

'I know, Father had a bit of a blow.'

'Your father is a very rich man but, as the bulk of his wealth is firmly tied up in family trusts, the damage has been strictly limited.'

'He was raging about it, though.'

'As I can well imagine, knowing your father as I do. He has indeed lost a considerable sum of money, although I was able to point out to him that it really only meant he would have to forgo the pleasure of habitually losing at backgammon in his club for a year or two.'

'He won't like that – he likes losing at backgammon.'

'So I have noticed,' said Mr Rankin dryly. 'However, I

am very much afraid that your situation is entirely different. Unfortunately, you have been involved with two very bad syndicates.'

'I know, and the bugger of it is that I was got into them by Franky O'Rourke.'

'Ah yes, the egregious Mr O'Rourke. He has truly been a bird of ill omen.'

'But he was a 13th Lancer.'

'What else would you expect from Line Cavalry, as I believe you like to say in The Life Guards.'

'So, what is the situation?'

'Grim I'm afraid.'

The spectacles got another vigorous polish and Mr Rankin applied himself to the file in front of him.

'To put it bluntly, your liquid assets will not cover your losses. As you know, the bulk of your capital came from your grandmother's legacy. This is free capital, and therefore liable to be offered up as a sacrifice on the Lloyds altar. You are a minor beneficiary from some of the family trusts, which Lloyds cannot touch, so you will not starve, but I fear that your lifestyle will require some modification.'

'What about the Army?'

'I am not privy to your mess bills, but it is no good my telling you that you can carry on as before.'

'Oh shit! I *am* sorry Mr Rankin.'

'Believe me, much worse has been said in this office. I think this is the moment for emergency measures.'

The 'man of business' rose from his desk, and opened a portion of the book case behind him. From the cupboard inside he extracted a bottle of Laphroaig and two glasses. He poured a large portion of the peaty straw-coloured liquid into a glass which he handed to his client.

'That,' he said gravely, 'is an emergency measure.'

Fred took an appreciative sip. 'Is there nothing else I can do?'

'Well, you can always apply to the Lloyds Hardship Committee, but I understand that it does indeed strain the quality of mercy.'

'A good party will do you the power of good, laddy,' said Jimbo Paxton, pouring more whisky into Fred's glass. 'The whole situation sounds like an entire skip of manure, and the worst thing you can do is sit about with your thumb up your bum brooding about it.'

Fred was sitting in the Commanding Officer's quarters at the Barracks. Jimbo and he were good friends, and it was natural for Fred to discuss his impending problem with him. It was the evening of the *Striders* party, for which Fred hardly felt any enthusiasm.

'Thank God that I stayed clear of Lloyds,' said Jimbo. 'That prat O'Rourke approached me, you know. Took me to lunch in the Captain's Room place. Bloody chef had absolutely ruined my Dover sole. I mean, it takes an absolute cunt to ruin Dover sole, so I reckoned any place that could put up with a chap like him must be suspect, and on top of that O'Rourke ordered a Muscadet that would take the shell off an egg.'

Jimbo's well-nourished and highly-coloured cheeks quivered with emotion. Pleasures of the cellar and table came somewhere between The Regiment and Hunting in the Colonel's list of affections; he was also very fond of his wife, who was an excellent cook.

'Then,' continued Jimbo, 'O'Rourke introduced me to a chap called Fossfat and said he was one of the most brilliant underwriters at Lloyds. Well, I was at school with 'Porky' Fossfat – you remember him, probably before your time? – a nasty little shit and the most frightful Pop Oil. "Well," I thought, "if they've got people like Fossfat running the place, then there's something rotten some-where." He one of yours?'

Fred nodded gloomily. 'A. E. Fossfat' was indeed one of the syndicates responsible for the more swingeing of his losses.

'Little bastard's done a runner to Nicaragua, they tell me. Living high on the pig's back from other people's money, including yours, Fred.'

Fred puffed at his cigarette in gloomy silence. Jimbo dropped himself into his large armchair, so that his plump little legs stuck out.

'Bastards! I'd like to send some Scorpions down to the City and shell the bloody place to the ground. That might sharpen them up a bit.'

Fred thought it a marvellous idea; after all, the Committee of Lloyds was about to pump several high explosive rounds into his life.

'Right, young Fred, party time. As your friend, I recommend it, and as your Commanding Officer, I command it. Any questions?'

'Splendid, lots of lovely Champagne! I made sure these publishers got some decent stuff. They whinged a bit about the price, but I told them they could not expect my officers of The Household Cavalry Mounted Regiment to drink the frightful plonk they had in mind.'

The nimble little man skipped out of his chair and called up the stairs. 'Come on, Emma! Sharpen up!'

There was some confused shouting in reply.

'Good God, she's been putting on her face for hours! You wait till you get married, young Fred.'

Fred thought that possibility fast receding.

The party was already in full throat when Fred des-cended into the Mess from the Colonel's quarters. Both Ante Room and Dining Room were packed with people. The sartorial dichotomy between the officers and the other guests was quite marked, what Major Smith-Watson liked to refer to as 'the media persons' being somewhat less restrained in their mode of dress. Fred took in the 'famous TV personality' in the Crimplene suit – it enabled him to push the sleeves back to the elbow – in frenetic conversation with a man sporting designer stubble, a pony tail and a most unfortunate green coat. He had a momentary, and most pleasing, fantasy of the two of them being consigned to the gentle and avuncular care of Regimental Corporal Major Williams; that great and good man would definitely have considered the TV person's shoes to be 'idle'.

'Thank you, Preston,' said Fred, taking a glass from a tray proffered by one of the Mess waiters. Jimbo was right; it was excellent Champagne.

Fred knew that he ought to mix and be affable. Soon he would, but just for the moment he felt like standing back and surveying the scene. He could see Jilly Cooper at the far end surrounded by admirers; he thought she looked pretty scrumptious. Many of the media corps of diary columnists, publishers and broadcasters were unknown to him, although he recognized one woman presenter he could not bear to watch on the telly. There was the unmistakable figure of Max Hastings towering above the throng. He had shot at Bardwick Hall, and the Marquis had approved: 'Decent feller, good shot, sound views – very.' He thought he might make his way across to Hastings in a minute.

'Hello, soldier,' squeaked a voice at his elbow. Fred looked down. A little roly-poly man, with dark hair *en brosse*, gave him a wide smile. 'I can *tell* you're a soldier – polished shoes and such a lovely suit – I *bet* you're an officer!'

'Well, yes, I am.'

'Oo lovely! I like a bit of class. Do you work here?'

'Yes, actually I'm the Life Guards' Squadron Leader.'

'Oo yummy! I had a Squadron Leader once – ever such a nice boy – he flew Jaguars. Like a jaguar he was too!' The little man pealed with laughter.

'Well, that's the RAF,' said Fred rather stiffly.

'I *know*, ducky, just my little joke,' and, putting a hand on his arm, 'I know *all* about the Army. I had a lovely Grenadier once, you might know him . . .' He mentioned a distinguished name that made Fred rear up. 'That shook you, didn't it? I really ought to be more discreet. *You* don't, do you?'

In spite of himself, Fred found himself laughing. There was something about this funny little man.

'No, I'm afraid I don't.'

'I should get so lucky. "No." I said to myself, "Bubbles," I said, "I bet he's as straight as an EU cucumber." But, nothing venture, nothing gain, that's what I say.'

'Are you really called Bubbles?'

'No, dear. My real name's Malcolm; I mean do I *look* Malcolm?'

'No.'

'Well, there you are. What's your name then?'

Bubbles, it was revealed, was a gossip columnist of renown and notoriety; even Fred recognized the name of the column.

'You're a dangerous man.'

'Oo, I love it when you talk dirty! Well, yes, I am to those who upset me. But I like you. I won't reveal your sins. Have you got any?'

'Well, I don't have anything very spectacular.'

'We'll have to do something about it. D'you fancy that?'

Bubbles pointed across the room to an exceptionally

pretty dark-haired girl, dressed in what was commonly known as a 'pussy pelmet'.

'Who is she?'

Bubbles mentioned a name that was vaguely familiar.

'She's in *EastEnders*. Now, if I get you off with her, you'll have a great fuck, and I'll get a great story.'

Fred cracked up with laughter. The night was improving. 'I suppose you know all these people,' he remarked, looking round the crowded and decibel-heavy Dining Room.

'Oh yes, dear, I know them all, and they all know Bubbles. Some of them would like to tie my balls in a knot. Wonder if I'd like that?'

At that moment Fred's attention was distracted. In spite of the noise, the happy baying of Subalterns rose up above it. He looked to see what was exciting the reptiles.

'Oh my God!' he gasped.

Katerina Kinsky was in a foul mood. She had no desire to go to a party. In particular, she had no desire to go to *this* party. She wanted nothing to do with the British Army at the moment. She had read and re-read her cousin's letter, and had wept over it. It lay in her handbag, and it felt as though tears and blood were oozing from it. However, Katerina's editor had insisted that she attend the party, and Katerina took her work very seriously. She showed her invitation to the Corporal of Horse at the gate, and ascended the steps, passing between the two Dismounted Dutymen in Full Kit – jackboots, cuirasses, helmets, swords at the slope.

'That,' thought Katerina, 'is about all the British are bloody good for.'

She took a drink from one of the Mess waiters – at least the Champagne was respectable – and surveyed the crowded, shouting throng.

'Get a word with Jilly Cooper,' the Editor of *Angelique* had said, 'and see if the publishers have dressed that lovely girl up like they did for *Riders*' – Mrs Cooper had been persuaded into riding boots and breeches for that occasion – 'Perhaps they have made her wear breeks and hiking boots this time. You really could go to town on that. Dip your pen in vitriol, Kat.'

It would certainly have suited Katerina's mood, but she was rather disappointed to see Mrs Cooper in a very smart cream silk suit – Katerina's professional eye placed it as by Ultima – and she could hardly pour vitriol on that. She would get a word with her later.

'Halloo,' drawled a voice at her elbow. 'I say, you look all alone and lorst, what?'

Katerina, who was tall, found herself looking down at a tiny and immaculately suited figure, who looked remarkably like an up-market version of David Jason.

'Hallo,' she said.

A tiny, soft hand was proffered, which she shook rather reluctantly.

'Piers Luckington,' said the owner of the hand, 'I sort of work here. Sort of soldiering, d'yersee.'

'What sort of soldiering?' asked Katerina in the honey-dripping voice that signalled danger amongst her acquaintances. 'How many men have you killed?'

'Goodness!' said Piers, rather shaken. 'Well, none actually. I mean not much going on for Queen and Country, d'yersee. We're on sort of ceremonial duties, actually, Queen's Life Guard and all that.'

'I am sure that your Queen must sleep easier in her bed for knowing you are guarding her. Do you sleep on the mat outside her bedroom door?'

Piers's brow furrowed with unwonted concentration: 'No, I don't sleep outside her bedroom. I don't even know where Her Majesty's bedroom . . .' His eyes lit up.

'Oh, I see, joke! Jolly good! Gosh, you're a sharp one! You're foreign, aren't you, what?'

'I'm Slovenian.'

'Goodness! Dracula and all that sort of thing.'

'No, that is Romania.'

Piers, whose grip on geography more or less allowed him to find his way from the Savoy Grill to the Cavalry Club – by taxi – puckered his brow again.

'Ah yes, Romania, yes, well, jolly nice place, I expect.'

'Not particularly.'

Piers felt he was floundering a little, but good manners – and the Commanding Officer – dictated that an effort must be made, and he knew it was the duty of a gentleman to put the lower orders at their ease. However, he felt he needed some help with this one: safety in numbers, d'yersee.

'I say, come and meet some of the chaps. Come and meet old Foxy, you'll like him. He went to Florence once. At least I think that's where it was.'

Lieutenants Oakeford (Jimmy) and Milton (Foxy) were overjoyed to meet Katerina.

'Phaaugh' they both said to themselves, and with Katerina – tall, high cheek bones, long blonde hair, legs that went all the way, and everything else where it belonged – the thought was absolutely warranted.

'Jolly good,' said Oakeford.

'Super!' said Milton.

'D'yer hunt?' asked Oakeford.

'You've a wonderful leg for a boot,' enthused Milton.

In spite of herself, Katerina found herself smiling. There was something about these young men, bumbling like puppies in front of her, that drew the poison from her mood. She even began to enjoy herself as she teased them and made them squirm a bit.

'Are you all virgins – the Virgin Soldiers?'

'Gosh!' gasped the Subalterns in chorus. Then, 'Of course not,' they claimed in unison.

We've all got women,' boasted Luckington modestly, 'and dogs,' he added.

'And which do you prefer?'

'You're teasing us,' said Milton.

'They're quite different!' observed Oakeford.

'I'm glad you have discovered that,' and Katerina burst out laughing.

'Whaugh! Whaugh! Whaugh!' chorused the Subalterns.

It was this combined peal of laughter that had attracted Fred's attention.

'Oh my God!' he said.

It could not be, never. And yet there was the same long golden hair, the greeny-blue eyes, the tall elegant figure; once again the vision of the girl he had seen on the television screen flashed in front of him. He stared, and stared again. No, it was not her, but the resemblance was uncanny. He had to meet this woman.

'Bubbles! Who on earth is that?'

'Katerina, darling! Nice to see,' cried Bubbles thirty seconds later, cutting ruthlessly through the encircling Subalterns and throwing his arms round her.

'Hullo, Bubbles, good to see you.'

Katerina was very fond of Bubbles; they had known each other for years. Sometimes she fed him juicy tit bits, and Bubbles had never bitten the hand that fed him. They had often cried on each other's shoulder whenever life and love turned sour for one of them.

'Now, darling, I want you to meet the most succulent man. He's dying to meet you, and he is totally impervious – *impervious* my dear – to all my charms.'

Katerina looked at the tall, dark man with the slightly solemn face and eyes with a sadness behind them.

'How do you do?' she said.

'How do you do?' said Fred, and smiled.

Katerina noticed that when he smiled, his whole face lit up, but there were still those eyes.

'Have these men been bothering you?' asked Fred, glaring at the Subalterns.

'Oh no, Fred.'

'Certainly not!'

'We've been entertaining her.'

'They have been very kind.'

'You all look like nice boys,' chortled Bubbles. 'Now, come and entertain me. We'll let the Squadron Leader – oh, it makes me all funny just saying it – talk to the nice lady. How would you like to meet a tart from *EastEnders*? East, west, any end will do for her!'

'Well, hullo Katerina.'

'Well, hullo Frederick.'

It is perfectly possible they could have kept this up for some time, but just then there came an almighty crash, followed by a cry of, 'My God! The Kaiser's down!'

'Like the barmaid's knickers,' said an anonymous but well-oiled voice.

Major Fergus Crichton was on what he subsequently described as a 'dammed sticky wicket'. The gallant major had retired from The Life Guards some years previously, but he had acted as a technical adviser for one of Jilly Cooper's earlier books. As such, the publishers felt he should be invited to the bash.

'I say, Marigold,' he said to his wife after reading the invitation, 'this looks rather fun. I think we ought to trot along.'

Marigold thought this a super idea.

The major's life was a somewhat complicated one:

besides The Wife who was lovely, there was The Mistress who was rather unlovely. The Wife knew of The unlovely Mistress, and the only thing they had in common was a mutual loathing.

What the Major did not know, as he hummed 'Colonel Bogey' and put the final polish on his shoes, was that The Mistress was even then putting the invitation card for Hyde Park Barracks in her handbag. Her position in a well-known publishing house had secured her the invitation.

The powder train was set; it needed only the match.

To say that the Major was nonplussed when The Wife and The Mistress came face to face at the party is to underestimate the resources of the seasoned old campaigner. His military training had taught him there are times when a tactical withdrawal is necessary. So, as the din of battle rose in high-decibel verbosity, the Major decided to shorten his lines of communication without delay, and began quietly to back away from the noise and fury. Unfortunately he had neglected another useful military dictum: 'time spent in reconnaissance is seldom wasted'. Had he done a recce, he would have known he was backing onto a flimsy trestle table, laden with glasses and canapés.

This table had been placed against the wall of the Dining Room on which hangs a very large and imposing portrait of the Kaiser. Before the 'difficulty' of the First World War arose, the Kaiser had been Colonel-in-Chief of The Royal Dragoons (1st Dragoons) who, in 1968, amalgamated with The Blues to form The Blues and Royals.

The assembled company at the publishing thrash had been called to silence in order to listen to the silken tongue of Mr Aidan Cruttche, Chairman of the publishers, and the man who continually winced at the quantity of Champagne he suspected was being consumed.

Mr Cruttche cleared his throat, and the company bated its breath. From the centre of the room came the sound of 'stern strife and carnage drear.'

Then from the back of the room came the unmistakable sound of a distinguished Major falling backwards on to a collapsing table of canapés. His flailing hands found the bottom of the heavy gilt frame of the Kaiser's portrait – found and gripped. With Imperial stoicism and dignity, the Kaiser proceeded to descend from his position on the wall and, without loss of composure, gave the Major severe concussion for his impertinence.

The Commanding Officer had been watching these horrid events with a sort of terrible fascination – the whole thing seemed to happen in slow motion – and could only take a large swig from his glass.

Things could not get worse.

'Excuse me, Colonel.' The Orderly Officer in his Blue Patrols was at the Commanding Officer's shoulder. 'The police have just telephoned. They have had a bomb threat. They want all civilians evacuated immediately.'

'Thank God for that!'

Fred escorted Katerina to the gate. As they came through the doors of the Mess, the Dismounted Dutymen snapped to attention and presented swords.

'At least your soldiers salute well,' Katerina remarked.

'You're very bitter about the British Army.'

'Yes.'

'Why?'

They stood face to face, their eyes locked as the chattering crowd flowed round them and out into Knightsbridge. Then Katerina's eyes dropped. 'It's not your fault. Perhaps one day I tell you.'

'Would you have dinner with me?'

'I think about it. Here, call me.'

She took a business card from her handbag and gave it to him. Then she turned and disappeared into the crowd without another word.

Fred stood looking at the card:

Katerina Kinsky

COMMISSIONING EDITOR

Angelique Magazine

So – Katerina Kinsky.

CHAPTER FIVE

'Ho! Ho! Ho! I've got a nice juicy one here!' chortled Marvin Sugden. The Office pricked up its ears. Marvin was a right card when he got going, and he didn't half make everyone laugh sometimes.

Laughs were not two a penny in the Committee of Lloyds Hardship Secretariat, which is tucked away in the hidden depths of darkest Chatham. It is here that the personal effects and affairs of those 'Names' who cannot meet their losses are picked over and scrutinised, rather as scavengers pick over the carcass of a once proud beast.

The myth of Lloyds of London is that those who put up their money as backing for insurance claims, face unlimited liability. If a Name is unable to meet his liabilities, then the theory is that Lloyds may rob the corpse of its fortune, yea! even down to that last cufflink. In practice, the astute Godfathers, who grow fat on underwriting insurance, and even fatter on 'losses' that do not always quite seem to correlate with claims, do not want a corpse. The last thing these splendid people want is for a chap – or a chappess – actually to go bankrupt; the bankruptcy of a Name would explode the myth of Unlimited Liability. The next thing there would be chaps going bankrupt all over the place, and the whole house of cards would come tumbling down. No, the Godfathers like to keep the mortal husk and myth alive. Those who cannot pay may surrender themselves to the tender mercies of the Hardship Committee.

The Hardship Committee makes the delicate decision as to how much financial blood the body needs, just to keep it ticking over in a more or less life-like state: no frills and furbelows, simply a table, a chair, a modest dwelling place, a bed to worry in and the frugal running of the teeth. With a flick of the wrist – the quickness of the hand deceives the eye – the Hardship Committee then removes the remainder of the money from the victim's wallet and, licking its fingers, counts it with practised ease, and shoves it away in its back pocket to give to the Godfathers.

The actual committee tends to consist of good chums of the Godfathers, people who have drunk deeply and satisfyingly from the well of Lloyds. This committee is but window dressing. It lunches richly, and then takes a rubber stamp to the recommendations of the Hardship Secretariat. This is the body that decides just how much flesh to pick from the bones. It is hardly a job to attract the superior sort of professional person – scavengers are rarely attractive animals – and if those who do work for the Secretariat are prone to *Schadenfreude*, then this is only to be expected. It cannot be easy to sit all day leafing through the personal documents and financial affairs of the upper classes – people who would not give you the time of day if they passed you in the street, people who, if they did speak to you, would patronise and sneer at your accent. No, it cannot be easy to have such power over a load of rich, rotten, snooty bastards. You might be entitled to think it served them right and gloat accordingly.

Marvin Sugden was gloating. Marvin loved his work. He had qualified as a Certified Accountant after something of a struggle. He was not a very good accountant, but then competence was not highly regarded at the Secretariat; after all, competence was hardly the hall-mark of its masters.

Marvin Sugden was definitely gloating. Fred's file had landed with a solid thump on his desk, and he was thrilled. He could scent blood here: good fresh young blood. Marvin could fillet ageing widows, ancient countesses and distinguished retired soldiers with the best of them, but they were poor meat, scrawny, shrivelled old bastards, and they would all soon be dead anyway, and past caring about Hardship. He always felt slightly cheated when the Grim Reaper pinched one of his 'clients'. Marvin liked his clients to have time to savour their changed circumstances. Now, Major Lord Frederick FitzHugh was a real bit of prime steak – Old Etonian, Household Cavalry, suits from Couch & Hoskin, shoes from Lobb, member of a lot of snooty clubs, nice little mews house near Eaton Square – lovely jubly! He would strip this bastard down to size.

'Ho! Ho! Ho!' cried Marvin. 'I've got a nice juicy one here!' and just then Dr Ernestine Crumb walked into the office.

Everybody at the Secretariat agreed that Dr Crumb was a caution. She was the Director of the Secretariat; she was also a Doctor of Sociology. She sternly maintained that work at the Secretariat provided many interesting case studies for her. One might think that the lady would seek the cloistered atmosphere of a university to pursue her work, but there had been one or two unfortunate 'incidents' in Dr Crumb's academic past that made centres of learning somewhat reluctant to employ her. Indeed, there had been vague rumours circulating in the office after a couple of female members of the staff had hurriedly left in tears, but the matter had been hushed up in the best tradition of Lloyds.

Dr Crumb was a large, brisk lady in her forties. There was a time when she had been quite comely, and her basic physical structure was sound. It was unfortunate that, like so many good basic structures, hers had been added to over the years, and not always in a way that was aesthetically pleasing; there had been quite a lot of development on Dr Crumb. It was not that she was 'fat', it just looked like that. Like all good sociologists – if that is not a contradiction in terms – she wore cropped hair and dangly ear rings.

Her attitude to her 'clients' was quite simple: they had known what they were getting into and, if they were too ignorant not to know, then they were stupid enough to deserve all they got – and Dr Crumb was the girl to see they got it, right on! However, she felt that there was no harm in combining her work and academic studies, and having a little fun as well; all work and no play might make Dr Crumb a dull girl. The staff were under standing instructions to bring her attention to cases that came into the category of 'interesting'; how a case came into this category is not generally known to the General Public, but then, that is the case with so many things pertaining to Lloyds.

Marvin Sugden felt that Fred's file might be worth presenting to the good Doctor, thereby earning himself several Brownie points. Dr Crumb indeed found Fred's file 'very interesting'. There was scope there, she felt, for some quite stimulating sociological exploration.

Fred was somewhat surprised to receive a summons to appear at Chatham. Mr Rankin had told him that negotiations with the Hardship Committee were almost always conducted by endless paper shuffling. Mr Rankin was also surprised when told about the summons, and polished his spectacles furiously; he did not know what such a summons might 'betoken'. Had he known, he would probably have taken immediate 'emergency measures'.

Fred took his personal appearance seriously. It was not that he was vain, it was just that he felt every occasion demanded its own kind of correct dressing: a form of good manners. He wasn't sure what the correct dress for Chatham might be, so he settled for a decent tweed suit and gleaming brown brogues. He was not to know that Dr Crumb had a 'thing' about tweed.

Fred's impression of the Hardship Secretariat was not favourable. The place seemed shabby, and the staff surly and scruffy. He had plenty of time to study both staff and surroundings as Dr. Crumb kept him waiting. He had arrived at the traditional 'five minutes before parade', and had been kept waiting for the traditional Secretariat hour – 'let 'em sweat a bit'. The shabby waiting-room had hard seats, and nothing to read but the house journal of the National Union of Public Employees. Fred found this less than exciting.

'Doctor Crumb will see you now,' said the girl with adenoids, and a skirt that seemed designed to restrict totally any movement of the legs; not that the legs were anything to write to mother about, Fred noted automatically.

His first sight of Dr Crumb was far from reassuring. 'My God,' he thought, 'it's Mrs. Toad.' She looked up at him through her large square spectacles which made one of her jowls wobble. From then on things got far, far worse.

Marvin and the others always liked to watch the departure of victims from the Doctor's office: the ashen cheeks, the stupefied expressions, the reeling walk. Dr Crumb really was a 'caution'. They went to the window to watch Fred stumbling out of the building, and had a good snigger.

Fred stumbled as far as the Goat and Compasses, fell

against the bar and ordered a treble Scotch. He knocked that back in one, and ordered another.

'Strewth, mate, you needed that!' said the barman.

Not too many double-trebles got ordered in the Goat and Compasses. Fred took his whisky to a table in the corner of the nearly empty bar, and sat down to take stock of the situation whilst sipping his second drink with more caution. The position looked bleak.

Dr Crumb had made it plain that Fred was in dire circumstances. If it wanted, the Committee of Lloyds could take him for his last shoelace, and by law were perfectly entitled to do so. However, the good Doctor pointed out, the severity of the sentence could sometimes be mitigated. The Hardship Secretariat could recommend that the Hardship Committee allow a modest annual income still to be paid to Fred: 'not enough to buy posh suits, I am afraid,' and always provided that 'certain criteria were satisfied'. Dr Crumb would be glad to enlarge on these criteria in the 'less formal setting' of her Battersea home: say 8 p.m. on Wednesday next. Fred was under no illusion as to the nature of the criteria he was going to have to satisfy.

As the whisky bit into the Major's system, he felt his own spirit reviving somewhat. The FitzHughs had stood firm at Agincourt, Bosworth, Blenheim, Waterloo, and all stations to Pirbright. Duty might well be unpleasant and onerous, but it had to be done. If duty meant him standing firm in Battersea next Wednesday at 8 p.m., then – by golly! – Major Lord Frederick FitzHugh would draw his sword, and do his bit with the best of them. In the meantime, he needed some fresh air, and something that would make him feel clean again. As he took out his wallet to pay for his drinks, Katerina Kinsky's card fluttered out of it on to the bar – Katerina Kinsky!

*

The young women and 'ever-such-nice-boys' who staff the editorial offices of *Angelique* were giving currently Katerina Kinsky a wide detour. She had never been a by-word for patience, or for suffering fools with even a pretence of pleasure. Even the Editor trod delicately in her presence; Katerina was very good at her job but suffered from a little Central European volatility. For the last week, Katerina had not just been volatile, but had been like a cloud of highly combustible vapour floating about the office. People were taking great care not to strike sparks.

Sharon Saunders was trying very hard not to be combustible. She was leaning over Katerina's desk, whilst the latter was checking through an article Sharon had written on 'Whither the Teenage Orgasm?'. Katerina was going through the piece with a fine tooth comb or, as Sharon thought uncomfortably, a sharp scalpel.

The telephone rang. 'Get that for me, please.'

Sharon picked up the telephone. 'Katerina Kinsky's phone.'

'I wonder if I might speak to Miss Kinsky, please?' Posh voice, and quite sexy, thought Sharon.

'It's for you.'

'Who is it?'

'Who's calling?'

'Frederick FitzHugh.' – Definitely posh.

'Someone called Frederick FitzHugh.'

'Tell him to fuck off!'

'I'm afraid that Miss Kinsky's in a meeting at the moment. Can I take a message? My name's Sharon, by the way.' – Waste not, want not.

Katerina threw down the pencil she had been sucking. 'Give me the thing. Katerina Kinsky.'

'It's Frederick FitzHugh – do you remember we met at the publisher's party at Hyde Park Barracks?'

'Oh yes, I think I vaguely remember.'

Katerina was being more than a little economic with the actuality. Fred had kept popping up in her mind, unwanted and uninvited. She felt that this was very poor manners on his part, and might well be sexual harassment. Now the wretched man was appearing in real life, ringing her up: cheeky devil.

'Do you remember you said that you might have dinner with me?'

'I don't think I said anything of the sort.'

'You told me to telephone you.'

'I think not. Goodbye, Major Lord Frederick FitzHugh!'

Three things then happened.

First, Sharon thought to herself: 'Ooh, a Lord! He must be stinking rich. *I'll* have dinner with him any time.'

Then Fred thought: 'I never told her all that. She must have looked me up.'

Thirdly, Katerina did not put down the telephone receiver.

'Are you still there?' said Fred.

'Yes.'

'Look, all I wanted was to ask you out to dinner. I did not want to start World War Three.'

'Perhaps World War Three is not a bad idea. Then a lot of you bloody Brits get killed.'

Fred decided that he had taken quite enough shit from the female sex that day. He wanted nourishment, not punishment.

'Look,' he said wearily, 'enough, enough. I'll bid you once, then I'll bid you goodbye. I intend to dine at the Savoy Grill at eight-thirty tonight, for what is probably the last time in my life. If you care to join me there, fine. If not, that's also fine. Now goodbye,' and he slammed down the receiver. 'Bloody women!'

After Katerina had had the telephone slammed down on her, she had sat for a moment, and then erupted in a spectacular flow of verbal lava and pyrotechnics. That bloody man! How dare he give her an ultimatum! How dare he hang up before she had had time to cut his balls off! Just because he was some kind of British Lord, did he think that he could treat Katerina Kinsky like some common strumpet? She would rather cut her nose off than go to dinner with him! She would . . . God! but she would make him sorry!

The only problem was that Fred was not there and now, and so it was the wretched Sharon Saunders who got the verbal cosh behind the ear, had her article torn up and fled in tears. Katerina felt she was then in just the right mood to go and discuss the problem of her expenses with her Office Manager. By the time she had finished her discussion, that good, hard-done-by man was also in tears and had to go home, where cold compresses were applied to his brow by his faithful – most of the time, unless there was something better on offer – Carlos.

Katerina then took her temperament out to luncheon, the Editor unlocked herself from the Executive Wash Room, and the office heaved a collective sigh of relief.

It was halfway through a soothing salad and a glass of Australian Chardonnay that Katerina began to think she just might go the Savoy that night, if only to make the bloody worm squirm. She would make him wait and sweat, though.

Fred had always loved the Savoy Grill, it had a very special atmosphere: a heady mix of food, wine, cigar smoke, money and power. Most of all, he liked the people who worked there. Fred was a connoisseur of morale and *esprit de corps*. The Savoy Grill was a 'crack unit' in military terms, and that was one of the reasons he enjoyed it. If the 'fish stinks from the head', then Mr Maresca, the long-serving Manager, was obviously a first-class Commanding Officer.

'Lord Frederick,' said Mr Maresca, his eyes twinkling, 'is lovely to see you here again, and looking so well. A little bit thin, maybe, but now you are here we do something about all that.'

'It's very nice to be here again, Mr Maresca. You are looking well.'

'You know how it is. In this kind of business you have to look well.'

'Any chance of my favourite table?'

'Lord Frederick, you know you have a lease on that table.'

Fred always liked to sit in one of the semi-circular booths along the back wall of the restaurant. From here he had good 'room domination'. He could watch the comings and goings of the rich and famous. He could watch the well-brushed silver heads, whispering over their beef and claret, and wonder what massive amount of money was hanging on the quality of the Yorkshire pudding – Mr Sharland's Yorkshire pudding was always a culinary delight. He also liked this station because it was on Rossetti's station, and just watching Rossetti – waiter extraordinary – was watching an artist at work.

'You have a guest coming, Lord Frederick?'

'I hope there is a lady coming, Mr Maresca, but I am not too sure.'

'Is not good to see you on your own.'

Mr Maresca escorted Fred to the table. 'I get Tony bring you one of his special Champagne cocktails, while you waiting.'

'Thank you very much.'

The Grill was crowded. Fred recognised many of the faces as being of the Great, the Good and the Definitely Not So Good. There were industrial moguls, kings of commerce, nabobs of newsprint and peers of the realm. Men were in the majority, but there were some power-dressed women, and one or two whose power was quite obviously exercised without the benefit of clothing.

'You would like to order yet, milord?'

'Thank you, Rossetti, I'll wait a bit longer, but it does look as though the lady may not be coming. Ask Tony for another of these, please.'

'Very good, milord.'

The bitch was nearly half an hour late; she was not going to show. Well, it had been a long shot anyway. It had looked like being a perfect end to a perfect day. He might just as well get on and enjoy his meal. The famous moustached author, with his napkin tucked into his shirt collar, was obviously enjoying his; he had never seen such a messy eater.

Fred stuck his nose in his drink and, as he did so, became aware of a stirring: something was happening by the door. There was a flutter of people, and Mr Maresca was leading someone between the tables.

'My God!' said Fred to himself.

It is a good moment for a man when he sits at a table in a restaurant, and watches a really beautiful woman being escorted through the assembled diners; when he sees the other men licking her with their eyes, sees the envious and disapproving looks from the other women, and knows that this object of lust and envy is being brought to him. Those who think this is a sexist attitude are damned right, and thank God for it.

Katerina was wearing a 'little black dress', an entirely proper little black dress, except that it only seemed to emphasise the parts that it sheltered. Those wonderful legs seemed to go all the way up, and the slim body all the way down, passing and including her breasts that were neatly covered. Katerina was a knock out.

She sailed through the tables, head held high, looking neither left nor right.

Mr Rossetti pulled the table out. Fred stood up. Katerina sailed into the alcove, and came to her moorings on Fred's right without a word to him, but flashing a brilliant smile for Mr Rossetti.

Fred sat down.

The pheromones began to waft.

It was a long dinner. From the initial sparring came talk, and from talk came engrossment.

He told her about his impending ruin – although not of his assignation with Mrs Toad – and the seeming certainty of having to leave the Army and the way of life that he loved.

She put her hand on his.

The alchemy was fizzing.

It was quite obvious to both of them, by the end of the evening, that they were to become lovers. It was a question of when. They both felt instinctively it was not to be that night.

'Call me,' she said simply, as Fred put her into a taxi.

Dr Ernestine Crumb prepared for what she called her 'Criteria Meetings' with some care. So far she had found them immensely refreshing and helpful to herself. She was not sure that her 'clients' left feeling the same way, but that was life, and there was no pleasing some people. She was very grateful to the Committee of Lloyds for giving her a job that provided her with such a fascinating set of specimens to study. After each session, Dr Crumb would sit down at the word processor and write copious notes on her evening's work. These notes were all stored on floppy disk, and she hoped that they would one day form the basis of a highly profitable book.

The table in her kitchen-diner was set for two, and a bottle of Liebfraumilch was cooling in the refrigerator. Dr Crumb did not lavish food and drink on her clients, but she had found that a modest meal and a glass of wine did help to relax them, and put them in the mood for what many had found to be a somewhat trying experience. She smiled to herself, and hummed a little Gershwin as she remembered one or two of those trying experiences; she found them highly diverting and a psychologist's absolute dream. She fondly remembered the expression on the face of General Sir Thomas Pole-Wiggley, Bt., DSO, when confronted with the reality of his situation. She was sure that Lord Frederick FitzHugh was going to be a guinea a minute; she did not often get her clients as young as that, and with all that firm, muscular young flesh. Dr Crumb sucked her teeth in anticipation, and went to check the contents of the 'Toy Cupboard'. Everything was ready.

Fred paid off the taxi and looked up at the block of flats. The cab had been a tumbrel as far as he was concerned. He had no idea what lay ahead of him at this 'little informal meeting', but he felt strongly that he was not going to enjoy it, which only goes to show how wrong a person can be. Still, if it enabled him to save something from the Lloyds débâcle, then anything – pretty well anything – was a runner.

He checked his piece of paper: No. 18b.

The lobby of the block smelled of piss and chips. The lift was out of order. Fred began to climb the stairs. He paused before the door of 18b, swallowed, stiffened his upper lip and knocked.

He had rather hoped that his impression of Dr

Crumb had been exaggerated; perhaps she would not look quite as like Mrs. Toad as he remembered. The creature that opened the door, clad in a long flowing dress, looked exactly like Mrs. Toad, but with badly-applied lipstick.

'*Do* come in, Lord Frederick. From now on I shall call you "Fred", and you must call me "Ernie" – short for Ernestine, you know. I want us to be absolutely informal and relaxed together. Now, I have prepared a small colla-tion and a glass of wine before we settle down to some serious business. How about a little drinky before we eat?'

'A drop of whisky, please.'

'A little whisky makes you frisky, eh, Fred?'

The awful Mrs. Toad burst into peals of baritone laughter.

'Oh, shit!' said Fred to himself.

He said the same thing throughout – and about – the meal, whilst doing his best to rise to the occasion, and make light conversation with the doctor who prattled happily on. 'Now, no business talk until after dins.'

The 'business talk', in due course, took place on the sofa in the 'lounge'.

Dr Crumb had found, from past experience, that it was no use poncing about; it was best to get down to the nitty gritty of the deal, and watch the buggers squirm – just as Fred was squirming at that moment. The deal was perfectly simple. The client (hereinafter referred to as the Client) of the first part, hereby contracted to submit him, or her, self to the sexual whims (unspecified) of Doctor Crumb (hereinafter referred to as the Doctor) of the second part or any other part as the Doctor may desire; all clear about that she hoped. In return for this, the Doctor undertook to 'use her best endeavours' to amelio-rate the Client's financial situation with the Hardship Committee.

'Now, is that all quite clear, Fred, dear?' – the Doctor spoke in the appalling 'little girl' voice she used on these occasions. 'You play your cards right, and you and Ernie will have a lot of fun this evening. Then Ernie will see what she can do about your monsey wonsey. You won't be the first one I've been able to help, you know.'

As she talked, her plump hand ran up and down Fred's thigh. Fred did not dare look at the Doctor; he thought that he might be sick, but his mind was racing. All right, she was a hideous old toad, but if it took a good poke to get him out of his present financial hole, then so be it.

'It's quite clear, er, Ernie.'

'That's a good boy! I knew you would be sensible. Now, you just take your clothes off, while Ernie gets herself all ready for you. Shan't be long!'

With a heavy heart, Fred took off his clothes and folded them neatly on a chair. He studied himself in a looking glass over the mantelpiece, and thought, 'Well Frederick, you are in deep shit, lad.' It was when he looked again at his reflection that he realised how deep was the manure that he was in. His mind might have come to terms with what was about to happen, but the body was resolutely holding out; his penis hung limp between his legs.

The bedroom door opened, and Doctor Crumb made her entrance. Fred experienced a spasm of horror. She was wearing a long leather overcoat – the kind that Gestapo officers wore in old war films – high-heeled leather boots, and a leer.

'Now, ducky, are you ready for a bit of sport with Ernie?'

Fred swallowed and shuffled his feet.

'Well, er, as a matter of fact . . .' He indicated his flaccid member.

Doctor Crumb trilled a hideous peal of laughter. 'Oh,

you silly boy, that doesn't matter in the least! You don't think I was going to let you put that nasty thing in Ernie, do you? Oh, no! Ernie's got a lot more fun than that in mind.'

With a dramatic gesture, the Doctor threw open her coat.

Fred gave a gasp of horror.

'Well, dear, what do you think of little Ernie now?'

'Bloody hell! What are you going to do with *that*?'

'Silly question, silly boy!'

At this stage the Doctor's voice changed. The trill disappeared, like the slipping of a mask, to be replaced by a deeper and commanding rasp.

'I'll tell you what I am going to do, Lord Frederick FitzHugh. I'm going to have some fun with you, and you're going to join wholeheartedly in my little games. Because, if you don't, I'll see that you don't even get a penny to scratch your arse with. Mind you, when I've finished with you, you won't feel like scratching your arse for quite a bit.'

She wheezed with laughter at this witticism.

'You don't think you're going to . . . ? With that?'

'I'll tell you exactly, Freddie Boy. First I'm going to put a little restraint on you, in case you get a bit carried away by passion' – at this point the Doctor flourished a pair of handcuffs from the pocket of her coat. 'Then, Freddie Boy' – thrusting her hideous face so close to Fred's that he got a whiff of rancid breath – 'I'm going to bugger you with my little toy.'

'Look here, I mean . . .'

'No! You look here! You know the old saying, "Get 'em by the balls, and their hearts and minds are sure to follow." Well, I've got you by the balls. I'm not worried about your heart or your mind, I just want your ass. Now, how about a nice kiss for Ernie?'

'Sod this,' thought Fred to himself, 'she can't possibly think . . .' Then it occurred to him that almost anything was possible in Doctor Crumb's mind. It was obvious, also, that the 'possible' must have become the 'actual' in the past. He wondered how many wretched people had submitted themselves to the Doctor in order to try to retain a small piece of their property.

'Come on, lad, you'll enjoy it. I bet you got buggered regularly at that posh school of yours. I bet you enjoy it, like all the upper class poofters. Well, this is going to be one to remember. Now we'll just put the nice handcuffs on you . . .'

Fred slapped her face. Hard.

'Ooof,' gasped the Doctor, sitting down equally hard on the floor, her spectacles flying off. 'You bastard!'

She began crawling across the floor to where her spectacles lay by the radiator. The handcuffs lay on the floor.

Fred was trained to react to violence. The training took over. He seized the handcuffs and fastened the Doctor to the bottom of the radiator.

The Doctor was alternately squealing pleas and growling threats. As she struggled and rolled about, the overcoat fell away to reveal her mountainous floppy buttocks.

Fred look at the massive bottom, and then at the cane in the corner.

'Right,' said Fred.

'You bastard,' screamed the Doctor. 'I'll get you – oooh! I'll ruin you, you miserable – owww! I'll get the police and – wooo! What are you doing? No! no! You can't! You wouldn't dare! Nooo!'

Fred was a kindly soul, on the whole, but he had been through a nasty experience, and the ancestral blood of the FitzHughs was now aroused. He was reminded of that great robber, Baron FitzHugh, whose motto was: 'If ye canne be hangit for *ſ*tealing one *ſ*heep, then *ſ*teal as many a*ſ* ye canne.' He was also reminded that the motto of the FitzHugh family was: '*Hostes Meis Defutantur.*'

The Doctor's bellows penetrated 18a and caused Deirdre Cudworth to turn up the sound on the telly.

'I suppose the doctor's having one of her parties again,' she said to her hubby who shoved another crisp in his mouth, his eyes never leaving the screen.

'Yeah, she's a right caution, the doctor. Gord streuth! Look at that one, Deird, look at them knockers!'

'Slags' is a cellar. A clever mind conceived the idea of making it into a club. The clever mind also realised that the essential thing for the success of a club is to make membership difficult to achieve, so that people will clamour to gain entrance. A trickle is then grudgingly admitted. Once the trickle is penned up in the cellar, he then compounds profits by making every glass of gooseberry champagne, every battery egg, and every piece of supermarket bacon cost an arm and a leg. This way the cellar will be tagged 'exclusive'.

Fred was a founder member of Slags. He had joined in the rather vague way that one does, when warmed with alcohol. The proprietor was a slight acquaintance, and had been anxious to recruit members from the Household Division to give his cellar the aura of a 'bit of class'. Founder members from the Household Calvary got in at a cheap rate. Fred joined, went a couple of times and found it little to his taste. As the membership expanded into exclusivity, Fred found the habitués less and less to his liking. However, it was a place where you could get a drink when the world was falling about you, and everything else was closed.

After his meeting with Doctor Crumb, Fred felt greatly in need of a drink, or two, or three. He could have had them at his house, but felt the need to be amongst a crowd, although not part of it.

So it was that he staggered into Slags that evening, ordered three fingers of whisky, and took himself to brood at a dark table. The elation of his defeat of Doctor Crumb was beginning to turn sour. He did not regret what he had done, but he realised that it had hardly eased his position. When the doctor was finally eased from the unfortunate position in which he had left her, he had a feeling that hardship – his hardship – was going to be much on her mind; she would not be a happy sociologist.

Fred was not a happy officer, as he glowered into his glass. His happiness was not increased as he looked up to order another very large whisky, and saw Katerina Kinsky on the diminutive dance floor, in the arms of a man. She looked happy, laughing and elated. The whisky turned to weed-killer in Fred's mouth, and he decided that Life and Katerina were both major bitches.

Katerina was still laughing as she left the dance floor. She was in a good mood. She had just arranged an interview with a famous New York designer, who was reluctant to give interviews and, when the designer's agent suggested they have a drink to celebrate, she had agreed to accompany him to Slags – not a place she particularly liked. She did not even mind him holding her in a somewhat familiar way on the dance floor, nor taking her arm in a possessive manner as he led her back to their table, although if he pushed his luck much further, he would regret it, interview or no interview. In fact, Katerina was rather regretting her agreement to come along, and felt the evening was approaching a cut-off point as far as her escort was concerned. It was at this moment that she saw Fred, and saw pain.

'You go on,' she said to the agent, 'there's a man there I must have a word with.'

'Don't be long, babe,' said the agent. 'I'll get some more Champagne ordered up.'

The little 'thinks' bubbles from the tops of their heads read respectively: 'I reckon I'm on a promise here,' and 'Dream on.'

'Hello, Fred, what are you doing here?' said Katerina with a happy smile.

'Getting drunk,' said Fred, sulking into his glass.

The little bubble above his head read: 'Sh'none of your damned business. Go and get lost with your fancy man, and if you really want to be poked by a frightful oik like that, then you can get stuffed too.'

Katerina was good at reading bubbles, and she could sense that there was something very wrong. She made a decision. 'I'm about to go home. Will you take me?'

Fred's head snapped up in surprise. 'What?'

'You heard what I say. I have enough of this place, and I want to go home, now.'

'But what about your fancy man?'

'He's not my fancy man, and I deal with him. You go and wait for me outside. Get a taxi.'

'Good night, my lord,' said the doorman, as Fred staggered out of the cellar.

'That'd be a bloody miracle,' said Fred, 'but thank you all the shame.'

Fred slumped in the taxi. He was deeply conscious of the girl who got in beside him: her scent, her golden hair, her long shapely legs. He would like to take her delicate hand and raise it to his lips. Should he? Shouldn't he?

Katerina sat with one hand laid on the seat between her and Fred. Why did the stupid Englishman not pick it up?

It was a busy night for the pheromones.

'Come in. I give you a drink and we talk.'

Fred talked. He told Katerina the whole saga of the Hardship Secretariat, and of the evening with Doctor Crumb, even unto the last note of the coda.

Katerina listened without interruption, curled up on the sofa opposite Fred like some gorgeous marmalade cat. Only at the end of the sorry tale did she sit upright with a – 'My God! You did that?'

Fred nodded dumbly, his eyes cast down.

The marmalade cat uncoiled itself from the sofa.

Katerina knelt before Fred, resting her arms on his knees.

Fred looked down into the amazing blue-green eyes.

'I don't think I would like that.'

Fred shook his head.

'And when you whipped her – did you enjoy that?'

Fred shook his head miserably.

'Perhaps,' said Katerina, 'you should try and see if you enjoy doing it to me.'

And she moved in between his thighs.

CHAPTER SIX

'It's a bloody shame,' said Lt. Col. 'Jimbo' Paxton, pouring another heavy-duty whisky into Fred's glass. You really think that you will have to go?'

Fred took a sip of the strong drink and sat forward in his chair, his forearms resting on his knees. He held the glass in both hands and looked down into it as he swirled the liquid round and round. He felt that the whisky was a bit like his life at the moment: swirling round and round. He sat in silence, staring into the glass, before he answered.

'Yes, I do. You know how it is in the Regiment, Jimbo. I've always been able to live pretty high off the pig's back, and people expect a certain standard. With just my pay, and a little bit of trust income that Lloyds can't touch, I wouldn't be able to keep up. It's no good saying that wouldn't make a difference, because I know it would and so do you. I certainly do not want to stay in the Regiment with people feeling sorry for me. That would be bad for discipline all round.'

Jimbo shook his head. He knew that Fred was right, but he was sorry for his friend and sad at losing such a good officer.

'It's such a waste – bloody Lloyds. Still, I would have given a hundred guineas to see that blasted woman's face when they found her.'

'I don't think that it was her face that was the main problem,' said Fred dryly.

Jimbo fell back in his chair, and waved his plump little legs in the air as he bellowed with laughter. The tale of Fred's brush with Dr Crumb had seeped into the barracks from the ether, and had kept the whole Regiment in chortles for days: 'Old Fitzy was a bloody caution and no mistake.'

Dr. Ernestine Crumb had not been amused by the unfortunate episode. She had determined to address Fred's case with extreme prejudice. She had come upon Marvin Sugden, who was seeking a new position, imitating to a convulsed general office the rather peculiar walk that adversity had thrust upon her. She was not a happy teddy – and Marvin Sugden was collecting his cards sooner than he anticipated.

'It's a bloody shame,' said Lt. Col. Paxton to Col. Bitterman, Silver Stick in Waiting to the Queen.

'I quite agree, we don't want to lose people like Fred. I'm sure that he would have commanded. But he's quite right, you know, it would be difficult for him. I expect that we could have found him some sort of Staff job, but he wouldn't want that. He loves the Regiment. No, I think he is doing the right thing, and I will pull all the necessary strings. At least he can go out on a decent note with the Birthday Parade. We'll get him away as quickly as possible after that.'

'It's a bloody shame,' said the Marquis of Fowey, 'I'm very sad for you, my boy.'

Fred and his father were sitting on the old stone bench on the ridge high above Bardwick Hall. This had been a favourite walk for father and son ever since Fred was small. The marquis always had a soft spot for his younger son who, apart from his poetry, was everything that he hoped his son and heir would be. Lord Tamar did not go for walks with his father, having found early in life that ill-health was a most useful weapon with which to guard against unwanted impositions, such as Work, Duty and Responsibility. When any of these dread sentiments were banded about, Lord Tamar took at once to his bed, where old Nanny Bardwick defended him against all comers with the ferocity of a tigress over her favourite cub. Even the marquis was somewhat in awe of Nanny, who had been nursery maid to *his* nanny.

The marquis sat with his chin resting on the horn handle of his favourite walking stick as he stared out across the Vale. Fred sat slumped beside him, absently chewing on a stem of grass. Although the world regarded the marquis as a human grenade, from which the pin had been extracted, Fred had always been able to ignore the storms of rage that frequently swept over the household and had always been able to talk to his father. They had hunted, stalked, fished and shot together. Fred had inherited his father's disposition to solitude, his love of the countryside and all that went to make it up. If they did not talk much when together, it was because they felt no need. When there was a need, Fred always found his father a good listener and sage counsel; there was need now.

'I wish I could help, Boysie,' – this was the marquis's childhood name for Fred, and only used in moments of great importance when they were alone – 'but you know the form. The whole lot's entailed to Tamar. I can't touch a penny without the Trustees giving the nod, and they're as tight as a duck's buttocks.' The marquis's battles with his Trustees were as legendary and bloody as a Norse saga. 'The bit of spare cash that I had went down with blasted Lloyds – Rankin will have told you that – and now yours has gone down the khazi as well. You know I always hoped that you would come back and run the place when Donkin' – the Agent – 'retires, and take on the hounds, of course. I mean, Tamar would make a complete balls-up of everything. But now your money's gone, we might have trouble with the Trustees – damn and rot the bastards! How that shit Wainwright ever became a trustee, I don't know. Did you know the bugger shoots foxes? And his wife's a veggie what-not. Bah!'

The marquis sat silently, seething that part of his life should be controlled by persons of such base and villainous disposition. Then he stirred, and said, 'So, what do you think you're going to do?'

'I don't really know, Dad. I mean, all this has come as something of a shock – I suppose I hoped that I might have commanded the Regiment one day.'

'Not as much of a shock as your Crumb woman got, eh, what? what?' The marquis dissolved into great spasms of mirth.

Fred had thought it proper to tell his father the story of his brush with the Hardship Secretariat. His father, whose sense of humour was broad, basic and somewhat cloacal, had not only thought it extremely funny but felt what Fred had done was meet, right and his bounden duty for the family honour.

'I don't know what to do, Dad. I mean, the only things I know anything about are soldiering and hunting, and neither look like growth industries in this country. I suppose that I shall have to go abroad.'

'Go to the colonies, you mean?'

'Not too many of them left, Dad,' said Fred, laughing. 'Oh, I expect something will turn up.'

He pulled a clasp-knife from his pocket, clicked the blade open, and started to whittle a stick of wood. It was

107

an old knife with yellowed horn scales on the handle, and a blade made thin by years of sharpening.

The hunter was gralloching the buck that he had just shot. His knife was old, with yellowed horn scales on the handle, and a blade made thin by years of sharpening. He cocked an ear, as though listening to some sound far away, and smiled gently to himself.

'Haven't seen that knife before,' said the marquis with interest.

'That's the knife that bearded chap gave me to take the brush off the fox after that brilliant hunt. I'd have given it back to him, but I've never seen him again and no one seems to know who on earth he was – very strange.'

The hunter smiled again and, slicing off the kidneys, put them in his pouch.

'Anyway,' said Fred, 'I've got the Birthday Parade to cope with. I'm not going to think of much else until that is over. You and Mama are coming, aren't you?'

'Wouldn't miss it for anything, Boysie, and we'll bring Annabel down with us.'

'Yes, of course. Annabel.'

'Darling, I *am* sorry about everything, my poor darling.'

Katerina was nestled in the crook of Fred's arm, with her golden hair spread across the tangled black mat on his chest. 'You should not have to leave the Army.'

'Well, I don't really, but I can't afford to stay on in the Regiment, and for me the Regiment is the Army. They're going to let me go straight after the Birthday Parade, send me on leave for a bit, then I just fade away.'

'You didn't fade away, just now,' said Katerina, delicately applying her teeth to one of Fred's nipples.

'Ouch, you bitch! You are coming to the parade, aren't you?'

'Darling, of course I come. I want to see you all dressed up with your big sword. Do you have a big sword, darling?'

'What do you think?'

'Mmm, I don't know. At the moment it seems a sad little thing. Perhaps if I . . .'

'You bitch! Your nails are very sharp! I can tell you you have absolutely no chance . . . Oh my God!'

'You know, you do have quite a big sword. Now, what shall we do with it?'

'Oh Lord! Not again! Damn it, woman, I've o-five-hundred stables in the morning.'

'One for the Queen, darling! In the morning you ride for *her*, but now it is *me*.'

The Queen's Birthday Parade or, as it is more generally known, Trooping the Colour, takes place each year near the beginning of June.

The Household Cavalry do not take a direct part in the marching and counter-marching. The job of the Cavalry is to wait upon Her Majesty at Buckingham Palace, and then escort her down The Mall to Horse Guards. Once they have discharged this duty, they fall-in into two ranks in front of the Guards' Memorial, to sit as still and steady as their horses will allow during the hour-long parade. At the end of the Trooping the Mounted Regiment does its own march past, first at the 'Walk Past' and then at the 'Trot'. It then escorts the Queen back to the Palace and retires for luncheon.

The HCMR consists of two squadrons: one of Life Guards with red tunics, white plumes, and one Royal Horse Guards ('The Blues and Royals') with blue tunics and red plumes. The Squadrons' command alternates year by year. The Squadron Leader, always a Major, whose year it is, becomes the 'Field Officer of the Escort'; his second-in-command is the 'Escort Commander'.

It was just after 4 a.m. as Fred pulled up at the gates of Hyde Park Barracks and waited for the duty policemen to let his car through. An early night was always a good idea before a big parade, but an early night with a beautiful journalist was not quite such a good notion; he could still smell the fragrant Katerina on his shirt.

'Morning, Kite.'

'Morning, sir.'

Fred's 'Blue Stable Dress' – blue tunic, blue overall trousers, whip and forage cap – was laid out for him in his room in the Officers' Mess. He changed quickly and, with Paddy at his heels – after a swift, sharp exchange of views with the Mess Corporal Major's cat – he set off through the June dawn for the stables.

'Morning, sir.'

A stamp of heels and a quivering salute.

'Morning, Corp'l Major,' and salute returned.

Corporal Major Bull – known to the Troopers as 'the Grim Reaper' – was Fred's Squadron Corporal Major.

'Nice cup of Rosie, sir?'

The canteen tea urn was seated on some straw bales with a pile of polystyrene cups. Fred gratefully swallowed a cup of hot, sweet tea and breathed in the wonderful smell of the stables as he took in the familiar scene that never failed to excite him. The three yards of stalls – one for each troop of the squadron – each held thirty black horses. Each was a region of organised chaos as troopers scurried about. The stalls were being mucked out, the dry straw being piled neatly in the passageway that ran down the centre of each yard. Horses were being groomed and feet were being picked out, white socks were being chalked even whiter. Impatient hooves stamped in the stalls, and sparrows cheeped in the roof.

Fred wandered about – checking a horse here, speaking to a trooper there – until he came to the loose box at the bottom of the yard. The big black horse tied up in the box turned his head and whickered as Fred entered. Trooper Rendall, his groom, came stiffly to attention.

'Carry on, Rendall. How is the old boy this morning?'

Tarrantino was Fred's charger.

'He's fine, sir, thank you, sir.'

Fred ran his hand down the silk-black shine of the horse's back and, pulling down an ear, whispered into it: 'Big day today, lad, behave yourself.' Tarrantino took a playful nip at him. 'You old bugger!' Fred stroked the velvet muzzle and felt a moment of sadness come over him; someone else would be riding Tarrantino soon, and this, all of this, that meant so much to him would be part of his history.

'Pull yourself together, man,' he said to himself and, doing just that, he went about his business.

An hour or so later, Fred stood in the middle of his room in the Mess, whilst Kite fussed about him in a practised manner. 'I wonder if this is what the ancestors felt like before a tournament, when the armourer was bolting them into their armour,' he thought. He had his gold-collard red tunic, white buckskin breeches, and black, mirror-shining jackboots and spurs on. Kite was strapping him into the breast and backplates of the gleaming cuirass, held over the shoulder by golden scales. Then came the gold epaulettes and the gold aiguillettes on the right shoulder, gold cross-belt with the cartouche on the back.

'There, sir, how does that look?'

Fred looked at himself in the full-length looking-glass; and Officer of The Life Guards in gleaming Mounted Review Order stared back, for the last time.

'Looks good, Kite. I hope the Commanding Officer agrees.'

'So do I, sir,' said Kite with feeling.

In the Household Cavalry, when the officers are inspected, their orderlies and grooms are also on parade, hoping they do not hear the dreaded words: 'This is a dirty officer.' This would result in much unpleasantness for the orderly concerned.

'Good luck for the day, sir.'

'Thank you, Kite.'

On the Barracks' Parade Ground, the Regiment was already drawn up in two ranks for the Commanding Officer's inspection. With him was his beady-eyed team of experts: the Adjutant, the Regimental Corporal Major, the Master Saddler, the Riding Master, the Squadron Orderly Corporal and two 'brushers down'. Not even the merest smudge or speck would escape that eagle-eyed group, or fail to bring down the terrifying wrath of Regimental Corporal Major Williams, who could make the destruction of Sodom and Gomorrah sound like a Girl Guides' picnic by comparison.

Down behind the NCOs' Mess, the officers were mounting and forming-up for their own inspection. Fred was very conscious of a knot in his stomach, although he knew the whole procedure forwards, backwards and sideways. The difference about today was that you only got to be Field Officer of the Escort once, and Fred wanted to do it perfectly.

'Fall in the Officers!'

'Open Order!'

'Escort to receive Standard – Walk March!'

'Receiving Standard!'

'Household Cavalry! General Salute! Draw Swords!'

As one, a hundred swords were drawn halfway from

their scabbards. Fred, with a sidelong glance to either side, gave a backward nod of his helmet, and the swords leaped, gleaming in the sunshine, to the 'Carry'.

Preceded by the Mounted Band, the Household Cavalry rides down the South Carriage Drive, through the Wellington Arch and down Constitution Hill. It never pauses, looking to neither right nor left, and disregards all traffic lights. A Sovereign's Escort does not concern itself with such things as road signs, and the Metropolitan Police take good care to see that other traffic is kept well out of the way.

The Escort forms up between the front of Buckingham Palace and the 'Wedding Cake', as Queen Victoria's Memorial is demotically known. The Field Officer then rides alone into the central courtyard of the Palace where he waits upon his Sovereign.

If Fred were asked to give a detailed account of the day, he would be unable to do so.

From the moment Her Majesty came out and got into her landau, to the moment back at the Barracks when, after he gave the order 'Return Swords', the Commanding Officer said to the Regiment, 'Thank you, gentlemen. Good parade. Enjoy your luncheon,' Fred was flying on autopilot.

Although he watched the video of the parade later, for him the day was a series of short memories: the band playing 'Scipio' as it approached Horse Guards; the agony of a breeches button digging into his shin bone; the sound of the Foot Guards NCO's blaspheming their men to keep their 'dressing' as they came down the back straight in front of the Cavalry; what Corporal of Horse Harris had snarled at Trooper Atkins. But the moment he always remembered was in the 'Trot Past' to the tune of 'Keel Row' when he had ordered: 'Household Cavalry! Royal Salute! Eyes Right!'

At that moment he felt that a part of his life had come to an end, and a new life, whatever it might be, was coming.

Fred tried very hard to enter into the spirit of the party in the Officers' Mess that evening. His father – who had also been in the Regiment – had enjoyed himself hugely. The Marquis of Fowey enjoying himself hugely was not a particularly pretty sight, or sound. Fred had a sneaking feeling of relief when his mother had, metaphorically, led his father away by the ear, before he started breaking things. Fred was more conscious of his Mess bill. Jimbo had told him not to worry and he was sure that the Sports Fund would cope, but then Fred was not quite sure that Jimbo had ever seen the marquis in full flow – he had the destructive inevitability of a flow of lava once he had erupted.

What with keeping a weather eye on his father, and trying to put up a good front, Fred had failed to notice that Annabel was not her usual jolly self. Annabel was a girl who enjoyed a good party – 'Darling, it was an absolute *shriek!*' It was only after his father had gone that Fred realised that Annabel had been unusually *piano*.

She was very quiet in the taxi when he took her back to the mews house, now in the well-manicured and nicely modulated grasp of Knight, Frank & Rutley. She was quiet while Fred undressed her, and offered no resistance when he made love to her – rather clumsily, because he was pretty drunk – but just lay there and accepted his attentions with no sign of enthusiasm; something or other was very wrong.

'What is it, Pudding?' said Fred, using the pet name given to Annabel when she was a plump, freckled child with braces on her teeth.

He put out a hand to touch her, but she shrugged it off and sat up with her hands clasped around her bent legs.

'What's the matter,' asked Fred again.

'There's someone else, isn't there?'

'Oh! shit!' said Fred to himself, and out loud: 'What makes you think that, Pudding?'

'Don't call me Pudding!' she said with a sudden flash.

'But I've always called you Pudding.'

'And I've always hated it.'

'I'm sorry . . . I never knew.'

'No, Fred, that's right – you never knew, and you don't know now. All these bloody years, and you still don't know.'

'Don't know what?'

'Anything really about me, do you? I'm just good old Annabel: dependable old Annabel. Always there when you want me – always good for a laugh. Ha! Bloody ha!'

'But, darling, I love you.'

'No, you don't, and I don't think you ever did. You simply got used to me, that's all. You were brainwashed into the idea of marrying me and, because you're bone idle, you just went along with it, but you never loved me. I loved *you*.'

'What makes you think that there's someone else?'

'Oh Fred! I may not be very clever, but I'm not stupid. I know there's another woman, because I *am* a woman. I can feel it. I can smell her on you. I am *not* a fool!'

'Oh, God!' said Fred, and sunk his head in his hands.

'Who is she?'

Fred blurted out the story of Katerina while Annabel listened in complete silence.

'Do you love her?'

Fred nodded.

'Do you love me?'

Fred buried his head in his hands.

Very quietly, Annabel began to cry.

Fred took her in his arms and she did not resist.

'Oh Fred, darling, it's all gone so wrong, and I don't know why, I really don't. But it's all falling apart, our engagement, your career. Oh, poor Fred, what will you do, will you marry this girl?'

'As things are, I can't marry anybody at the moment. And I don't know what I'm going to do, I don't know what on earth *we* are going to do.'

'Well, I know what I am going to do. I'm going to make us a nice cup of tea,' said Annabel, throwing off the duvet in a determined manner.

They sat shoulder to shoulder in the bed and sipped their mugs of tea in silence.

At last Annabel spoke: 'I think that I shall go and visit Charlotte. She's always on at me to go out and stay and now would seem a good time.'

Charlotte was Annabel's sister who had married a cattle station in Queensland.

'And you, Fred, what will you do?'

'I just don't know. Oh Pudding, I'm so sorry.'

Fred realised that for the first time in many years he was crying.

Annabel put down her mug, and gently took Fred's from his hand.

'Poor darling,' she said, 'come here. Poor us.'

And they lay in each other's arms like two lost children, and their tears mingled as they cried themselves to sleep.

'Can I have a word with you, sir? Quiet like?'

'Yes, Kite, of course.'

'Well, sir, all the lads are choked about you going and that, and I'm choked and all, sir. I mean, you're the best fucking officer – begging your pardon, sir – what I've ever had, and I just wanted to say that if you're going, could I sign off and come with you? I mean, begging your pardon, sir, but you're goin' to need a party to look after you. You need keeping an eye on, if you don't mind me saying so, sir, and that's wot Corp'l Major Bull was saying – same thing, sir.'

This was the longest speech that Fred had ever heard the normally taciturn Kite make, and he was completely flummoxed but very touched.

'But Kite, I don't know where I'm going, or what I'm going to do, and I certainly couldn't afford you anyway.'

'That's all right, sir, I know you. You'll sort something and Paddy and me'll just tag along – won't we Paddy, mate? Now, then, where are you? You know, sir, I think the little bleeder's hooked to the Cook House again. Permission to retrieve dog, sir!'

'Carry on, Kite,' said Fred, sinking wearily on the bed, and putting his head in his hands once more.

Kite's head re-appeared round the doorway: 'One other thing, sir. I don't want no other bleeder messin' up your toe caps.'

'Carry on, Kite!'

Fred was not drunk. He should have been, and it was not for want of trying on the part of the Warrant Officers' and NCOs' Mess. He was not drunk, yet it is possible that his path across the Parade Ground to the stables, in the small hours of the morning, was not entirely straight.

He paused at the end of the first yard, breathed in the wonderful smell, and looked down the two lines of resting horses, some lying, some standing with an eased leg.

Trooper Hopkins, the Night Guard, came swiftly to attention.

'All well, Hopkins?'

'Yessir.'

Fred wandered down the yard, listening to the sound of hay being munched and the occasional rattle of rack chains.

Tarrantino was waiting at the door of his loose box. As Fred let himself in, the big horse nuzzled his pockets for the Polo mint that he knew would come. Fred stroked his muzzle, then, putting his arms around the hard-muscled neck, he buried his face in the silky coat. 'Goodbye, old boy.'

And when he left, Tarrantino's neck was wet.

CHAPTER SEVEN

They caught Francis on a steep wooded hillside in Bosnia.

His motley patrol of half-trained and ill-armed volunteers had been sent to try to outflank a Serb position that was bringing down withering fire on the Croatian positions. The patrol was led by an ex-school teacher who was drunk, frightened and incompetent in roughly equal measures. The Serb regulars had spotted the Croats' amateurish manoeuvrings at an early stage, and had had plenty of time to spring an ambush. It was very efficient.

Francis was fortunate to find a place amongst some rocks where he had some cover and was able to put his skill with a rifle to good use. There were two other members of the patrol crammed into the tiny space with him. Francis realized their position was hopeless. The patrol was cut off and surrounded. The Serbs were cutting it to pieces at their leisure and pleasure.

The agricultural student on Francis's left was the first to die. He took a bullet through the temple, a shot that blew the back of his head off, splattering blood and brains all over Francis.

'Well,' thought Francis grimly, 'he won't be needing them any more.'

He took a swift shot at a figure scrabbling from one rock to another. The impact of the high velocity round lifted the Serb off his feet momentarily, then he crumpled on a slope like a scarecrow.

Francis's remaining companion was a peasant boy of eighteen. He had never left his home village until he joined the Army. He was not likely to see his village again. He called alternately on his own mother and the Mother of God, and closed his eyes every time he fired his rifle.

The Serb fire was intensifying, whilst the return fire dwindled as more and more of the doomed patrol met their end. The Serb regulars with their 'fire and movement' were getting closer and closer.

Francis and the peasant were in a hell of noise, ricochets and bullets zipping overhead. The place stank of cordite.

Francis ejected a spent magazine and slapped a new one into his AK-47.

Several things happened at once.

A Serb appeared from behind a tree only forty yards away.

Francis aimed and fired.

His AK-47 jammed.

The words of the Hunter flashed through his mind: 'In the time of the wolf, you cannot afford to miss.'

He saw the grenade curving through the air towards where they lay. The young peasant was killed outright by the grenade: he was the lucky one.

Colonel Vlavic was a happy man who loved his work. He was not a nice man, but then that would have been a positive disadvantage in his position. He was the Security Chief in the area where the Croatian patrol had been cut up. He was feeling especially cheerful that evening. Not only had an enemy patrol been wiped out, but there was a report of a wounded prisoner who was not only a mercenary, but quite possibly a German mercenary. Colonel

Vlavic rubbed his hands and poured himself another glass of slivovitz. The colonel's father had been shot by the Germans. He did not like them, and he especially did not like them playing the mercenary. He was looking forward to interrogating this specimen.

Francis was floating on a sea of pain. His peasant comrade had taken most of the force of the grenade, but there was enough remaining to shatter Francis's left shoulder and lacerate his back. From somewhere deep inside, he heard himself screaming. The detached Francis thought, 'Surely Czernys don't scream?' The undetached Francis screamed again as a heavy boot slammed into his wounded shoulder.

Through the waves of agony that washed over him, he heard a heated argument taking place. He knew it was to do with whether he should be killed or not. He wished they would get on with it. He tried to think of Tatiana and home, but the red waves washed out all thought except pain.

A new voice joined in: a voice of authority. Francis tried to turn his head, but got a boot in the nose. He heard the name Vlavic mentioned and a silence fell, followed by laughter.

'He'll wish we had killed him,' said a voice slurred with alcohol.

Colonel Vlavic lit a small cigar. 'So you are a German.'

'I am Slovenian.'

'You have a German passport.'

'I live in Slovenia,' mumbled Francis.

He mumbled because his lips were bloody and swollen. He had swallowed two teeth. Colonel Vlavic was a great believer in starting how you meant to go on. To help things go with a swing, Francis had been put in a chair with his hands cuffed behind in a manner as to produce maximum discomfort to the wounded shoulder. The pain was so great at times that he travelled in and out of consciousness. The colonel, who did not want any of that sort of nonsense, had summoned a doctor to give Francis an injection to wake him up.

'You are an agent of the German Government and the NATO scum.'

'I came here as a volunteer.'

'Why?'

'Because you bastards raped and killed my cousin, and killed her family.'

'Lies! We Serbs do not do such things! You are a spy!'

'I tell you . . .'

'Oh yes, mein Herr! You will tell us all right – everything.'

The colonel sorted through the papers on his desk that had been taken from Francis. He picked out a photograph. 'Who is this?'

Francis raised his head and looked through pain-blurred eyes at the beautiful face of Tatiana. He realized that he would never see her again.

'My wife.'

'She is very beautiful,' said the colonel. 'I wonder how I can persuade her to come and visit me, eh? Shall I tell you what I would do to her?'

'No, for God's sake!'

'There is no God here but me, my little German, and I promise that you will pray to me before I have finished with you. Now, listen to what I shall do to your wife.'

He bent close to Francis, smelling of sweat, garlic and slivovitz.

The detail was graphic, if crude.

Francis spat in the colonel's face. In return, the colonel stubbed his cigar out on Francis's cheek and shouted for his aides.

*

Francis did not die well. No one dies well who has the soles of his feet whipped through to the bone; who has been tied to a metal bed frame and had electrodes applied to various parts of his body. A slow dying in those circumstances is not good. Francis had been trained to resist torture when he was in the Special Forces. 'Think beyond pain,' they had said. 'Think of the things that you love. Think of the good things.' He became two people. His inner self desperately sought memories of his wife, of his green fields, of cool forests, whilst all the time he could hear himself screaming. He also thought of the little gold crucifix that had hung round his neck: Tatiana had given it to him when he left. Colonel Vlavic had ripped it from him with a satisfied grunt. 'That's not going to help you now, Kraut,' he had said. But the good colonel was wrong, Francis could still see it. 'Hold thou thy cross . . .' he thought, and formed the image of the cross in the red mists of pain. Even so, it was a relief when they finally cut off his genitals, and choked him with them. At least that ended it.

Colonel Vlavic had thoroughly enjoyed his bout with Francis. The evening's works had appealed to his robust sense of humour, and had been much appreciated by his staff. They had particularly liked the colonel's little refinement at the end. How they had laughed when the Kraut spy had been made to choke on his own wedding tackle; so should perish all enemies of the Greater Serbia. Opening more bottles of pivo, they made a merry night of it.

The next morning, the good colonel sat once more at his desk sorting through Francis's papers. He kept returning to the photograph of Tatiana. She really did look a fantastic bit of tail. Just supposing she could be persuaded over into Serb territory, or, more specifically, Colonel Vlavic's territory, there might be yet more sport to be had out of the German spies: teach the bastards a real lesson.

'Mischa!' he shouted.

The door of the office opened and a bleary-eyed unshaven face peered through the crack.

'Yes, Colonel?'

'What have you done with the carcass of the spy?'

'It's lying outside, Colonel. We're going to tip it in the cellar of one of them burned houses, sometime.'

'That cold-room still working down at the abattoir?'

'Dunno, colonel, I think so.'

'Well hang the bastard up in there, along with the pigs.'

'Very good, Colonel.'

Mischa retired shaking his head – fucking officers, who could understand them? But he did understand that you did not disobey the colonel, not with his sense of humour.

The colonel shuffled through Francis's papers again, and set about composing a telegram.

After Francis had gone, Tatiana had a good weep. Then she dried her eyes and determined that she would weep no more. There was work to be done, and she was there to do it. Each day for the next few weeks she worked herself to exhaustion the better to get through the aching void of nights in the large empty bed. The better to avoid waking up in the dark and reaching out for the great warm body that was no longer there. Exhaustion saw her through the small dark hours when fear and anxiety prowl about seeking their prey.

For the first few days, Francis was able to telephone Tatiana, but once he moved further inland, the calls stopped. He wrote every day, but the letters arrived spasmodically, sometimes a bunch arriving together. In his letters, Francis tried to put a good face on the situation, but Tatiana knew him too well to be deceived; she could see things were not going well. Francis had done his national service in the Bundeswehr. He had done Special Forces training and had been commissioned. He felt he had a lot to offer to the Bosnian Army, which at that moment was too demoralized and disorganized to make proper use of the skills and training he could offer. Thus it was that Francis found himself on the front line as part of a makeshift and ill-trained unit. He knew for certain there was disaster waiting and, although he tried to keep his letters light and cheerful, Tatiana was able to read through the lines, and sense the despair and fore-boding that lay there. She flung herself even harder into her work.

There was a big flap of ewes and lambs on one of the upland pastures. Normally old Felix the shepherd and his gaunt, savage dogs, spent the day wandering the rolling grassland with the flock, bringing them back to the fold at night. However, long hours in the cold and wet over the years had finally caught up with Felix and he was laid low with the rheumatism. Although he struggled to get up, he got scant sympathy from either his wife or the Frau Gräfin, both of whom ordered him back to bed with a flea in his ear. The old man lay there grumbling about the perverse nature of womankind, and at least that took his mind off the ache in his joints.

Little Felix, the grandson, was sent to look after the sheep, but he was only twelve years old and somewhat simple. His grandfather's dogs refused to go with him. They lay by the old man's bed, growling at anyone who went near.

'*Quis custodiat, ipsos custodes,*' said Tatiana to herself, adding to her tasks that of riding out to the pastures to see that Young Felix was all right. One day the young lad was obviously upset.

'There is a ewe and her lamb missing, Frau Gräfin,' said Young Felix.

'You're sure?' said Tatiana, because she knew he could only count to ten with difficulty.

Young Felix shrugged. He knew. What he did not know was how he knew, except that he came from thirty generations of shepherding stock.

'Stay with the flock,' said Tatiana. 'I will go and have a look around.'

Turning her horse, she cantered across the rolling grassland to where the trees marked a little valley, with a rushing stream in the bottom. For half an hour she rode along the valley, searching.

The Hunter was leaning against the time-sculpted trunk of a large beech tree; Tatiana could have sworn that he had not been there the moment before. He raised his battered hat. '*Grüss Gott*, Gräfin. You have lost a sheep, perhaps?'

'*Grüss Gott!* Yes, we have. Have you seen it? It has a lamb with it.'

'Yes I have, and no it hasn't, I'm afraid. Follow me.'

The remains of the ewe lay by the stream; there were bits of bone and wool scattered over the muddied, bloodied grass. Of the lamb there was no sign.

'My God!' said Tatiana. 'Was it wolves?'

'It was one wolf – a very big wolf.'

'A Devil Wolf?' asked Tatiana in a small voice.

'The Devil is certainly hard at work these days,' said the Hunter, taking off his hat and scratching his mat of tangled locks.

Then he paused, as though listening, and his face hardened suddenly.

'You must go home at once, Gräfin – at once. I will help Felix shift the sheep lower down the hill where they will be safer. Then I will come to the Schloss. Do nothing till I come, absolutely nothing. Is that clear?'

'Yes, but what –?'

'Don't blether, woman – ride! Now!'

Tatiana swung her horse and touched him with her spurs. They took off like a rocket. It was only as she galloped away that she suddenly thought, 'How dare he speak to me like that! Who the hell does he think he is?' then, 'Who the hell *is* he?' But she galloped on just the same.

As she reined in the sweating pony in the courtyard of the castle, old Tomislav appeared waving a telegram.

'My dear old thing! You can't possibly go over there. I mean, you shouldn't even be here.'

Captain Leo Wisden of Princess Louise's Own Dragoon Guards – known to the rest of the Cavalry as 'The Plods' – was perplexed. Captain Wisden was quite often perplexed, but all this was more perplexing than usual. He had not much wanted to come to Bosnia. It was quite obvious that it was a shambles, and that UNPROFOR was an absolute shower; the former Yugoslavia was a shit heap, and the best thing to do, in Captain Wisden's opinion, would be to nuke the whole bloody lot, and get home in time for the hunting season. He did not want to have two damn good horses eating their heads off at Melton all season whilst he was sitting in this hell hole – and he was running out of cigars! He had also thought the blue beret was too Charlie for words, until Fiona had pointed out it was jolly near Eton Blue. Good old Fiona, she knew how to cheer a chap up. Anyway, a soldier has to do his duty, and his duty had brought him to this checkpoint between the remains of two villages.

The Bosnian Army was slouching about in the village behind him – 'bloody idle lot of buggers, want a bloody good gripping,' his Troop Sergeant had said – and 'Caspar Chetnik' was getting pissed as a rat in the village in front of him. A pretty shitty situation, and now he had this woman who had appeared in a Bosnian Army car, and was wittering on something about going to collect her husband's body from the Chetniks. Mind you, she was a looker; a bit grimy and smudged, but even so he wouldn't mind . . . he pulled himself together.

'Absolutely out of the question, my dear old thing . . .' he began again.

'I am not your Old Thing, you stupid little English prick,' said Tatiana.

'I say! Gosh! That's a bit steep! I'm only thinking of your safety. I mean, I can't let you go over there.'

'You don't have the authority to stop me.'

Captain Wisden thought about this one, and concluded that she was probably quite right. Then he brightened. 'I'll have to check with HQ. C'prl Thomas!'

A head appeared from the turret of a Scimitar CVR.

'Sir!'

'Any contact with Sunray?'

'No, sir, the comms are still on the blink.'

'Fuck!' said Captain Wisden, then to Tatiana, who really was a super-looking girl, 'But how did you get here anyway?'

'In Captain Ahmed's car. I have the full authorisation of the Bosnian authorities.'

'How did you get that?'

Tatiana shrugged.

Wisden looked at Captain Ahmed who was leaning against the Merc, sulkily cleaning his fingernails with a match stick. He was sulking because he had thought that escorting this blonde bombshell was a gift from Allah. On the way, he had suggested that it was time for a little taste of Paradise. He had even placed the bint's hand on his crotch to show her the path. When he had finished screaming, the bint had a knife at his throat, and his driver was laughing so much he nearly turned the car over. Captain Ahmed was sore both mentally and physically. As far as he was concerned, the bint could go to the Chetniks, and Gehenna – good luck to her, them and it. He did not know how she had got authorisation either.

The commander of the Bosnian detachment had been looking at the papers that Tatiana had produced. They seemed in order, and came from his Headquarters. The woman must have had some clout to get clearance and a staff car, even one with Captain Ahmed as escort.

'This is not good,' the Hunter had said when Tatiana showed him the telegram. 'You should not go.'

'I must – I must bring Francis home.'

'The body is not important. It is only a husk. It is not your husband.'

Tatiana stared at him, dry eyed and stony faced.

'When you shoot a deer, you make a ceremony over the body to honour the soul of the departed beast.'

The Hunter was silent.

'How can I honour the soul of my husband unless I have the body? How can I grieve? Oh, Hunter, I want to grieve!' She looked up at the kindly weather-beaten face above the bushy beard.

The Hunter reached out a hand and smoothed her hair. 'Then,' he said, 'this is what you must do.'

'You understand,' said the commander of the Bosnian unit at the checkpoint, 'that I am authorized to let you pass, but my orders are quite specific: I cannot help you in any way. You will be on your own.'

'I understand.'

'I really think I should arrest you or something,' said Captain Wisden.

'You would cause an international incident, Captain.'

Captain Wisden looked at Tatiana's taut, determined face. 'Oh, shit! C'prl! Are the Serbs on net?'

'I raised them earlier, sir.'

'Well get hold of that chap who speaks English – Vlavic – tell him he's got a visitor.'

'Colonel Vlavic is expecting me.'

'Well, all I can say is the best of British luck, my dear old thing.'

The road between the two shattered villages had been gouged out of a steep hillside. Above the road was steep woodland, and, below was a rocky scrub-covered slope that dropped to a tumbling stream. The distance was only about half a mile, and the two villages were in plain sight of each other. It was the longest half mile of Tatiana's life. She was very frightened, but she strode along with her back straight and her head held high – although her legs were trembling. A brisk breeze in the face whipped her golden hair so that it rippled in the sunlight. She was determined that anyone watching should detect no weakness, and there were many people watching.

'By Jove! She's a cracking mover!' said Captain Wisden as he watched through his field glasses.

'Nothing we can do for her, sir? Not if the Chetniks cut up rough, like?' said Sergeant Hammond.

'They will be rough,' said Captain Ahmed, with a certain note of satisfaction in his voice.

'Not a bloody thing, Sar'nt – she's on her own.'

Captain Ahmed said; 'She won't be on her own for long!'

'Sergeant Hammond!'

Captain Wisden kept his eyes glued to his glasses.

'Sir!'

'If that beastly man utters another word, stick a monkey wrench up his arse.'

'It'll be a pleasure, sir!'

'It would be a pleasure for me to stonk those bastard Chetniks,' said Captain Wisden, with a note of longing in his voice. 'Any luck with Sunray, Corp'l Thomas?'

'Dead as a NAAFI sandwich, sir.'

'Shit.'

Colonel Vlavic was beside himself when he got the radio message from the UNPROFOR detachment; he had never thought she would really come. He grabbed his field glasses and hurried to an observation post. He focused on the tall, slim and upright figure striding up the road towards him, with her face set. She was truly beautiful! He watched the wind-blown hair and the firm outline of her breasts. He felt the same stirring in his groin as he had when Francis was screaming and writhing on the iron bed. The colonel just knew that this was going to be a good day.

At the first sight of the Chetniks manning the barricade across the road, Tatiana nearly faltered; she could feel their eyes licking her body. She was very frightened and would like to have turned and run, but her pride gave her strength and determination. She had come to take her husband home, and she would not go home without him.

High up on the wooded hillside, the bearded man sat crouched with his back against an ash tree. He was in a little grove. With his binoculars he watched the little figure striding on the road down below him.

'Brave girl!' he thought. He watched the grimy, unkempt men rise up from behind the barricades to meet her, surrounding and leading her to the jeep where a plump colonel waited.

The man eased the fighting knife in its scabbard, and checked the magazine on his machine carbine. He gestured with his hand, and men moved out of the shade of the ash trees; they had been so still and silent that they might have been part of the trees themselves.

They began to move downhill, without disturbing a stone or twig.

'Welcome, welcome, Frau Gräfin,' said Colonel Vlavic as Tatiana climbed into his jeep.

She was shaking now, and could not help it. As soon as she had walked through the barricade, grimy hands had seized her arms, and she was surrounded by dirty, un-shaven faces. She smelled the breath – foul with garlic and alcohol – but the eyes were worse: wolves' eyes, leering and lusting. She knew she was in deep trouble.

Many hands had led her to the colonel's jeep, hands that strayed over her body as she was propelled along. Now there was the colonel; sleek, shaven and stinking of cheap cologne, he laid a hand on her knee as she sat beside him. He was smiling, but his eyes were as still as the eyes of a snake.

Tatiana's mouth was dry with fear. She was only able to speak with effort. 'You said that if I came, I could have my husband's body.'

'And so you shall, my dear. Igor Vlavic is a man of his word. Your husband was a very gallant soldier, but stupid to come here. I have his body ready for you. We will go and see it at once. Once we have completed the for-malities, you may then take it away.'

Tatiana swallowed. 'What formalities? You said I could just take him away.'

The colonel spread his plump hands. 'Alas, in this world, there are always formalities, always a price to pay.'

'How much do you want? I do not have much money with me.'

'Do not concern yourself. There is always a way. Now I will take you to your husband.

*

Tatiana screamed and went on screaming.

The Serbs who had gathered in the abattoir to watch the fun, roared with laughter and slapped their thighs. Colonel Vlavic was a caution, and no mistake. He had, of course, explained to Tatiana that he had – kind, thoughtful man that he was – arranged for Francis's body to be kept in cold storage pending her arrival. He did not tell her of his little surprise. Tatiana was not only now looking upon the naked, mutilated, burned and beaten body of her husband, but there it was – and this is where the colonel's famous sense of fun came into play – hanging from a meat hook through its chin alongside the carcass of a pig. As an extra refinement, his genitals had been tied round his neck.

Tatiana fainted. When she came to, she found she was sitting on a hard chair.

Someone was pulling her head back by the hair. Someone else had forced a bottle between her teeth, and was pouring slivovitz down her throat. The fiery liquid made her cough and gag back to consciousness.

Sitting on the other side of a rough table was Colonel Vlavic, smiling happily. The room was full of men who stank.

'Are you feeling better, Frau Gräfin? I am afraid the sight of your husband came as a bit of a shock to you. I am sure that we all offer you our condolences.'

The room giggled.

'I ... I ...' began Tatiana, but she could go no further.

'The lady is trying to say that she is touched by our sympathy. Give her another drink.'

Once again Tatiana's hair was pulled back roughly, and once again the bottle was thrust between her teeth. The liquor burned and choked her.

'Now,' said the colonel, 'it is time for the formalities.'

'But what is it you want?' sobbed Tatiana, who felt she was falling apart. 'Just let me take my husband and go.'

'Your husband was a stinking spy,' the pleasant mask had now gone, 'and you are probably another. I should interrogate you, as I did him.'

Tatiana hung her head. She was speechless with terror, and desperately trying to control her sobs.

'Look at me!'

Her hair was pulled back.

The colonel was smiling again: an unspeakable smile. 'There may be a way round this unpleasantness. That is all I want from you, a little pleasantness – a little gentleness – you understand?'

'No!' said Tatiana.

'Hold her!'

The colonel rose to his feet and came round the desk to stand in front of Tatiana. Very slowly he unbuttoned his flies, and took out his erect penis.

'Suck me, Kraut bitch!'

'No! No!'

Her head was forced towards the already glistening tip.

Summoning all her courage, Tatiana snapped at the penis.

The colonel leaped back, and there was a roar of laughter.

'Perhaps she is Jewess, Colonel. Maybe she thinks it's pork!'

More laughter, but the colonel was not laughing. 'I think that she needs breaking in a bit first. Hold her!'

Strong hands held Tatiana back in the chair.

The colonel reached forward and ripped her blouse open.

'Great tits!' he said, and seizing a nipple between each finger and thumb, he squeezed hard.

Tatiana screamed.

'Now I'll really give you something to scream about, you common sow.'

Tatiana was dragged to her feet, and the rags of her shirt were pulled off her. She was forced face-down across the table and held there, the rough wood scraping her injured nipples. Hard hands pulled down her jeans and pants.

The colonel ran a hand down between her buttocks, fondling her anus with his finger.

'Now, my little German whore, I am going to break you – and I am going to start by breaking-in your arse-hole – and when I'm finished the others can have a go. You won't be snapping then.'

There was a cheer.

Tatiana could feel the stiff hotness of the colonel's penis rubbing in the cleft of her buttocks. 'You like the feel of that?' he grunted.

The door burst in, and the room became a hell of screams, smoke and explosions.

A body fell across Tatiana, pinning her to the table, and she felt the warm gush of blood across her naked back.

She fainted.

Rough hands were pulling up her pants and jeans; more hands thrust her into a camouflage jacket to cover her nakedness.

There were bodies, blood and smoke everywhere, and the room swarmed with men in camouflage and bala-clava helmets.

A giant man peeled off his hood and put his great arm around her.

'Hunter!' she exclaimed. 'But how –?'

'Hush! No questions! We must get out of here.'

'What about him, Boss?'

Colonel Vlavic had taken two rounds through the

shoulder, and was propped up in a corner with his trousers still down by his ankles; he was groaning, but still conscious.

'Finish him!'

'No!' shouted Vlavic and Tatiana simultaneously.

'Give me your pistol,' she turned to the Hunter.

'No! Please!' screamed Vlavic.

'Are you sure?' asked the Hunter gently.

'Yes.'

She took the pistol and crouched in front of the colonel, the barrel pointed at his sagging, naked, belly.

'In the name of God, no!' cried the wretched man.

'You have no god,' said Tatiana.

She lowered the pistol and pressed it against the now flaccid penis.

'No!'

She carefully squeezed the trigger.

Part of a letter from Captain Wisden to his wife Fiona, which began 'Darling Pudding,' and in which he described the events of that interesting day:

'. . . then we heard lots of firing from the Chetnik village and I said to Hammond what the hell's going on Sergeant and he said buggered if I know Sir but it sounds like a right old bundle over there. Then this party of blokes appeared and the Bosnians got very jumpy and I told them steady on as I can see the girl is with them and they are carrying a body bag and then this big chap at the front of the party starts waving the Bosnian flag and they all jump around very excited. So these blokes come marching up to our checkpoint and I must say they did look a hard lot of bastards and I said so to Hammond and this big bearded cove who was obviously the Head Honcho turned to me and said in perfect English, 'yes, we're straight out of the trees, Old Boy. Now I wonder if you would be kind enough to look after this lady, she's had a bit of a rough time actually.' And there was this girl I told you about and she's all bruised and shaking and wearing a cammo jacket four sizes too big for her and Hammond sits her down and shouts for the medic and a mug of tea and I just start to ask the big chap a question or two when all hell breaks loose. The TV people arrive and the Colonel arrives and a lot of UNPROFOR brass and the big chap winks at me and says 'Toodle pip Old Boy' and he and his chaps just fade away into the trees, I mean one minute they were there and the next minute they had gone. There was a lot of shouting and arm waving and the Adie woman tried to interview the girl who was still drinking her tea and shaking and my word, Pudding, didn't she give the Beeb an ear bashing almost as bad as your Aunt when some silly bugger kicked one of her hounds. And the Colonel takes me aside and says what-the-hell's-been-going-on-here? so I told him and he looked very thoughtful and said that I was not to tell any of this to anyone, but I knew he wouldn't mean you Pudding, but I must say it was all a pretty rum do, with that bearded chappie and everything. I do hope Misty's got over the colic . . .'

Katerina was in America at the time of Francis's funeral, but she wrote to her cousin and in return received a full account of all that had happened, except that Tatiana claimed to have no knowledge of the identity of her rescuer. Katerina was a woman of the world, and there were some things that the world was just not ready for.

PART TWO

CHAPTER EIGHT

Fred's life was eddying. His military life had closed behind him. His financial structure was being dismantled around him. He had no idea where he was going. The only certain thing in his life seemed to be Katerina. Their affair had blossomed and flourished, even although it sometimes got singed at the edges – Fred had found mid-European mood-swings more than a little confusing at first.

'You're a bit like a blood horse,' he said to Katerina, as she lay, satiated and purring.

'You mean fast and beautiful and wonderful to ride?'

'Well, I really meant you can be quite nasty in the box sometimes; but you've a good mouth, you are a straight mover and, provided I watch your oat ration and don't misuse the whip, you are not a bad ride.'

'Bastard!' she rolled on top of him, growling. 'Bastard! As if I could get too much oats off an impotent English like you!'

That wasn't what you said just now. *Ow!*'

Katerina had dug her nails into his pectoral muscles.

'Not a bad ride!' she snarled and, letting her golden hair hang over Fred's face, she lowered her slightly parted lips to his. 'Just what did you mean about judicious use of the whip?' she murmured.

Fred could not bear the thought of showing yet another

version of 'Henry-and-Caroline' round the mews house. he had telephoned Hugo at Knight, Frank and told him he could damn well get off his well-upholstered backside and start earning his commission.

'Don't you want to sell the house?' Hugo grumbled.

'Not much,' said Fred. 'You're too bloody idle and so are your shoes.'

'How do you know?' said Hugo, guiltily looking down at his, perhaps, less than lustrous toe-caps.

'Because you always were an idle little officer.'

Fred rang off and went to the Club to read the papers. Life could not consist of Katerina alone, he realised as he walked up St. James's; one way or another, he had to find himself some sort of gainful employment, and that meant soon. He had had one or two offers: County Red Cross Organiser, another as the Secretary of the Central Midlands Agricultural Show, but there was not much to stimulate the adrenaline in either direction. He had even been approached by an old Army colleague about training counter-insurgency forces in Turkmenistan – that would certainly get the adrenaline pumping – but from what Fred knew of the present Turkmenistan Government, it undoubtedly deserved all the insurgency it was going to get.

Fred knew beggars could not be choosers, but he had not yet quite joined their ranks and he was certain that something would turn up. He would have a good scan through the 'sits vacant' and, besides, you never knew whom you might run into at the club.

'. . . then, you see, the feller – that's the other feller, not the feller I told you about first, d'yersee – no! no! it wasn't him, it was the merchant banker, well, he says . . .'

Fred groaned inwardly. The Club Bore was in full

142

spate. He had been concealed behind a newspaper in the club's otherwise empty reading room, when Fred had poked his head in before making for the bar, and he had failed to penetrate The Bore's disguise. All he had seen was a large bottom half, and an unfolded *Daily Telegraph*. However, The Bore had scented prey and, with the grace of a tiger, which was surprising considering his bulk, he had leaped up, tracked, and sprung.

'. . . and one for me, too,' said the voice behind Fred, who was just ordering a glass of Champagne. Fred groaned.

'No, no, I'll do these, old boy – haven't seen you for ages. You know, I heard a jolly funny story the other day . . .'

That was the trouble with The Bore; you could not meet a nicer or a kinder man, but never a worse story-teller whose tales went on, and on, ad infinitum.

Rescue!

'Hello Fred.'

'Barney!'

'Barney! I was just telling Fred about this merchant banker feller . . .'

'You mean the one who waved his John Thomas about in the Stock Exchange?'

'Oh, you've heard about it?'

'You told me last week, old thing, and a right cock up you made of it too. Now, Fred, you're just the man I want to see. May we have a quiet word?'

'But Fred hasn't heard the end of the story.'

'Yes, he has, I just told him. Now come along, Fred.'

'Very good! Ha! ha!' Fred mouthed over his shoulder as he was led away from the disconsolate Bore.

Barney Napier had been at school with Fred, and now ran many broad acres and a family pack of foxhounds somewhere in the distant North. Fred had hunted with him, and knew that he was on the Committee of the Masters of Foxhounds Association.

He led Fred to a pair of side-by-side armchairs. 'Now then, I've got something that might interest you,' and settled down to give Fred the background.

Mr. Oates had come highly recommended to the Mastership of the Old Wessex. He had ascended, like a rocketing cock pheasant, from the relative obscurity of a county in the south-west of Ireland, which someone had once described as acres of flooded bog stitched together with wire. He was, by all – not the least his own – accounts, a 'coming man', and this on no less an authority than that great Irish MFH, The Knight O'Rafferty. This recommendation mightily impressed Colonel Sir William Nately, Bt., the Chairman of the Old Wessex Hunt. Sir William had once briefly met The Knight at a drinks party during the Royal Dublin Horse Show, and this transient encounter allowed Sir William to rank the Irishman as one of his dearest friends; Sir William was like that. He adopted Mr. Oates's candidacy with great enthusiasm, bullied it through the Hunt Committee and thoroughly endorsed Mr. Oates in local society.

It has to be said that Mr. Oates was a man of immense persuasion and charisma. He was charmingly reticent about his background.

Major Simkin, the grim-visaged ex-Gunner who performed the role of Hunt Secretary with nit-picking efficiency, said he thought Oates had been in the Irish Guards. Sir William felt it could have been the Grenadiers, but it had certainly been Household Brigade.

Jim Scuttle, who had been put on as the Old Wessex First Whipper-in and Kennel Huntsman, muttered the opinion, after seeing the new Master's performance with hounds, that more likely it was the Fire Brigade.

Mr. Oates smiled, flannelled and charmed, and gave

nothing away. He especially enchanted and flannelled Lady Nately in whose life there had not been too much of that sort of thing. It was she who spearheaded Mr. Oates's campaign to have the entire season's guarantee paid up front. 'It would so help poor Rufus' – for such was his given name – 'in planning his gross margins.' Sir William, who had no more idea what a 'gross margin' was than his wife, vaguely thinking it was a headland left round an arable field for the hunt to ride on and therefore 'a good thing', heartily ratified Mr. Oates's request. Major Simkin might have had misgivings, but was persuaded both by Sir William and by Mr. Oates's charm – after all, the chap had been in the Micks – and paid the requisite sum into the Master's account.

The next morning the money was gone – along with two horses, the hunt Land Rover and trailer, and Mr. Oates himself. It was midsummer and the Old Wessex had no master.

'So,' concluded Barney, 'the Old Wessex have no Master. Wondered if you might be interested. I mean you're a pretty houndy chap and you go well. It's quite a riding country – a lot of hunting farmers and retired soldiers who want a good gallop – with a lovely bit of vale and some niceish downland. They need a Gent too. There are one or two bobbery sort of chaps who have been sniffing at it, but frankly they just would not do.'

'I know it a bit,' said Fred. 'I've hunted there a little over the years but, Barney, I couldn't possibly afford it. I mean, you know my position. Pretty well everything has gone down the tubes at Lloyds. I've still got a couple of horses at Bardwick, which the buggers are not going to get, but that's about all.'

'But you could run your teeth, and buy the odd bottle of whisky?'

'Well, yes, just about.'

'I don't think money is a major problem. There's plenty of cash washing about down there, and that ass of a Chairman is doing the right thing at last by rooting in his wallet for the funds that little red-haired bugger decamped with. They'll pay to get the right chap.'

'What happened to this Oates, anyone know?'

'Buggered off to Florida with an American widow old enough to be his mother, so I'm told. Better than being in gaol, I suppose, but not much. Serve the little shit right.'

'Can I think about it? I must say it is rather tempting.'

'Of course. Give me a ring. Why not go down and talk to them anyway? You can't lose anything by that. Let's have another drink and bag a table for lunch before the geriatric brigade gets in and pinches them all.'

Fred poured himself another cup of tea, lit a cigarette, and lounged back in his chair with a contented sigh.

'Oh, come on, then,' he said to Paddy who was wagging his tail in a hopeful manner. The little dog took a flying leap into his master's lap, licked his face and curled up happily.

Katerina looked over at them, smiling from the other side of the table. 'Happy, darling?'

'Well slept, well fed, and well fucked – yes, of course I'm happy.'

It was Saturday morning. Fred had spent the night at Katerina's flat. The mews house had been sold to 'Henry-and-Caroline', and he was in the process of getting his things together. The little house that had been home was now full of packing cases and rolled up carpets. No longer was it home.

'Come and stay with me, darling,' Katerina had said.

'What about Paddy?'

'It is Paddy that I want. Who would want a greedy, untidy bear like you in their flat.'

'Bears have their uses.'

'Show me one.'

They had slept late, made love, and were now enjoying a leisurely breakfast in their dressing gowns.

They had talked late into the night about the Old Wessex.

'The idea excites you?'

'Well, I do love hunting. It's probably one of the few things that I am good at, and there seems to be nothing much else about. They're in a bit of a hole.'

'Then I think you should go and have a look, darling. Also, it's not too far away from London. I don't want you too far away.'

'Would you come and visit me?'

'Of course, darling, I come and see you in your little rural hovel.'

'That'll give the locals something to talk about.'

'It is good for the bourgeoisie to be shocked occasionally.'

The rattle of the post box now interrupted their calm.

'I go, I do not wish Herr Paddy to be disturbed.'

Paddy's tail thumped at the mention of his name. He liked Katerina, but could not understand why he was not allowed to sleep on the bed with his master and the mistress.

Katerina returned with a handful of letters.

'Ah! there is one from my cousin.'

'Which one?' asked Fred, with a slightly weary intonation. He had been taken through the labyrinth of Katerina's family, had got lost amongst the aunts and uncles, and given up completely in the complications of cousins. 'Is it the one in New York who lives with two queers? The one in Vienna who can't resist cream cakes? Or . . . ?'

'No, it is the one in Slovenia.'

'I don't think I have heard about that one.'

Katerina paused, looking at him, her face sombre. Then she said, 'You remember when I first met you at the Barracks and I was angry?'

'I do indeed! You were hating all Brits, and especially hated soldiers.'

'Yes, that was because I had just had a letter from this particular cousin.'

'But why should you and she hate the Brits?'

Katerina got to her feet and went to her desk. From a drawer she took a letter and a photograph. She put the letter in front of Fred and sat down again.

'Read it,' she said.

Fred read the letter, twice, without comment. As he did so, he felt the tingle of recognition at some of the horrific details it spoke of. He looked up. Katerina was watching him, her face firmly set.

'What does your cousin look like?' asked Fred quietly.

Without a word Katerina threw the photograph across the breakfast table.

Fred looked.

'Dear God! It's her! It's the woman on the television. Dear God, I never thought! You know, when I first saw you that night I thought from a distance that you were her. You're so alike!'

'Her mother and my mother were twin sisters. We are very alike, but I am perhaps a little more beautiful,' said Katerina matter-of-factly.

'She had a hell of a rough time – what a woman – I'm very sorry about her husband.'

'If the bloody British Government had allowed the Bosnians to arm themselves properly, he might not have died. And if your bloody soldiers had blown that Chetnik village away, as they should have done, then my cousin would not have had to suffer at their filthy hands. But what can you expect from the bloody British, eh?'

Katerina's voice took on an edge that Fred had learned betokened trouble.

'Look, if you're spoiling for a row, then I'm off. I don't need this shit from you. I wasn't there, and even if I had been I would have done exactly the same as that poor bloody captain – what all soldiers do – obey orders!'

'You mean you'd have done nothing to save my cousin?'

'Your cousin was very brave and very foolish, but if anyone had started shooting, she would have been very brave, very foolish and very dead. She was bloody lucky to get out. Does anyone know who the chaps were who rescued her?'

'No, but it certainly wasn't the fucking Brits!'

'How do you know? It says here that their commander spoke perfect public school English.'

'Anyone can do that.'

'No, they can't. So, for all you know, it could have been the Hereford Gardeners who rescued your cousin.'

'It is possible, I suppose,' said Katerina sulkily.

'So, do you still want to have a row?'

'No.'

'No what?'

'No, darling.'

'Right, then, get on and read the cousin's letter.'

Katerina opened the letter and read.

'Oh God! As though she didn't have enough trouble!'

'What's happened to her now?'

'She says that the area is being plagued by wolves.'

'Wolves? I didn't realise they were still a problem in middle Europe.'

'They think that the war is moving them.'

'I once read a splendid book about wolf hunting in Brittany in the last century. It sounded incredibly exciting. I wonder if your cousin would like me to go and hunt her wolves?'

Katerina did not look up. 'She would cut your balls off.'

'Well, in that case, the Old Wessex sounds a better bet. What is your cousin called, by the way?'

'Tatiana.'

'Another one?' said Tatiana.

Tomislav nodded silently.

They were in what had been Francis's office in the castle where Tatiana now struggled to pull together all the paper threads of the estate, and to plough through the mass of documentation occasioned by her husband's death.

'Where this time?'

'In the high summer pasture above the Wolf's Slack, Frau Gräfin. A fine heifer calf, they say.'

'Should I ride up and take a look?'

'There is not much left to see.'

'That is the third calf this month. Do you think we should move them out of the high pastures?'

'Where would you move them to, Frau Gräfin? We need the lower pastures for hay and, besides, who is to say that the wolves would not find them there? They are becoming bolder all the time. I think that the Devil himself is driving them.'

'At this rate they will clean us out of calves before the autumn. Can we not get someone to shoot some wolves? What does the Hunter say?'

'I have not seen him for some time. You never know with the Hunter.'

'What about the men from the village? Can they not shoot a wolf?'

Tomislav shuffled his feet and looked out of the window. 'They are frightened, Frau Gräfin.'

'Why?'

'Because of what Albert told them.'

'And what did Albert tell them?'

Sometimes getting information out of Tomislav was like quarrying granite, Tatiana thought.

'Albert took his rifle and lay out one evening, watching the carcass of the last calf to see if the wolves would come back. He saw this great big wolf come to the remains. He took aim, and as he fired, he says that the wolf turned and stared at him, and the bullet came whistling back past his ear. He turned and ran home as fast as he could. He says that the wolf is bewitched, and that ordinary bullets cannot harm it.'

'Rubbish! I have never heard such nonsense! I expect Albert was drunk as usual, hit a stone and got a ricochet.'

Tomislav shrugged. 'Perhaps, Frau Gräfin, but the villagers believe Albert.'

'And you, Tomislav, what do you believe?'

Tomislav shrugged again and said nothing.

'Of course, I'll come with you, darling,' said Katerina. 'I want to have a look at these people and stop them trampling on you. I wouldn't trust you to organise a piss-up in a whelk stall.' Katerina's grasp of demotic English was interesting.

They were discussing an invitation from Sir William Nately: 'Come and meet some of the worthies of the Old Wessex. A bit of a drinks party so they can have a look at you, then a few of the old and bold stay to dinner. Just a suit.'

'But you hate the country.'

'Darling, that is because I have spent all my life escaping from it. But I want to see where my Fred is going to live, and see if I approve.'

'They might not take me on.'

'Don't be so fucking stupid, darling. All those leathery old ladies will want to eat you alive, especially when they see what sort of a mistress you've got. I am very glamorous,' said Katerina modestly.

'There's no argument about that,' said Fred to himself, as Katerina rippled about the flat in a pair of skin-tight jeans and a silk shirt. Aloud he said, 'We'll drop Paddy off at Bardwick on the way.'

'That is good. I think your father likes me.'

'Too bloody sure of it – the randy old goat.'

'He wants to bring his girl friend with him. I couldn't really say no,' said Sir William Nately.

'Oh dear! I really don't think there will be enough beds,' said Her Ladyship. 'Really William, I do think you might have consulted me first.'

Sir William coughed, shuffled his feet and consulted his carpet slippers. 'Well, actually, I did mention that, and the feller said not to worry, they would share a bed. He said the girl gets claustrophobia in bed on her own.'

'I'll have none of that in this house!' exclaimed Lady Nately, at the same time thinking to herself that chance would be a fine thing, and if only that lovely Rufus had not turned out to be such a rotter. Rufus Oates had caused a flowering of seeds long lain dormant in Phoebe Nately's ample bosom.

'Humph! Yes, well look, old girl, you know I don't approve of that sort of thing, but we can't afford to scare the feller off. He's the only real hope. We don't want to run the thing with the Committee again.'

Sir William still bore the scars of the awful season when the Old Wessex had been run by the Committee under his Chairmanship.

*

'Oh, that's lovely! Oh, that's *lovely*! Now lick my nice big hairy boggles!'

'Not if I can't go with you. You won't get any more nice lickies from Jeremy!'

Bryan Skevings sighed deeply; he had seen this argument coming. Really, Jeremy could be very difficult at times and if it were not for his manifold talents, he would happily dump the little bastard back on Hampstead Heath where he had first found him.

Jeremy was always wittering on about Bryan 'coming out' and being a 'torch bearer'. The trouble was that Bryan, as the sitting Tory member for Mid Wessex, knew exactly where that particular torch would finish up were he to start waving it about. Tory Party Central Office might be pink and soft enough to inflict him upon an unwilling Mid Wessex – he had succeeded a much-loved and long-standing Knight of the Shire – but he was under no illusion as to what would become of him should his 'proclivities' become known. It had been said that Mid Wessex would vote for a donkey if you stuck a blue rosette on it, but Bryan knew full well that, if it ever came out that the Conservative Member was both gay and anti blood sports, he would be slid out on his ear pretty sharpish. So, very patiently, he explained again to his catamite that the time was not yet right, and they could best serve the causes, in which they both believed, from within the system. In the meantime, he had to wear his disguise in public, especially if he were to retain his seat at the forthcoming General Election, with its anticipated Labour landslide. Then, once the Comrades were in power, there would be a sympathetic climate for their political aims.

Surely Jeremy could understand that, and that Brysey just had to go down for this dinner party for the new MFH – Brysey would be a fifth column, a Trojan horse – Jerry must understand.

Jeremy pouted his lovely sulky lips and then, rather grudgingly, put them to better use. Bryan Skevings moaned with pleasure.

The traffic on the M4 had been quite ghastly, making Fred and Katerina late and flustered for their arrival at Nately Hall. They had been effusively received by Sir William, and with some reserve by Her Ladyship, with whom Katerina formed an instant bond of dislike. The arrivals had glasses thrust into their hands before being hustled upstairs to bathe and change, as 'guests will be arriving shortly'.

Sir William's slightly bulging eyes bulged a bit more as he watched Katerina's rear view undulating up the stairs. Phoebe's instinctive dislike was cranked up a couple more notches.

Phoebe had enforced her disapproval of Fred and Katerina's cohabitation by consigning them to two very meagre single beds, and Katerina's first act of defiance was to shift the furniture and push the two of them together.

'I don't think we shall have much joy in those beds,' said Fred doubtfully.

'Joy doesn't come in to it, darling, I just want to stain the bitch's bed linen.'

Fred sighed. The evening was starting badly. Coal was glowing white in the furnace of Katerina's temperament.

The party was gathering in the withdrawing room. Old Colonel Wiley, accompanied by his ever tongue-tied wife, had backed Bryan Skevings into a corner, and was discussing his favourite political issue.

'When are you chaps goin' to do somethin' about all those darkie wallas, eh?'

Bryan Skevings winced. As Chairperson of CARS

(the Conservatives Against Racial Stereotyping), he had been instrumental in producing the slogan: 'If he's black, pat his back.' An over-enthusiastic application of this slogan had led to a race riot in Bristol, for which Bryan felt he had been unjustly blamed.

Lord Warknock, celebrated ex-Master of the Old Wessex, was talking to his ex-Joint Master, Diana Pettigrew. Diana was a handsome old lady in a weather-beaten sort of way, with a command of the English language that had held her in great respect in the country. 'Miss Diana's giving the buggers their tea in a mug,' the car followers would say, whenever she reasoned with her field in a Christian spirit.

Warknock was deaf, and he therefore thought everyone else was similarly afflicted. 'What a mean bugger William is,' he bellowed at Diana. 'He always gives us this frightful sweet sherry in these bloody little thimbles.'

Across the room, Sir William went puce.

Fred and Katerina entered. There was a sudden drop in hubbub – Katerina was wearing her 'little black dress'.

As Phoebe said to a crony the next day, 'My dear, she might as well have been *naked*!'

'By Jove!' spluttered Bertie Warknock in his storm force whisper. 'What an absolute corker!'

Katerina flashed the ageing peer her most brilliant smile.

The drinks party passed for Fred in a blur of faces, names and handshakes. He thought them a very pleasant bunch, but his head was beginning to spin when the crowd thinned until only those invited to dine were left. He recognised the pinched little Hon. Sec., Simkin, and his pinched little wife – what the hell was she called? Lord Warknock and Miss Pettigrew he knew; they had both been to puppy shows at Bardwick Hall. There was that fearful old Wiley, and the wife who never uttered. Then there was that trendy-looking MP who seemed paired off with the big jolly girl who ran the Pony Club, Jennifer Something.

He took Katerina by the wrist. 'Are you all right, darling?'

'Of course.'

'Do you like them?'

'They are peasants, but pleasant enough peasants.'

Fred sighed. Katerina was in her mischief mode – anything could happen.

'He's not a peasant,' Fred nodded towards Skevings.

'No, he's a queer.'

'How do you know?'

'I smell these things. Now I am hungry. Do you think these people will fodder us?'

'Dinner is served, milady,' announced the butler.

CHAPTER NINE

Fred settled happily in Old Wessex. Lord Warknock, who owned the kennels, lent him a little cottage just a mile away – 'only a labourer's cottage, I'm afraid, but it will do you for the time being.'

The little place, that had once housed an under-keeper, was quite adequate – two bedrooms, a bathroom, a large sitting room and a kitchen – and perfectly suited Fred and Paddy: 'plenty of room for a bed, a kettle and a bottle of whisky'. It was also isolated, standing alone up a little lane; this was fortunate, as Fred pointed out to Katerina, in view of the noise she was inclined to make at moments of crisis.

Katerina sniffed. 'That is because the bed is so fucking uncomfortable, darling. Leave it to me.'

A few days later, a Harrods van drove gingerly up the little lane. After it had got stuck whilst trying to turn, and had been pulled out by a tractor, it disgorged a king-size bed that almost completely filled the little bedroom.

'It does not leave much room for anything else,' said Fred to Katerina on her next visit as she bounced up and down on it pleasurably.

'What else to you want to do here, darling – swing cats?'

'Well, at least you can't use discomfort as an excuse for making a noise like one.'

'Then you had better provide me with another

excuse,' said Katerina, unfolding and stretching her supple body on the bed, and raising her knees so that her skirt fell back to reveal her superb thighs . . .

Afterwards, as Fred looked down at her and gently brushed the golden hair away from a forehead damp with passion-induced sweat, he realized how deeply he had come to love her.

'I never want to lose you,' he said, and he meant it.

'I will never leave you, darling,' and, at the time, she meant it too.

Tatiana lay in the big bed. She had woken as the first rays of sunlight shone through the eastern windows of the big circular room in the tower; here the sun always shone through one of the room's windows until it set in the west.

As usual, when she came up from the troubled depths of her sleep, she reached out a hand to where the great bulk of Francis used to lie. She had loved that first touch of the great warm, hairy body. She had usually woken first, whilst he was still shaking the room with his snoring or the funny little grunting noises that he made in his sleep – 'just like a bear'.

She had liked to cuddle up to his massive body and stroke him awake, covering his arms and shoulders with little kisses. If this did not work, she had other ways of ensuring that Francis came awake fully aroused and rampant.

'Dammit woman,' he would grumble, 'can a man never be left in peace?' Whereupon she would increase her efforts until Francis groaned with pleasure and would take her roughly.

The early mornings had been a special time for Tatiana. Now she came out of sleep and, as always these days, her searching hand found only cold, lonely emptiness. She would usually counter this by getting out of bed quickly, leaving memories behind. She fought her loneliness by hard work.

This morning, however, she lingered as the first rays of the sun played across the duvet, bringing an early warmth. She thought of Francis, as she always did, and the memory of his body kindled a matching warmth in hers. She felt a sudden, desperate need that burned her. Her finger went down to between her legs. She was already wet and swollen with remembered desire. She began to touch with her finger, trying to bring a little blessed relief to the fire that now raged in her. Then, with a despairing cry, she leaped from the bed and, pressing her forehead against the cold stone of the window sill, she wept bitter scalding tears until the fire subsided. She knew it could not be quenched like that.

Fred wrote to Trooper Kite:

. . . so there is a job going here for a terrier man/fencer. It only pays agricultural wage, I am afraid, but there is a free cottage, coal and light. Let me know as soon as possible if you are interested.

He got a postcard almost by return:

Sir – Course I'm coming and don't let any other bugger near your boots – Yrs, T. Kite (ex LG)

Every summer morning at 0630 sharp, Fred would arrive at the Kennels to go on hound exercise. The hounds, with their naturally musical hearing, soon learned to pick out the individual sound of the Master's Land Rover and would be up at the kennel rails baying with excitement and joy.

Fred was a natural 'dogman' and the Old Wessex hounds thoroughly approved of him.

Jim Scuttle also approved of him. Jim had started with the Old Wessex as a boy during Lord Warknock's Mastership, and had worked there throughout his hunt service. When the old huntsman had retired with rheumatism and disgust at the coming of Rufus Oates, Jim had been put in as First Whipper-in and Kennel Huntsman. Jim was a trained gentleman's servant and, with his jaundiced eye, had seen straight through Mr. Oates.

'This bloke's a toff,' he told the bar in the Warknock Arms, 'not like that bloody Irish git. This one's all right. He's a proper hound man.'

There was no higher praise in Jim's terms of reference.

The two steady old ponies who lived in the kennel field would have been saddled and bridled in time for Fred's arrival. He and Jim, dressed in bowler hats and white kennel coats, would mount.

The noise in the kennels would reach a crescendo.

A nod from Fred, and Kite would open the gate and a tide of joyous hounds – white, black and tan and wheaten – would flood out and surround Fred's pony, baying and gambolling with pleasure. Old Ben, the pony, who had done this for years, would stand steady as a rock with his ears cocked. He did not even blink when Paddy tried to swing on his tail.

Kite put a stop to that. 'You stupid old bugger! You'll get your brains kicked out one day!'

Then, away down the lane they would go, the young hounds racing away in front of the horses, then turning to gallop back, tumbling and playing the while. The older hounds, more steady, trotted happily along around Old Ben.

Down the lane they would go, sometimes through the village and out through the thickly-fenced lanes of the Vale, other times up on to the Downs where they could walk for miles on the old chalk drove roads.

Fred loved the Downs with their rolling hills and steep-sided combes. They could jog along the ancient chalk tracks, with larks rising from the fields alongside, and the sun warm on their backs. Up there they would meet no traffic and see no human beings, except for the occasional shepherd with his dogs, or a farmworker chugging along to his work in his tractor: or the gypsies.

'But how long are you going to be away?' asked Fred.

Katerina shrugged. 'A week, ten days – I don't know exactly. All I know is that Guggenheim wants me to attend this conference at Head Office. He does the paying, so he does the saying.'

Katerina had received a summons to the head office in Los Angeles of the magazine group to which *Angelique* belonged.

Fred poured her some more wine and looked sombre. 'Oh God, but I'm going to miss you!'

'Darling, I'm only going to be away for a week or so.'

'I know, but I don't know how I'd have got through the last months if it hadn't been for you. I love you so much.'

'I know, my sweet, and I love you too, but I am a working girl – remember? I have a career to follow.'

'Dammit! I just wish we could be together all the time.'

'That is not possible. One day it might be, but meantime I must work.'

'I shall miss you.'

'Absence and abstinence will sharpen you up, darling, for when I return.'

'I might not abstain.'

'Then I will stick a knife through you and the slut when I get back.'

'Do you really love me?'

Katerina came round the table in front of the chair where Fred was sitting. She knelt before him, and pushed his knees apart. 'Light your cigar,' she murmured. 'You know that I like you to smoke a cigar whilst I am doing this.'

'I shouldn't go down that drove, sir,' said Jim Scuttle one morning. 'That's where the Pikeys are.'

Jim and Fred were out on hound exercise on the Downs, jogging along the main ridgeway, the hounds flooding around them, sedate now in the increasing warmth of the morning sun.

'Gypsies? What's wrong with them? They often camp on Bardwick Common, and Father gets on well with them.'

'It was that prat Oates, begging your pardon, sir. Bloody useless with hounds he was. We went down there one morning, and young hounds took off after one of their lurchers. Very nearly tatered it. There wasn't half a bloody row.'

'In that case, we best get it sorted,' said Fred, turning down the drove road in question.

The gypsy encampment sprawled along both sides of the drove: a litter of vans, lorries, half-dead cars, tethered ponies, lines of grubby washing and open fires sending their blue smoke into the still morning air.

As they approached, a mass of nondescript dogs came hurtling out to meet and abuse them.

'Hold up!'

At Fred's order, the hounds obediently formed into a tight bunch behind Old Ben.

'Steady, Gadfly, steady!' growled Jim to a young bitch who looked like breaking away. Surrounded by a circle of frantically yapping dogs, the Old Wessex moved into the encampment.

The barking of the dogs brought forth people: silent women with babes in shawls, less than clean children with thumbs in their mouths, hard-looking men with tangled hair and muscular tattooed arms. One of these stepped out in front of Fred.

'Blimey, Guv'nor,' muttered Jim Scuttle, '*we're* going to get tatered.'

Fred stopped.

'We told you not to come here no more,' said the man, his hands on his hips.

Out of the corner of his eyes, Fred saw another man pick up a large spanner.

'Not me, you didn't,' said Fred cheerfully. 'I've never been here before.'

'Then you better not come again.'

'Look, I know there was a problem. That was nothing to do with me, but I've come to apologize just the same.'

'Then you can bugger off just the same.' The man spat.

Fred could now see a couple of pick handles as well as the spanner.

'Jacob!'

Behind the group of men was a caravan obviously a cut above the others. It was richly decorated with gilt and chrome, with rows of cut glass displayed in its net-curtained windows. The man who had spoken was on the step of the caravan. He was hugely fat. He was wearing a battered trilby hat, a vest and a vast pair of brown trousers that were kept in place by a set of braces that could have towed a lorry. He was a man of respect.

'What's all this bleeding row about? Mum and I were just having a cup of tea.'

'It's the bloody hunt! We told them not to come again after they chased them dogs.'

'I don't see 'em chasing no dogs.'

'This twat said they come to apologize.'

'Watch yer language, boy! If he come to apologize, then he ain't a twat. Might be a gent. Let 'em through!'

The crowd of men parted sullenly, and closed in behind the hounds as they rode up to the big man.

'Good morning, sir,' said Fred, politely raising his bowler.

'And good morning to you,' said the fat man, and raised his grease stained trilby, 'and who might you be?'

'I'm Frederick FitzHugh. I'm the new Master.'

'They got rid of that Paddy tinker's git, then?'

'Yes.'

'Good job! You be the Marquis of Fowey's boy?'

'Yes!' said Fred, vastly surprised.

'I've camped on your dad's land. He's all right. Fancy a cup of tea.'

The tea came in delicate Crown Derby cups and was heavily laced with whisky. The hounds stood still and patient until the children, their shyness gone, got amongst them and had their faces comprehensively licked. The threatening atmosphere had evaporated, and the growling curs were kicked and sticked back under the vans.

On chains at the end of Fat Man's caravan were two of the finest lurchers that Fred had ever seen: big rough-coated dogs.

'That's two smashing lurchers,' he remarked.

'Like lurchers, do you?'

'Yes, very much.'

'Hmm!' said the Fat Man.

'Well, thank you very much for the tea I think we'd better get on now. Look, I'm sorry, but I don't even know your name.'

'I'm Mr. Smith.'

'Thank you so much, Mr. Smith.'

'Call in any time, Lord Frederick, you're always welcome,' said Mr. Smith.

★

The fine, dry weather continued throughout that summer. Farmers and gardeners grumbled about the lack of rain, but still the sky remained blue and the sun shone. The harvest was early and quick, so that Fred was able to reckon on starting cub-hunting before the end of August.

Because of the weather, the autumn cub-hunting takes place in the early mornings, at first light, before the heat burns the dew off the grass and dries up the scent with it. The weather was still and settled, making for good scenting conditions. There seemed to be plenty of litters of well-grown foxes all over the Old Wessex country.

No huntsman ever forgets his first morning hunting hounds. Fred was in a fever of excitement and hardly slept. He lay awake, listening to hounds singing in the kennels, as they always do before hunting. They always know.

The first meet was at the kennels at 5.30 a.m.

There is magic in a misty autumn morning, with dew hanging heavy on the blackthorn and the clear dawn heralding another fine day. It was a great moment for Fred, on Old Ben, as he took his excited hounds down the lane from the kennels to the big withy bed beside the river.

Hounds were already whimpering on the dew-soaked grass of the meadow as they approached the covert, touching on the overnight drag of a fox which had presumably gone to lie up in the withies. As soon as they were in the withies, the whimper grew into a full roar of hound voices as the first fox of the season took to his feet.

At the end of the morning's hunting, three foxes had been killed fair and square. Fred sat on his horse in the stream, the sun warm on his back, the smell of sweat and leather in his nostrils, the now tired hounds relishing the cooling swirl of water; and autumn tints were already starting to show in the hanging woods on the slopes of the Downs above.

Fred thought of the excitement of the morning. He

thought of the massive breakfast he intended to have, and he thought of his lovely Katerina who was coming down that evening. He was the happiest man in England at that moment.

'Los Angeles!' exclaimed Fred, sitting bolt upright. 'Los Angeles! My God, it's the other side of the bloody world!'

Katerina had arrived that evening carrying a magnum of Dom Perignon and some news; both had been put on ice while Fred took Katerina in his arms. She was shaking with desire and an excitement that related to something else. Absence and abstinence had, indeed, sharpened both their appetites. Their love-making was urgent and rather brutal, even with an edge of desperation as Fred thrust into her again and again. Again and again Katerina cried for more and harder, as though Fred's driving could exorcise some inner hurt from her. She knew what was to come and she dreaded the final moment of confession. She knew it was going to hurt, and hurt both of them.

Limp, satiated and exhausted, they lay in one another's arms. Fred cradled her smooth brown body in the crook of his left arm as he lay back on the pillow, spent, contented and deeply in love. Katerina had her face buried in the black mat of his chest, her golden hair spread across his white skin. Katerina smelled the sharp male scent of his sweat; she loved this smell, all male and musk. In fact she loved Fred more than she had loved any man, but . . .

'Darling,' she said, her voice muffled, 'there is something I have to tell you.'

Katerina had been offered the Editorship of *American Angelique*.

Fred sat bolt upright, spilling Katerina back onto the bed.

She lay there watching him as the shock took hold.

For a moment he just sat there, blank-faced, as he took

in the news and its implications. Then he sunk his head in his hands, his body rigid with misery.

'Oh, darling, *don't!*'

She came behind him, put her arms around his neck, and gently began kissing his bare shoulders.

His body was shaking.

'Oh, darling! darling! What have I done to you? Come here, my sweet, my pet!'

She pulled Fred's unresisting body back and laid his head between her breasts, whilst she stroked his hair, and crooned the little endearments in Slovenian dialect that he loved so much.

Fred still said nothing, but his body continued to shake and Katerina felt the warm wet tears on her skin.

'Please don't, my sweet! I love you and I am hurting you. I love you! You know that, don't you?'

'I thought I did.'

It was not a happy evening, but they talked and talked. Not even the Champagne could lift their mood. Of course she must go, Fred said, it was a wonderful chance and she would be mad not to take it. It was just that he had never loved a woman the way he loved her, and he would miss her dreadfully.

Katerina cried.

She said she would never have believed she could love anyone as much as she loved Fred. No man had ever pleased her as he had done. Her great, greedy, orgasmic bear – how could she leave? But . . .

They made love several times that night, with a passion born of desperation. Finally, they lay curled up in each other as the pale morning light filtered through the bedroom window and, as the new day dawned, both knew that their love affair was dying.

★

Tomislav beat the rain water off his hat and limped into the kitchen of the Schloss.

'Don't you go treading mud all over my kitchen floor,' screamed Katya, looking up from kneading some dough. 'There are enough troubles in this house without you adding to them.'

'Women are the trouble in this house,' said Tomislav sourly, 'women within, and wolves without. How about a cup of coffee?'

'Get your own coffee, you old fool! Can't you see I've got dough on my hands?'

'You're lucky that's all you've got on your hands, old woman, you should have my worries.'

'You're my biggest worry, you silly old man. You, and that poor child through there, worrying her heart out because the estate is being ripped to pieces by these here wolves. And you useless parcel of men won't do anything about it.'

Tomislav hung his sodden coat and hat close to the old-fashioned wood burning stove that roared all day in the great arched kitchen. He helped himself to a mug of coffee from the pot on the stove, and sat down opposite his wife at the big table. Katya was shaping the dough into rolls.

'Can't, not won't,' grunted Tomislav.

'Devil wolves, is it?' she jeered. 'The only devils round here are the ones like you and Albert who believe such nonsense.'

'We're trying!'

'Oh you're trying all right. You've been trying my patience ever since I was fool enough to marry you!'

'Old woman, you don't understand.'

'Oh, I understand all right! I understand that the poor slip of a girl upstairs is working her heart out for this estate. She's not eating. She's not sleeping. She's just a rickle of bones covered in skin. And what are you useless load of sheep doing to help? Nothing! That's what.'

'She should get herself a man,' grumbled Tomislav reaching out his spoon for some more sugar, then: '*Ow!* Sweet Mother of God!'

The heavy wooden spoon had cracked across his knuckles, sending sugar and spoon scattering across the table.

'She *had* a man, remember?' screeched Katya. 'And when I look at you, you old fool, I wonder what any woman wants with a man.'

'What all you bitches want!' roared Tomislav, slamming his fist on the table.

'Then there's not been much joy out of you these last thirty years! I'd have had more fun with a carrot!'

Bang went the wooden spoon.

'I'd be sorry for the carrot!'

The two old people glared at each other across the table, and then, as they had done for the fifty stormy years of their marriage, they began to laugh.

'She wants to see the Hunter,' said Katya.

'It's tipping down with rain,' grumbled Tomislav.

'That won't worry him.'

'It worries me.'

'I'll worry you, you old eunuch, if you don't get straight out there.'

'Dried up old bitch!'

Tomislav reached for his sodden hat.

'I hope the wolves get you!' yelled Katya. 'And take your boots off when you get back!'

'I must say, he's one hell of a huntsman,' said Sir William Nately, pouring a thimbleful of dubious sherry into Major Simkin's glass.

The Chairman and the Hon. Sec. of the Old Wessex Hunt were having one of their regular meetings.

'Old Warknock says it's the biggest tally cub-hunting since the war.'

The Major looked gloomily at the tiny glass of liquid; William really was very mean. 'I just hope there will be enough foxes left for the season.'

'Oh, there are plenty about. "The more you kill, the more you find," Bertie Warknock says.'

'And I suppose the more money you spend, the more you find you have.' Major Simkin tended to have a rather negative view of life, but then he had a lot to be negative about.

'I must say, our Master does seem to have been a bit out of sorts lately,' said Sir William, with feeling.

His new horse had kicked one of Fred's hounds during the previous week, and Fred's comments about the horse and its rider had been short, to the point, and very, very pithy.

'I haven't seen that girl of his about lately.'

'I gather she's got some job in America.'

'Ah, so that's it! Unlucky in love, eh?'

'Who isn't?' said Major Simkin, looking at his empty glass without major expectations.

Meanwhile, in the pub, Jim Scuttle was also discussing Fred. 'The poor bugger's just plain bloody miserable,' he said to the Public Bar. 'Oh, he's right enough with the hounds and me, but all the spark's gone out of him, somehow.'

'That girl of his has buggered off, ain't she? Gone to America, they say,' said a Guinness.

'Phaaugh! She were a bloody looker! I wouldn't have minded carving a round off her!' said a Mild and Bitter.

'You, you old bugger?' said Jim scathingly. 'You

couldn't carve a soggy chip. I heard about you and Mavis Soady. They don't call you "Limp Dick" for nothing.'

'Haw! Haw! Haw!' chorused the Public Bar.

'That's what comes of taking up with a foreign tart. They all buggers off in the end,' said a Lemonade Shandy.

Jim banged his pint pot on the bar. 'She weren't a tart. She were a nice lady, and her and Lord Fred were real fond of each other, you could see that. Even my missus liked her, said she were a proper lady.'

There was silence for a moment as the Public Bar considered this. Such an endorsement from the formidable Mrs. Scuttle was not to be treated lightly.

'She still buggered off, though,' observed the Lemonade Shandy.

Fred had indeed been miserable since Katerina's departure. His life had been taking a sharp upward turn as their love affair deepened and strengthened, and all the unhappiness and emptiness he had felt, after the loss of his capital and leaving the Army, seemed to have been cleared away; his love for Katerina had cancelled it all out.

Then, suddenly, his life was a void. They still talked lovingly to each other on the telephone, and wrote each other longing letters, but the simple facts could not be ignored. Katerina was on the other side of the world, and Fred retired every night to a cold and empty bed. He had kept Katerina's pillow and would often bury his face in it but the scent of her was beginning to fade. He knew that the affair was fading too.

The hunting was the one thing which kept him going, and made him tired enough to sleep at night. All his thoughts and dedication were put into his work. His hounds sensed this, as hounds always do, and they responded by giving the Old Wessex foxes a towsing such as they had never known. In the process, they provided the Old Wessex fields with the sort of fast, galloping hunting that had not been experienced since pre-war days.

'Bloody young feller!' said Lord Warknock to Miss Pettigrew. 'D'yer know, I've hardly had time to finish my port and sandwiches once out hunting this season.'

'He's a damned good huntsman.'

'I just wish the feller was a bit happier. He used to be jolly when he first came. Now he goes about with a face like a busted boot, what?'

'His girl friend has gone to work in America.'

'Ah! *Cherchez la femme*, what?'

'I wish he would.'

'Well, I expect some of them will damn soon *cherchez* him, what?'

The first frosts had already turned the leaves of the beech woods which hung on the escarpment above the River Lipp. A strong north-easterly gale had brought the leaves showering down. As Tatiana rode up the steep twisting track that led from the Schloss to the top of the escarpment, her horse had to plough through great banks of wet leaves, reminding her of her childhood when she and her cousins used to roll with gleeful abandonment in such great piles. Memories of childhood brought a brief smile to her face, a face that was now almost gaunt with worry, and becoming etched with the lines of anxiety and strain. There was not much to smile about now.

The Hunter sat on the rocks above the escarpment, his heavy cloak wrapped round him against the chill of a biting wind; not that cold worried him too much. The wind snatched away the smoke from his foul old pipe as he watched

*the girl and her horse emerge from the trees onto the open
pastureland and turn towards him.*

*He was shocked by the woman's appearance. She was
beautiful still, but worn and drawn – too much worry, not
enough to eat, not enough sleep and no man. All the sparkle
and zest had gone out of her. Something would have to be
done. He did not like interfering in people's lives, but there
were times. This was time to take a hand.*

*He carefully tapped out his pipe on the rock and rose to
greet Tatiana.*

'Grüss Gott,' *he said, raising his disgraceful hat.*

Letter from Tatiana to Katerina in Los Angeles:

Dearest Cousin,
. . . so you can see, I have terrible problems. If I cannot
resolve them, then it will be impossible for me to continue at
Lippitz. We have tried everything with these wolves, traps,
poison, but they do not work. The men are superstitious peasants and will not shoot them. They are convinced there is a
Devil Wolf protecting them all. It is nonsense of course, but old
Tomislav says that only the 'hounds of heaven' can help. There
seems to be a legend about how one of the old gods brought a
mysterious stranger with his hounds to kill the Devil Wolf. He
saved the countryside.

Katya says all old legends come out of schnapps bottles. I am
so tired and alone I fear I will start believing this nonsense
myself.

I must do something. I have been advised that hounds might
help, and a friend said I should look in England for wolf
hounds. You know what I think of the bloody English, but I
trust this man. I know nobody over there, so can you help
me?

How is your new job going? At least it has got you away from
that pig of an English! How you could . . .

173

Letter from Katerina to Tatiana:

. . . he is not a pig, he is a great big randy lovely bear and I miss him terribly, but I am so busy that I do not have much time to think, which is a good thing. Anyway my 'Pig of an English' just happens to be the very man who might be able to help you with wolf hounds. I have written to him and asked him to contact you. Be nice to him. If you are nice to him, maybe I could even give him to you . . .

Letter from Tatiana to Katerina:

. . . I cut his balls off . . .

Letter from Katerina to Tatania:

. . . be nice, cousin, be nice . . .

Letter from Major Lord Frederick FitzHugh, MFH, to the Gräfin Tatiana Czerny:

Dear Gräfin,
Your cousin has written to me enclosing your letter about your wolf problem. I do not think that pure 'Wolf Hounds' would be the answer to your problem. The breed has been somewhat degraded and, as there have been no wolves in this country for some four hundred years, there is no 'working strain' to look for. I think that you might do better with Lurchers. These are sort of cross-breds, although this is too simple an explanation of them. Suffice to say that they are excellent working dogs. I do know a possible source of the sort of big lurchers that you would require, but this source is Romany. The gypsies have very good dogs, but are loath to part with them. I shall make enquiries, but can promise nothing.

I must say, I have always rather fancied hunting wolves. For two pins, I would pick up my hounds and nip over. It would be

174

very nice to meet you. I heard so much about you from Katerina . . .

Fred did not mention that he had also seen Tatiana on television. He had felt an odd frisson when he saw from whom the letter had come; Katerina had sent it on to him.

'Pig English!' said Tatiana, as she read the letter. 'It would not be nice to meet *you*, milord! Well, you would never be *my* lord! I bet you are bloody useless like all the English, hah!'

Yet, she could not help thinking of some of the things that Katerina had told her about Lord Frederick.

CHAPTER TEN

The tide of hounds flooded down the lane. In the middle of them, Fred walked at ease, his whip tucked under his arm and his hands in the pockets of his stained brown kennel coat. Hounds were on their twice daily 'walking out'.

Behind him, Jim Scuttle chattered away, scattering titbits of local gossip, of which he was a bottomless mine. Fred attended with half an ear and grunted occasionally to show that he was listening. In fact, his mind was divided: part of it concentrating on what his hounds were doing, and part of it far away in sun-drenched California.

He had noticed the change in Katerina's letters; they were getting shorter, less charged with longing and sparser. In the beginning of their parting, Fred had convinced himself that their love could survive the distance and changed circumstances, and that one day they would be reunited to pick up where they left off. Reality began to assert itself. Fred was a realist, and he began to understand that it was no good torturing himself by continuing to suck the sore tooth of their parting. The facts of life were that Katerina was six thousand miles away, was caught up in a busy, demanding and exciting job, and was a beautiful and passionate woman, whose needs none knew better than he. With all that sun, sand and adrenaline, the facts of life could not be ignored.

There was another thing too: even after a few weeks, Fred found that the image of Katerina had faded a bit.

Increasingly he found that, in his memory, her face became confused with the picture of her cousin, Tatiana, as he had seen it on television and in the photograph. 'After all,' he told himself, 'they are closely related and very similar.' So when, in the dark of the night, his hand strayed for a brief ersatz relief, it was hard to say just who was the golden blonde girl, tumbling and moaning in his imagination. This made him even more depressed.

His dark mood had hardly been lifted by a somewhat peremptory letter from Slovenia which asked just what the hell 'the bloody useless English' was doing about some lurchers. The letter was couched in terms of brittle politeness, but that was the sense of it. Fred did not think that Tatiana would like to know she was featuring in his fantasies, even in confused and composite form.

The sound of a diesel engine grinding up the road woke him from his reverie. 'Car up! Get over!' he ordered.

Hounds obediently formed up in a tightly-knit group at the side of the road.

The battered pick-up chugged into sight from round the corner. It had the sad remains of a car lashed onto the back. The cab contained Jacob Smith and two other Smiths, in convoluted degrees of cousinship, tangled hair and tattoos. The pick-up ground to a halt beside Fred.

'Morning, mate,' said Jacob cheerfully. 'Taking your dogs for walkies, then?'

Fred was now on good terms with the clan Smith. 'Just the man I want to see,' he replied.

'Want me to take that old wreck of car off you before you fall through the bottom?' chortled Jacob.

''Sno wonder your woman did a runner, you with a car like that,' added a cousin with jovial brutality.

Fred winced.

'Shut it, mush!' said Jacob evenly. 'What do you want then, Boss?'

'You know those big rough lurchers your dad has? Do you think that he would ever consider selling a couple?'

The pick-up cab rocked with laughter. It was the funniest thing the cousins had heard for days.

'Sorry, Boss,' said Jacob when he had stopped heaving. 'but I reckon you've got more chance of Dad selling Mum than selling one of them dogs. I'll tell him what you said, but I ain't going to tell you what *he'll* say. Oh Sweet Jesus! But that's a laugh! Ta-ra, Boss. Nice seeing yer.'

The ancient pick-up coughed and grunted away down the road.

'Trot on, dears!' said Fred, releasing the hounds.

'Never get bugger-all from them Pikeys,' muttered Jim Scuttle disapprovingly. 'Did I ever tell you about the time they pinched the copper out of the kennels, back in His Lordship's day that was . . .'

Katerina stood on the balcony. The hugh Pacific rollers thundered onto the beach in front of her, a full moon laying a streak across the water. Katerina's mood was as restless and unsettled as the ocean.

'There you go,' the man came up behind and handed her a glass. 'Well, what do you think of my little place?'

'It's beautiful,' said Katerina truthfully.

'So are you, honey.'

'Art, I –'

'I know, I know. You're in love with this English guy – this Lord Fred. You plighted your troth to him, or whatever it is you guys do over there. Now you got to admit that I been good. I been patient. But, baby, I got it real bad for you! Real bad!'

Katerina stared at the ocean. She had met Art soon after she arrived. Art was a 'suit' at the company, a man on his way to the top. He had made no secret that he was 'hot' for Katerina, and had pursued her doggedly, but pleasantly. That was the trouble: Art was a nice guy – he was rich, good-looking and a widower. He was also amusing, and – well, yes she had to admit it – sexy; he had grown on her. This was the first of many invitations to his beach house that she had accepted. She had been true to Fred but, oh dear, Fred seemed a very long way away and in what now seemed a different world. She knew that her future lay here in crazy, exciting, adrenaline-pumping California. She also knew that she felt very, very randy.

Art stood behind her, and started working her shoulder muscles with his strong fingers.

Neither of them spoke.

Katerina did not resist and began to writhe gently under the firm pressure. A huge wave thundered onto the beach, its white crest gleaming in the moonlight.

Katerina turned to Art.

'Fuck me!' she said.

Letter from Katerina to Fred:

Darling Fred . . .

'Darling Fred, my arse!' exclaimed Fred, screwing up the letter in a fury. 'It's a bloody "Dear John" – the bitch.'

Letter from Tatiana to Katerina:

. . . I just do not understand you, cousin – first an English, which is bad enough, but now a Yank! What will you do for an encore? A Russian?

Your bloody English is being as useless as I thought he would about his lurchers. He writes me pathetic letters about not being able to find them. He is limp, useless, and I'm not surprised that you left him. Who would want a man like that? But an American! Jesus, Mary and Joseph!

'Dad wants to see you.'

Jacob Smith had called at Fred's cottage just as he was finishing his lunch. Fred thought that Jacob looked odd: he was not his usual cocky self. He looked shifty, even frightened.

'Did he say why?'

Jacob shuffled and looked at his feet. 'He just said to go and ask you to come up to the camp.'

'Right.' Fred stuffed the last bit of bread into his mouth. 'You go on and tell him I'll be up shortly.'

'You will come? It's important.'

'I'll be there.'

Fred was good at sensing atmospheres. He sensed there was something different as soon as he walked into the gypsy camp towards the end of the afternoon. After his first meeting with the Smiths he had often called in for a cup of spiked tea, and had even dined there on occasion – he had not asked the provenance of the excellent roast pheasant. On this occasion, there was definitely a feeling of tension.

An evening mist was rising from the surrounding fields and the air was dank. Mr. Smith was sitting on a rough bench by a large fire that kept the late autumn chill at bay. Beside him, with his hands held out to the flames, was a huge bearded man, wearing a disgraceful hat and with a foul pipe clenched between his teeth.

'Now, boy!' growled Mr Smith, without looking up.

'Good afternoon, Lord Frederick,' said the large man.

Fred recognized him at once. 'Good heavens! It's you!'

The big man took out his pipe and grinned widely. 'It's me.'

'I tried to find you after that day's hunting – you remember?'

'Oh, I remember it well.'

'I wanted to give you your knife back. Look, here it is,' said Fred, fumbling in his pocket and producing the horn-handled knife with the honed thin blade.

The man grinned again and took from his pocket a knife that was exactly the same as the one Fred held.

'Keep it. I have plenty of them. It might bring you luck.'

'I'm afraid that I don't even know your name.'

'Call me Hunter,' said the Hunter. 'Now, I believe you are looking for a couple of good lurchers for a certain purpose.'

'Yes – but how on earth did you know?'

'These things get about,' said the Hunter vaguely.

'Jacob!' shouted Mr. Smith, who had not uttered since his greeting. 'Bring Bonnie and Clyde over here.'

He saw the Hunter wince.

'Sorry about that. It were Mum's idea – she'd just watched the video when we come to name the pups.'

The thin daylight was declining as Jacob came up to the fire with the two great rough-coated lurchers that Fred had noticed at his first meeting with Mr. Smith. Jacob took them up to his father, who took each dog's head between his hands and, leaning down, seemed to whisper something in each dog's ear. For a long moment, in turn, man and dog stared into each other's eyes. Then Mr. Smith coughed, spat and threw another log on the fire. A shower of sparks rose into the air.

'There, they'll go with you now. Didn't want them taking your hand off.'

'But I can't take them!'

'You take 'em, boy, and put 'em to good use. Now, I'm going to have a bit of a lie down.'

Mr. Smith got to his feet, and hobbled to his caravan.

'But . . .' started Fred.

The Hunter gripped his arm. 'Not a word, and certainly not a word about money. This is an act of friendship for you and me.'

'Have you known the Smiths for a long time?'

'The ancient of days. Now, take the dogs and go.'

'Shall I see you again, Mr. Hunter?'

'Oh, I'll be about, here and there.'

Fred held out his hand to each of the huge lurchers. They sniffed it politely, giving a cautious wave of their feathery sterns.

Jacob took the chains off them. 'You'll not need them, not now Dad had a talk with them.'

As Fred made his way back to his car, the two lurchers walked at his heel as though they had known him for ever.

Bonnie and Clyde and Paddy were having a tremendous game in the kennels paddock, the two lurchers chasing each other round and round with their great strides, twisting and turning almost in their own lengths. Paddy was doing his best to stay in contention – but his little legs, although moving like a blur, could not go fast enough. Suddenly the lurchers turned and started ragging him. Paddy lost his temper and, leaping up, managed to get a mouthful of the great mane of hair from Clyde's neck. Bonnie took a playful nip at Paddy's tail, and away the lurchers went again with Paddy in hot and furious pursuit.

Fred and Kite were watching from the door of the kennel valeting room where Kite had been busy shining a pair of Fred's shoes.

'Bloody lovely dogs, sir. Just look at 'em move, bloody wonderful!'

'The problem is getting them to Slovenia.'

'That's the top of Juggo, isn't it?'

'What we must now call "the former Yugoslavia".'

'Yer, right. Well, I don't think that's a problem, sir.'

'I knew you'd have an idea, Kite. You always were a bloody good fixer.'

'When you're looking after officers, sir, you've got to be. Now, you remember old Nobby Thomas?'

'C'plhorse Thomas?'

'That's the one. Well, when he come out the Regiment he started off a bit of a transport business. Done really well, he has. In fact, if you hadn't sent for me, I was going to tap him for a job. Well, I know he has trucks running regular to Greece and Turkey and places like that. I bet we can get the dogs on one of his rigs, no bother.'

'Someone would have to go with them.'

'I'll go if you like. I fancy a touch of the duty-frees. Johnny Tab can do the terriers while I'm away. I'll be back inside a week or so.'

'Well, if you don't mind, Kite. I obviously want someone reliable.'

The dog game debouched from the paddock, the two big lurchers flying the paling fence with Paddy shooting underneath, trying to nip Bonnie as she landed. The whole lot ended up in a panting, grinning heap at the feet of the men.

'Well, then,' said Kite, smoothing the great rough heads of the lurchers, 'who's coming on a trip with their Uncle Trevor, then? And it's not you, Paddy, you little sprucer.'

With a slight shock, Fred realized that, in all the years he had known Kite, he had never before known his Christian name; he felt rather ashamed.

★

Letter from Major Lord Frederick FitzHugh to the Gräfin Tatiana Czerny:

. . . so the dogs should be with you within a week. Kite is a very reliable man and was my orderly for many years. I do hope that the dogs will do the business for you. I know from your letters that you have been getting a little impatient, but dogs like these are hard to find and even harder to acquire.

I expect that you have heard that Katerina has finished with me. I do not blame her, and from what she has told me, you will approve of her getting rid of the 'Pig English' anyway. It has left me pretty desolate, but I know that you have your own desolation to cope with, and I shall not bore you with mine.

You can become fond of the dogs without denting your prejudices as they are gypsy dogs, and may be regarded as non English – a neat little Jesuitical casuistry for you. Hunting here has been good . . .

'Dammit!' said Fred to himself, 'I don't see why the bitch has to be so snotty with me.'

'Pig English!' snorted Tatiana. 'I"ll give him "Jesuitical casuistry". It's a good thing he's not coming here. I would have him burned as a heretic. Tomislav, would you mind roasting a fat Protestant?'

'It would be a pleasure, Frau Gräfin.'

'It would be the first bit of work you have done today!' screeched Katya from the hall door, where she appeared wiping her hands on her apron. 'If you don't get some wood in, Old Man, there will be nothing roasted in this house, pork or Protestant.'

'Hold your tongue, you Old Witch, or the Gräfin will hunt you with her new English dogs, instead of the wolves.'

'English dogs! Holy Mary!'

'They're gypsy dogs,' said Tatiana.

'And that makes it better? English, German, gypsy or Jew – they had better stay out of my kitchen.'

'The Gräfin will feed them on wolves.'

'I'll feed you to the wolves if you don't get me that wood.'

'Huh!' said Tatiana to herself as the tumult and shouting faded away down the passage to the kitchen, and she returned to Fred's letter. 'Why does he bother to write to me of his problems and his pathetic foxhunting?' But she read the letter through twice just the same.

'Bloody'ell, Butty Bach!' said Laurie the Lorry. 'If this road gets any narrower we're in dead lumber. They never thought of artics when they built this goat track!'

'Get on with you, you hairy Welsh git,' said Kite. 'You'd know all about goats and goat tracks – the only way you Taffies ever get your end away, innit?'

Laurie said something regrettable in Welsh.

It was true that the road up to Lippitz did represent a bit of a challenge for a large articulated lorry, but it was quite passable, with care.

Ex-Corporal of Horse Thomas had come up to expectations and the transport had been 'jacked up' in short order. A temporary kennel had been installed at the back of the lorry trailer, and Bonnie and Clyde had settled down with good grace for their journey to Slovenia.

Laurie dropped another gear as the big diesel snarled to the top of the incline and then, there before them lay the village of Lippitz in its broad valley. Beyond the village, where the tree-covered escarpment soared away, was the steep roof and the four round towers of the Schloss on its little bluff above the River Lipp.

'Bloody 'ell, boyo! Fantasia, innit? Bet there's a fairy princess lives there.'

'What lives there, my lovely old Taffy, is a fierce female

called a Grayfin and we don't get these dogs across there bloody juldi she will bite our balls off, my son.'

'Dhu! look there's a bloody reception committee, isn't it?'

And so it was.

Kite had telephoned ahead from the lorry's mobile and, after a mutually incomprehensible skirmish with Katya, who hated answering the telephone anyway, he had spoken to Tatiana and given her estimated time of arrival.

The news had spread round the village.

'I hope the natives are friendly,' said Kite.

They were.

As Kite and Laurie got out of the cab in front of the castle, they were surrounded by smiling faces; their hands were shaken, their backs slapped, bottles of schnapps were thrust into their hands. There was hubbub.

The circle of people suddenly parted and, as Kite reported to Fred later, his first thoughts were – well, electric.

'Bloody stroll on! what a smasher! and she really is, sir, a real bloody stunner, but nice with it, you know. Well, she come through the crowd and she shook hands with me and Taff and she speaks English real well, you know. Well, we got Bonnie and Clyde out and all the crowd went Oo! and Ah! so I let them go for a leg stretch and you know how they play them two, well they galloped all round this, like a green, in the middle of the village and all the people laughing and cheering and the Grayfin standing there all smiling. Then I calls them and they come bounding up and I puts the leads on them and hands them to the lady and I says to Bonnie and Clyde, "This is your boss now and you've got to do good for her, otherwise Uncle Trevor will come and give you a right bloody rollocking", and they wags their sterns like they do when I talks to them. Then the lady gets down on her knees and she talks to them both, sort of whispers in their ears and they wag their sterns again.

'Then we all march up to the castle and the old bloke who works there starts dishing out the schnapps, but the lady takes me and the dogs into the big hall there and the dogs settle down straight away by this great log fire, like they always lived there.

'Then the lady asks all sorts of questions about the dogs and then she starts asking all sorts of questions about you and what you were like. And I don't know, sir, but I think she hoped a bit that I would say you were a bit of a wanker, begging your pardon, sir, but I said I had known a lot of officers, but I reckoned you were about the best of the bunch, you know. All she find to say was "Oh", and then she thanked me very much and gives a bloody great tip for the pair of us and when I left the dogs were fast asleep by the fire so I reckon that's OK, sir.'

There was no doubt but that the Old Wessex was the 'form pack' that season. It was a good scenting season. Foxes live by scent and they know what the conditions are like; when scent is good they do not hang about. That season they worked hard and fast, but not as hard and fast as the Old Wessex hounds and their Master and Huntsman. Fred's skill as a huntsman swiftly became a legend, as did his daring horsemanship. Fred was a beautiful, natural horseman who slipped across the big Vale fences with a deceptive ease. He seemed to have no fear, taking on places that had become accepted locally as unjumpable.

'You'd think the bugger wanted to kill himself,' said one of the more notorious of the Old Wessex thrusters. 'The bastard certainly nearly killed me.'

This was after the man, his mettle roused, had tried to follow Fred over a well-known fence with a huge drop and an arm of the sea on the landing side, into which the thruster had landed conclusively. His horse was lamed, and both his top hat and his pride considerably crumpled.

Fred certainly seemed careless of his own neck. He had become grim and silent. He refused all invitations, and sat each evening in his cottage with only Paddy for company. He wrapped himself in his loneliness and felt very sorry for himself.

'I hear he's drinking himself to death,' said some.

'No, no! He's having a wild secret affair with A, B or C,' said others.

It being an accepted fact that all Masters of Hounds must be doing one or other or both, Fred in fact was doing neither. His name was often linked with Phoebe Nately. A lot of names had been linked with Lady Nately in the past, and this was hardly surprising considering the complete ghastliness of her husband.

'You can't blame poor Phoebe for having a bit of a fling,' said some.

'I wouldn't want to share a house with William, let alone a bed,' said others with a shudder.

'They don't, you know.'

'What?'

'Share a bed. My dear! Haven't you heard about William's, er, habits . . . ?'

'No! Really? Gosh how *awful*! You mean he . . .'

'Yes!'

The Christmas Eve meet of the Old Wessex was always at Bulbarrow Wood which was generally accepted as a 'bloody awful meet'. Bulbarrow Wood was a large stretch of woodland with bottomless bogs for rides, and lots of foxes, which always went round in circles. This gave an excuse for a 'short day', so that the Hunt Staff could get 'done up' early on Christmas Eve. It was also an excuse for followers to do last-minute Christmas shopping, secure in the knowledge that they were missing nothing.

Fred was not in festive mood. Several people had asked him for Christmas, but he had declined. He was under a three-line whip to drive to Bardwick for the festivities. 'Stop feeling sorry for yourself, Boy. You can damn well come and be festively miserable with the rest of the family.'

At the meet, Fred sat grimly on his horse with his hounds around him. He was in a foul mood, which matched the weather – driving sleet and damp cold that chilled the bone. The hunting would be bloody awful, and he thought he might have influenza.

'Good morning, Frederick. You look out of sorts.'

Fred looked down, startled out of his gloomy reverie. The Hunter was leaning on his stick beside the horse. Sleet was dripping off the disgraceful hat.

'Mr Hunter!' said Fred, with genuine pleasure. 'How very good to see you! I've never had a chance to thank you for all your help over those lurchers. I know it's thanks to you that I got them. I haven't heard how they are getting on. I keep meaning to write to the woman, but I have not got round to it.'

'I think the Gräfin is very pleased with them.'

'You know her then?' asked Fred with great surprise.

'I have a wide circle of friends,' said the Hunter with a bass chuckle. 'Yes, the dogs are well and about to prove themselves, I think. Perhaps even today.'

'Well, I hope that they are going to have more luck than we are going to have in this bloody place, and this bloody weather.'

'Ah, but you never know with hunting. That is part of the fascination – the Glorious Uncertainty. Now may I offer a little bit of advice?'

'Please do. You seem to bring me luck.'

'Draw down towards the west end of the wood, where the strip runs out onto Bulbarrow Down. You never know, you might just get a hunt from there.'

'It would be an Act of God if we did.'

'Ah well, you never know with gods.'

'Now, you all understand what you have to do?' said the Hunter. He was standing on the snow-covered step of the church at Lippitz. In front of him, the men of the village shuffled their feet and rubbed their gloved hands to keep out the bitter winter cold. The men were carrying a variety of rifles, shotguns and sticks. Tatiana stood beside the Hunter with Bonnie and Clyde, shivering in the chill wind.

'You drive the woods down towards the high meadow. The Gräfin and I will be waiting in the rocks. Shoot a wolf if you get the chance but, I warn you, do not shoot me – you will go straight to Hell on Christmas Eve if you do.'

The men chuckled.

'Remember, this is the sacred eve of Christmas, and coincidentally the eve when the old men said Wotan rode out in the Wild Hunt. So from every point of view it must be a good day for God's work, which is to protect ourselves from the evil of the wolf. Now, Father,' he turned to the old priest beside him, 'if you will give us a blessing, we will be on.'

It is an acknowledged truth in foxhunting that great hunts often happen from bad places. 'The Great Bulbarrow Wood Run' has gone into history, and those who chose to go shopping instead did indeed 'think themselves accursed they were not there'.

Hoping against unreasonable hope, Fred did what Mr. Hunter had suggested. He drew down towards the west end of the wood, where the strip runs out onto Bulbarrow Down. There they found and Jim Scuttle holloaed away what he excitedly described as, 'Blimey, Guv'nor, the biggest bloody fox I ever seen – like a bloody wolf he is! He'll tater us!'

Foxes hardly ever run in a straight line, but the 'point' of a hunt is the straight line than can be measured on a map between the start and finish of a hunt; a 4-mile point is respectable, a 6-mile point, remarkable. The Great Bulbarrow Run was a 10-mile point, and anyone's guess as hounds ran in between. It ended with hounds being defeated by a howling wind, blizzard conditions and darkness; they were indeed tatered.

'He was a bloody good fox, Guv'nor, he deserved to get away.'

'I'm not sure that we were ever meant to catch him,' said Fred thoughtfully. For some reason an image of Mr. Hunter flashed across his mind.

The Hunter slowly scanned the hillside with his binoculars. The wintry sun made the fresh snow sparkle. Nothing moved. He and Tatiana were crouched behind a tumble of boulders overlooking the undulating expanse of pasture. Bonnie and Clyde sat beside Tatiana quivering with cold and excitement; they knew that something was up.

'Nothing,' said the Hunter, lowering his glasses. 'We must be patient, eh, my children?'

He ruffled the shaggy heads of the dogs, and two feathery sterns thumped the snow.

'They like you.'

'Dogs like Hunters.'

Away to the right a murmur of sound pressed on their consciousness and grew. As it got louder, it separated into shouts, whistles and tappings; the beaters were getting nearer.

The lurchers pricked their ears.

There was a sudden eruption of shouts.

Then a shot – shouts – another shot.

The dogs quivered, and Clyde gave a little whimper.

'Hold his muzzle! No noise!'

The Hunter's glasses were glued to the rocky cut that led into the field from the direction of the noise.

'Hah!' he said suddenly.

Tatiana saw it: a lithe loping form, not unlike a large German Shepherd.

She tensed.

The dogs saw the wolf and were straining to be off.

Tatiana could not keep Clyde's muzzle shut as well as hold the two big eager dogs.

The Hunter's huge hand closed over hers, his strength pulling the dogs back.

'Wait!'

The wolf paused to listen to the sound behind him. He was a young wolf and confused. The sound of the men was getting nearer now.

The wolf set his mask across the open snow, towards the woods at the far side. The snow was fresh and powdery. It was not good travelling for him.

The wolf was clear of the rocks now, in the open.

'Now!' barked the Hunter.

Tatiana slipped the leads – and the two big lurchers were gone.

Like two arrows they converged on the wolf, their greater length of leg getting them faster through the soft snow.

The wolf got a peripheral glimpse of movement.

He turned with a snarl.

It was too late.

Clyde hit the wolf like a thunderbolt, his strong jaws instinctively seeking to snap the spine.

Bonnie went straight for the throat.

The three disappeared in a flurry of thrown up snow.

Within seconds the wolf was dead.

Fred was exhausted, cold and wet through when he got back to his cottage later that Christmas Eve. He got a reproachful greeting from Paddy who had had a day at home and resented his exclusion from the terrier Land Rover.

'Poor old man,' said Fred, picking up the little dog and stroking his head, ' you missed a hell of a hunt.'

Paddy licked his master's face.

Fred put him down and threw some logs into the wood-burning stove. They quickly flared up, and the flicker of flames showed through the transparent door. Fred poured himself a large glass of whisky and stood with his back to the warming stove; steam started to rise from his wet breeches.

He knew that he ought to get out of his sodden clothes and have a hot bath. It was his usual custom to hunt the day again in his bath, and submit the performance of himself and the hounds to minute analysis; Fred was his own sternest critic. He ought to have a bath, and some more whisky to celebrate what had undoubtedly been a historic hunt. He ought to think about cooking himself some supper – he had eaten nothing since early morning. But he did not feel celebratory or hungry; he felt flat, lethargic and lonely. He knew that he ought to be getting over Katrina by now. But there was always a sound, a smell, or some memory of shared happiness that brought things flooding back. He had fallen badly.

It had still been snowing when he had come in and the knock on the door surprised him. Who the hell could that be at eight o'clock on the night of a blizzard? He was not in the mood for visitors and, grumbling to himself, he went and opened the door.

'Good heavens,' he said, 'what are you doing here? You're covered in snow. Come in.'

Phoebe Nately came in.

'I hear you had the most wonderful hunt today – what a fool I was to miss it,' she said quickly and brightly. 'So I've come to congratulate you, and wish you Merry Christmas.'

She held out a bottle of Champagne.

'It shouldn't need much chilling,' she said with a nervous little laugh.

'That's very kind of you. Shall we open it now, or would you rather have some whisky?'

'I'd love a glass of Champagne.'

'And what did William say about you turning out on a night like this?' asked Fred, as he twisted the bottle neck round the cork.

Sir William's proprietorial attitude to his much younger wife was well known, especially as the first Lady Nately had bolted, to the surprise of no one except the Baronet.

'Oh, William's been shooting in Gloucestershire, and he rang to say that the weather was so bad that he would not try to come home tonight.'

Fred filled the glasses, handed one to Phoebe, and raised his in salute. For perhaps the first time he looked properly at Phoebe Nately. She was really rather a comely woman, he thought – looked well and went well out hunting – and now, as she perched rather nervously on the edge of her chair, he could see that she had fine black hair, very good legs, and her shirt was very nicely filled. No more than forty, he decided, but, by the lines on her face, she was hoeing a hard row.

They looked at each other over the tops of their glasses.

Phoebe really had very nice eyes.

Fred felt a sudden stirring of warmth under his sodden breeches; it had been a long time.

'Goodness,' said Phoebe, 'you're still in your wet clothes! You ought to have a hot bath and change. You'll get pneumonia.'

'Oh, I'll get changed after.'

'After I've gone?'

'Well, yes.'

Phoebe dropped her eyes. 'What if I don't go?' she asked in a small voice.

'Good heavens! Do you really mean what I think you mean?'

'Yes,' the voice was tiny.

'My dear old thing, it really wouldn't work! My God! Here, have another drink.'

Fred realized that he was babbling. He then pulled himself up short. 'Look,' he said gently, 'it just wouldn't work. I mean, I know that Masters are supposed to screw all their female followers, but life is not like that, and I'm not like that, and I'm in love with someone else.'

'She's left you.'

'That does not mean I am going to start screwing everybody's wife.'

'I don't want you to screw everybody's wife. I want you to screw *me*.'

Phoebe was crying now. Still perched on the edge of her chair, her head bent, silent tears ran down her cheeks.

Fred could sense her desperation.

'Oh, Phoebe,' he said.

Kneeling in front of her, he took her face in his hands and gently kissed her wet eyes. She came into his arms and they huddled on the rug in front of the stove. The whole story of her unhappy and miserable marriage came pouring out, and Fred felt a great warmth of pity.

'Come on,' he said, getting up and taking her hand.

Phoebe undressed quickly, with her back to him.

Fred was able to admire the shapely curve of her buttocks before she dived under the duvet, where she lay with just her large frightened eyes peeping out as he pulled off his wet breeches and underpants.

He climbed under the duvet and began, very gently, to caress Phoebe's body. She was rigid with tension, but as Fred's hands gentled her, she began to relax and he could feel her spreading wetness around his softly probing finger.

'Oh Fred! Oh Fred! Do it now, *please* do it *now*!'

Fred spread her legs and knelt between them. His face was heavy with lust. It had been a long time since there had been a woman in this bed: a woman with her legs spread, aching for him to thrust into her.

He had a sudden vision of golden hair spread on the pillow: a dagger of memory.

His penis went limp.

'My poor, poor Fred, I'm so sorry.'

'Oh God, I'm sorry. I've disappointed you.'

'No, no, it's my fault. I shouldn't have come. I'm sorry, so very sorry.' Phoebe leapt from the bed and began to dress frantically as she sobbed.

'Look, don't go.'

'I must go. I shouldn't have come. I'm so sorry!'

Wiping fresh tears from her face. Phoebe grabbed her coat and fled from the room.

Fred followed her down stairs, and stood naked in the middle of the room as the door slammed shut.

'Oh shit!' he said, looking down at his flaccid cock, 'and Merry Fucking Christmas.'

As he reached for the whisky bottle, a tear rolled down his own face.

CHAPTER ELEVEN

As the winter wore on, morale rose in Lippitz. There were three wolf skins nailed to the castle gates. The depredations continued, but were not as frequent as they had been. The wolves seemed to be shying away from the area of the village. Bonnie and Clyde were the toast and boast of the whole area.

The two great hounds had settled into the life of the Schloss as though they had never been anywhere else. They adored Tatiana and followed her everywhere. In the evening they would lie stretched out in front of the fire in the hall. At night they slept in her room. Tatiana found it a great comfort, when she woke up in the night, to put out a hand and feel a great rough head on the floor beside here, and have a wet tongue lick her hand. In the morning she was often woken by a wet nose nuzzling her face, telling her that it was time to be up and about. She grumbled and groaned, but it pleased her. For the first time since the awful death of Francis, she felt an easing of her loneliness.

The dogs had a good effect on the poor scattered mind of Aunt Helga, with whom they formed the bond that dogs often have with those whose minds had started wandering. She would spend much time crooning to them and stroking them. This seemed to ease her mental anguish, and her lucid moments became more frequent, as though they were helping her back into the world.

Bonnie got off to a bad start with Katya. Prolonged screams from the kitchen brought Tatiana running to the door in the hall that opened onto the kitchen passage. As she opened the door, Bonnie came bounding through with a joint of meat in her mouth, snatched from the kitchen table, closely followed by Katya waving a large ladle and demanding blood, reparation and damnation for all gypsy dogs. The joint was restored to Katya. Order was restored to the house. Bonnie was severely admonished and Katya retired grumbling and triumphant. Tatiana did not feel it politic to enquire into the provenance of the stew that she ate that night: 'what the eye does not see, the heart does not grieve about.'

The theft was not repeated, and it was not long before 'the gypsies' had wormed their way into the kitchen and into the affections of Katya. Tomislav complained that they got more cake than he did.

'That is because they are more useful than you, Old Man. They don't believe in fairy stories.'

The hounds always went with Tatiana when she rode her daily round of the estate, trotting with their sling jog beside her horse and being treated with respect and admiration by everyone they met. As they said in the pub: 'If them dogs were human, they'd be up for canonisation.'

One particular February morning dawned bright, crisp and clear. The recent snow had melted slightly in the warmth of the previous day's sun, and had then frozen again in the night, making a thin crust that shimmered in the sunlight.

The sun was warm on Tatiana's back as her horse picked its way up the snowy path, crunching through the ice crystals. Bonnie and Clyde followed, using the horse's tracks to make their own travelling easier.

'Frau Gräfin! Frau Gräfin!'

The distant shouts startled Tatiana who had sunk into a reverie brought on by the sun and the beauty of the winter countryside, and the sight of an eagle soaring over a distant crag.

'Frau Gräfin!'

The small figure, stumbling and hurling itself down the track, resolved into Young Felix, the shepherd boy. Scarlet in the face and blown with running, he stood panting by her horse. The dogs sniffed him, their ears and sterns erect.

'Wolf!' he got out, as he strained and sobbed for breath.

'Where?' said Tatiana, instantly alert.

'In the meadow by the pines,' Felix panted out. 'It's killed a sheep and is feeding on it. I saw it and Grandfather saw it. We had gone up to bring the sheep down because of the snow. It's a big wolf, a huge wolf!'

'Where's your grandfather?'

'He's watching the wolf. He's up in the rocks. He did not want to disturb it. He sent me for help.'

'Right! Down to the village and get every man you can. And guns. Now run!'

The boy was away down the track like a hare.

'Come on, children!' urged Tatiana.

At a touch of her heels the horse burst into a gallop, spraying snow to either side, with the dogs loping easily after it.

'Dear Lord! Let the wolf still be there,' Tatiana prayed to herself. The adrenaline was pumping in her now as the icy air burned her face and lungs. She realised that there was little chance of surprising the wolf, out in the open as Young Felix had described. Then she saw it: a black spot in a circle of reddened snow.

Surely it must see her now?

Had the dogs viewed it yet?

Surely it would take off?

Could she get the dogs near enough before it did?

Not much hope!

Nearer! Nearer!

It was almost as though the wolf were waiting for her!

Old Felix crouched in his hiding place in the rocks. He could see the wolf some two hundred metres away. It was the biggest wolf he had ever seen, and he sensed that it knew full well that he was there and was not in the least concerned. It stood there in the trampled blood-stained snow, tearing flesh from the pathetic carcass of the old ewe.

Suddenly the wolf became alert, head raised, ears pricked, a piece of bone protruding from its mouth, its nose working: something was coming.

From Old Felix's vantage point, he could see down the meadow towards the place where the track from the valley debouched from the woods. Three black specks were moving fast across the white expanse.

'What's the wolf waiting for,' thought Old Felix. 'It has surely seen the Gräfin and the dogs! No ordinary wolf would hang about like that! No ordinary . . . Oh Holy Mother of God!' and the old man crossed himself.

'Wolf! Wolf!' cried Tatiana.

It was as though an electric shock went through the two dogs – and they had gone. They were streaking across the snow like two bolts from a crossbow.

The wolf saw them coming, turned and loped away towards the dark line of the pine trees.

The big lurchers were bounding through the snow. They were gaining, their extra length of leg giving them an advantage.

'Go! Go!' cried Tatiana from where she sat on her horse.

Old Felix rose from his hiding place, waving his hat and uttering cracked screeches of encouragement.

The lurchers were closing on the wolf.

But the wolf was nearly at the trees.

The lurchers were still twenty metres behind when one, two and three disappeared into the dark forest.

'February Filldyke' was living up to its reputation in the mild, wet west of England. The wind was battering the rain against the windows of Fred's little cottage. Inside, Fred was sitting contentedly, his slippered feet spread in front of the open door of the roaring stove. There was a glass of whisky at his elbow, Paddy curled up in his lap. He was re-reading, for the umpteenth time, *The Experiences of an Irish R.M.*, that wonderful book whose gentle humour age had never withered, nor custom staled. Fred was at peace with the world.

The knock on the door scattered his peace. Paddy scrambled from his lap and stood barking furiously at the intrusion. The door thundered again.

'I'm coming! I'm coming! Who on earth can that be on a night like this?' Fred grumbled as he rose from the chair.

When he opened the door, Paddy's threats turned to ecstatic welcome. Mr Smith stood on the doorstep. Behind him in the lane, Fred could see the lighted cab of a pick-up with Jacob at the wheel.

Fred was amazed. He had never seen Mr Smith away from his camp before. His huge bulk was wrapped against the weather in an enormous ankle-length overcoat.

'Mr Smith! Come in! Come in!'

'I'll not stop.'

'You can't stand there, man. Come in and have a glass of whisky.'

Mr Smith visibly wavered.

'Is that Jacob with you? I'll give him a shout.'

'No, let him bide there. I'll not be stopping, but I'll take a glass with you.'

Mr Smith stood himself by the stove where his coat dripped onto the floor. He made no attempt to remove it.

Fred poured a large glass of whisky which Mr Smith took down with one swallow.

'It's them dogs,' he said.

'What, Bonnie and Clyde? They're doing frightfully well, I hear.'

Fred had received a letter from Tatiana the previous week. In fact, they had come to exchange letters on a weekly basis without realizing how the habit had become established. The letters remained extremely formal, but, as week had followed on week, the tone of the letters had undergone a certain lightening. Tatiana wrote at length about life on the estate and the wolf hunting. Fred wrote about his life and times. Tatiana often asked questions about foxhunting which she found a strange and interesting concept.

'They're in trouble,' said Mr Smith.

'What sort of trouble?'

'I don't know.'

'But, I mean, how do you know?'

'I just knows. I wants for you to find out for me.'

'I will, of course.'

'Right then – I'll be off. Ta for the drink.'

Mr Smith picked up his rain-spotted hat from the floor by the stove where he had dropped it, clapped it on his head and rolled to the door.

Fred turned to open it for him.

'Ta,' said Mr Smith. 'You find out about them dogs for me. Mum's worried.'

Without another word, he waddled down the short path to the lane, heaved his bulk into the waiting pick-up and was gone.

With the adrenaline pumping through her system, she had galloped on the track of the lurchers and the wolf, the three tracks plain to see in the sunlit snow, to the edge of the dark trees. There were no convenient trails which might take her in the approximate direction of the hunt, and it became quickly obvious that there was no way she could force her path through the tangled branches on her horse.

She returned to the edge of the trees, and tied her horse as a sign for those who were following. Then she set off on foot, ducking and weaving through the snow-laden branches.

At first the tracks had been easy to follow. She knew that the lurchers would be unsighted in the tangled woods, but she knew that both dogs had excellent noses, and that the taint of the hunted wolf would be strong. The tracks led upwards. The ground became steeper and rockier, with great clusters of boulders protruding through the snow. The tracks became more difficult to follow, but she struggled on and, by casting round the bits of bare rock, she managed to pick the trail up again.

Then she came to the scree.

A great river of small stones and boulders flowed down the rocky face in front of her. Tatiana knew that these scree slides were very treacherous, especially when covered in snow that concealed what was underneath. Anyone trying to cross one of these faces was in danger of setting off a slide of rocks and snow which could turn into an avalanche and bury the unwary and unwise.

The tracks led onto the scree.

She paused for a moment.

She had to go. Her dogs had gone – had gone for her.

A stunted fir sapling grew out of a cracked rock beside her. Tatiana cut it with her hunting knife and trimmed off the branches.

With her stick she ventured gingerly onto the scree.

It was the little ash tree that saved her.

The little ash tree had taken root amongst a cluster of rocks at the edge of the scree. The big overhanging boulder at the top of the cluster had forced the little tree to grow out horizontally.

It was a moment of sick despair and frantic fear that overwhelmed Tatiana when she felt the rocks start to move beneath her. She was only a few metres onto the loose stones, but she knew she was too far.

She turned to get back to the firm ground – but realised that she was too late; the hillside was beginning to move. Fifty metres below her were the ragged boulders of an ice-strewn river.

She made a desperate move for the firm edge, but her feet sank in a shifting mixture of snow and stones.

The whole slide was on the move and gathering speed.

She lost her balance and, as she fell, a rolling stone the size of a turnip bashed into her shoulder.

She was sliding faster.

Then she saw the little ash sapling that grew out of the side of the scree slope and was bent across her path.

With a desperation born of terror and determination, she rolled sideways and grabbed. Her flailing hands found the wood: found and grasped.

The sapling bent, bent more and bowed with her weight and momentum, but it was tough and rooted deep in the rocks.

It held.

With horrified eyes, Tatiana watched as the hillside slid past her, faster and faster until it exploded in a fountain of snow and rocks in the icy water of the river below. But for the little ash tree, she would have been at the bottom of that pile of debris.

But she was not safe yet. She did not know how much longer her aching arms could hold out, and what she was going to do next.

'You do get yourself in some awkward places,' said a voice above her.

She looked up and saw the familiar beard and the disgraceful hat.

'Hunter!'

'At your service – and a very interesting one it is proving to be.'

'My arms!'

'I know. Now, I am going to lean over and grasp your wrists. when I say "Now", you let go. Understand?'

Tatiana closed her eyes to concentrate on her weakening grasp and nodded.

She felt the Hunter's huge rough hands slide down over each of her hands and seize her wrists in a mighty grasp.

'Now!'

The woman let go of the ash.

For a moment she swung and, in spite of herself, gave a small scream. Then she was being hauled up over the rough surface of the boulders to land, scratched, bruised, winded and sobbing, in a heap on the firm ground.

The Hunter crouched on his haunches beside her, a wry smile on his rugged bearded face. He felt in the pocket of his tattered coat and pulled out his flask.

'I think this calls for a drink.'

The Hunter then brought her back to the rendezvous

as the first vehicles arrived from the village, full of armed men. He handed her over to the care of Tomislav with strict instructions that she was to sit in the cab and keep warm. Shock from her recent experience was now setting in, and Tatiana was content to huddle in the warmth of the truck and wait.

The Hunter then disappeared.

The winter darkness came quickly on the uplands above Lippitz, and with it came fresh snow, drifting down from the now leaden sky in huge feathery flakes. The snow drove the search party back to the rendezvous in the meadow where Tatiana, white and exhausted, sat huddled in the cab of the truck.

The search party straggled back to the huddle of vehicles. Snow was falling steadily now, and the head-lights were switched on to guide in the searchers. The men stood about, stamping their feet and beating their arms to generate warmth in the gathering cold. Bottles of schnapps were passed around, but the warm flood of alcohol did nothing to lift the general air of gloom from the company. They had been unable to follow the tracks and now the snow was covering everything. Of Bonnie and Clyde there was no sign.

Tatiana sat slumped in misery whilst Tomislav did a roll call to make sure that all searchers were accounted for.

'Where is the Hunter?' asked Tatiana, arousing herself from her lethargy.

Tomislav shrugged: 'He is not here. With him, you never know. Here, Frau Gräfin, drink – it will help.'

He thrust a mug at her which held a generous portion of schnapps. Tatiana sipped the fiery liquid and felt its warmth flood down through her.

'All the men have returned, Frau Gräfin. We must move down to the valley. This snow is really setting in.'

Tatiana nodded unhappily; she knew he was right.

Then there was a shout from one of the assembled men. A headlight beam picked out a large figure emerging from the darkness.

It was the Hunter.

He looked like a walking snowman, but moved through the snow with his long stride unaltered. Tatiana scrambled out of the truck as he came up.

'Have you found anything?'

He shook his head. 'It's not good, I'm afraid. Before the snow started I managed to follow the trail to the Wolf Lair.'

'Oh dear God!'

The Wolf Lair was a huge jumble of boulders at the head of the Wolf Slack. It covered perhaps a hectare of mountainside. The great rocks formed a jumble of passageways and caverns, some of them big enough for a man to crawl through. This had been the lair of the legendary 'Devil Wolf'. Tatiana had only seen the place once, at the height of a sunny summer's day. Even then, the place had an air of brooding menace that had made her shiver in the warmth of midday. Now her poor dogs were in there somewhere.

'Can we do anything?'

'Nothing, Gräfin. By now the place is cut off with the snow. If the dogs are in there, there is nothing we can do. Now you must get these people back down the hill whilst you still can. It is a matter for the gods.'

'I shall pray,' said Tatiana.

'That is always a good thing,' said the Hunter gravely.

No one went to bed at the Schloss that night. Tatiana, Aunt Helga – moaning gently with grief – Katya and Tomislav all sat round the big stove in the kitchen which

Tomislav kept well banked up. Katya made constant brews of tea laced with sugar and schnapps. Tatiana could not face the prospect of her bedroom, even lonelier now without the two great dogs.

She blamed herself:

If only she had not met that boy.

If only the wolf had gone before she got there.

If only she had realised what a giant wolf it was.

If only . . .

At last, some time in the small hours, she allowed her head to fall on the rough wood of the kitchen table, and exhaustion took her off into a troubled dream-laden sleep.

Katya and Tomislav dozed and nodded fitfully in their chairs. Only Aunt Helga, in the rocking chair that she loved, rocked and moaned gently to herself; sleep was not a thing that came easily or pleasantly to her.

It was she who first heard the noise.

But no, the night was still, under the persistent snow.

Then, there it was again.

The old lady sat up in her chair, her keening stilled. Without waking the sleepers, Aunt Helga padded through the scullery behind the kitchen to the great outside door which gave onto the central court of the Schloss. Very cautiously she opened the door.

The snow had stopped falling, but lay deep and white in the bright moonlight that lit up the courtyard. Something dark was slumped in the snow at the foot of the steps where she was standing. From it came a feeble whine.

Aunt Helga screamed.

Bonnie was in a bad way. Her coat was matted with dried blood. Her near foreleg was smashed from a massive bite. The skin and flesh were torn from a flank so that the bones shone through in the lights of the kitchen.

The bitch had lost a lot of blood and was obviously

near to death. She had used up almost the last of her strength to struggle home with her dreadful wounds.

They laid her on the table.

'My God!' cried Tatiana, her eyes wide. 'What can we do?'

Katya burst into tears. 'The poor child. She is . . .'

'What's born, must die,' said Tomislav with the fatalism of his kind.

'Stuff and nonsense!' said a voice.

They all turned.

It was Aunt Helga – but a different Aunt Helga. Gone was the moaning mental invalid. Something had snapped in her wandered mind at the sight of the dying Bonnie, rather as a dislocated bone is snapped back into place.

All three looked in surprise and awe as the new Aunt Helga appeared or, to be more correct, the old Aunt Helga re-emerged from the prison of her mind. This was now a determined and knowledgeable old lady who took command.

Katya was told to stop snivelling and get some water on to boil.

Tomislav was told to stop looking like a piece of ham at a Jewish wedding and find something to use as splints.

Tatiana was told not to just stand there, girl, and to look for bandages, sticking plaster, antiseptic, and when she had done that . . .

They all leaped to obey.

As she ransacked the cupboards to find the necessary things, Tatiana remembered Francis had told her that Aunt Helga had had a great reputation for her herbal remedies and healing powers.

Bonnie was going to benefit from the time she had spent reaching Helga's sick mind.

*

Letter from the Gräfin Czerny to Lord Frederick FitzHugh:

. . . and I had forgotten that Aunt Helga used to be an absolute wizard with herbs and things. She set Bonnie's crushed leg. She had Katya boiling up the most extraordinary concoctions and made some amazing poultice which seems to have drawn all the poison out of the wounds, which she stitched up so beautifully. The poor lamb is very weak, but she is definitely out of danger now. I am afraid Aunt Helga says that the foreleg is too badly crushed and that Bonnie will never be able to hunt again. Not that I would want her to, not after that awful day. There has never been a trace of Clyde. The Hunter took a party of men up to the Wolf's Lair – they would not go near it without him. The fools have got all worked up over this 'Devil Wolf' business again – but there was no sight nor sound. I miss him so much, but Bonnie is managing to hobble round the house after me and . . .

Letter from Lord Frederick FitzHugh to the Gräfin Czerny:

. . . what a truly terrible thing to happen, I am so sorry for you. When I got your letter I took it up to Mr. Smith – the chap I got the dogs from – and you remember in my last letter, I told you that he was worried about the dogs. Anyway, I read him your letter and he sat there puffing his pipe.

Then he said that the dogs were bred to work and he reckoned that they did a pretty good job and the only certain thing in this world is that we all die before we get out of it. He said it's better to die doing something you want to do. Make sure to breed from the bitch, he said, he'll be looking out for a dog for you.

Then he said that if the wolves be such a nuisance, it would be better if I took my hounds out there – they won't be much use, he said, when we get Socialist government.

So I asked him if he was sure that we would get a Socialist government – we have got an election coming up in the autumn – and he said yes, Mum had seen it in the tea leaves and he had won money on bets on all the elections for the last 30 years with Mum's tea leaves; she 'weren't never wrong'. So I asked him if a Socialist government would stop hunting in this country and he said, 'does water run down hill?' so that is not a cheerful prospect.

Fancy having a pack of hounds and a keen huntsman? The season is getting towards the end now . . .

'Bah!' said Tatiana after she had read the letter to Aunt Helga. 'The arrogance of the Pig English! The idea of having him and his hounds here, it's a joke, *Ja*?'

Aunt Helga did not look up from her embroidery. 'There's many a true word spoken in jest,' she said.

'Bah!' said Tatiana again, and stamped off to find something to bully Tomislav about.

Aunt Helga bent down to stroke Bonnie's head. 'You aren't the only bitch that needs breeding from.'

PART THREE

CHAPTER TWELVE

'A pack of hounds is not such a bad idea,' said the Hunter, puffing his pipe. He and Tatiana were sitting on the pile of boulders in the meadow above Lippitz.

The Hunter was still a great mystery to Tatiana, but one that she had given up trying to solve. She suspected that Tomislav knew at least some of the answers, but to ask any questions was to meet a great wall of silence and much shrugging. She knew that if she wanted to meet the Hunter, Tomislav always seemed to be able to arrange it. She also knew that only in the most extreme emergency would he come to the Schloss.

The pile of rocks had become their tacitly acknow-ledged meeting place, and it had become her habit to ride by the rocks as part of her morning round. Sometimes the ragged figure in the cape and hat would be sitting there, wreathed in pipe smoke and apparently oblivious of the weather. His presence was a sign for talk that she never ignored. The Hunter, whoever he was, had become too important a part of her life – which he had saved twice – to ignore, but she could no more account for him than she could account for wind, rain, or sun; he was something elemental.

She had become accustomed to discussing all manner of things with the huge, grave man, and amongst them were Fred's letters, inviting him to share her scorn for the 'Pig English', but all he did was to give his big bass chuckle and smile wryly as she ranted on. Also, and she just had to admit to herself – but not for the riches of the world to anybody else – that she had come to look forward to Lord Frederick's rather rambling missives. In spite of her scorn, she had become rather interested in foxhunting and the Old Wessex. However, she was properly scornful when she mentioned Fred's light-hearted suggestion that what she needed was a pack of hounds. At that point, the Hunter had just smiled his smile and made no comment.

The year had progressed from winter, through spring to the pleasant warmth of early summer. With the coming of summer, the wolf problem had diminished. The wolves had moved further back into the mountains. The bitch wolves would want to be far from men when they had their cubs, and there were plenty of deer to keep their milk flowing.

The troubles would start again in the autumn, the Hunter said. Then he added: 'A pack of hounds would not be such a bad idea.'

Tatiana was struck dumb for a moment. 'But how on earth would one find such a thing? There has been nothing like that round here since before the last world war.'

The Hunter puffed silently for a moment, his eyes staring away into the blue distance. 'You never know. The world shifts and swings about.' He turned to look at her. 'But listen to me. If a chance does occur, don't shilly shally, take it, and worry about it afterwards.'

Hounds were splashing happily in the river by the bridge below the kennels.

Fred and Jim Scuttle were leaning on the stone parapet of the bridge, the sun warm on their backs. Every now and then Fred would take a couple of dog biscuits from the pocket of his kennel coat and drop them into the lazy stream. There would be an immediate splashing and flurry as hounds swam out to grab them.

'So there'll be an election in the autumn, Guv'nor?' asked Jim.

'There's got to. The Government's run out of time.'

'That ain't all they run out of – what a load of wankers. A lot of these bloody Conservatives are no better about hunting than them Labour bastards. I'm a working man and they want to do away with my job.'

'Neither you, nor your job, are politically correct, Jim.'

'Political Correctness – that's just yuppie shit. A lot of tossers who never done a decent day's work in their lives!'

'That's the Chattering Classes for you, Jim.'

'I'd make the buggers chatter – Driver! Steady now, lad! Don't want you sloping off into that withy bed. There's a litter of cubs in there – if we ever get to hunt the buggers. Do you think that Labour will stop hunting if it gets in?'

'As Mr. Smith says, as sure as water runs down hill.'

'What would happen to the hounds, then?'

'I expect they'll let you keep a few to go draghunting. The rest will be shot.'

'Draghunting! It's like wanking, I reckon! I mean, would you be happy with it, Guv'nor?'

'No, Jim, I wouldn't.'

'What would you do then?'

'I think I would go abroad and look for something to hunt.'

'Take me with you then.'

Fred laughed. 'And what about Mrs Scuttle?'

The formidable Mrs Scuttle, pillar of the Women's Institute and the Mothers' Union, was known to hold strong views on just about everything, including the oft-proclaimed fact that, in marrying Scuttle, she had married beneath herself.

A spasm crossed Jim's cheerful weather-beaten face: 'Blimey, Guv'nor, she'd be so busy making jam and singing "Jerusalem", she'd never even know I'd gone.'

Both men burst out laughing.

'So, Persons, in conclusion, I promise you on behalf of the next Labour Government that we shall, immediately upon taking office, and as a matter of urgency and with the full backing of the Cabinet, push through the necessary legislation, which is already framed in 'The Small Furry Animals Protection Bill' – we shall push through the necessary legislation to ensure all so-called "Blood" so-called "Sports" are finally consigned to the dustbin of history.'

The packed meeting of the Hornsey Chapter of CLAW – Council for Loving All Wildlife, except rats; rats are not PC, and it was accepted that they could quietly be poisoned because they had the decency to die out of sight and mind – rose to its collectively and expensively trainered, middle-class feet, and gave the Shadow Minister for Rural Interference a standing ovation. Bryan Skevings and Jeremy Dibbings applauded enthusiastically.

The Shadow Minister raised his hands. 'But that's not all! *But that's not all!*' The audience waited expectantly. 'The next Government – a truly Socialist Government, Brothers and Sisters – also intends to introduce a "Flesh Eaters Registration Bill". Anyone who wishes to eat the carrion flesh of murdered animals will have to register with the Ministry of Health and wear at all times a badge that says: "Meat is Murder". They will become the pariahs of our new, caring society, and will thus be shamed into joining hands with us as we march to the broad sunlit uplands, where we will all live in harmony with our animal brothers and sisters.'

Tumultuous applause, although it was more restrained on the part of Bryan Skevings who was very fond of a good rare steak.

As they sipped their carrot juice after the meeting, Bryan spoke to the Shadow Minister. 'Wonderful speech, Ron! I'm with you all the way!'

He faltered momentarily, and wondered if 'Omelettes Arnold Bennett' at the Savoy Grill would still be allowed under the new dispensation, and – horrid thought – would the Savoy Grill itself still be allowed?

'I'm with you all the way, but I am sure you understand that I cannot "come out" just yet. I must keep up my pretence of being in favour of these cruel and ghastly practices, otherwise the retarded peasants in my constituency won't vote for me. But I promise you that, after the election, your Government can count on my whole-hearted support for these bills.'

'Don't worry, Brother,' said the Shadow, 'the Comrades understand your position and you have our fraternal support. You are "The Enemy Within", as it were.'

'Be "within" me soon, won't you, Bry?' giggled Jeremy, as they turned to leave the meeting; carrot juice always had a powerfully libidinous effect on him.

The Shadow watched them go. 'I hate bloody queers,' he muttered to himself.

Bryan himself cringed, and dropped his catamite's hand which was horribly hot and clammy.

Fred continued his hermit-like existence. Indeed, since his failure with Phoebe on Christmas Eve, he had retired even further into his shell. He had, of course, seen Phoebe out hunting, and they had exchanged bright and rather brittle pleasantries. However, he had not managed to get her out of his mind. His sleep was often disturbed by lustful dreams in which blonde and black-haired women whirled about in the most confusing manner. Fred was a normal lusty man and he did not find his self-imposed chastity easy. He sometimes thought of popping up to London – where there were both attached and un-attached women who had made it plain that the lean, pale and interesting major, so strong and silent, did not have to continue lurking in his monkish cell if he did not want to. Inertia prevented Fred from taking up these chal-lenges, however; inertia coupled with hurt and, now, a fear of having another flop. Fred was a proud man, and his masculinity had been badly dented.

It was the 'Galloping Majors' who finally managed to prise Fred out of his carapace.

The 'GMs', as they were known in local shorthand, were two retired Cavalry officers – albeit 'Line Cavalry' – who both 'farmed vaguely and hunted three days a week'. It was one of them whom Fred had buried in the 'arm of the sea.' They were desperately keen hunters, went like smoke, and Fred spent a lot of time cursing them; this was water off the proverbial duck's back to the GMs, who had been roundly cursed by Masters in all the better hunting countries. They were connoisseurs of curses and rated Fred very highly in that category, as in other mat-ters of the chase. They both had plump, jolly wives, and they were always bombarding Fred with invitations to drink and dine, generally to put his hair in a braid and have a bit of fun.

At last the breakthrough came. Fred succumbed to an invitation to dine with GM number one. GM number two was inevitably present. They all got 'hog snarling pissed', and Fred laughed more than he had laughed for a long time. He also succumbed to pressure from the plump and jolly wives, agreeing to join a party to the Old Wessex Summer Dance. This he bitterly regretted the next morning, but all his attempts to wriggle out of the festivity were greeted with good-humoured ripostes.

'Bugger off, Fred, you're coming.'

'We've got a smashing girl lined up for you.'

Letter from Lord Frederick FitzHugh to the Gräfin Czerny:

. . . so we are all very worried about this election. It does look as though the Socialists will get into power and then things could be bad for hunting. Our local Conservative MP will almost certainly get back in – the locals here would vote for a donkey as long as it wore a blue rosette. I only met the chap once with Katerina and I did not take to him. He is really a townie. Katerina said he was queer – I do not know about that, but I have certainly never seen him with a woman in tow. He makes all the right noises about hunting (he has to here) but he has a bad eye. If he was a horse, I certainly would not buy him. I do not trust him. Now look, I know that this is the most frightful cheek, but we have been writing to each other for some time and I thought it would be interesting to know what you look like. I mean, I know what you look like, because I saw you on the television and I saw that picture that Katerina had of you, but sometimes it is nice to know the face that you are writing to, and I just wondered if you might have a photograph. I mean, I know it is rather a cheek, but anyway this is a picture of myself with my hounds and . . .

'A cheek! A cheek! I'll say it's a bloody cheek! What does this fucking English think I am? Some cheap whore from a whore's magazine, that I would send him a picture? Is that what he thinks? The man is a pig, and he thinks that I want his bloody picture? Mother of God!'

Aunt Helga put on her spectacles and inspected the photograph that Tatiana had hurled down on the table.

'He is quite a nice-looking young man,' she said mildly.

'Nice looking! He looks like the back end of a pig! A pig English!'

'Shall you send him a picture?'

'Never! Never! Never!' and Tatiana stormed out of the room.

Aunt Helga sighed. She got to her feet and went to the big wooden cupboard in the corner. From one of the drawers she took a file full of photographs. After some consideration she extracted a copy of a portrait photograph of Tatiana, a blown-up version of which stood on a table in the drawing room. It was a good likeness. She went to the desk and got an envelope.

Letter from Lord Frederick FitzHugh to the Gräfin Czerny:

Thank you so much for the picture. I must say that is just how I remember you. I remember Katerina said that she was more beautiful than you, but I am not so sure . . .

'The bastard, how dare he! And how did he get my photograph? I never sent it!'

Aunt Helga, quite unperturbed, did another stitch or two of her embroidery and replied without looking up, 'I sent it.'

'*You?* You! Aunt Helga, how *could* you? How *could* you?'

Tatiana was boiling up into a fine old rage, but the fact remained she was now somewhat in awe of Aunt Helga and so, with considerable effort, she reined in her temper.

'But why, Auntie?'

'It seemed like the polite thing to do.'

Tatiana stood fuming for a moment and decided that she would go outside and scream at something – anything. As she went she fired a Parthian shot: 'Anyway! I *am* much more beautiful than that hussy Katerina!'

As the door slammed, Aunt Helga smiled at her embroidery.

For Fred, the Old Wessex Hunt Summer Dance in the middle of June was not being a great success. The Galloping Majors and their plump jolly wives had been as good as their words. They laid on an extremely good, and liquid, dinner party before the dance, and they had produced a 'smashing girl' for Fred. In fact, she was definitely what is known as a 'nice gel' and would one day make somebody a plump jolly wife; the one thing Fred was quite certain about was that she was not going to be his. Fred was fond of horses, but did not want to talk the horse, the whole horse and nothing but the horse. However, he found that by nodding and grunting in a sympathetic manner, he was excused further attempts at conversation; he just had to sit back and let the tide of fetlocks, martingales and twisted snaffles flow over him, and this he found pleasantly soporific.

It was a cheerful and noisy dinner party, and Fred found that his flagging spirits were somewhat uplifted by the general haroosh. He was even prevailed upon to tell the story of the Farriers and the Major's watch, a House-hold Cavalry story that the Galloping Majors thought was the funniest thing since Sir William Nately was pitched from his horse head first into a muck midden. So it was in general good humour that the party set off for Nately Hall.

Sir William had agreed for the dance to be held at Nately Hall provided that most of the action took place in a marquee, loosely attached to the house. Sir William had been caught out some years before when he had agreed to have it inside the house. Not only had he found his own bed rather vigorously occupied when he decided to retire from the revels, but something very nasty had turned up in one of his Ming vases when it was being dusted a few days later. This time, he had barbed wire put across the staircase, and stationed his dour Kirkcudbrightshire keeper behind it with a bottle of whisky and a shotgun.

The Summer Dance was a jolly affair, and Fred arrived in quite cheerful mode. Then he saw Phoebe Nately and his mood nose-dived. However, he pulled himself together, dutifully dancing with the female members of his party and doing his best to chatter brightly until the ever-so-merry leader of the band announced an eightsome reel. Fred refused. Whatever the Scottish nation might have contributed to the advance of civilization, Scottish Dancing, in his opinion, was not part of it; besides, he had once nearly had a leg broke by a hulking tartan harpy whilst attempting to dance a Strathspey or some such horror. He had certainly pulled a riding muscle and missed a ride in a point-to-point as a result. Eightsome reels were a no-go area. He resisted appeals of the rest of the party to join in and, with a feeling of relief, sat down at his table and poured himself a stiffening glass of whisky: definitely a Scottish contribution to civilization.

He lit a cigarette and, hands in pockets, looked contentedly at the ceiling as the company whooped and skirled their way round the floor to the tune of 'The Muckle MacGregor of Auchtermuchty'.

Someone sat down beside him.

'Good Heavens! Phoebe!'

Fred started to struggle to his feet. 'Sit firm.'

'Why aren't you dancing the light barbaric?'

'Oh Fred! I'm exhausted. I just wanted to sit quietly for a moment. Do you mind?'

'No, no, of course not – lovely to see you! I mean, I haven't seen you . . . I mean I haven't seen you to talk to . . . Oh, shit!' Fred concluded miserably.

Phœbe looked at him with her big black sad eyes. Then, under the table cloth she gently laid her hand on his.

'Darling Fred, it doesn't matter – it really doesn't. Now give me a drink and do stop babbling.'

Suddenly they both smiled at each other, and all the tension fell away as they sat for a moment sipping their drinks in companionable silence.

Then Fred asked, 'Would you like to dance?'

This took them both by surprise.

'Well, I'm not very good at that – and anyway we couldn't just barge in now.' Phoebe gestured at the Albannach capering.

'Bloody dangerous, I reckon. But isn't there a night club or something?'

'Yes, there is. But, look, you don't have to, you know.'

'I want to.'

'All right, then,' and Phoebe gathered up her bag.

The night club was in a little sub-marquee, with music and an atmosphere that were dark and soothing. It was full of couples in various versions of the Clinch or Clutch, some of which reminded Fred of his Close Combat Training.

He and Phoebe went into a decorous, non-tactile clutch. Neither spoke. They just looked at each other.

Then they pressed their bodies together.

Fred could feel his cock hardening.

She could feel her nipples tightening.

Fred slid his hands down her back until they rested on her buttocks. Phoebe ground her pelvis against him, and they both gave a little moan. Then she suddenly pushed back from him and, for a moment, they both stood quite still, looking at each other.

Then, still without a word, Phoebe took Fred's hand and led him from the tent. A full moon rode in the cloudless sky. The grass was wet with dew. Phoebe removed her shoes and handed them to Fred.

Silently, and hand in hand, they crossed the moonlit lawn, the music of the dance receding as they went, and the noises of the night taking over. A tawny owl hooted in the copse, and somewhere a nightingale sang its passionate warble.

Rounding the corner of a yew hedge, they came to a little summer house with a table and chairs.

Phoebe led Fred inside.

She turned and they kissed. It was a long kiss.

Fred could feel Phoebe's hand exploring his groin – and then stroke the hardness.

'Phoebe! I . . .'

'Hush, Fred, hush. It'll be all right.'

She undid his fly buttons.

Her warm hand gently caressed his balls, and then began to move up his stem. All the while her lips were pressed to his, her tongue exploring his mouth.

Fred slipped his hands under her dress – stockings! He felt over the smooth, soft skin of her inner thighs.

His hand came to a flimsy covering. It was quite wet.

'Take them off!'

Fred obediently eased the knickers down over her knees, and Phoebe kicked them off. With one deft move, she lifted her skirts above her waist and bent over the little table. The ivory-white globes of her buttocks gleamed in the moonlight.

As Fred entered her soft wetness, she gave a soft cry.

Fred gasped as he slid further inside.

He could feel the tide rising within him.

He rutted like an animal.

Phoebe cried out again, half stifling the noise.

He came in great shuddering spurts – it had worked, it had worked! Praise God, he was a man again!

It was a long, hot summer, with the prospect of a general election hanging like a pall of political pollution on the horizon. It was generally accepted that the chances of the long-standing Conservative administration's survival were almost nil. It was sinking in a slough of deceit, hypocrisy and ineptitude. Its members seemed so weary that they could not even be bothered to step aside from the banana skins.

The voters were weary and sullen from years of broken promises and inefficiency. No one had any great hopes of 'Bambi' Blair and his toothpaste smile, because everybody knew that behind him the Neanderthal Socialist class warriors were lurking quietly in their caves, sharpening their knives and waiting for the moment of triumph. As they honed their blades, they licked their lips at the prospect of the juicy victims whom political victory would allow them to devour.

One of their juiciest prizes would be the countryside which they intended to turn into a theme park for the urban proletariat. As for the reactionary peasants who lived and worked in the country, well, the history of the Socialist struggle showed what should be done with them. One of the more humane suggestions was that the Ceauçescu system should be copied: villages would be bulldozed and the inhabitants rehoused in urban tower blocks where they could be strictly regulated. Other Socialists thought that their Serbian Comrades had demonstrated a much more efficient way of dealing with the programme. The one thing upon which all activists were agreed was that an essential start to breaking the spirit of the countryman was to do away with all country sports. This would be a matter of urgency for any incoming administration; it was, after all, a question of Political Correctness.

In spite of the approaching storm clouds, business continued as usual in the country. Hay time came and went and by August, the farmers were well into the harvest. As the weather seemed set fair, Fred had calculated on an early harvest and therefore an early start for hunting. With this in mind, he set about gradually working up the long slow hours of exercise to bring the hounds to fitness. He also decreed that the horses should be brought up early from their summer ease in the water meadows, in spite of the Hon. Secretary's grumbling about additional expense.

Ever since the Summer Dance, he and Phoebe had also been exercising each other whenever the opportunity presented itself. This was quite often as Sir William was always going up to London for a 'committee meeting' or to 'see his man of business'. The pressures of this business must have been intense because the baronet often had to be shovelled off the train from London in a highly emotional state.

Sir William's emotion became more heightened as little whispers began to reach him about how his wife was occupying herself in his absences. Anyone who thinks that there is any such thing as a 'private affair' in the country is deluding himself quite seriously.

'I yeard thic old vixen screaming again around the Maser's cottage,' said the Public Bar of the Warknock Arms. 'Ho! Ho! Ho!'

In fact, there was not too much 'Ho! Ho!' about it. It was an affair based on hopelessness rather than love. Fred found that making love to Phoebe only deepened his own sense of despair and loneliness. It made him realize all the more how deeply Katerina had hurt him, and how he was still haunted by her memory. To try and exorcise it, he used Phoebe. The result was not happy for either of them.

One evening in late August, they were naked on the bed. Phoebe sat with her head bowed and her hair hanging down. Fred lay on his back with his arms across his face.

They were silent.

Then Phoebe said, 'It's not working, is it?'

'No. Look, I'm so sorry. It's just . . .'

'It's Katerina, isn't it?'

'Yes, I'm afraid so.'

Phoebe said no more. She got up and dressed quickly. Then she came round to where Fred was still lying, as though frozen. She pulled his arms away from his face and, bending down, kissed him gently.

'Don't worry, darling, it's my fault. I thought it might make things better for both of us, but it's only making things worse. Don't worry, I won't bother you again.'

'Phoebe! I . . .'

Phoebe put her hand gently over Fred's mouth.

'Goodbye, darling.'

And with that she was gone.

Fred lay like a stone as he listened to the door closing and the sound of the car starting in the lane; then he was overwhelmed by a tide of black misery.

Fred wrote to Bryan Skevings asking his support for country sports, and received a reply indicating the MP's unwavering support for all matters pertaining to Hunting, Shooting and Fishing and hoping, therefore, that he could count on Fred's vote in the forthcoming 'democratic struggle'.

'I don't know how you can do it, Bry – Jeremy Dibbings was helping Skevings with his campaign.

'Politics, my sweet. Now, you just get on with your

envelope licking and, if you're very good, I'll find something better for your sweet little tongue to do later.'

Jeremy pouted prettily.

Skevings blew him a kiss across the table, and thought to himself that, once the election was over, it might be time for a change of partner; Jerry was really getting rather plump, and Bryan Skevings liked his meat close to the bone.

In the west country, Fred perused Skevings's letter. 'Hmm – I just wish I though that chap was trustworthy. I don't think we'd shoot tigers with *him*, young Paddy, my boy.'

Paddy, lying panting in the sunlight from the open door, thumped his tail in agreement.

Aunt Helga had put the discarded photograph of Fred with his hounds behind a large brass candlestick on the mantelpiece above the great fireplace in the hall.

Tatiana studiously ignored it, except for the occasion when Katya, during one of her periodic dusting blitzkriegs, inspected the picture and ventured the opinion that the English Lord was not half bad looking and sat his horse like a gentleman.

Tatiana's subsequent explosive comments on so-called English gentlemen, and Slovene so-called cooks who did not know their place – anyway the horse was much better looking than its rider – made Aunt Helga and Katya, who was impervious to the Gräfin's moods, screech with ill-suppressed mirth. This roused Tatiana to even greater paroxysms of fury, and made her stamp out of the hall loudly, consigning all stupid old women and all Englishmen to the nether regions of the inferno. This made the old ladies laugh even more.

Aunt Helga remarked that the English Lord succeeded in getting under the Gräfin's skin, even though they had never met. Katya gave Fred's picture another flick with her duster before suggesting that, in fact, the Gräfin had quite another place in mind for the Englishman. This made them cackle in a most disgraceful manner.

A few days later Aunt Helga, with her noiseless tread, entered the hall and saw Tatiana standing by the fireplace studying the photograph intently. The old lady had not been detected, and she withdrew silently smiling to herself.

The predicted Socialist landslide in the British General Election might even have been described as an avalanche but for the fact that very few people could even be bothered to vote. The electorate was disgusted with the fatuous antics of politicians of all parties.

'A plague on all your houses,' it said, and stayed at home in droves.

Great Britain had a Socialist government, and the Neanderthals came snarling and slavering out of their caves, baying for Class War. Mr. Blair had signed a contract with Rupert Murdoch's News Corporation for a world tour, lecturing on 'The European Union – A New Holy Roman Empire'. Naturally, he could not have afforded to upset such a powerful patron by cancelling the tour, so being Prime Minister would have to wait until he got back. He was keen to keep the troops happy at home, so he decided to leave a carcass or two for them to gorge on in his absence.

The 'Small Furry Animals Protection Bill' was rushed through Parliament on a three-line whip and to rapturous urban acclaim. The *Sun*'s headline read: BAMBI BUTCHERS BLOOD SPORTS. The *Guardian* was more restrained with: TONY – THE NEW ST. FRANCIS.

Bryan Skevings, in his ultra-safe seat, was one of the

few Conservatives to be re-elected. He promptly voted for the Bill, and told his outraged local party association that, as far as he was concerned, they could get stuffed; he was considering taking the Labour whip anyway. He did not tell them that his chum, Ron – now in the Cabinet – had hinted at a minor ministerial appointment as his thirty pieces of silver.

It looked as though hunting would become illegal before the Opening Meet.

The letter was signed 'A Friend'. The friendly writer felt that it was his friendly duty to inform Sir William of the disgraceful state of affairs that existed between Lady Nately and the Master of the Old Wessex. The write felt that 'poor darling Phoebe' had been grossly misled by the scheming, saturnine, ne'er do well that Frederick FitzHugh undoubtedly was.

Sir William sat in his study, snarling and chewing his biro until he got a mouthful of ink.

The bitch! He had thought that something fishy was going on – a chap gets a nose for that sort of thing, especially if he has been cuckolded before. The bitch! He ought to give her a good thrashing, but he was a bit leery of that line of action; he had tried it with the first Lady Nately, and had only just missed out on intensive care.

The swine! He ought to horsewhip *him*, but that was ruled out by the thought that, if he tried such a thing with someone of Fred's build and training, he might *not* miss intensive care this time.

The swine! He would get Fred thrown out of his club! But, no, go steady there: there might be those to point a finger at some of Sir William's more arcane habits – which he had nous enough to confine to the Metropolis – and, anyway, if clubs started chucking out chaps for adultery, there would not be many clubmen left.

No! Revenge there must be, but . . . Sir William had never heard of Machiavelli, but he would have agreed with his dictum about vengeance being a dish best eaten cold. He must think of a way of hurting FitzHugh, preferably somewhere way below the belt. Now, what was the feller fond of . . .

He picked up the telephone and dialled Major Simkin's number. Simkin, the hunt's Hon. Sec., was a mean-spirited, devious bastard – just what he needed.

'What are we going to do, Guv'nor?'

Jim Scuttle, Kite and Fred had convened a spontaneous meeting in the valeting room.

Fred scratched his head. 'I really don't know. I mean it will be a bit of time before the Bill actually becomes law, and I suppose that we just go on hunting until then.'

'But then what?'

'God knows!'

The Hunter and Tatiana were sitting on the rocks. There had been a frost the night before, and the warmth of the rising sun was tempered by a definite bite in the air. With the coming of the colder weather, there had been reports of wolf sightings.

The Hunter had sent a summons through Tomislav for Tatiana to meet him at 'the usual place'.

'The wolves are returning,' said the Hunter. 'You remember we talked about a pack of hounds?'

'Yes, but I said that I knew nothing of such things.'

'Just remember what I told you: if a chance comes your way, take it and worry afterwards.'

'It would be a gift from Heaven!'

'Another satisfied customer!'

★

'What's this special Hunt Committee meeting about, then?' one of the Galloping Majors asked Fred.

'I don't know. I haven't heard anything about it.'

'Aren't you supposed to attend meetings, ex-officio and all that?'

'Yes, I am, but I've heard nothing.'

'Very rum. Ah well, hate bloody meetings myself – those silly old farts, Nately and Simkin, binding on and on.'

Major Simkin looked glumly at the glass of sherry that Sir William had issued to him: what a mean bastard.

'So, d'yer think it will work?'

A strategy planning committee of two was taking place in Sir William's study.

Simkin nodded. 'I've sounded out some of the key Committee members. Everybody's got their tails between their legs over this Bill. They can see the point about there being no use maintaining a pack of hounds if they are going to become illegal.'

'And are they happy about having them shot immediately?'

'Well, no one's happy about it. But there doesn't seem to be much alternative. There's no point in feeding them for nothing. Someone did suggest that we try to sell the pack to America, or some such . . .'

'No! No! I want them shot, and I want that bastard FitzHugh to do it. I'll learn the bastard! But mind now, he mustn't get wind of what is happening.'

Major Simkin nodded gloomily. William really was a mean bastard.

It was the schemers' fault for not closing the study door properly. Phoebe had been passing by on her way upstairs to change for dinner. She had not meant to eavesdrop. But sometimes you just could not help overhearing, especially when she knew that William was up to something.

The enormity of exactly what he was up to took her breath away.

William really was a mean bastard.

Without further pause, she grabbed her car keys from the hall table and set off for the kennels.

CHAPTER THIRTEEN

'So what do we do now?'

An evening Council of War had been hastily convened after Phoebe's fluttered visit. She had laid information against her husband's dastardly plot. Kite and Jim Scuttle were there. Fred had also roped in the Galloping Majors, on the basis that they were both daft enough for anything. The council was ranged around Fred's kitchen table and a bottle of whisky.

'This meeting's tomorrow night, is it, Guv'nor?'

'That's right, Jim, so we have not got much time.'

'You don't think that the Committee would really agree to the hounds being shot, do you? I mean, what about His Lordship and Miss Pettigrew? They'd never allow it, and a lot of farmers would never stand for it.'

'They've timed it well. Lord Warknock's on his annual pilgrimage to Scotland, and Miss Pettigrew's staying with a cousin in Ireland. I've also discovered that a lot of farmers on the Committee are on an NFU trip to France.'

'But what about the rest of the Committee?'

'They don't amount to much, and they are all pretty well beaten down about this Bill. You've got to remember that Nately puts a great deal of money into the Hunt, and he's got that devious bastard Simkin on his side to preach doom and gloom. I reckon they'll get their way.'

'But surely the hounds belong to old Warknock,' said one of the GMs.

'Used to, but he gave them away to the country – that effectively means that they belong to the Committee and they can dispose of them as they wish.'

'Can we get them away somewhere, sir?' asked Kite.

'Well, if we did, we would be stealing them and as Nately is doing this to spite me, he'd just love that.'

'In the slammer goes the Master, loaded in chains, what?' said the other GM.

'That's about it.'

'You remember what you said, Guv'nor, about going abroad if hunting went pear-shaped. What about that, then?'

Fred looked around the weather-beaten faces, lined with worry. He took a deep breath. 'There's just one chance, and it's a faint one. if we did it we would have to move bloody fast – like tomorrow night during the meeting. We would have to create a diversion, and be loaded up and out of the country by morning; and I couldn't do it alone. So what about it Kite?'

'You know me, sir, I ain't got nothing here, and you'll need someone to keep an eye out to you.'

'Jim? And what about Mrs. Scuttle?'

'Blimey, Guv'nor, don't worry about my missus. I reckon she'll be glad to get rid of me. Give her something to moan about for a month. She'll be like a pig in straw!'

'Smashing!' chorused the GMs. 'We'll help, of course, and when you get settled, let us know and we'll come and gallop all over you. What? Whuff! Whuff! Whuff!'

'Right then! I've a call to make. But mind, this is a bloody long shot and it's about our only one.'

*

Katya hated answering the telephone but it was late in the evening and the ladies had gone to bed. She and Tomislav were sitting comfortably by the stove in the kitchen whilst Tomislav finished his pipe.

The telephone started jangling in the hall.

'Well, answer it, Old Woman!'

'Why can't you answer it, you lazy old stick?'

'I never touch the damned thing. It is always bad news.'

'You're as much use as a bad tooth.'

Katya rose grumbling to her feet, and hobbled down the passageway.

Very gingerly she lifted the receiver. '*Grüss Gott*,' she said.

'Do you speak English?' said a voice far away.

Katya held the receiver away from her ear, shook it to get rid of the incomprehensible sounds, and tried again: '*Grüss Gott.*'

This time the voice came in halting German, which Katya could more or less make out.

The voice wanted to speak to the Gräfin Czerny.

The Gräfin was in bed, said Katya in the satisfied manner of justified refusal.

Could the Gräfin be woken?

The very idea was an outrage; the Gräfin must sleep.

It was an urgent matter, said the voice.

Was it indeed? The Gräfin was not to be disturbed lightly; the voice could ring at a Christian hour in the morning.

The voice persisted; it really was *most* urgent.

And who was it, who sought to rouse such an important lady from her bed, pray?

The voice explained that it was Lord Frederick FitzHugh from England.

Katya held the receiver away from her ear and stared at

238

it for a long moment. Then, 'Are you the English Lord on the horse?'

Fred paused for a moment in puzzlement. 'Ah! You mean the photograph! Yes, that's me.'

'Jesus, Mary and Joseph! Wait, English Lord, wait!'

Tatiana was woken rudely from a deep and pleasing sleep. Katya had obviously gone mad, shaking her like that. Either that, or the castle was on fire. No, she had definitely gone mad. She was shouting about 'the English Lord' and gibbering nonsense.

Tatiana was seldom at her best on first waking, but she got the bit about the telephone.

Telephone! At this hour! Grabbing her dressing gown, she sleepily groped her way downstairs. She looked at the receiver as though it was lying in wait for her, but picked it up.

'Hello,' she said drowsily.

Aunt Helga had been roused by the frantic Katya. She had come wide awake at once and, unlike Tatiana, had grasped the situation immediately.

The two old women were now hanging over the banisters listening to the one-sided conversation.

'Of course, I speak English!'

'Who is this?'

'What!'

'You?'

'You want to do *what*?'

'Are you *mad*?'

All the time Tatiana's voice was rising as wind becomes a gale.

'*Do you really think that I . . .*'

It was at this moment that the echo of another voice came into her mind.

'*But listen to me. If a chance does occur, don't shilly shally. Take it and worry about it afterwards.*'

Tatiana paused and, for a long moment, held the receiver in front of her, staring at it. She had been right; something had been lying in wait for her. At last, putting the receiver back to her face, she said in a small – now trembling – voice, 'All right, come!'

Then she slammed down the handset, staggered to the table, sank into the chair, put her head in her hands and burst into tears.

For a long moment Fred stood staring at his telephone. 'I must be fucking mad!'

When he went back to the kitchen a circle of faces looked at him expectantly.

'Bingo!'

'Where?'

'When?'

'How?'

Fred raised his hands to still the babble. He picked up his glass, and there was an expectant hush.

Fred raised his glass. 'Gentlemen! I give you a toast: to the Gräfin Tatiana Czerny, and to Wolf Hunting in Slovenia!'

There was an awed silence.

'Fucking stroll on!' said Kite.

The next day the kennels was one of frantic, but concealed, activity. Ex-Corporal of Horse Thomas rose to the occasion, like a true cavalry man. Laurie the Lorry appeared at the wheel of a large articulated cattle lorry in the farmyard of Galloping Major A. He tucked it out of sight behind a Dutch barn.

A large van, which proclaimed itself to be carrying 'Bonzo's Bonzer Dog Foods', arrived at the kennels and backed up to the building. Into this was packed all the necessary kennel equipment and tack for the horses. Into the van also went the men's suitcases and personal kit.

Jim Scuttle was aided by the fact that Mrs. Scuttle was conveniently absent on a visit to a WI in Yorkshire, which was keeping her nicely out of the way.

Major Simkin lunched at Nately Hall. Lady Nately was absent on a shopping expedition, which included doing Fred's packing for him. Chairman and Hon. Secretary were able to discuss their forthcoming coup without being inhibited by her presence.

'The main thing,' said Sir William through a full mouth, 'is that the blighter does not get wind of what is happening, what? You don't think that he knows anything, do you?'

Major Simkin forced down another mouthful of spam fritter – a dish of which Sir William was inordinately fond, it was cheap too – and shook his head. 'Don't think so. I passed the kennels on my way over and they were delivering another batch of hound food – seems such a waste.' A spasm of parsimony shrivelled his face.

'Capital! Capital! We want everything to look normal. I don't anticipate any problems at the meeting, with Warknock and La Pettigrew away and all those farmers boozing it up in Belgium or some such place. We shall have enough for a quorum at the meeting, and they are all in shock from this Bill. I must say, good comes out of everything. That bugger FitzHugh was costing me a bloody fortune, apart from anything else.' Sir William's face darkened at the thought of a cuckoo in his nest. 'This will be – what do you call the thing? – a double whammy for the bastard. I can't wait to see his face when you tell him.'

Major Simkin choked. '*Me* tell him? I thought you would tell him that as Chairman.'

'No, no. You break the glad tidings. I'll be there to back you up, of course.'

'But suppose he gets violent? I mean, he did the Hereford course, I understand.'

'Don't be such a wimp, Simkin! You were a soldier too!'

Major Simkin thought rather sadly that a blameless career in Coastal Defence Batteries had not included being trained in crushing an opponent's windpipe.

'I wonder if we ought to have the police there?'

The Hunter roared with bass laughter. 'So he's coming! Splendid! I thought that my young falcon would stoop to the lure.'

'So I'm a lure, am I?'

The Hunter had made one of his rare visits to the castle. At first light, a grumbling Tomislav had been sent to find him by a near hysterical Tatiana who gave graphic descriptions of what might happen to the old man if he returned empty handed. In fact, the Hunter had been easy to find, as the whole village knew that he was having one of his periodic breakfasts with the old priest. He could not have been more conveniently placed if he had planned the whole thing himself.

'What red-blooded young man could resist the plea of a damsel in distress?'

Tatiana spluttered. 'But it was not a plea! And I am not in distress!'

'You will be if the wolves get back in strength.'

'But how do I know that this English and his hounds will do what we want?'

'I think you will find that he will supply all your needs,' said the Hunter rather cryptically. 'And talking of needs, this schnapps of Katya's is really quite excellent.'

He looked at his empty glass.

Tatiana sighed and filled his glass. The Hunter must have consumed at least half a bottle without any visible effect. She felt deflated.

'All right, I suppose so, but where am I going to put all these dogs and horses and men?'

'That is no problem. There are the old kennels where Francis's grandfather kept his hounds before the Hitler War. It will take them about three days to arrive here. The old building is sound, as you know, and has been used as a storehouse. I told Tomislav to organize a party from the village to clear them out and clean them up. As for the horses, you have enough stable room here for a squadron of cavalrymen.'

Tatiana sat bolt upright. 'You don't think that I am having that English in my house?'

'Why not? Are you afraid of your virtue?'

'Certainly not! I have my revolver and my knife. It, it, it is . . . it is just unthinkable. You know what I think of the English!'

'You are all part of Europe now, Gräfin, and you must look on this young man as a refugee from political persecution. Surely, knowing what you know, you would not refuse shelter to a refugee?'

Aunt Helga had been sitting quietly at the end of the table, busy, as usual, with her embroidery. 'Think what Francis would have done,' she said gently, 'and don't forget you told the English to come.'

Tatiana once more buried her face in her hands. 'My God! What am I doing?'

The Hunter reached across and refilled her glass.

'We're going to need a diversion.' It was a lunch time meeting at Fred's cottage. 'We need something to concentrate the minds of the Hunt Committee and the police tonight.'

'Sorry I'm late!' Galloping Major B came bustling through the door. 'I say, do you know what? I came past the cottage that that frightful oik Skevings rents and, do

243

you know what, the little shit is there. He's got the gall to show up here after what he did, the treacherous bastard, and he's got some ghastly little poofter with a pony tail with him. They were walking up the path as I drove by, and I swear that they were holding hands – *holding hands!* Dammit, the chap's a brown hatter as well! I mean, we've got to do something about *him*, what?'

There was a grumble of agreement.

'Ah ha! Well, they might just come in handy as another diversion.' Fred turned to the GMs. 'Now, how are you two on doing a bit of evil?'

The two red faces glowed with eagerness. 'You mean bangs and black balaclavas, cheese wires and things like that?'

'Negative the cheese wires, but you get the drift.'

'Wizard!'

'Smashing!'

'Can we have just a little bang?'

'Only if you're very good. Now, Phoebe, I don't think that you should be involved in any of this.'

Phoebe flared up. 'If I hadn't told you in the first place, you wouldn't know any of it. Of course, I'm involved!'

'Thank you. Right then! What I have in mind is this . . .'

The Old Wessex Hunt Committee was accustomed to meet in the upstairs room – rather grandly referred to as 'The Conference Suite' – of the Whistle and Flute. The Whistle and Flute liked to be called an 'Olde Worlde Coachinge Inne', which meant that it was heavy on phoney horse brasses, and that the dispirited waitress wore a mob cap whilst serving the deep-frozen scampi and soggy chips. In fact, the hotel was a thoroughly dispiriting place. This suited the mood of the Committee members who crept into the meeting room; they looked utterly whipped. This condition suited the purpose of Sir William who sniffed the miasma of despondency with some relish. The meeting looked thoroughly malleable.

Major Simkin, who was gloomily picking his nose over the minute book, looked at his watch, looked at Sir William, and coughed.

Sir William was away in a happy day dream, which had Fred on his knees clutching the baronet's ankles and making incoherent pleading noises.

'Ahum! Yes, well, I think everybody's here that can be here. I think that we should make a start.' Sir William rose to his feet. 'There is only one item on the agenda of this Extraordinary Meeting, which is – er – the disposal of the Old Wessex hounds in the light of the Government Bill to ban all forms of hunting. I should say, at this stage, that I understand even draghunting may be under threat with this Bill, as certain members of the Government feel that even this might be cruel to horses, is elitist, and might tend to deprave and debauch those who take part. In those circumstances, as I see it, there can be no possible case for further maintaining our pack of hounds, and the proposal before the meeting is that, in these circumstances and having regard to all the relevant facts, and having weighed and balanced all the avenues open to this committee, it would appear that we have no realistic alternative . . .'

There is no saying how long Sir William might have continued. He was, in the speech-makers' form book, ranked as a 'stayer'. However, at that moment there was a knock on the door and a uniformed Police Inspector entered the room.

'Sir William Nately?'

'Yes! Yes!'

'I wonder if I might have a quiet word, Sir William.'

*

Bryan Skevings and Jeremy Dibbings were having a lovely evening in Bryan's cottage.

Jeremy had prepared a scrumptious vegetarian meal straight from Marks & Spencer to microwave, which had tasted like a microwaved supermarket vegetarian meal. They had soaked themselves in a couple of bottles of organic wine, that tasted, well, organic. They had then rounded off this culinary delicacy with some 'illicit substances'; each had 'popped' a capsule of amyl nitrate. The 'sudden vigour' occasioned by inhaling the fumes put them both in high good humour, and also in a state of considerable randiness.

Hand-in-hand they scurried to the bedroom.

Jeremy liked to be wooed on these occasions, and the tradition was for him to be chased round the room and over the bed, emitting little squeals of delight. Experience had shown that this routine seldom failed to arouse the somewhat portly Skevings. It worked well that evening and, when Jeremy finally assumed the posture of maximum submission, Bryan fell to with greased vigour.

It was at this unsuitable moment that the bedroom door burst open, and the coupling couple were confronted with the unhappy sight of two men in boiler suits and black balaclavas, both with rampant pistols.

'Don't move either of you! Just stay right where you are!'

Jeremy squealed and immediately found a pistol pushed into his face.

'Don't move!

The unhappy couple remained – almost – entirely rigid in their unfortunate position.

Bryan tried a little bluster. 'Look here! Don't you know who I am?'

'Yes, and shut it!'

Bryan noted that the man had a heavy London accent.

Then the other balaclava produced a large roll of parcel tape.

At the kennels there was frantic activity. The articulated cattle truck arrived in the darkness, and Laurie the Lorry reversed it expertly up to the building. The excited hounds romped up the tail board and into a deep bed of shavings partioned off at the front. The horses clattered up the ramp in their turn, well-rugged and wrapped round with leg and tail guards.

The little convoy – the cattle truck, the equipment van still labelled 'Bonzo's Bonzer Dog Foods' and Fred's car – was assembled.

Fred, Kite and Jim Scuttle stood for a moment looking at the old brick-built kennels which had been home to the Old Wessex hounds for nearly one hundred years. The deserted buildings looked lonely and forlorn.

'All my working life, I been here,' said Jim mournfully. 'Never thought I'd work anywhere else, and now . . .'

Fred put a hand on his shoulder. 'The main thing is, we've saved the hounds.'

Jim perked up. 'Aye, that's right, Guv'nor, we've got the hounds. Them's the thing that matters. The Old Wessex lives on – right?'

'Right!'

Laurie was looking at his watch. 'If we're going to catch that ferry, like, we'd better be moving.'

'Right! Mount!'

Jim climbed in with Laurie.

Kite got in with the driver of the Bonzo van.

Fred had Paddy on the front seat of the car.

The engines roared.

The headlights came on.

The convoy set off.

★

'We're treating it as a bomb threat, Sir William,' said the Inspector, as the speeding police car sirened and flashed its way through the lanes. 'Lady Nately phoned us. She got back this evening and found this suitcase on the doorstep. It had a hand-written sign on it that says, "Up Yours, You Cruel Bastards". We suspect it could be some of the Animal Rights loonies. They're still very active in spite of the Bill. The *Old Wessex Mail* was rung up by something calling itself the "Furry Animals Rights Militia" saying that you had to be "cleansed". Special Branch have never heard of this bunch, but they spring up like toadstools. Anyway, the Bomb Squad's on its way, but it will take them a couple of hours to get here from Hereford.'

'But why me? Why me?'

'I suppose with you being Chairman of the Old Wessex Hunt, and a prominent local personage.'

In better times, Sir William would have liked being referred to as a 'prominent local personage', but just now he wished that his prominence would detumesce.

'Frau Gräfin! Frau Gräfin!'

Katya's screech echoed round the castle. Tatiana came running, expecting some new disaster. Bonnie came hirpling along on three legs behind; she did not like letting her mistress get too far away from her.

Katya was standing staring at the receiver of the telephone that she had put down on the table and backed away from. As Tatiana approached she saw Katya cross herself.

The old woman pointed at the receiver as though she expected it to rise up and strangle her with its cord. 'An English!'

'The Milord?'

'No, a lesser English.'

Katya's sense of social stratification was instinctive.

Shaking her head and trying not to laugh, Tatiana picked up the telephone. 'Hello.'

'Is that the Grayfin Czerny?'

'Yes.'

'Good evening, madam, my name is Thomas, Corporal of Horse Thomas. The Major asked me to telephone you and tell you that the convoy has started. Operation Wolf-scare is go.'

'*What?*'

'Operation Wolf-scare, that's the code name for the operation, madam.'

Tatiana pulled herself together. 'Yes, I quite understand, Mr. Thomas.' Her voice dripped honey now. 'You are a clever man who has provided, how you say, "logistics", yes?'

Thomas was mollified. 'That's right, madam, rolling and on time to RV with the ferry at Southampton. I sent them that way because I thought we should get them away and out of the country, juldi, juldi.'

'Jildi? What is this jildi?'

'Er, "quickly", madam. It's an old Indian Army word, you see . . .'

'Thank you, Mr. Thomas. I understand your colonial traditions. So, all is well, so far?'

'That's it, and the Major said he will report progress once they are Europside.'

'I can hardly wait. Thank you, Mr. Thomas.'

'Thank you, madam.'

The telephone clicked.

Tatiana ruffled Bonnie's head and had her hand nuzzled. 'Holy Mother! What have I started?'

Katya had been hovering. 'The English are coming?'

'The English are coming, Katya. They will probably rape you and do unspeakable things to Tomislav.'

'In that case, things are looking up round here.' Katya hobbled off to the kitchen, cackling; she always liked to have the last word.

Nately Hall was a blaze of light. Police cars were scattered about the gravel in front of the house, and in the middle of the spacious lawn lay a solitary suitcase, with spotlights turned on it. A sergeant approached the Inspector's car as it crunched up the drive.

'We've moved everybody into the back of the house, sir. Lady Nately and the staff are all in the kitchen, should be safe enough there.'

'Thank you, sergeant. Any panic amongst the civilians?'

'No, sir. Lady Nately's playing poker with the butler and the cook.'

Sir William winced. 'Is that the bomb?' he asked.

'That, sir,' said the sergeant reprovingly, 'is the Suspect Package.'

'Any news of the Bomb Squad?' asked the Inspector.

'ETA one hour, sir.'

'Then we just have to wait.'

Thomas had provided the convoy vehicles with two-way radios.

Fred's set crackled. 'Wolf Two to Wolf Leader. Message. Over.'

'Wolf Leader. Send message. Over.'

'Laurie says you should see the signs for the docks at the next traffic lights. Follow. Over.'

'Roger. Out.'

The little convoy rumbled through the scattered late night Southampton traffic towards the docks.

'There! That should do it,' said the balaclava with the London accent.

'Aye! Happen it will.' The other balaclava had a highly improbable Yorkshire accent.

Neither Jeremy nor Bryan were in the mood, or the position to quibble about accents. They were bonded, in every sense of the word. The two balaclavas had taped them together, with yard upon yard of sticky tape, in the position that they had found them. The two lovers also had their mouths taped.

The balaclavas stood back and admired their handiwork. Then they clasped each other and, before the horrified eyes of their victims, fell into great spasms of convulsive laughter.

Then Balaclava A spotted the bottle of amyl nitrate on the table. He pointed. The other one nodded.

Still shaking with laughter, they taped the bottle onto Skevings's back and, with a wave to their victims, left them to their own devices.

Downstairs, one of the balaclavas picked up the telephone and dialled a number:

'*Daily Telegraph*. Can I help you?'

'Newsdesk,' said the heavy London voice.

The Bomb Squad sergeant rubbed his chin as he studied the flood-lit suitcase. 'Could be anything. I don't reckon trying to open it. It's been moved about so I reckon we needn't worry about a trembler switch. I reckon a nice little controlled explosion to blow the lock and the lid off would be favourite. OK with you, sir?'

The Inspector nodded.

'What about my windows?' asked Sir William.

The Sergeant shrugged. 'All depends what's inside.' He glanced at the broad, many-windowed front of the house. 'Could be some lucky glazier's birthday if that lot goes tinkle, tinkle.'

Sir William groaned.

'Right! Everybody take cover!'

'A pack of hounds and four horses?' said the Customs Officer.

'That's right, sir, and all documentation present and correct.' Laurie handed over the papers. Ex-Corporal of Horse Thomas had performed a minor miracle to get the export papers through so quickly.

'Well, bloody roll on, that's all I can say. Go on then! Bloody roll on!'

As the convoy rolled onto the Cherbourg ferry, the hounds in the lorry began to sing.

The Customs Officer took off his cap and scratched his head. 'Bloody roll on! I wonder what the Frogs will make of that lot?'

There was a sharp pop as the lock and top of the suitcase blew off.

For a long moment nothing happened.

Then, inside the suitcase, a cylinder that had been activated by the explosion began to hiss.

Something began to move and squirm.

The 'something' rose slowly from the inside as the gas inflated it.

It rose and swelled, and began to assume a definite shape.

A face swelled and assumed a ghastly smile.

Its breasts swelled to pneumatic improbability.

The thighs and buttocks blew into a shape of hideous invitation.

There was a long astonished silence.

'It's a fucking woman!' cried a very young police constable.

The Bomb Squad Sergeant grinned a happy grin.

'That, Sunshine, is exactly what it is – we've all been well and truly stuffed.'

The laughter started small, then spread and swelled into a great wave of mirth.

Sir William fled.

'Your accent was bloody awful, old boy.'

'Not as bad as your attempt at Ecky Thump, my dear old thing.'

The Galloping Majors, boiler suits discarded and balaclavas burning in the kitchen stove, were restoring their tissues with rather a lot of whisky in the house of GM A.

'I almost forgot, where's your shooter?'

'On the table with yours.'

'I had better sort them.'

GM A rose to his feet and took the two pistols from the table. He crept upstairs. He sneaked into the bedroom where his small son lay in the deep sleep of sweet innocence, and restored the pistols to their rightful place in the holsters that hung on the end of the bed.

There would be domestic hell in the morning if the 'Dirty Harry – Make My Day' – cap guns were missing.

CHAPTER FOURTEEN

'About a thousand miles from Cherbourg to Ljubljana – Paris, Metz, Stuttgart, Salzburg, up over the Alps and motorway all the way, my lovely boys. After Lub it's about another fifty miles up into the hills, and motorway it is not.'

Laurie was briefing the members of the convoy on the dockside at Cherbourg, his finger stabbing out the places on the map.

'Never let an officer near a map,' muttered Kite, sotto voce. Then out loud: 'You're right there, me old Taff. More like a goat track, that last bit to Lippitz, but Taff here knows all about goat tracks, don't you, me old sheep shagger?'

'I'll shag you in a minute, you cockney git. Bloody walk you can if I have any more of your lip.'

The two men grinned at each other.

'How long will it take us, Laurie, bearing in mind drivers' hours and we shall have to stop twice a day for feedaway and a bit of leg stretch?'

'I reckon on about three days, Major.'

'Very good. Well, lads, we better get started. Hounds seem to be all right, Jim?' Jim Scuttle had been checking round the open ventilation ports of the lorry. The Old Wessex hounds were accepting the journey in a philosophical canine way by curling up and going to sleep.

'Right then. Mount!'

★

Tatiana was inspecting the renovated kennels. All the odds and ends that had been stored there over the years had been removed. The work party from the village was hard at it, scrubbing, painting, hammering and talking. Since the news had been announced that the English Milord was coming with his hounds to hunt the wolves, the village had talked of nothing else.

Tatiana found herself being bombarded with questions which she was not able to answer.

'How big is a foxhound?'

'What do they eat?'

'They must be very savage!'

'Will they eat the children?'

'How big is the Milord? As big as the Herr Graf?'

'Is it true that English Milords expect, as a matter of right, to take their pleasure with the women of the village?'

This was not helped by Katya going round cackling with glee and assuring everyone that the Frau Gräfin had told her that the English would assuredly rape all the women.

At last, in desperation, Tatiana got the photograph of Fred and his hounds, and the priest tacked it up on the door of the church. He remarked dryly, as he watched the crowd jostling each other to look at the picture, that he hoped they would be as eager to get through the doors to Mass on Sunday.

The picture caused a great deal of comment and one or two ladies, having looked at Fred's picture, were heard to say that the idea of '*droit de seigneur*' was not all bad.

Katya was enjoying the fuss hugely. 'I told them, Frau Gräfin, that the castle staff had the right to get raped first.'

'Who would want to rape you, you shrivelled old sow!' grumbled Tomislav.

'Well, I can tell you who wouldn't be able to! So don't talk to me about shrivelled!'

'Old fool!'

'Old bullock!'

Tatiana fled, leaving the battle raging happily in the kitchen.

Aunt Helga was cleaning the silver in the pantry.

'Milord this! Milord that! I tell you, Auntie, I am sick of this man before he even arrives. I should never have said that he could come. I must have been mad. He has turned the whole village upside down before he even gets here. But don't worry! I will sort him out! I will put him firmly in his place!'

Aunt Helga could see herself smiling in the silver tray she was working on. She carefully straightened her face. 'You might even like the young man when you meet him.'

'Like him? *Like him?* Mother of God, Auntie, don't tell me you are as mad as the rest of the fools! I'm going out!'

Aunt Helga's reflection smiled back at her.

'Bugger! That's something we never thought of!'

'Well, we can't feed without it, Guv'nor. We got the meal and we got the troughs, but it's no good without hot water to make the porridge.'

'*Bien sur, monsieur,*' said the manager of the Relais Routier fifteen minutes later, 'of course you may have some hot water from the kitchen to mix your dog food. How many little doggies do you have?'

'Sixty-three.'

'*Mon Dieu!*'

Jim Scuttle made his report to Fred: 'The horses are all right, sir, but they're bound to get a bit leg weary travelling this sort of distance. Nothing wrong that a couple of days' rest and a decent stable won't put right.'

It was Aunt Helga who answered the telephone and listened to the halting German.

'Everything is ready for your arrival, Lord Frederick,' she responded, 'and I can assure you and your men that you will receive a great welcome. Goodbye for the moment.' She put down the receiver.

Katya tended to hover about when she heard the telephone ring, usually appearing very busy dusting something, anything.

'That was the English. They will be here this afternoon. I must tell the Gräfin.'

Katya forgot about her dusting and scuttled away to spread the tidings around the village.

'There it is sir. Welcome to Lippitz, as they say.'

The convoy had paused at the head of the pass. All the men had got out of the vehicles and gathered on the road. The valley lay spread out before them, the fields white under a covering of snow, with the trees standing out black and stark against the whiteness that glittered in the wintry sun.

In the middle of the valley, the village showed as a huddle of snow-covered roofs, with the smoke from the chimneys rising in the frosty air and then combining into a cloud that drifted slowly across the fields.

Behind the village, where the hills rose and rolled away towards distant mountains, the Schloss stood out square and white against the background of hanging beech woods. The afternoon sun caused the castle windows to glitter.

'Blimey, Guv'nor, it's like a blooming Christmas card!'

'It'll look better with some red coats in it, Jim.'

'Well, I hopes the natives are friendly. It's a bloody long way from home.'

'I don't think you need worry about your welcome,' said a deep voice.

The little party turned, surprised.

The huge man in the disgraceful hat was leaning on his stick by the side of the road.

'Where the hell did he spring from?' thought Jim.

'Good heavens! Mr. Hunter!'

'Very good to see you again, Lord Frederick. Welcome to Lippitz! All of you, welcome to Lippitz!'

The Hunter shook hands with each of them and, as he did so, the hounds began to sing.

The sweet but savage sound of the singing hounds carried across the frosty stillness to the villagers assembled on the green.

'That's a wild sound,' said Albert. 'It is almost like the wolves themselves howling.'

The old priest listened to the sound as he stood on the steps of his church. 'These men have come with their hounds from a foreign country. They are far from home and we must make them welcome. God has sent them to help us.'

'The Hounds of Heaven, eh, Father?'

'Something like that, my son.'

A short while later, Fred's car led the convoy into the village.

'Golly! What a lot of people!'

The Hunter had got into Fred's car and Paddy was standing on his lap with forefeet on the dashboard so that he could bark at the crowd.

'The whole village has turned out for you.'

As the convoy halted, the villagers formed a circle of curious faces, staring at these strange beings from another world who had come into their village; it was almost disappointing to see that they looked quite normal. They all recognized Milord from his picture; he was a fine big man, and handsome.

'He looks a choice stallion,' said Katya to Tomislav. 'He should scatter some rare stock about the country.'

'Handsome is as handsome does,' grunted the old man. 'They say that all the English Milords are queer, anyway.'

'How do they breed, then? You tell me that.'

'Is that all you think about, old woman?'

'Thinking about it is the most I can hope for with a husband like you, you old capon!'

'Bah!'

The presence of the Hunter thawed the villagers' shyness, and Fred suddenly found himself shaking rough hand after rough hand. Kite and Laurie, who were well remembered from their previous trip, were being slapped on the back and kissed by the women. Bottles of schnapps appeared from nowhere.

The crowd in front of Fred suddenly melted and a passage was formed for the two women. Tatiana was holding Aunt Helga's arm. She told herself that she was doing this purely to steady the old lady amongst the crowd; not for one moment would she consider that she was seeking a little reassurance for herself.

The crowd parted before them.

Fred and Tatiana faced each other.

Once, many years ago, during Close Combat Training, Fred had been kicked in the gut. As he bent double, gasping for breath, the little gamecock of an instructor had danced around him shouting. 'Come on! Come on! It's only pain!'

The blow and the pain, this time, were mental and not physical, but real enough.

He had seen Tatiana on the television. He had seen her photograph. But nothing could protect him from the stunning force of the real thing that stood there, her long golden hair framing the beautiful face beneath her fur hat. Even with her face set determinedly in its severest mode, she was quite simply the loveliest woman that Fred had ever seen.

'Damn him, he looks like a hawk!' thought Tatiana, as she looked at the tall, muscular figure in front of her, with the lean face, the firm mouth and the dark brooding eyes. 'I hate him! I hate him for an English! I hate him because I said yes to him coming here! I hate him because he is here! I hate him because, because . . . well, I just hate him!'

The space between the two crackled with electricity. Afterwards, Katya always maintained that she had actually seen the lightning flashes.

The silence was broken by the Hunter who stepped forward, and said, 'Gräfin, may I present Lord Frederick FitzHugh – *Jäger* extraordinary!'

Without taking their eyes off each other, Tatiana and Fred clasped hands.

'How do you do?' they both said with glacial politeness.

'You don't mean that we should *feed* the brute as well, Auntie?' scowled Tatiana a while later in the kitchen.

'Of course, dear. He is your guest.'

'Oh, very well, but just tonight mind.'

'Don't be silly. The man has come here to help us. Of course, he must eat with us. You would not expect him to eat in the kitchen, would you?'

'He can eat in the ash tip for all I care.'

'And to think that the Czernys were always famous for their hospitality.'

'I don't feel like being famous.'

'Stop pouting, Tatiana. You're behaving like a spoilt child.'

'Oh, all right.'

Fred had been given an apartment at the back of the castle. It consisted of a bedroom, bathroom and a sitting room. They were large rooms that had obviously not been used for some time and, equally obviously, had been cleaned up in a hurry.

The rooms were gloomy from long desuetude. Their only decoration was some rather dreary prints of flowers in the bedroom, and a somewhat ragged tapestry of a stag at bay in the sitting room.

The old four-poster was a cavern of creaks and it groaned as Fred sat down on it, after dropping his kit on the floor.

The adrenaline of the escape and the journey had evaporated. He felt exhausted and depressed.

He was over a thousand miles from home, where there were probably criminal charges pending against him.

He had a pack of hounds and two men, for whom he was responsible.

He had done all of this on a whim.

Suppose it failed. It was truly the act of a madman.

The sad shadows in the room, formed by a single light bulb, did nothing to lift the mood.

There was a knock on the door, and Tomislav poked his head in.

'The Frau Gräfin says you're to dine with her; half an hour,' said the old man gruffly.

And to himself as he closed the door, he muttered, 'The mood she's in, you'll be lucky if she doesn't eat you.'

It was not a happy dinner. Aunt Helga pumped Fred for all the details of his flight from the Old Wessex. Fred, tired as he was, did his best to make the story entertaining.

Tatiana sat icy and remote, eating little and crumbling bread in her fingers. She answered Fred's questions with cold formality.

She also tried very hard to stop her eyes straying to him. The trouble was that she was not always successful and, when they did stray, she usually met Fred's eyes straying towards her.

Tatiana had spent a lot of energy blaming the English as being partly responsible for the death of Francis and her own subsequent misery. The English had been a very convenient target when they were impersonal and far away.

Now she had an Englishman sitting at her table.

He was rather a good-looking Englishman.

He was quiet, rather diffident and dryly funny in that self-deprecating English way.

It was quite difficult to hate him.

He really was quite handsome.

His mouth, now . . . It was a sensual mouth – the sort of mouth that . . .

Then there were his hands: strong, sensitive hands.

And the voice: deep, dark and – she could hardly bear even to think the word – *sexy*.

Tatiana felt a totally unbidden and rebellious warmth between her legs.

No! No! No!

How dare he?

Now she really hated the Englishman.

The kennels were a long range of buildings and the hounds settled happily into their new home, and the village quickly became accustomed to the chiming of hound voices floating down across the river.

Kite and Jim Scuttle settled equally happily into the cottage which was attached to one end of the kennels. Tatiana had appointed a widow woman from the village to minister to their needs. She was a jolly, elderly woman, hugely fat and, as Katya so delicately put it, with a 'face like a busted boot'. This fact was not unconnected with her getting the job, as Katya also liked to point out in less delicate terms. Whatever, she was an extremely good cook and housekeeper.

'We're like pigs in a spud field, Guv'nor,' Fred was told.

The villagers were fascinated by the hounds. There were always faces pressed against the bars of the kennels as Jim and Kite went about their daily routine. When Fred came to 'walk out', the pack was accompanied by a throng of villagers. They were amazed by the happy obedience of the hounds and by their friendliness.

It took a couple of days for Fred to realize, however, that there were never any children amongst the watchers. He questioned the Hunter – who paid regular visits – about this.

The big man laughed. 'They think that the hounds would eat them.'

'Bugger that!' said Fred.

The next morning, the hounds arrived at the village school while the children were having their morning break in the playground. There was immediate pandemonium as the children fled indoors.

Fred spoke to the teacher in his frightful German.

'And you are sure there is no danger?'

Playboy had his paws on Fred's chest as he stroked the old dog hound's greying muzzle.

'You see what danger I am in. I will give this bar of

263

chocolate to the first child who is brave enough to come and meet the hounds.'

Little Stanko was small and somewhat backward. He got teased a lot and was consequently rather withdrawn. He had a great affinity with all animals, however. He had never thought that the hounds looked very savage, but his parents told him sternly that in England they fed the hounds on naughty children who did not do their sums properly, so he was a little bit frightened. But – he loved chocolate.

The teacher felt a tug at her skirt. She looked down at the silent Stanko. 'You! You want to go?'

Stanko nodded, his eyes wide.

Then the English Milord held out a hand to him.

Stanko took the big hand and let himself be led into the milling pack.

His face was licked.

Wet noses sniffed him all over.

He felt no fear.

He felt happy.

There was a big rough-coated hound called Brutus, who came and nuzzled him; his nose was almost on a level with the boy's face. Instinctively Stanko put his arms round the big hound's neck, and ran his fingers through the rough mane.

It was wonderful!

The other children watched in amazement, but not for long; if Stanko could do it . . .

Soon the playground was aswirl with happy hounds and children.

Stanko was a hero. He shared his chocolate bar with Brutus.

Hounds and horses had been at Lippitz for a week and were now well rested after their arduous journey.

'Jumping out of their skins, Guv'nor. When are we going to have a little action?'

The same question was on everyone's lips. The village was taut with anticipation and excitement.

Fred raised the question at dinner in the Schloss that evening. He had worked very hard during the past week to lighten the atmosphere. He had no problem with Aunt Helga. The old lady had now well and truly emerged from the land of shadows, and had become quite her old self. That old self, as Fred discovered, had a very earthy sense of humour. She had rolled with laughter as Fred retold – with certain rather purple emendations – the story of houndknapping the Old Wessex. Tears ran down her face as Fred related the saga of booby-trapping Sir William. She had near hysterics over the 'bonding' of Bryan and Jeremy. She pumped Fred for details of life in England, his career in the Army and his family.

Tatiana sat through all these revelations with unbroken hauteur, responding to Fred's attempts to draw her into conversation with icy politeness. Her only visible sign of emotion was the crumbling of bread. An awful lot of bread got crumbled that week, 'enough to feed the hounds', as Katya muttered when she swept the table after dinner.

In spite of herself, Tatiana found herself listening to Fred with an interest that she refused to show. She found herself covertly studying Fred's melancholy dark eyes and watching his strong hands as he ate or illustrated some anecdote. There was the dreadful evening when she nearly laughed at a joke, but caught herself just in time. She had to keep reminding herself that she hated and despised the English.

She hated him even more when she awoke sweating from a dream that involved those strong hands doing unspeakable things to her, to the extent that she realized it was not just sweat she was wet from. She had got up, walked round the bedroom, and pressed her burning cheek against the cold stone of the window sill until the unbidden warmth subsided.

She felt a wet nose nuzzling her hand. Bonnie was disturbed by her mistress's distress.

Tatiana knelt and put her cheek against the bitch's rough head. 'Oh Bonnie! Bonnie! How dare he do such things to me? You should defend me.'

In fact, Bonnie adored Fred and had given him a rapturous welcome of remembrance. She adored Paddy even more, and the two of them had tremendous games of chase as they had done in England. Bonnie would always limp from her wound, but was as sound as she ever would be.

The two dogs were curled up in front of the fire when Fred raised the question of hunting. At the word 'wolf' Bonnie raised her head and pricked her ears.

'The thing is,' said Fred, 'these hounds have never seen a wolf. I don't imagine that we shall have much trouble getting them to hunt them, but for the first time we want to take them somewhere where we know for certain that a wolf is lying.'

Aunt Helga nodded. 'Ah ha! Then we must get the Hunter. He will know.'

She told Katya to get Tomislav to find the Hunter in the morning. 'And bring some schnapps, Katya. We will toast the hunting.'

It might well have been the schnapps that loosened Fred's tongue enough for him to tell the story of Dr. Crumb.

Aunt Helga nearly fell out of her chair, laughing.

Poor Tatiana! As she listened, she felt the laughter begin to rise within her in a way that it had not done since the death of Francis. It bubbled inside her in a most intolerable way. The man was funny as well! She must put a stop to it! She rose to her feet, just managing to retain her glacial calm.

'That was a truly disgusting story,' she blurted. 'How dare you!'

Then she fled to her room.

Then she laughed.

Then she cried.

On three sides of the Schloss, and looking into the central courtyard, there was a first-floor gallery with open arches, where one could lean on the parapet and look down into the courtyard. The rooms on the first floor opened from this gallery. Tatiana often came and stood in the gallery to look upwards at the night sky. She found the stars a comforting sight.

Now, after she had recovered her composure and washed her face, she went out onto the gallery to let the frosty cold and the starry sky steady her confused mood. It was a night of full moon and the courtyard was bathed in light. She leaned on the parapet.

Then she saw the glow of a cigar on the other side of the courtyard where Fred's apartment was.

Fred was also leaning on the parapet.

The sight of Tatiana in the moonlight made Fred catch his breath; he could not believe anything could be so beautiful.

Tatiana nearly bolted – but it was *her* gallery and *her* castle, and . . .

'May I come round?' he said, in a voice that seemed like deep dark velvet.

'If you wish.'

The glowing cigar tip moved round the gallery, and Fred stepped into the moonlight.

Tatiana looked rigidly in front of her.

The man came and stood beside her. She could smell the maleness of him in spite of the aroma of the cigar. She could *feel* the presence as he leaned on the parapet beside her.

'Look, I'm very sorry if I upset you at dinner.'

'You were disgusting.' 'I wonder what his hand would feel like on my breast.'

'I do apologize.' 'My God, but she's beautiful! I want to take her in my arms.'

'Well, I suppose that's all right, but I do not find that sort of thing funny.' 'I wonder what his hand would feel like . . . like in the dream?'

'I apologize, Gräfin, it will not happen again.' 'Bugger it, Tatiana! I want to make love to you.'

'I accept your apology, Lord Frederick.' 'My name is Tatiana, and I want to hear you say it again, and again, and again when you . . .'

'Look this is silly! I mean . . .' He put his hand on her arm.

For a moment Tatiana looked at the hand, felt its hard warmth, felt an answering warmth inside her. She turned to him, eyes wide, lips parted. It would happen!

Then she panicked.

Her hand caught him a stinging slap on the cheek. 'How dare you touch me, you English Pig!'

She turned and fled to her room where she buried her face in her pillow and . . . screamed.

For several seconds Fred stood quite still with his mouth open. Then he rubbed his burning cheek. 'Young Paddy, women are very kittle cattle!'

Paddy wagged his tail.

Fred realized that he still held his cigar; he puffed it into a glow and turned wearily towards his bedroom.

'I'll tell you something else, young Paddy. A woman is only a woman, but a good cigar is a smoke. Remember that, little dog.'

Paddy wagged his tail again and followed his master to bed.

The ruined castle stood on a promontory that looked over a steep forested valley. The hillside below the castle was a jumble of boulders, heather and scrub. The Hunter had been watching the hillside for some two hours. He was tucked in behind some stunted ash trees on the opposite side of the valley where he could not be seen. The wind was blowing in his face. Once again he raised his binoculars and slowly scoured the facing fellside, moving his glasses up and down the face of the slope so as to miss nothing.

The binoculars traversed, stopped and moved back. They fixed on a particular spot.

The Hunter gave a grunt of satisfaction.

The bitch wolf was lying in her usual spot amongst the rocks, where she could get the benefit of the morning sun. He watched her for a few minutes, then began a cautious and silent withdrawal through the trees.

The whole village had turned out: young and old, sound and halt. Such a sight they had never seen before.

The English Milord and Jim Scuttle in their red coats and black caps, sat on their big shining horses, whilst the glad hounds frolicked and bayed around them, and the children ran excitedly and, now, fearlessly amongst the pack; there could be no school on the day of the first wolf hunt.

Then there was the Frau Gräfin, well wrapped in furs on her horse. She looked pale, some of the women said. Katya had told her friend Eveca that there had been hard words said at the castle, and that the Gräfin had refused to speak to the Milord all yesterday. Perhaps he had tried to creep into the Gräfin's room at night? Perhaps the Gräfin had threatened to shoot him? Was it true what Tomislav had said, that English Milords only like other men? Someone else had heard that English Milords were like bulls. Eveca said that, in that case, she certainly wouldn't threaten the Milord with a gun if he came creeping round *her* bed. Katya said that Eveca would need a gun to get a man anywhere *near* her bed.

Herr Kite was also on a horse, but why was his coat black instead of red?

The Hunter came striding down the hill. He would have news of the wolf. The hunt was surely on.

'The bitch wolf is lying in the rocks below the old castle.'

Fred was bent in his saddle, as he leaned down to listen to the Hunter.

'You cannot ride along the valley bottom, it is too steep and too rough. There is a forest track which will take you right out to the point below the ruins. You will be able to see hounds in the rough below you. I suggest that Jim goes with the Gräfin along the opposite side of the valley.'

'You're sure we will find there?'

'I'm sure. After that, matters are in your hands, and in the hands of the gods.'

'I hope the gods are friendly. I must admit I'm a bit nervous. Almost as bad as the opening meet at home. I'm also a bit nervous about the followers,' Fred jerked his head towards the villagers, all of whom seemed to be armed to the teeth. 'Do you think you can persuade them not to shoot me?'

The Hunter grinned and slapped Fred's thigh. 'Don't worry, I won't let them shoot you. Of course, if you don't catch the wolf . . .' The big man roared with laughter.

'Ha, bloody ha!' said Fred to himself.

'Are you ready, Gräfin?'

Tatiana gave a silent nod.

*

'Leu in! Leu in try!'

Fred's voice encouraged hounds to spread out on the rough hillside before him. He mused briefly that, for the first time, he was using the traditional huntsman's cheer in its proper sense; it was derived from the old Norman-French '*E loup*' – 'After the wolf'.

The eager hounds were soon spread out below him on the rugged boulder-strewn ground, their sterns waving and their subtle noses questing as they moved through thicket and deep, snowy heather.

It was little Gossamer who hit the unfamiliar taint first. It was strong *and* unfamiliar. The bitch had been true to the scent of a fox all her life – but, but, *but*! It was a wonderful smell: a dark, tempting, rank smell, that roused some deep-seated atavistic urge buried in her bloodlines. She took another sniff and decided that, whatever it was, it was good. She gave a high-pitched whimper.

Little Gossamer's whimper was twenty-two carat. Other hounds flew to her and tested the wolf taint: tested it, and found it good. Rather uncertainly, they joined their voices to hers.

The Hunter was striding easily beside Fred's horse. 'That is good and true. That is the line the wolf took when she came in from feeding early this morning. Your hounds are right.'

'Leu at 'im, my darlings!' Fred cheered

Encouraged by her master's voice, Gossamer surged forward on the line. The rest of the pack came tumbling to the cry and joined in. The valley rang and echoed to the ancient sound of hound voices.

The bitch wolf had been curled up in a sheltered corner of the rocks; she was replete and sleepy. When the unfamiliar sound came faintly to her, she was instantly awake, her ears pricked.

The cry came nearer.

The wolf was familiar with the barking of dogs from her foraging round the outskirts of farms and villages, but this was different; this was a threat noise. She rose to her feet and listened again. It was time to move away from the sound.

Jim and Tatiana sat their horses on the far rim of the valley, watching hounds on the opposite slope.

They heard Gossamer open.

'That is good?' Tatiana asked.

'Best bitch in the pack, madam.'

The cry swelled and rose. They could see the hounds crowding onto the line, and heard Fred's cheer.

Jim's experienced old hunt horse stood rock still with his ears cocked, but Tatiana's blood horse began to snort and plunge at the excitement of the savage sound. Jim noticed how effortlessly she sat, and then soothed the fractious animal.

'Nice little woman on a horse,' Jim thought.

'Look! Look!' cried Tatiana, pointing with her whip.

The big, grey shape slipped out of the rocks, and dropped lithely down the hill towards the thickets by the river. Jim stood up in his stirrups, and gave one of his famous and blood curdling – view holloas.

'On! On! On! On!' cheered Fred in immediate response.

Carried away by the excitement, the line of villagers, beside Tatiana and Jim, all added their various screeches to the tumult.

'Like a fucking football match,' said Fred.

Hounds were settled on the scent now. They came roaring and tumbling down the steep hillside on the line of the wolf.

The wolf was accustomed to the easy avoidance of village curs. For a long time she dodged about the thickets by the river, but for every turn she made the pursuing noise went with her and, indeed, was getting closer. It was time to shake it off. She straightened her neck and set off at a steady lope alongside the river.

She was in plain view to the watchers on both sides of the valley, as were the hounds singing and swinging on about five hundred metres behind her.

Jim and Tatiana galloped along the rim, keeping an eye on the wolf. Fred kept level with his hounds, cheering them on occasionally and doubling his horn.

In the frenzy of the chase, the villagers ran, hobbled and stumbled along the crest of the hill.

'See the wolf!'

'The evil rascal!'

'See the brave hounds, how well they follow the scent!'

'Hear the Milord cheer! Let us cheer too, comrades!'

'Who would think the tiny trumpet could make such noise!'

'Oh my back!'

'Oh my legs!'

'Oh for young lungs again!'

'Run, comrades! Run!'

'They certainly seem to be enjoying themselves!' The Hunter was running with an apparently effortless stride beside Fred's horse; he seemed to be able to run, talk and laugh all at the same time.

Down the river went the wolf, the narrow valley behind her ringing and echoing with the cry of the pursing pack. As the valley descended, it gradually widened out. The valley sides became less steep and woodland crept down the slopes. There were open pastures in the valley bottom.

With the cry of the hounds getting remorselessly closer, the wolf's instinct was to leave the open. From his vantage point, Fred saw the distant loping figure turn away from beside the river and head up across the open for the cover of the trees.

The Hunter had also seen her.

The hounds were now spread across the pastures, flying like a flock of dark birds across the snow-covered ground.

Fred and the Hunter stood in the white forest ride at the top of the slope, and listened to the hound voices in the trees below. Although the hounds could not be seen on the forested slope, it was obvious from their cry that the hunt was no longer heading straight.

The Hunter leant on his stick and listened. 'She's tiring. The wolf is starting to run short.'

There was a new note on the voices now. 'They're running for blood,' said Fred.

Jim and Tatiana, and a straggle of panting villagers, stopped on the hillside and listened to hounds in the woods opposite. The cry was now awesome in its savagery as it moved up and down the wood.

Tatiana crossed herself. She could feel the hairs on the nape of her neck stand up.

'The wolf is tatered, madam,' said Jim quietly.

'Look! Look!'

The wolf broke from the wood with hounds only yards behind her. As they viewed her, the cry died as every hound put on speed. The wolf made the river and put in a great leap for a flat boulder in mid-stream.

Big, rough-coated Brutus matched the leap.

He seized the wolf in mid-air and snapped her spine with one bite of his mighty jaws. Other hounds piled in to worry the carcass oblivious of the icy stream.

'They've killed!'

Fred set his horse to slide down the snow-covered bank.

'They've tatered him!'

'My God.' Tatiana put a hand to her mouth.

'It was Brutus! My Brutus!' shouted little Stanko, who had run until he thought his small legs would drop off, and had then run some more.

'They've killed the wolf! They've killed the wolf!'

A fusillade of joyous shots rang up in the frosty air.

Fred leaped from his horse.

'Dead! Dead! Dead!'

He pulled the mangled remains of the wolf from the river and let the triumphant hounds worry it some more, whilst he cheered them and rattled his horn.

Jim and Tatiana scrambled their horses down from the crest of their ridge.

'Bloody marvellous, Guv'nor!'

With a broad smile on his face, Fred doffed his cap and addressed Tatiana. 'I hope that pleases you, Gräfin.'

'Your hounds have ruined the skin,' said Tatiana icily.

Fred's smile faded.

The Hunter turned away to hide his.

CHAPTER FIFTEEN

Through the short, dark days of November and December, the Old Wessex Hounds harried the wolves of Lippitz. The snowy forests rang to the cry of the pack and the hunting was fast and furious. The tally of wolf noses on the castle door grew.

The people of Lippitz and the surrounding area took to hunting with tremendous enthusiasm. Each day's hunting was the main talk in the Gasthof. The merits of individual hounds were argued over loud and long. The performance of the hunt staff was also the subject of great talk, and Messrs Scuttle and Pike were the heroes of the bars. It was a good job that both men were mature and level-headed, otherwise they might have drowned in adulation and slivovitz.

As for the quiet, brooding Milord, he became an almost god-like figure.

All this was reported faithfully to Tatiana by Katya, who never let the truth interfere with her reports.

Fred's popularity in the countryside did nothing to thaw his relationship with Tatiana; it remained glacial. However much she might have admired Fred's skill as a huntsman, she was hardly prepared to admit it, even to herself. As to his popularity, she resented it. After all, she told herself, *she* had been responsible for getting the hounds to Lippitz. *She* ought to be getting some of the credit; and she allowed this to stoke her resentment of the English.

She also resented the fact that he seemed almost to ignore her, except for polite discussion of practical matters. There had certainly been no repeat of that night on the gallery. Not, of course, that she wanted any contact with Fred – she shuddered at the thought – but it would have been nice to find him curled up outside her bedroom door, if only so that she could give him a good kick.

As for Fred, he reckoned that once slapped, twice shy: 'Damn the bloody woman,' he thought. 'Why are women always so contrary?' He channelled all his energies into his hunting, and the long days in the wild, rough country brought him home exhausted enough to prevent him thinking too much. There was also added danger to pump the adrenaline, as he discovered when they hunted a big dog wolf.

So far, hounds had found and hunted mostly bitch wolves and young ones; these they were able to pull down and quickly kill. The big dog wolf was a different matter.

One day, they had hunted this big one for nearly three hours, until he stood at bay against some rocks. Fred heard the cry change to the steady baying that is known as 'marking' – as hounds would do at a fox's earth.

Fred and Jim arrived at the crest of the hill. They could see hounds spread out in a semi-circle around the clump of rocks. Every now and then a bolder spirit would dart forward, then leap back again, and the baying would increase.

Fred jumped from the saddle. 'Here, take my horse. I'd better get down there.'

He slid and tobogganed his way down the snowy hillside and arrived at the hounds just as Kite came panting up from the valley bottom, with Paddy straining on his chain.

The wolf had his back end in amongst the rocks, and was snarling at his pursuers.

'Blimey, that's a licker, sir! We better do something quick, or we'll have some hounds hurt. I've got me pistol.'

'Not in amongst those rocks – not safe.'

Fred took from his pocket the thin-bladed, horn-handled clasp knife which the Hunter had given him at another time and place.

'You're never going to try and take him with that?'

'You see that gap between the boulders behind the wolf?'

'Yessir.'

'You reckon Paddy would get through there?'

'Bloody stroll on, sir.'

'It's our only chance.'

It all happened very quickly.

Paddy wriggled through the crack and sank his teeth into the wolf's quarters.

The wolf turned with a snarl.

Fred was in like a snake.

He sank the blade in behind the shoulder and into the heart.

The hounds piled in behind him.

'Bloody hell!' said Jim Scuttle. 'I thought the Guv'nor was tatered there!'

The story flashed round the village, and penetrated the castle long before Fred had seen his hounds fed, pulled off his boots, knocked back an officer's-size slivovitz and sunk into his bath.

His hands were still shaking.

He decided he would not mention the incident at dinner.

In the hall, however, Katya was already laying informa-tion against him to Aunt Helga and Tatiana, who had not been out hunting that day. 'The wolf was tossing hounds right, left and centre, they say, when the Milord arrives and the wolf goes straight for his throat – and the wolf and the Milord roll down the hill and the Milord pulls out this little knife like the Frau Gräfin uses to sharpen her pencils, and cuts the wolf's throat with it, and . . .'

Tatiana put her hand to her mouth. She felt sick.

'Suppose he had been hurt?' she thought. 'Suppose he had been killed? He was brave! How dare he frighten her! He was a fool!'

Being angry stopped her being sick.

'It was a bold thing to do,' said Aunt Helga.

'The man is a complete lunatic!'

Fred entered the hall, and Tatiana turned on him, her eyes blazing. 'You are a fool! A fool! *A fool!*'

Fred was brought up all standing by this unexpected attack, but he suddenly felt drained and weary.

'If you say so, Gräfin.'

'I do say so! Suppose you had been hurt? What then, eh?'

'I did not have time to think.'

'Think? Think? Of course you don't think! And, if you had been hurt, who would have looked after you, eh? Answer me that!'

'Well, I'm quite certain that it wouldn't be *you*, Gräfin.'

Tatiana seemed to be winding up for a further pyro-technic display, but Aunt Helga put a hand on her arm. 'Peace, child, peace. The man is tired and needs a drink. Come and sit by the fire, Frederick.'

She led Fred away, and Tatiana subsided.

She remained quiet and thoughtful during dinner, but she listened as Aunt Helga skilfully extracted the full story from a somewhat reluctant Fred.

Tatiana got up suddenly, and walked to the end of the hall where she took something off the wall. She came back and laid the object on the table in front of Fred.

Fred stared at it. It was an ornately decorated short sword, with a snarling boar's head on the hilt. He pulled it out of the sheath and an eighteen-inch steel blade glowed dully in the lights of the hall. He had seen similar weapons in France – '*couteaux de chasse*' – used for the dispatch of the quarry. Astonished, he looked at Tatiana.

'That was the hunting knife belonging to Francis's grandfather. If you are going to behave like a complete idiot, at least you should be better prepared.'

Before Fred could say anything, she turned and left the room.

'The thing that puzzles me is that we don't seem to have seen hide nor hair of that very big wolf that everybody talks about – what the locals call the "Devil Wolf". Must be a load of nonsense, that.' Fred was talking to the Hunter one day at the kennels.

The Hunter stroked his chin thoughtfully. 'Evil comes in all sorts of packages. That big wolf is undoubtedly about, but he has not been showing himself lately. I don't doubt but that he will make his entrance in due course. I have told everybody to be watchful.'

Little Stanko's grandfather had been a forester, and had lived in a small house deep in his beloved woods. After being badly injured in a felling accident, he had lived in agony for a painfully short time and then, mercifully, died.

The family had tried very hard to persuade Granny to leave the remote house and to move into the village. The old lady had stubbornly refused to leave her home. It was now part of Stanko's duties to visit the old lady regularly and help her with her chores: to see that she had water from the well, and a plentiful supply of firewood to keep her stove going through the bitter winter nights.

Stanko liked visiting his grandmother. He realized that

he was not quite as bright as other young people, but Granny never made him feel this. She treated him as an equal, and this made him feel good. She was also a fund of old stories about gods and fairies and monsters, which she told to the entranced Stanko as he ate the wonderful spicy buns that she baked.

To Stanko, the old stories were very real; sometimes too real when he was running home through the dark forest. There was that old bridge, under which he was quite certain a troll lived; he always put on a burst of speed when he crossed it, in case a huge leathery hand should reach up from the dark shadows, seize him by the ankle and . . . Well, Granny had told him what happened to children when the trolls caught them – they became supper.

Stanko had strict instructions that he was always to be home in the village before nightfall but, sometimes, there were so many chores to be done, then Granny's stories were so interesting, and the buns so delicious, that darkness caught him on his homeward journey. Then he just ran faster. Stanko might not have been good at sums, but he was one of the fastest runners in the village, and no old troll was going to catch *him*.

It was a few days before Christmas and a thick blanket of snow covered woods and fields when Stanko paid one of his regular visits to Granny, this time on skis. He filled her water buckets and chopped a lot of wood for her, as he knew that he would not be able to come the following day. Stanko was in the church choir, and the next day the choir was going to visit the shrine of the Black Madonna of Kollmitz. The Black Madonna was famous for her miracles and Stanko longed to see a miracle. Although he was not sure what a miracle was, he hoped it might be something about his getting the new clasp knife for Christmas that he had prayed for so fervently.

On this occasion, Granny had baked a particularly delicious apple cake and he had gorged himself on it. So, what with one thing and another, darkness was already falling when he kissed his granny and set out on the three-kilometre run back to the village. Stanko knew the track, even in the dark, just as he knew his way in the dark round the little bedroom which he shared with his two brothers.

He put on his skis and set out, moving easily and fast over the frozen snow.

He whizzed over the troll's bridge: 'Ha! Ha! Old Troll! You can't catch me.'

At first it was just a feeling of uneasiness. Stanko was a child of the forest, and had the sharpened instincts of those who spent a lot of time alone in remote places. He pressed on.

The feeling came again: stronger this time.

He was being followed.

The moon was now rising in the clear sky – it was a few nights off full. The moonlight threw strange shadows across the lonely track. Stanko stopped for a moment and, greatly daring, looked behind him: nothing. Nothing moved in the shadows or on the white track behind him. The frosty air was still; there was no sound.

But . . . *but* . . . something was there.

Something was watching him.

He could feel it.

Stanko dug his ski sticks into the snow, and set off along the track as fast as he could, ploughing through the shadows on the white surface.

It was one of the shadows that caught his eye.

The shadow was moving.

The shadow slid through the trees on his left.

It was keeping pace with him.

More speed! He must go faster – another kilometre

and he would be clear of the trees, and see the lights of home in the valley below him.

He had noted the fallen branch on his way into the forest; it lay across part of the track and was lightly covered in snow. He had made a mental note to remember to avoid it on his way home.

But the shadow was still moving through the trees. He forgot the branch.

It was a bad fall, and he knew immediately that his leg was hurt. One of his skis had slid away from him. Moaning a little, he clutched his leg and looked around him. The forest was white, still and silent in the moonlight.

He sighed with relief and started looking for his ski.

It came fast, and terrifyingly silent.

Stanko had a momentary impression of a hurtling shape. He got a whiff of carrion-foul breath. The rest was great yellow teeth and eyes: great green eyes from the bottom of a nightmare.

Stanko screamed.

Fred and the Hunter stood together at the funeral and, after they had watched the pathetic little coffin being lowered into the grave whilst the villagers stood, bowed and shocked, Fred said to him. 'I didn't think that wolves attacked human beings?'

'There have been a few recorded cases in western Europe in recent centuries, but we are on the boundaries of Europe here and, with the war, the perimeters of civilization have become badly bent. Who knows what nasty habits a wolf might pick up in war zone?'

'But poor little Stanko!'

'Exactly. He was small and weak. In the cruel world of nature, he was a natural prey for a predator.'

'Well, natural or not, we have got to do something about *this* predator.'

'That is also the way of nature, my dear Frederick.'

This was the first time that the Hunter had addressed Fred by his Christian name; he felt flattered.

'So how do we go about it?'

'It may not be so easy. This wolf is a lone wolf. He does not run with the pack. He is not only physically large, he also seems to have exceptional intelligence. My feeling is that he will lie tight for a day or two, and will be extremely difficult to find in that time.' The Hunter scratched his beard. 'After all,' he added grimly, 'he has fed well.'

Fred thought of the blood-stained snow, the pathetic scraps of scattered clothing, and . . .

He shuddered.

Fresh snow had fallen on the night of Stanko's killing. For two days, parties of villagers – no one wanted to go alone to the forest – searched for wolf tracks in the new snow. Some tracks were discovered which always generated great excitement. The Hunter would be sent for, or would suddenly appear. He shook his head. Wolf spoor, certainly, but not the feetings of *the* wolf.

'Perhaps he has gone back to Hell where he came from,' said Albert, a friend of Tomislav's from the village.

Tomislav shook his head. 'That one won't go back to Hell unless we send him there, and the sooner the better he has tasted human flesh.'

'Well, he wouldn't get very fat on you, old man,' Katya banged her ladle on top of the stockpot, 'but I suppose we could use the bones. A bit of poverty soup for a nunnery is about all you'd boil up into.'

Fred kept the hounds and horses at instant readiness. He could feel the tension and the excitement building up inside him. He knew that when something did happen it would probably be explosive. He hated the waiting.

He had been in his room trying to write a letter to his father, with whom he corresponded regularly – 'Old Nately is permanently blotto, they tell me, these days . . . Even the Socialists would not touch that vermin Skevings after the piece in the *Telegraph* . . .' – but found that he could not concentrate.

Deep in thought, Fred clattered down the spiral stone staircase that led from the gallery to the courtyard. So wandered were his thoughts that he bumped into, in the literal sense, Tatiana who was coming up the stairs. If Fred had not grabbed her, she would have fallen.

Fred had seized her by the upper arms.

For a moment, in the gloom, he held her in his arms.

For a long, long instant, they stared at each other.

Then Fred dropped his hands and waited, rather resignedly, for the wrathful tirade that he was sure would follow. Instead, Tatiana stood silently looking at him, her back pressed against the curving wall of the staircase. Her face looked drawn.

She spoke quietly, and dropping her eyes. 'You are ready for the hunt, Lord Frederick?'

'Just waiting for the "off", Gräfin.'

They fell silent, but neither offered to move.

'This wolf . . .'

'Yes, Gräfin?'

'I have a bad feeling about it. There is something . . . Oh! I don't know, but I am sure that this is the wolf that killed poor Clyde. You must be careful.'

The softness of her tone surprised Fred.

'I will be careful.'

Still they did not move. Fred could smell the subtle fragrance of her hair.

The next question also surprised him. 'Shall you miss your family at Christmas?'

'Good heavens! I hadn't given a thought to Christmas!'

'Tomorrow is Christmas Eve.'

'Bless me, so it is! It won't be much of a Christmas for poor little Stanko's family.'

A little bit of the old fire blazed in Tatiana. 'The best present you can give them is to kill the wolf.'

'I will do my best.'

'But, be careful.'

They stared into each other's eyes again for a moment. The memory of the night on the gallery flared up in both of them.

Finally, Tatiana spun on her heel and fled up the stairs. 'My only concern is that my arrangements for Christmas should not be disrupted,' she said over her shoulder.

You never saw old Josip without Stalin trailing along at his heels.

Stalin had been with Josip since he was a puppy. He had been the runt of the litter; a small, misshapen and bad-tempered dog of nondescript breeding, which is how he had come by his name. He and Josip had grown old and fat together. Every day old Josip hobbled from the little hamlet where he had lived all his life, up to the edge of the forest to gather a bundle of sticks to take home and dry out for kindling. Josip's family pointed out that it was quite unnecessary for him to perform this chore. His many children and grandchildren always made sure that the old man had a good supply of logs to keep his stove warm through the winter, and he had no need to go scrabbling around the wood for soggy kindling. Old Josip took no notice. He had collected wood all his life, and would continue as long as the good Lord allowed him to do so – although, from the aches and pains that now plagued him in the cold weather, he was beginning to think that the good Lord might be giving him notice to quit. However, he still hobbled out, grumbling and coughing, his large belly wobbling. Always at his heels came Stalin, as stiff and fat as his master.

The wolf was hungry. He had lain up comfortably for a couple of days, and now the hunger pangs suggested that he should go out and forage.

The wolf had little fear of men. Experience had taught him that there were often good pickings to be had round the dwellings of humans. He worked his way along the edge of the forest inside the screen of trees, his keen nose whiffing as he took in the various scents of fur and feather, and sorted them out in his brain. Then came a different waft and the wolf paused, his head raised, his nose working: man, certainly, and dog. Yes, definitely dog.

The wolf liked dog.

Josip bent over the pile of stocks he had gathered. He took a length of cord from his pocket, and began to tie the bundle.

Stalin sat in the snow behind him, idly scratching an ear.

Josip heard the crash and Stalin's yowl of pain and fear. He turned quickly, falling over his bundle of sticks.

He saw the wolf.

Not just a wolf, but a WOLF – a monster as it crouched there with poor dead Stalin at its feet.

For an awful moment, man and wolf stared at each other.

To his dying day, Josip would never forget the great yellow fangs or the large eyes in which, as he said many, many, many times, 'all the fires of Hell burned bright'.

Then, before the old man's horrified eyes, the wolf picked up the limp body of the little dog and trotted off into the darkness of the forest.

Josip scrambled to his feet, and ran for the nearby houses as he had not run since years out of memory.

As he ran, he shouted, 'Wolf! Wolf!'

'Vlaz,' said the Hunter, 'you have been past it. Just a few houses in a valley about four kilometres east of Lippitz.'

'And it's definitely *the* wolf?'

'According to the message, it's the size of a buffalo. But, yes, I think this is the one.'

'Kite! Saddle up!' Fred shouted, then, turning to the Hunter, said, 'Do you remember last Christmas Eve, Hunter, when we had that great hunt at the Old Wessex, thanks to you? I wonder if today is going to be like that?'

The big man put his hand on Fred's shoulder. 'I think that it will certainly be a day of surprises, but be careful, Frederick.'

'You are coming?'

'I would not miss it for anything. After all, this is Christmas Eve when Wotan and the Wolf Hunt are abroad, or so people say.'

'What do *you* say?'

'I say that if you catch this wolf, your hounds will indeed be the Hounds of Heaven. Now, go!'

As Fred and Kite clattered out of the courtyard, leading a third horse for Jim Scuttle, Tatiana came running, her face flushed and her golden hair streaming behind.

'What's happening?'

'The wolf's been sighted – killed a dog at Vlaz an hour ago,' Fred shouted over his shoulder as the hooves echoed in the archway.

'Why wasn't I told?'

'You just have been!' came the distant reply.

'Pig, English!' screamed Tatiana, beside herself with fury and frustration.

But Fred was gone.

'Don't worry – your horse is saddled and ready,' said a deep voice.

For the first time, Tatiana noticed the Hunter standing by the stables.

'Oh, thank you, Hunter. I'm sorry I lost my temper. It's just –'

'You don't have to explain to me, and don't worry, you'll be there.'

'Right!'

Tatiana turned towards the stables.

'Just one more thing,' said the Hunter, 'do you have your pistol on your saddle?'

Tatiana, surprised, shook her head.

'Then I think that you should go and fetch it.'

There had not been a great deal of excitement in old Josip's life, but that Christmas Eve made up for it. With many a word and graphic gesture, he explained to the English Milord on his enormous horse just how the Devil Wolf had crept up on him, how poor Stalin had been snatched before his very eyes, and how, had it not been for his presence of mind in forming a cross with two broken branches, he had no doubt but that the beast would have mauled his body and would be dragging his soul into Hell at this very moment.

'Poor old Stalin,' and here the old man wiped away a tear, 'a better, more faithful companion a man had never had, and to finish up as breakfast for a wolf . . . So go! Go, Milord! Save us from this evil beast on this Holy Day, and may all the saints, and the Christ Child yet to be born, go with you to aid your efforts!'

It was easy to follow the tracks of Josip's headlong rush from the forest in the snow. They led the hounds into the trees, and to the place where the bundle of kindling lay, and where blood stained the trampled snow. As they reached the spot, a tremor ran through the already excited pack and they opened on the line of the wolf with a great roar of hound voices.

At this point, the three horsemen were joined by Tatiana, pink with cold and impatience.

'Ah, Gräfin! Good of you to join us. Would you like to take Jim with you, and Kite can come with me. Splendid!'

Tatiana opened her mouth to point out that leaving her behind like that was very far from splendid, and what was more . . . But Fred was already spurting away up the ride in pursuit of his hounds.

Tatiana closed her mouth, turned to the poker-faced Jim and said in a tight voice. 'Well, Jim, we had better do as our Master bids us!'

Jim grinned his huge grin. 'He can be a bit of a bugger at times, madam.'

'How right you are!'

The hunt was on.

It was a good day to make a legend. The sun shone in a cloudless sky. The still frosty air made the mind effervesce. The crisp snow sparkled, and to the north of the snow-covered uplands, the distant Alps stood out sharp and clear.

As always seems to be the case in remote areas, news of the hunt travelled through the ether from village to remote farm, and down to the next valley. Soon every hilltop had its crowd of waters. Ancient tractors and battered four-wheel-drive vehicles ploughed through the snow on the upland roads and tracks.

From the deep forest-clad valleys, the cry of hounds rang clear as church bells.

The villagers marvelled at the strange, savage echoes. The Wild Hunt of Wotan rode on in the nighttime storms, but this, too, was a wild hunt and on a Holy Day; the Lord's Day for the Lord's work – the Lord's work being the annihilation of the evil that had come to their land in the form of the Wolf.

Sometimes the watchers could see the wolf as he slipped across open pasture, then their cries and holloas would echo from hill to hill. The wolf was the Devil, and he was on the run.

Then they would see the hounds flying across the snow – 'like avenging angels' – and they too would be cheered on. They were, as the old priest had said, 'truly the Hounds of Heaven'.

The pace of the hunt was tremendous and inexorably it shifted higher and deeper into the hills.

There was no way in which the four riders could attempt to follow the track of hounds as they hunted from one steep valley to another. They had to cut corners and they had to keep to the high ground to save their horses. Fred remembered the old Exmoor adage: 'tis quicker to go round the rim of a bucket than to try to ride over the handle. Steep slopes tire horses.

They had to make guesses when hounds disappeared out of hearing and Tatiana's local knowledge stood them in good stead. They would stand on some high point, listening to the hound voices as they grew fainter and further away in some deep valley below them. At times the cries from the distant watchers on their hilltops helped them choose a direction.

When the hounds disappeared from sight and sound altogether then the three men would turn again to Tatiana.

'We go this way,' she would say, pointing with her whip, and they would set off in a direction that seemed opposite to that taken by hounds. Her long hours spent riding the countryside now paid dividends. After trotting through the snow across some ridge, with Fred bursting with the impatience of a huntsman who wants to be near his pack all the time, they would come to look down into another valley, and would hear the cry of hounds in woodlands on the far side.

'Well done, Gräfin!' Fred would say.

'Bloody marvellous, madam!'

'Now didn't I tell you the lady would find them, young Paddy?' Kite would say to the little terrier, who was travelling tucked down the front of his coat with his head sticking out.

Tatiana accepted the plaudits serenely, and did not show her inner satisfaction; the English did not know it all.

They came to a steep valley, and could hear hounds on the other slope. The four riders slipped from their saddles to ease their horses who were now growing weary. They had been ploughing through the snow for several hours now, and still the relentless cry came back to them.

Fred took off his cap and mopped his brow with his sleeve; it was warm work in spite of the cold:

'This is one hell of a wolf. I wonder what distance he's covered.'

'You'd think the bugger must be tatered by now. I wonder where he's heading?'

A worried frown creased Tatiana's forehead: 'I think I know where he's heading – and it is not a good place. We shall have to cross this valley and the river crossing is not good.'

'Where's this place he's heading, then?'

'It's called the Wolf's Lair.'

Without another word, Tatiana swung herself into her saddle and set her horse to pick its way down the steep slope before them.

The river was fast-flowing and rocky, with steep banks. The four riders paused.

'This looks a bit of a knacker job, Guv'nor. Any better crossing place, madam?'

Tatiana shook her head. 'Not for a long way. We must cross here or we lose the hounds.'

'Well, we better have it then,' said Fred.

He found a place a few metres upstream where the bank was not quite so steep. His trusty old horse looked at the scudding water, tumbled with ice-covered rocks, and snorted his disapproval.

'Steady, old man!'

The horse snorted again, then edged his way down the steep, slippery, snow-covered bank, making the last few feet into the river by sitting back on his hocks and tobogganing into the icy water. With the caution and skill of experience, the horse began to pick his way across.

It was that steadiness and experience that prevented tragedy.

Tatiana's blood horse was furious at being left behind and was fretting and sidling around on the bank. Tatiana was watching Fred as he picked his way across the torrent, with the water foaming up to his boots. Impatience finally got the better of her horse and it suddenly launched itself from the bank into the river.

It landed with a great splash and a clatter of rocks just behind Fred. The blood horse struggled to find a footing amongst the slippery rocks and rushing waters.

It was going down.

Tatiana, loose in the saddle from the unexpected leap, was thrown up on the horse's neck.

She was going down with the horse.

Fred's reaction was lightning. Tatiana felt herself seized by the waist, just as she was on the point of falling. She was whisked through the air and dumped unceremoniously, face down, across the withers of Fred's horse.

She started to struggle. 'Keep still, damn you, woman, or we'll all go down.'

She obeyed.

The blood horse, relieved of Tatiana's weight, managed to regain its footing and scrambled out on to the far bank, where it stood shaking. Fred's horse, with its double burden, crept and heaved its way up the rough bank.

Tatiana was lifted by her coat collar and dumped on the ground.

Her fur hat fell off.

Her reaction was bred of fear out of fury. 'Don't you dare swear at me, and don't you dare call me "woman"!' She rammed her hat back on her head but, in her agitation, it went on crooked.

Fred could not help himself. The combination of the release of tension, the furious face, the arms akimbo and the crooked hat, was too much.

He doubled up with laughter.

'Blimey, Kitey!' chortled Jim Scuttle, 'I reckon we better get over there sharpish. She'll shoot the Guv'nor if she gets that pistol before we do!'

As they climbed, the ground got rougher and the snow deeper. Added to this, the horses were now very weary and the glory of the day was rapidly departing. A freshening wind had risen in the north-west, bringing scattered flakes of snow.

Rags of cloud began to blow across the bleak hillside above the riders who were picking their way up the slope. The air seemed suddenly dismal and foreboding.

From somewhere above them in the enclosing mist came the steady baying of hounds.

'Thank heaven! They're marking!'

'I wouldn't thank Heaven yet, Frederick.' The deep voice came out of the mist, and was followed by a large shape in a disgraceful hat. 'Your hounds are marking at the Wolf's Lair, and we must get there quickly before mischief is done. You must leave the horses here.'

The Hunter turned and was quickly swallowed in fog.

Tatiana took her pistol from its saddle holster and stuck it into her belt.

CHAPTER SIXTEEN

They left Jim Scuttle – under protest – with the horses.

Tatiana, the Hunter, Fred and Kite, with Paddy tugging on his chain, began to climb.

They could hear the hounds above them, but by now the swirling mist had closed around them and visibility was only a few yards. It was cold, miserable and dreich as they stumbled through the snow-covered rocks on the hillside. The damp cold seeped into their bodies and their souls, tempering adrenaline that urged them onwards towards the baying of the hounds.

The Hunter led the group. 'We must keep high to avoid the scree face – the Gräfin may remember that,' he said dryly.

Tatiana remembered and shivered at the memory. The thought brought back another memory: that of Clyde who had disappeared in this desolate place.

Breathing hard as they struggled upwards through the snow, the three followers had to work hard to keep the mist-shrouded figure of the Hunter in sight.

'There!' the Hunter paused. The sound of the hounds was immediate now.

The mist parted for a moment and the three had their first view of the Wolf's Lair.

It was a massive borran; a huge pile of large boulders heaped in a fissure on the mountainside – some of the boulders were the size of small houses. The rocks were loosely piled as though some superhuman hand had carelessly emptied a sack on the hillside. Because of this haphazard formation, the huge mound had many cracks and passageways between the great stones.

Hounds were crawling all over the mound. Some had their heads into the cracks, baying at the scent of their unseen adversary far below them.

Old Seamstress came wriggling and whining to Fred as though urging him to make haste and get things sorted out for them.

'Jesus Christ, sir! That's a hell of a place.'

'Hellish is right, Kite!'

It was obvious, as the four of them scrambled round the borran, that many of the hounds were deep inside. A steady, but muffled, 'Woof! Woof! Woof!' came echoing up through the cracks.

The Hunter took off his hat and ran his hand through his long grizzled hair. 'Well, Frederick, that is where your wolf is – under that little lot.'

'Oh shit!' said Fred.

He then noticed that there was a gap between the two larger boulders at the bottom of the mound. Getting on his hands and knees, he looked through the gap. Beyond the gap there was definitely a tunnel that led into the heart of the tumbled rocks. The tunnel looked large enough for a man to crawl in on hands and knees, anyway as far as he could see.

The tunnel sloped up into total blackness – and the sound of hounds came echoing loud and clear from that blackness.

Fred go to his feet. 'I think I can crawl up there, but I'm not sure how far I can get.'

The Hunter was impassive, but the other two looked at him in disbelief.

'You've got to be joking, sir!'

'You are mad!'

'Look, those are my hounds in there. They've brought their wolf all this way and I'm damned if I can just leave them in there.'

'You also may be damned, if you go in there,' said Tatiana quietly.

'The Gräfin's right, sir. You get in a bother in there and there's nothing we could do to get you out.'

Fred shrugged. 'Well, I'll just have to be like Pooh Bear. When I've starved for a day or two, you'll be able to pull me out.'

'If you go in there, you might not get the chance to starve. There is a wolf in there and he will be in a poor temper,' said the Hunter grimly.

Fred gave a crooked smile. 'Some of my hounds will be in tatty fettle. I've *got* to try.'

'I forbid you to go!' Tatiana's voice came rather shrill.

Fred said nothing.

He took off his knife belt. Then he took off his red coat and spurs, and handed them to Kite, together with his velvet cap.

He buckled the belt back on, and undid the strap that held the knife in its sheath. He eased out the blade to make sure that it would draw smoothly. Then he swivelled the belt round so that the knife lay in the small of his back where it would not interfere with his crawling.

Tatiana stood in front of him, barring his way. 'I forbid it!'

Fred looked down at her: the small determined face, ringed with golden hair and crowned with the fur hat.

They stood facing each other for a moment, in silence.

Then Fred reached out and gently removed the hat.

Equally gently he took her by the shoulders.

Then he pulled her to him.

For a moment Tatiana resisted him, her mouth and eyes wide with surprise.

Suddenly she threw her arms around his neck.

Her mouth found his. On the dreary snowbound mountainside, they kissed with all the passion that had been pent up inside them for so long.

Then, still in each other's arms, they stood staring at each other.

'Please!' Tatiana's voice was tiny.

'I have to.'

The memory of her parting from Francis came flooding back to Tatiana. Her mind shouted, 'Oh, dear God, not again! Not again!'

The thought made her furious, and she snatched away from Fred. 'Then go, you stupid Pig English! Go!'

Fred smiled his crooked smile again as he looked at the lovely angry face, down which the first tears were already running.

'That's more like my Tatiana!'

'Ahem!'

It was the Hunter, he held out a small, battered and rather rusty torch. 'I always carry one of these. You might find it useful.'

'You think of everything.'

'I try.'

Fred took the torch and turned to the tunnel.

'This,' thought Fred, 'is going to bugger the knees of my breeches.'

The cave up which he was crawling was wider than he had first thought, and he was able to make reasonable progress. The floor of the tunnel was well beaten with the passage of animal feet, and was obviously the main entrance to the borran.

He was relieved that the passage seemed to incline

upwards and, for a time, a certain amount of grey light filtered down through the stones from outside. This gave Fred some hope.

He was also encouraged by the fact that the boulders, which formed the rough tunnel, were large and well-seated; the chance of rockfall seemed unlikely. *But* – Fred tried not to think about it.

In fact, Fred tried not to think of anything very much; he wanted to keep his mind blank. If he started thinking, then he might start to consider what a bloody stupid thing he was doing, and then the fear would come flooding in – the childhood fears that Fred did not like to admit even to himself: the fear of the dark, the fear of being trapped in the dark, the fear that stemmed from the time when he was small and his brother had locked him in the dark cupboard for hours. Over the years, Fred had confronted his fears; he had had to suppress them especially during the course at Hereford. He believed that he had conquered them.

The passage turned to the left.

Even for a slim man it was going to be a tight squeeze to get round that corner, and who knew what lay beyond?

Fred came to the corner and saw what lay beyond. It was total blackness.

Fred began to scream silently.

In the enveloping mist outside the borran, the others crawled from place to place amongst the rocks, listening at cracks and holes to the savage sounds that came up from the depths. It was Kite who found the spot.

Towards the top of the borran, there was a wide gap between two huge boulders. The gap formed a chimney that disappeared into the blackness below.

'Up here! Up here!'

The Hunter and Tatiana scrambled up the rocks to where Kite was gesturing. They all gathered at the mouth of the chimney.

The baying of the hounds welled up from below – and they could even distinguish the snarls of the wolf.

'I don't reckon that they're very far below us here.'

Tatiana looked at the huge tumbled boulders. 'They might as well be a million miles.' Her voice was small.

The Hunter put a hand on her shoulder. 'We must wait and pray.'

The skull nearly did it for him.

Fred had screwed up his courage, and silenced his screaming nerves, to force himself round the bend in the tunnel. He had the Hunter's little torch out, and the thin feeble beam showed the passage in front of him. It was getting lower, and Fred knew he would have to continue to crawl, but at least it was no narrower; a man with steely nerves could do it.

Fred's nerves were shredded.

He began to inch his way on up the tunnel.

It was lying in the tunnel, its eyeless sockets staring at him, its fleshless jaws set in a ghastly grin in the torch light.

Fred felt a dark wave of panic surge through him. This was nightmare made real.

He must get out!

He must go back!

Oh shit!

This was hell!

He made a convulsive wriggle backwards and felt a sob of fear rising in his gorge.

He buried his face in the ground.

Playboy saved him.

As Fred fought a real scream rising in his throat, he felt

a cold, wet nose nuzzling him and a warm tongue licking him.

Fred reached up a hand and felt the rough coat. The torch showed him Playboy's grinning face. The old dog had obviously heard his master crawling up the tunnel, and had come back to encourage him.

A warm flood of relief coursed through Fred. He was not alone.

He ruffled Playboy's head. 'Come on then, old dog, let's go get him!'

Fred pushed the skull to one side. Alas, poor Clyde!

Other figures emerged out of the mist.

The word that the hounds were in the Wolf's Lair had flown round. The country people were there to help. The tough peasant men looked at the boulders and shook their heads.

'The Milord gone in there?'

'Holy Mother!'

As each group was told, they crossed themselves.

They would not see the Milord again.

The baying of the hounds was deafening now as Fred crawled onwards and upwards.

Suddenly, he was there.

The tunnel opened up into a chamber, high enough for Fred to crouch in. There was some grey light in the chamber: daylight was seeping through from a funnel in the rocks above. It must be quite near the surface, Fred thought.

The light was enough to see what was happening inside the cave.

The chamber was full of leaping, baying hounds. They were leaping at a large boulder which formed a four-foot high shelf at the back of the cave.

On the shelf was the wolf.

'Oh shit!' said Fred.

'A guinea to a gooseberry, madam, they are right below us here – if only we had a torch.'

'A torch! A torch!' the message was passed round the growing crowd.

An old farmer bustled forward.

He had a torch.

The wolf was massive, and from his position on the shelf, he could fight off any attempt by the hounds to dislodge him.

Even as Fred watched, Brutus, emboldened by his master's presence, took a great leap at the wolf.

He almost managed to get onto the shelf.

There was a moment of snarling, worrying, mayhem – and Brutus fell bleeding to the floor. The wolf dripped blood from a torn ear.

Fred's position was not good. He could only crouch. If he approached the wolf, then his face would be on the same level as those slashing, grinding, snapping, yellow teeth.

But!

But!

If he delayed, he would have more injured hounds. Fred found a small rock from the ground, then he reached behind him and slid the knife from its sheath. He began to inch his way through the struggling mass of hounds.

The wolf gave a hoarse snarl of hatred.

'Right, boss, let's have a dekko with your torch.'

Kite took the farmer's torch and, lying on the rock, shone it down the funnel.

★

It happened very quickly.

Fred was about a yard from the wolf.

He was crouched.

The wolf snarled.

Fred was going to get only one chance.

The small rock was in his left hand.

He flung the stone to the right of the wolf.

The yellow beam of light from above, split the gloom.

'There they are! I can see them! Oh, my God!'

The wolf sprang.

Its huge weight knocked Fred sprawling backwards amongst his hounds. The knife flew from his hand into the darkness.

He was momentarily conscious of great green eyes, foul breath, great teeth. He flung his head desperately to one side, and his right hand seized the great mane of the beast.

He tried to roll – couldn't.

He saw the teeth flash.

The teeth sank into his shoulder.

He screamed.

It was all black and full of pain.

'The pistol, madam! For fuck's sake, where's the pistol!'

Tatiana dragged the pistol from her belt and crouched down beside Kite.

It was a scene from Hell at the other end of the torch beam. She could see and hear the circle of furiously baying hounds.

She could see the wolf worrying something on the floor.

That something was Fred.

'Shoot, madam, shoot!'

'I can't! I can't! I might shoot him!'

'Fucking shoot, or the Major's dead meat!'

Down the torch beam Tatiana took aim.

Her hands were shaking.

Suppose she killed Fred.

'Fucking *SHOOT*!'

She closed her eyes. 'Hail Mary, full of grace!'

Her hand steadied.

She lined up on the shoulder of the wolf and squeezed the trigger.

The explosion filled the chamber with din.

Through his pain Fred felt a wet warmth gush on his face and suddenly the weight of wolf was gone as the hounds rushed forward and dragged the body off him.

He passed out.

'I've killed him! Oh, Jesus and Mary! I've killed him!'

All that could be seen in the torch beam now was the straggling mass of hounds as they dragged the body of their adversary to and fro.

Tatiana staggered to her feet. The Hunter put an arm round her, and she buried her face in his chest, and the hot scalding tears came.

'I've killed him!' she wailed.

'Well, if the Major got in there, I certainly can. I'm much thinner than him.' The Hunter clapped Kite on the shoulder. 'We've got to get the wolf and the hounds out, and then we can sort out the Major. Now, if you can get some of the skinnier blokes to help me, sir. And I'll need another torch.'

Kite explained to the Hunter what he had in mind.

*

Fred swam back into consciousness and pain. Through his half-closed eyes he registered the torch beam shining through the roof-chimney.

The hounds were still worrying the carcass and dragging it to and fro. To and fro in the confined space included over him. A hound trod on his shoulder.

Fred swore.

'That's better, sir, means you must be still alive.'

'Kite! Where the fuck are you?'

'Just coming up your tunnel, sir. We're going to get the hounds and the wolf out of the way, and then I'll be back in a jiffy for you. Don't go away, sir, will you?'

'Fuck off, Kite!'

'Sir!'

Kite crawled in beside Fred and got hold of the wolf by one of its hind legs:

'Dead! Dead! Dead! Dead and leave it, hounds! All right, lads, haul away!'

A pair of boots stuck out of the end of the tunnel where Tatiana and the Hunter were waiting. The farmer, who was keeping his torch shining down the chimney, shouted to the Hunter.

'Right, pull!' the big man bellowed.

Many hands seized the boots and legs, and pulled. As the man owning those boots and legs was pulled from the tunnel, another pair of boots appeared.

'Pull! Pull!'

Man by man, the human rope was drawn out, until at last came the triumphant Kite towing the body of the wolf. He was followed by the triumphant hounds who tumbled one by one out of the end of the tunnel.

A spontaneous cheer went up.

'Fucking roll on!' said Kite.

Tatiana was on her knees beside the breathless Kite. 'Tell me!'

'He's alive and swearing, but he's hurt.'

'Oh, Mother of God! I shot him!'

'No, not this time, madam, the wolf got him first.'

'I must go to him.'

'No, I think you'd better stay with Mr. Hunter. I know me way about in there now. He's only got a wing down, by the look of it. I can help him out.'

The torch light was still shining down the chimney when Kite crawled back into the chamber.

Fred was still slumped on the floor, he was covered in blood, and Kite quickly realized that it was not all wolf blood.

He shone the torch on Fred's face. His guv'nor's eyes were closed, his breathing quick and shallow. He moaned as the light hit his eyes.

'Oh, bloody Norah!' said Kite to himself, then aloud, 'Sir! Sir!' He gently shook Fred's good shoulder.

Fred moaned again. Then, 'Kite?'

'That's it, sir, come to get you out.'

'Bit groggy, Kite.'

'I know, sir, but we can't stay here, now, can we? Do you reckon you can crawl?'

'Bloody well have to!' Fred rallied himself.

Kite helped him onto all fours. Fred tried to put some weight on the injured shoulder and cursed roundly.

'That's better, sir. Now how much use do you think you got in that arm?'

'Not a hell of a lot.'

'Right! Well look, see if you can hang onto my belt with the bad hand, and use the other one to crawl with. I'm going to take it real nice and easy.'

Very slowly, they began to inch their way back down the tunnel, with Kite chatting gently – urging, soothing and, sometimes swearing.

'Come on, sir, for fuck's sake. You can hack it!'

Fred said nothing, except for the occasional expletive when the pain hit him badly. He was sweating with agony, and there were moments when he felt that he was going to faint.

Suddenly, out of the red mists of his mind, there appeared the leering face of that bloody little bantam cock, the Close Combat instructor.

'It's only pain,' the little man had shouted at him. 'Come on you bloody public school pouf, it's only pain.'

'Fuck you, Staff!' Fred shouted out loud.

'That's the stuff, sir, you tell the bastards!'

The crowd of villagers was gathered anxiously round the mouth of the tunnel. There were more torches now. There was a cheer as Kite's head was seen, and many willing hands reached to help him out.

'For God's sake be careful with the Major! He's hurt bad! Watch his shoulder!'

'Hail Mary, full of grace . . .'

The ghastly, fouled and blood-stained figure of Fred appeared from the tunnel.

He looked up at the circle of faces.

Then, with Kite supporting him, he made a supreme effort and got to his feet, swaying.

A great sigh went up from the crowd, and then a massive cheer. They surged forward.

'Keep back! Keep back!' roared the Hunter.

Fred looked around him blearily. 'The hounds! Where are my hounds?'

'It's all right, sir, Jim's got them.'

Tatiana could stand it no longer.

She flew to Fred and threw her arms around him. 'Oh darling! Oh my darling!'

'Oh, my fucking shoulder!' said Fred, and collapsed in her arms.

★

'Put him in the Gräfin's bed and stoke the stove up. Her room is warmer than that awful kennel he sleeps in. He must be kept warm.' Aunt Helga was in full charge. 'Now you, child, go and sit by the fire. Katya, give the Gräfin some schnapps.'

'I must stay with him!'

Tatiana had arrived back at the Schloss in a state of near hysteria. She had insisted on accompanying the unconscious Fred all the way, and was blaming herself for the state he was in.

Aunt Helga took her by the shoulders, shook her, and then pushed her into a chair by the fire. 'Sit there, have a good weep, and then pull yourself together. You are going to be of no use to anyone in that state!'

Tatiana sat and, through tear-wet eyes, watched the makeshift stretcher on which Fred had been brought back being carried across the hall.

The courtyard of the castle was full of people. They stood silently in the snow – waiting and watching.

'Now, we had better have a look at the damage,' said the Hunter.

Fred had been laid on Tatiana's bed. Only the Hunter, Aunt Helga and Katya were in the room. Everybody else had been shooed out. The Hunter tugged off Fred's boots and breeches, while the injured man moaned fitfully in his coma. His shirt was a mass of filth and dried blood.

'Scissors,' said Aunt Helga, 'and, Katya, hot water – constant hot water – and poultices. You know how to make them.'

Katya bustled away, but moments later the door opened and Tatiana came in quietly.

'How is he?'

Then she saw the bloody mess. 'Holy Mother of God!'

Aunt Helga was grim. 'Now, child, this is no place for the vapours. You've seen worse than this, I know. Now pull yourself together and lend a hand.'

As gently as possible they cut and then soaked the blood-stiffened shirt away. Albert and Eveca kept the supply of hot water coming from the kitchen.

There was a hum of muted voices as the latest bulletin was passed from mouth to mouth and out to the waiting crowd in the courtyard.

At last the clotted blood and muck was cleaned away from the wound. Even in his coma, the pain penetrated Fred's brain.

Every cry and moan made Tatiana wince, but she controlled herself.

'That', said Aunt Helga, 'is a mess.'

The Hunter's huge hands were very gentle as his fingers probed and cleaned the wound made by the wolf.

Fred shouted incoherently.

'Nasty!' said the Hunter. 'But no bone damage, I think. It was lucky that you are a good shot, Tatiana, it could be a lot worse.'

'Infection,' said Aunt Helga, 'that will be a problem, that and fever. He is burning' – she felt Fred's brow – 'we must draw the poison. Tatiana! Pass the message to Katya to send up one of her poultices, and we shall need plenty.'

Some thirty minutes later, the Hunter stretched himself hugely. 'Well, I don't think that there is much more I can do now. Katya makes a good poultice. It is now a question of time, care and a lot of prayer.'

'But will he be all right?' Tatiana's voice was small.

'It's all in the hands of the gods.'

The Hunter flexed his mighty hands and cracked his knuckles horribly. He walked across to the window and looked down into the courtyard; it was thronged with people.

'The best thing I can do now is to persuade all those good people to go home. It is nearly time for Midnight Mass anyway. I will tell them of the Milord's need for prayer. I think they will follow me,' he said matter-of-factly. 'If you need me, I shall be at the priest's house tonight. I hear the old man has some excellent French brandy in for Christmas.'

He was halfway through the door when he turned. 'Oh, by the way, Happy Christmas!'

All through the night and through Christmas Day, Fred's fever ran high. The only things that were cooked on Katya's stove that day were poultices and a rather foul-smelling infusion of herbs. This was one of Aunt Helga's patent remedies for fever, and the unconscious Fred was drenched regularly.

Helga and Tatiana took turn and turn about to watch but, even when it was Aunt Helga's watch, Tatiana would not leave the room, but tried to doze in an armchair.

At one point, Aunt Helga shook her out of a fitful sleep. 'He is running with sweat. Fetch some towels and some dry linen.'

The weary Tatiana stumbled off, and shortly afterwards together they lifted and turned Fred's burning naked body.

Tatiana could not help noticing that it was a hard, lean body, with dark hair running down from the chest, right down to . . . With a flash of guilt, she lifted a limp leg for Aunt Helga to dry.

'Yes,' said the old lady cheerfully, 'he's got a good set of tackle. Big balls – I like that in a man.'

'Auntie!' Tatiana was deeply shocked.

'Don't be silly, child, I saw you looking at it.'

'Auntie! I never . . .' She felt her face burning.

'Look, Tatiana, I'm an old woman. When you've been where I've been, and seen what I've seen, life boils down to a few simple things. People try to make them complicated. You've been making all this as complicated as you can. I've seen the way you look at Frederick, when you think no one is noticing. You've been aching to get him in your bed, even if you would not admit it to yourself. Well, girl, you've got him that far – all you've got to do now is keep him there. Right, I'm off for a cup of coffee and a sleep.'

Gathering up the sodden towels and linen, the amazing old lady bustled out of the room, leaving Tatiana with her mouth open in surprise.

The bad weather blew over on the evening of Christmas Day, leaving a night of frosty stars and a full moon.

The moonlight was streaming through the windows of the bedroom when Aunt Helga woke Tatiana from a light sleep.

'Praise be to God, it is over!'

'Oh Holy Mother!' Tatiana's hands went to her mouth in horror.

'The fever, child, the fever has left him. He is sleeping now.'

'Oh, dear God, I thought . . .' For a moment Tatiana buried her face in her hands.

The old lady gently squeezed her shoulder. 'All is well, child, our prayers have worked – they and Katya's poultices. You keep an eye on him now. I will be back in an hour or so with fresh dressings.'

She left the room.

Tatiana moved her chair to the side of the bed so that she could look closely at the sleeping Fred. He was very pale and drawn, but his face was no longer contorted or wracked with the heat of the poisons. He looked almost childlike as he lay on his back, breathing deeply and easily, and making the occasional little grunting noises.

Tatiana rested her elbows on the edge of the bed and held her face in her hands so that she could gaze at the drawn handsome face.

She felt a deep sense of peace and tenderness as she watched him, but after a while a great weariness swept over her. She tried very hard to keep awake, but her head kept falling forward and she would have to jerk herself up.

At last she could stay awake no longer.

She laid her head on the sleeping body, and slept the sleep of utter exhaustion.

It was a lovely dream.

Her hair was being stroked, gently and lovingly, in the way that Francis used to do it. And yet, it was not Francis, it was . . . but the dream did not tell her. There was only the hand – a strong hand – stroking so gently; so gently that she wanted the dream to go on and on for ever.

She swam up from the depths of the dream to semi-wakefulness. It was then she realized that it was not a dream; it was real. Someone was stroking her hair.

She opened her eyes very slowly.

Fred was lying propped up on his pillows, his dark eyes watching her, and that funny crooked grin on his face. His good hand was stroking her hair as her head lay on his chest.

She gave a little start and a cry, and sat up.

She would have leaped to her feet, but the big hand gripped her wrist, forcing her gently back into her chair.

'I'm sorry, I did not mean to wake you. I just wanted to stroke your hair.'

'But you shouldn't! You mustn't! I mean, you're ill! You're hurt!' Tatiana knew that she was babbling.

'That doesn't stop me stroking your hair.'

Fred released the wrist.

Tatiana sat motionless – rigid.

His hand came up and very gently smoothed the hair from her face. The fingers were strong and hard but, oh so softly, they began to trace the outline of her face, her eyes, her nose, her mouth . . .

Tatiana gave a little sob and, seizing the hand, she held it to her lips and began to kiss the fingers, then the palm. As she did so the tears trickled down her cheeks.

'Hey, hey! Why the tears?'

'I thought I was going to lose you.'

'I'm not so easy to get rid of.'

With a little wail, Tatiana buried her face in his chest. Fred stroked her hair until the sobs subsided. Then very carefully he took her hair and raised her face.

They looked at each other.

'Kiss me!' said Fred.

Tatiana was stroking his face when she felt his hand exploring her breast. She sat bolt upright in her chair.

'Lord Frederick!'

The hand strayed out to her breast again.

'Gräfin.'

Tatiana felt herself going pink and confused – 'like a little virgin,' she thought to herself. Then aloud 'May I remind you that you are a sick man.'

'I am convalescing.'

Tatiana could feel the massaged nipple hardening.

She gave a little moan.

The hand switched to the top button of her shirt – her favourite white silk Dior shirt which she had put on to cheer herself up. The hand fumbled with the button.

Tatiana could stand no more.

She pushed the hand away and rose swiftly to her feet.

Fred's expression combined lust with disappointment.

Tatiana said nothing, but slowly and deliberately she unbuttoned the shirt and let it hang loosely from her shoulders.

Still without speaking, she came to the edge of the bed and stood there, proud and erect.

The shirt fell away from her full, firm breasts, the large nipples standing hard.

She did not look at Fred, but heard him gasp.

His hand found her breasts, not so gentle now, squeezing and rubbing.

Tatiana closed her eyes and concentrated all her senses on what was happening. She gave little moans of pleasure, and could feel the warmth flooding through her body.

His hand left her breasts.

She felt his fingers tracing a line down her front, towards her navel, and coming to a stop at the buckle of the belt on her trousers.

The hand began to unbuckle the belt.

Tatiana looked down. Fred was still lying on his back.

His eyes were hooded, and his face had a hawk-like fierceness to it.

Tatiana gave a little shiver.

Not taking her eyes from his face, she gently pushed his hand away, unbuckled the belt herself then shrugged and stepped her way out of the constricting trousers.

Only a wisp of ivory silk remained between the two of them.

She felt a finger hook into it.

She stood proud and nearly naked in front of the man.

She felt the finger, the gentle, probing finger.

She opened her legs to give it free passage.

It probed into her moist depth and then found the magic place, as it had once done in her dreams.

Tatiana closed her eyes, arched her back, and moaned. 'Oh my Lord! My Lord!'

Fred was shuddering from a combination of love and pain. He could scarcely believe the beauty of the woman who was writhing at the touch of his finger.

He wanted her more than anything in the world at that moment.

His voice came out as a croak. 'Come to me, please!'

Tatiana pulled back the duvet.

There was a sheen of moisture around the tip of his penis. Tatiana bent over it.

'Oh, that's wonderful!' Fred writhed with pleasure. Then 'Oh shit!' as the pain hit him.

'Oh, I'm so sorry!' Tatiana was stroking his face. 'I hurt you!'

'No! It just hurts a bit when I move – come back, I want you so much!'

'Oh darling, darling! I want you! But what about your poor shoulder?'

Fred put out his good hand. 'Help me up.'

'No, No! You'll damage yourself. Just lie there and I'll . . .'

'No! I don't want that! Not now! I want *you* I have a *need*! Do you understand?'

Then, with a sudden change from almost anger to gentleness, he put up his hand and stroked her face. 'Oh God, I love you, but I need . . .'

Tatiana looked at him gravely. 'You need to take me,' she said quietly.

'Yes!'

She helped him to kneel on the bed, conscious of the waves of pain that washed over his face and, then, without a word, lay down with her head in the warm hollow of his pillow.

She spread her legs either side of the man, and held out her hands.

His shoulder ached abominably, but desire blocked out everything.

He felt her gentle hand drawing him forward.

He felt her tightness and heard her cry out.

Then he was sinking deeper and deeper into a velvet wetness.

Urgent lust was driving him on – harder, deeper, faster – as he crouched over her.

Oh God! It was a great, burning rod, thrusting right into her depths, into her very soul.

She abandoned herself to the fire, screaming every time it burned her, yet again and again and again.

It was savage; it was lovely; it was beauty; it was – oh God! – another scream.

She watched the transfigured face above her.

She saw the eyes go green with passion as he thrust into her. Again and again and again.

The pain came back in a flooding tide.

He could no longer support himself and pitched forward onto her writhing body.

As he did so, the red waves of pain and pleasure made him roar with the agony and ecstasy.

She heard the roar and felt him collapse on top of her.

As he did so, she could feel the great spurts of warmth flooding into her. 'Dear God! Oh my God!'

At the same time, she felt another wet warmth seeping into the silk of her shirt.

His blood was staining her.

★

Aunt Helga and Katya were coming from the kitchen with a fresh poultice. The noise from upstairs filled the stairwell.

They stopped.

'About time too!' said Aunt Helga. 'But I hope that girl's being careful of his shoulder.'

'Yes, it's a poor midden without a cock to crow on it,' said Katya. 'I'll keep this poultice warm. We'll likely need it later.'

The two old women turned back to the kitchen.

Fred's shoulder had been dressed again. He and Tatiana had been scolded, fussed over and put to bed, as Fred said, 'like a pair of teddy bears'.

'Now,' said Aunt Helga firmly, 'no more nonsense tonight! You, Frederick, must be like a monk, and you, Tatiana, like a Mother Superior.'

This had made them both giggle, and Katya cackle.

Then they were alone.

Fred put his good arm around Tatiana and drew her to him. She nestled her head in the crook of his shoulder and took a delicate nibble at his chest.

'Aunt Helga will be cross!'

'Aunt Helga is not here,' said Tatiana sweetly.

Then they just lay quietly, side by side, watching the moonlight streaming through the window, content in the soft warmth of each other's bodies.

Fred suddenly became alert. 'Quick! Help me up!'

'Darling, whatever is it? What's the matter? Are you hurting?'

'Stop wittering, woman, and help me up!'

Confused, and rather frightened, Tatiana got out of bed and gave Fred her hands. With a wince and a groan, he pulled himself upright and padded across the room to the window.

Tatiana watched in consternation as he threw open the window, letting the frosty air rush in on his naked body.

'Frederick, darling. Are you mad?'

Tatiana scooped the duvet from the bed and rushed to Fred, wrapping it carefully round him.

'What is it?'

'Shush! Listen!'

He wrapped the duvet round her as well, and he pulled her to his side. 'Listen!'

Through the frosty air came the sound of hounds singing in the kennels, their wild voices rising and falling in perfect harmony. At moments the song would fall away, then a hound would take it up and the whole pack would join again, their bell-like voices floating across through the clear air.

Tatiana clung more tightly to Fred.

'Oh, my love. It is truly heavenly!'

The Hunter stood with the old priest on the steps of the priest's house in the bright moonlight. They too listened to the singing.

'The Hounds of Heaven!' said the old priest.

The Hunter was silent, listening . . .

'And a hunter's moon,' continued the priest. 'It would be a great night for the wild hunt of Wotan.'

The Hunter grunted. 'Wasn't last night's hunting wild enough for you? Anyway, you shouldn't believe such old stories. You, a man of the cloth!'

'Old stories form the basis of Faith. It comes in many ways and in many guises.'

The Hunter grunted again, then stretched and yawned hugely. 'Time I was going.'

'I imagine even gods get tired.'

'You never know with gods.'

The Hunter took the old priest's bony hand in his own great paw. 'Thank you, Father, and good night.'

The old priest watched the big figure walk down the steps and into the moonlit street. Then there was nothing, nothing but the empty moonlight and the song of the hounds. The old man smiled –

'And, good night to you, Father!'

SIGNET

Published or forthcoming

Mark Crompton

In the slick world of the conman, there's only one way to catch a thief . . .

Patrick Old, late of Army Intelligence, is now a private detective and a missing-persons specialist. Fed up with tracing errant spouses, he's intrigued by a new commission – to track down a conman who duped Barry Mee and nine of his friends out of a great deal of money.

Barry Mee ought to have known better: a multi-millionaire porn-king, he's no stranger to the seamier side of life. And nor is Patrick Old. As he delves deep into the world of conmen, he encounters a variety of people who make a very healthy living out of being dishonest. And when Old eventually finds his man, he knows that the only way to catch him is to sell him a scam that will prove irresistible . . .

SIGNET

Published or forthcoming

A KILLING JOKE

Mark Daniel

The stakes are high in the Pardubice, Czechoslovakia's historic Grand National. One error at the towering fences can spell death for horses and men . . .

Londoner Jago van Zeller thought he had a chance in the Pardubice with Burlington, the faithful old chaser he'd kept when his business went bust. And in the other crazy scheme that just happened his way: teaming up with a fellow jockey and a beautiful woman to recover an aristocrat's lost fortune in jewels.

Except the great Havlik treasure is the cruellest of jokes. It is a cause some will kill for – a race for survival that makes the Pardubice seem tame . . .

FEAR OF THE DOG

Neil Tidmarsh

In the art world, there's more than one way to make a killing . . .

Tony Acton, flamboyant and ruthless young art dealer, clocks up one blistering success after another. Artist Nicholas Todd should be delighted: Acton sells his work too. So why does he hate Acton? Hate him enough to consider the unthinkable? Enough to take pleasure in his early demise . . .

Fear of the Dog is a fiendishly clever thriller set in the darkest depths of London's art world. Neil Tidmarsh weaves a cunning web of love and hate, deception and forgery . . . and murder.

SIGNET

Published or forthcoming

THE EAGLE HAS LANDED

Jack Higgins

It was to become known as the most daring enemy mission of the entire war. Operation Eagle: SS Reichsführer Heinrich Himmler's audacious plan to kidnap Winston Churchill on British soil in November 1943.

But, despite spectacular secrecy, there was to be no surrender without a fight. In a remote corner of Norfolk, an élite force gathers together. Ready to do battle for a nation against the most ruthless task force ever assembled.

THE CHAMELEON

Sean Martin Blain

An anti-Soviet activist gunned down in Czechoslovakia . . .

A lunchtime killing in the centre of London . . .

A high-flying businessman shot in cold blood . . .

Three perfect murders, with one striking link. In each case the police authorities are handed a ready-made suspect – someone the victim knows well – and damning forensic evidence for conviction.

But new findings unearthed by Irish detective 'Cowboy' Johnson point to only one killer. A contract killer, able to appear and disappear at will. Able to command the highest price. Able to guarantee someone else is convicted.

The ultimate killing machine.
The Chameleon.

SIGNET

Published or forthcoming

NIGHTRIDER

Sheila Holligon

Only her desire would allow him to live . . .

Photographer Rose Thorpe has reached a crossroads in her life – and finds herself ready for escape. Haggabacks is a godsend – a cottage high on the Yorkshire moors, the final strange bequest from a father she'd last seen as a child.

But here the dreams turn to shadows and Rose's nightmare begins. As an outsider, she is viewed by the locals with mistrust and scorn. And inside the four damp walls, something is watching her . . . following her . . . wanting to make love to her: a creature of animal passion that has come from beyond the grave, forcing her to respond with a hunger she has never known before . . .